Diane T. Ashley *and* Aaron McCarver

Jasmine

SONG OF THE RIVER

Book No. Three

BARBOUR
PUBLISHING

© 2013 by Diane T. Ashley and Aaron McCarver

Print ISBN 978-1-61626-544-1

eBook Editions:
Adobe Digital Edition (.epub) 978-1-61626-999-9
Kindle and MobiPocket Edition (.prc) 978-1-61626-998-2

All scripture quotations are taken from the King James Version of the Bible.

This book is a work of fiction. Names, characters, places, and incidents are either products of the author's imagination or used fictitiously. Any similarity to actual people, organizations, and/or events is purely coincidental.

Cover credit: Studio Gearbox, www.studiogearbox.com

For more information about Diane T. Ashley and Aaron McCarver, please access the author's website at the following Internet address: www. dianeashleybooks.com

Published by Barbour Publishing, Inc., P.O. Box 719, Uhrichsville, OH 44683, www.barbourbooks.com

Our mission is to publish and distribute inspirational products offering exceptional value and biblical encouragement to the masses.

Printed in the United States of America.

Dedication

Diane—It is funny how things turn out sometimes. I wrote this dedication to be used in *Camellia* before deciding to save it for the final novel in the series. It breaks my heart that you died before you ever saw it. Rest in peace, darling, until we are reunited in heaven. For Edward Gene Ashley, April 15, 1952–November 28, 2012:

For Gene—the man who holds my heart. If I had looked the world over, I could not have found a spouse better than you. You enrich my life beyond anything I could have imagined when I was single. It took a long time for God to bring us together, but I cannot regret those years because I know He was molding each of us to become what the other needed. Thanks for forgiving my shortcomings, overlooking my faults, and encouraging me to pursue this dream of writing novels. Each day I get to spend with you is a treasure. We may not always see eye-to-eye, but that does not matter because we love and respect each other. You have taught me so much about patience, peace, and how wonderful love can be between a man and a woman. No one gets me like you do. No one else sees my warts with quite so much clarity. Yet you still love me. You are my hero. If I started today and filled up every hour telling you all the reasons I love being your wife, I would never get to the end of the list. I hope we get to spend many more years loving each other. I love you. . .more.

Aaron—I honor my friend who fully supported his wife's writing in a partnership. Thank you, Gene.

Acknowledgments

We would like to thank Becky Germany, Becky Fish, and the team at Barbour for believing in us and our journeys along the Mississippi River. We also thank our agent and friend, Steve Laube, for helping to make our writing dreams come true. For our support group, the Bards of Faith, God put you in our lives for many reasons beyond writing. Thank you for being His instruments. And for our readers, we thank you so, so, so much. We do it for Him, but we have you in mind always.

Chapter One

Sandwich, Illinois
April 15, 1870

Ducking behind a horse trough, David Foster pulled out his weapon and aimed it toward the opposite side of the street. A bullet dug a hole in the dirt a bare inch from his foot. David narrowed his eyes against the dust it kicked up and pulled his body in tight. "Put down your weapon and raise your hands."

He could see Cole Hardy's face peeking past the curled brim of a hat—a lady's hat with posies tucked into the headband. The poor woman wearing the incongruous headpiece was an innocent passerby Cole had grabbed when David first tried to arrest him. The outlaw brandished his pistol and laughed. "You're not going to take me alive, Pinkerton."

Even though it wasn't his name, David had grown used to the title in the past weeks. The others employed by the famous private detective agency said it was a part of the job.

David looked around the end of the trough to judge the distance between him and Hardy. "Let the woman go, Cole. She has nothing to do with this."

"My name's the Whiskey Kid." The man's voice held a plaintive note.

A grin slid across David's face in spite of the dangerous situation. Criminals could be so childish. As if their development had ended at age five even though their bodies continued to mature. Perhaps by appealing to the outlaw's ego, he could diffuse the situation. "How did you get that name, Whiskey?"

The woman he held whimpered, a sound combined of fear and pain.

"Shut up," Cole hissed at his hostage.

From his limited view of the pair, David could see her face pale even further as the outlaw tightened his hold. While he waited for an answer to his question, David considered how to protect her. If he shot at Cole, he might hit her instead. His best option was to get the man talking. "If I'm going to call you something other than the name your ma gave you, I want to know why."

"It's because I kin drink more than anyone else around and still keep my wits about me."

"Is that right?" David wondered if the man was drunk right now. If he was, his aim would be shaky. Of course his temper would be on a short fuse. "And I guess your skill has gotten you a lot of admiration over the years."

David risked leaning out a few inches farther and studied what he could see of his opponent. The kid looked only fifteen years old, but he was probably about twenty-one, the same age as David. The leader of a local gang of outlaws terrorizing the area, Cole Hardy had shot down the former sheriff and two of his deputies to establish control. He might be young, but he was still a murderer.

The day the town of Sandwich buried their law enforcement officers, a telegram from the local bank president arrived at the Pinkerton National Detective Agency—a plea for help that David had been selected to answer.

"Come on out here, Pinkerton, and I'll show you my real skills."

Another bullet struck the ground and made David duck for cover. At least the bullet had missed him again. Sweat trickled down his face, mixing with the dust. He would need a bath when this was over.

Wiping his face with his free hand, David pushed his hat back. It was time to see if he couldn't push Cole a little harder—see if he could get the lady free. "Where I come from, real men don't hide behind women's skirts. Why don't you let her go, and you and I can discuss the matter man-to-man."

The only response to his taunt was silence. He leaned forward again, hoping Cole wasn't smart or sober enough to be waiting for his face to show once more.

Something had happened to draw Cole's attention away from the trough where David hid. He was looking over his shoulder, maintaining the barest grasp on the back of the woman's neck.

David waved a hand to make sure she could see him and gestured with a jerk of his head to run. Fear entered her eyes, gleaming through a sheen of tears. He smiled for encouragement and received a whisper of a nod from her. He held his breath as she pulled away with a sudden jerk and went running down the street.

Cole Hardy whipped his head back around, cursed, and pointed his weapon at David. In the split second before the outlaw fired, David squeezed his trigger. The other man spun in the opposite direction as the bullet tore through his thigh. His shot went wild. David was up and running toward him as the outlaw hit the dusty road.

"You shot me." Pain twisted Cole's face, and he curled up into a ball, his spent weapon forgotten. "It hurts."

David picked up the gun and shoved it into his belt. He holstered his own weapon, looking to see what had taken Cole's attention away from his captive in the moments before she had escaped. Illinois Bank was painted on the plate glass window, but no one stood there.

With a mental shrug, David bent to inspect Cole's wound. "You're lucky I didn't shoot you in the heart. You'll live to face a judge for the murders you committed."

A door creaked open, bringing David's attention back to the bank. Two men, their hands raised high, stepped across the threshold, followed by a grim-faced man who held an ancient-looking shotgun in his hands. "Git on out there so the Pinkerton man can escort all you to jail."

David stood and settled his bowler on his head more firmly. "I'll take those men off your hands, but the doctor will have to sew this one up before he gets carted off to jail." He pointed his pistol at the two uninjured outlaws and marched them toward the end of the main street to the sheriff's office.

People stepped outside and watched them move past the various businesses of Sandwich. Their faces showed varying degrees of relief, shame, and hope. A young boy dashed past, shouting for his pa to come look. Ladies stood in little groups of two or three, their bonnets shading their faces but not obscuring their admiring glances.

He reached the jailhouse without mishap and herded the two men inside. An empty desk and two barred rooms greeted them. Where was the sheriff? Or whoever represented the law since the sheriff was murdered.

"Both of you can get in that cell." He closed the door behind them and walked to the desk, opening the drawer and fishing out a ring of keys.

By the time he had them secure, the grim man who had held his shotgun on the two gang members entered the sheriff's office. He looked different now—more jovial and relaxed. David assumed he was the banker who had sent a wire to the agency.

"Now our law-abiding citizens won't have to hide themselves anymore." The man held out his left hand. "I'm Mr. Morton Winthrop at your service. I don't suppose you'd consider staying here in Sandwich for a spell? We need a new sheriff."

David waited for Mr. Winthrop to pause before introducing himself. "Where is your sheriff?"

"Dead." One of the prisoners answered him with a cackle, exposing a number of broken or missing teeth. "Cole done kilt him last week."

The other gang member, shorter and meaner looking, nodded. "And yer next."

Mr. Winthrop shook his head. "You can see why we're having a bit of a problem choosing a new sheriff. . .but a man like you can handle himself. And Sandwich has a fine collection of pretty young misses, any of whom would make you a good wife."

An image sprang to David's mind. A girl with coal black hair, violet eyes, and a complexion as fair as a bowl of milk. "I'm not interested in finding a wife or in staying in Sandwich."

"Woo-hoo, I'd like me one of them gals." Tall-and-toothless stood with his face pressed between the bars of the cell.

"Mind your own business." Mr. Winthrop sneered at the man. "I wasn't talking to the likes of you or your partner."

The front door swung open, and two men brought Cole Hardy in on a stretcher.

One of them looked to Winthrop. "Where should we put him?"

As Winthrop sputtered, David slipped past the men with the stretcher, feeling Cole Hardy's angry stare all the way out the door. Turning right, he walked down the street to the hotel, the only two-story building in Sandwich.

The sun would set soon. He couldn't get back to Chicago tonight, so he decided he could get that bath, eat some supper, and retire early. Tomorrow he would get an early start. The people of Sandwich could handle the Whiskey Kid and his followers. David had done what he was hired to do.

Breathing a sigh of relief to enter the relative coolness of the hotel, David tossed a couple of coins on the front counter and asked for bathwater to be delivered to his room.

"I'd be happy to bring it myself." The girl at the counter was the daughter of the proprietor—single and dangerous. She was rather pretty, if a man liked his women with wheat-colored hair and glittering blue eyes. He was more fond of dark-haired women.

Besides, like he'd told Mr. Winthrop, David had no intention of finding himself a wife here. "That's all right. If you don't have a servant to carry the water, I can go to the barbershop." He ran a hand over his chin. "I need a shave anyway."

She pushed out her red lips in a pout. "Pa can bring the water."

"That's okay." The hair on the back of his neck rose in response to the predatory look in her eyes. He would also ask the barber if he could get a decent meal at any other place in town. David had plans for his future, plans that had nothing to do with being caught by a man-hungry female in Sandwich.

ᢀᢤ

Chicago

PINKERTON CODE:
ACCEPT NO BRIBES
NEVER COMPROMISE WITH CRIMINALS
PARTNER WITH LOCAL LAW ENFORCEMENT AGENCIES
REFUSE DIVORCE CASES OR CASES THAT INITIATE SCANDALS
 OF CLIENTS
TURN DOWN REWARD MONEY
NEVER RAISE FEES WITHOUT THE CLIENT'S PRE-KNOWLEDGE
APPRISE CLIENTS ON AN ONGOING BASIS

David could recite by memory the words stitched on the framed handwork hanging on his supervisor's wall. They had been drilled into his head when he joined the agency. They were the first thing he was taught, along with the methods for catching criminals.

Homer Bastrup glared at him over the top of his wire-rimmed glasses for a moment before nodding. His bulldog face relaxed into a smile. Removing the glasses, he carefully folded the legs and placed them in a leather case.

"Good job." The large man's voice boomed through the suite of offices located on the second floor of the Pinkerton National Detective Agency. Several of the detectives whose desks were stationed outside his door raised their heads. "This is the kind of report I wish all my men would turn in."

The heads dropped again, and David thought he could hear the scratch of pens on paper in the sudden silence. "Thank you, sir." The approval on his supervisor's face brought home the importance of his recent success. It made his hard work worth the effort.

"Mr. Winthrop was very complimentary. He sent a letter saying you did an excellent job in protecting the citizens while addressing the problem." Mr. Bastrup tapped a sheet of stationery with a beefy finger. "He even asked if you might be willing to return to Sandwich as their sheriff."

"That's very kind of Mr. Winthrop. He made my job easier by holding a weapon on the gang members after I shot their leader."

"Are you interested in returning to Sandwich?"

"I don't think that's a good idea. I like living here in Chicago." David hoped to make a career for himself with the Pinkerton agency. Chasing down criminals and making sure they were put in prison was a noble occupation, and one he seemed to have some aptitude for.

He was proud to be a Pinkerton detective. The agency had the largest collection of information anywhere about crimes and criminals in the United States. Thanks to their efforts, America was a safer place for law-abiding citizens. "We never sleep"—the motto of the Pinkerton agency—was proven true over and over as murderers, thieves, and anarchists were arrested in ever-growing numbers.

The older man reached for a fountain pen, scratching his name at the bottom of the final page of David's report with a flourish. "Those men who held up your stagecoach last fall got quite a surprise. Your story is much like Allan's. He got involved in detective work when he helped the Kane County sheriff capture a gang of counterfeiters."

David was familiar with the story of how Mr. Pinkerton had become a deputy sheriff before forming the agency with his brother Robert. The three-story building that housed their agency was a testament to their hard work and success. "As they say, 'It's an ill wind that blows no good.'"

The trip back from San Francisco had been difficult even before the incident Mr. Bastrup mentioned. David had traveled out there to reconcile with his father. That was a mistake that had cost him both time and money. On the long trip back, a pair of masked riders held up the mail coach. All the passengers were ordered out of the coach and told to empty their purses and pockets. Waiting for the right opportunity, he managed to pull his weapon, wound one of the robbers, and capture the other.

"How would you feel about a trip to New Orleans?"

The question caught David off guard. Most of the cases he'd worked were much closer to home. "Sir?"

Mr. Bastrup's wise brown eyes seemed to see right through him. "You're familiar with that part of the world, aren't you?"

Memories flooded David. The flavor of fresh fish; the smell of burning coal; warm, lazy days watching the splash of a paddlewheel. . . "I grew up in the South."

"You still talk like your mouth is full of cotton."

David had heard that complaint often since making Chicago his home. "The people back there say I sound like a Yankee."

A hint of a smile lighted Mr. Bastrup's face as he opened one of his desk drawers and pulled out a thick folder. "You may remember hearing about a rash of bank robberies in Chicago last year. Just about the time our agency was hired, before we could find out if the robberies were connected to each other, they stopped."

David watched the older man's face as frustration and anger replaced his moment of humor. Mr. Bastrup was dedicated to his job. For him it was a personal insult for someone to get away with a crime. As tenacious as a snapping turtle, he rarely failed.

"Now the same thing is happening in New Orleans. One of the bank officers wants to hire our agency. They need help getting their money back, and it seems the police force down there isn't having much luck. When I talked to Mr. Pinkerton about this assignment, I told him I think there may be a connection between the robbery there and what happened here. He agreed and told me about another incident in Vidalia, Louisiana, across the Mississippi River from Natchez. Isn't that where you're from?"

David didn't want to nod. He had no desire to discuss Natchez or even think about the people there. But Mr. Bastrup knew the answer. He tilted his head.

"I thought so." Bastrup slammed a fist on his desk for emphasis, making David's shoulder even more tense. "The robbers take their time and hit the banks when they are most vulnerable. We have to stop them.

Let people know their money is safe. I want an agent down there who can put them in jail where they belong."

An odd mix of feelings assailed David as he listened to his supervisor. He was equally anxious to catch the bank robbers, but he wasn't certain if he wanted to return to the South. He had come to Chicago for many reasons, not the least of which was to start a new life. He no longer had any family ties. He was free to go anywhere, even to Europe if he wanted. Was going back to the area where he'd grown up a good idea? His heart said yes; his mind, no. "Do you need an answer now?"

A frown drew Mr. Bastrup's eyebrows together. "Most of the detectives out there would jump at the chance I'm offering you. I thought you were a man of ambition. Do you really want to become a manager here, or are you satisfied working small cases in remote areas?"

When his supervisor laid out the options, David realized he didn't have much choice. "I'll do it."

"Good." Mr. Bastrup handed him the folder. "Here's all the information we gathered in Chicago. Maybe you'll see something we missed. And you should probably check out that bank that was robbed in Vidalia. They might have some new lead. If nothing else, it'll give you an opportunity to visit your family in Natchez before you continue on to New Orleans."

David started to correct him about his family situation, but he simply said, "Thank you for trusting me." He stood and tucked the folder under his arm. "I'll do my best."

Bastrup grunted. "I expect good things from you. If you want more responsibility, you'll have to earn it. Mr. Pinkerton demands it from himself and from his agents."

As he walked from the room, David wondered at the irony. He had thought he could break free of his past. Unresolved questions returned to his mind. Would the people in Natchez treat him differently now that he was a full-fledged detective? His life had taken so many turns that it made him dizzy to consider all the twists and turns. Where would this venture take him?

Chapter Two

Natchez, Mississippi

"My dance card is full." Jasmine Anderson snapped together the spines of her fan so David wouldn't see that several of them had no partner written on them. Why had Camellia decided to order fans instead of using the traditional dance cards that could be more easily hidden? Dangling from her wrist, its weight seemed to chide her for being untruthful. She wished she could use the silly thing to cool her cheeks. Why was the room so warm when the month of May had barely begun?

Jasmine set her jaw and glared up at him. She would not yield to temptation. David had no right to expect her to swoon with excitement because he had shown up at the last minute. At one time she might have considered a proposal from him—a temporary bout of madness, no doubt. She had been foolish enough to listen to his plans and dream of a future together. But no more. She was done pining for him.

A slight smile emerged from the corner of his lips but did not continue up to his eyes, eyes as green as maidenhair ferns. Eyes that held a hint of sadness. Why should he be sad? He was the one who had gone adventuring and left her to molder here in the backwaters.

Something had changed in him since he decided to move to Chicago and become a detective. And she didn't like it at all. In spite of her determination to remain at arm's length from him, she wished David could remain the staunch friend and ally he'd been. She was the same, after all. What had happened to the boy who had known her better than anyone else? Was he still inside there somewhere? Or had he ceased to be her David the moment he left town?

No matter the answers to all those questions, he should not have appeared so suddenly tonight. He should have had the decency to call on her yesterday or at least earlier this afternoon—before the ball started—like her other dance partners. Did he think he should get special consideration because of a handful of empty promises?

If that's what he thought, she would disabuse him of the notion right now. "I'm sorry, David. If I'd known you would be here. . ." She let the words trail off.

"Of course. I understand." His voice was steady and his smile widened, but his green eyes stayed sober. He bowed briefly. "I apologize for my presumption."

She was saved from further conversation with him by the appearance of William Smalley, her next dance partner. She welcomed his arrival with a determined smile. She refused to compare him to David. A proper gentleman, Mr. Smalley had called on her several days ago and secured her hand for this dance. Never mind that he was not as tall or broad shouldered as David. He was a very nice man, and she was looking forward to their dance.

"I believe our quadrille is beginning." Although William held out his right hand in invitation, his uncertain brown gaze darted from her face to David's.

"Of course." Jasmine put her hand on his arm and allowed herself to be swept onto the dance floor as the music began.

"You are looking exceptionally lovely this evening, Miss Anderson." William's smile was much more flattering and genuine than David's had been. It soothed her ruffled nerves.

Jasmine curtsied to him before turning to the gentleman on her right and curtsying again as the dance required. "Thank you, Mr. Smalley."

The orchestra's music could not quite drown out the conversations in the crowded ballroom, but at least out here they had room to breathe. Waiting for their turn to cross the square, she pulled at the cuff of her elbow-length glove. What was wrong with her? She should not be so nervous. It wasn't like this was her first ball. Since the end of the war she had attended dozens of similar affairs with her sister Camellia. At the age of twenty some would consider her an old maid, but Jasmine was determined to take her time before selecting a husband. Or she might decide to remain single. No law demanded that she marry, after all.

Tapping her foot in rhythm to the music, Jasmine swept out onto the floor with all the enthusiasm she could muster. As she and her partner neared the far end of their square, she held out her left hand for him to grasp. His right hand rested lightly on her waist as they executed the turn. In perfect coordination, they crossed the center once more to return to their original position. Then it was time to promenade.

Mr. Smalley was an excellent partner. Jasmine was beginning to enjoy herself in earnest, her gaze sweeping the room for sight of either of her older sisters. Both Lily and Camellia were dancing in another square, their husbands at their sides.

The turn of a man's blond head drew her attention. David! He was leaning toward another female and smiling. His eyes crinkled in the way she remembered. The way they should have crinkled when he was smiling at her.

Betrayal swept through her like a spring flood. Jasmine missed her next step and stumbled. If not for Mr. Smalley's tightened grip on her waist, she might have actually fallen to the floor like a graceless child.

"Are you all right, Miss Anderson?" His whispered question brushed past her ear.

She answered him with a nod. "Thanks to your quick thinking, sir."

"It's kind of you to say so." His face beamed, and his chest expanded with pride and satisfaction.

"I apologize. I must have been distracted. I promise I'm not usually so clumsy."

His eyes widened, and he swallowed hard. "You're never clumsy, Miss Anderson. Quite the opposite, in fact."

They reached the point in their square where they had begun, and Jasmine breathed a sigh of relief. Concentrating on the other dancers, she refused to let her mind wander to what she'd seen David Foster doing. It was none of her business anyway. Let him flirt with whatever girl he wished. He'd made it quite clear when he moved to Chicago what their friendship meant to him—nothing. He may have hinted at returning for her, but he'd never done so. And her heart had mended.

The quadrille came to its conclusion without further mishaps, and Mr. Smalley escorted her from the dance floor. Jasmine was quickly inundated with other young men who wished to dance with her. Laughing with all the skill she could muster, Jasmine allowed one or two to pen their names to the empty spines on her fan. No green-eyed traitor was going to ruin her night.

By the time the orchestra took its first break, her feet ached and her lips felt cracked from all the smiling she'd done. She spied a pair of empty chairs next to a large vase of cut flowers and hurried toward them. Sitting down with a sigh of relief, she stretched her toes as far as her shoes would allow. It would be nice if she could reach down and rub her arches, but Camellia—ever the stickler for proper behavior—would have a fit of apoplexy if she saw her sister doing anything so gauche.

"You seem to be the belle of the ball tonight." Lily's voice interrupted her moment of solitude.

Tucking her feet away, Jasmine glanced up at her oldest sister. Lily's light brown hair was pulled back into its usual bun, but it gleamed in the light of nearby candles. "Isn't that what you and Camellia want? Both of you seem insistent on introducing me to suitors so I'll wed and no longer be a burden to you."

"Don't be a goose." Lily sat down in the chair next to her, the dove gray silk of her dress sighing like the flutter of birds' wings. "You'll never be a burden to me. All I want is for you to be as happy as I am."

"And marriage is supposed to make that happen?"

Before Lily could answer, a shadow fell over their corner. Jasmine frowned as her other sister approached them. Camellia was resplendent as always. A true Southern belle, she wore a gown of light blue watered silk that matched the color of her eyes. Her golden hair was dressed in the latest style—pulled straight back to the crown of her head and allowed to cascade around her face in a profusion of ringlets. "Here the two of you are. I wondered if you were hiding."

Jasmine sighed. If she tried to arrange her hair that way, it would have looked like a rat's nest. But Camellia's natural curls could always be depended upon to look just right. "I believe you can count your ball a success."

Camellia's blue gaze swept the ballroom. "Who would want to miss such a festive evening? Did I see David here awhile ago?"

"I saw him at the docks this afternoon and invited him to come." Lily unfurled the fan each of the ladies had been given at the beginning of the ball—it was noticeably empty of partners' names—and waved it back and forth. "He didn't seem certain if he could make it. Did you speak to him, Jasmine?"

"Only for a moment." Jasmine's hands clenched in her lap. "I've been so busy dancing."

Camellia frowned at her. "I hope you weren't rude. David considers us his family, you know."

"I don't know why." Jasmine rolled her eyes. "He and I may have been playmates as children, but he's hardly been here since last summer."

"I'm sure it's been difficult for him. I wish his father had not died before David tracked him down." Lily's brown eyes moistened. "We all know what it's like to be separated from our parents."

Guilt assailed Jasmine. She grew up thinking her father had died in the same accident that took their mother's life. When he had reappeared eleven years ago, all their lives had changed. Lily had let go of her bitterness, Camellia had focused on her future, and Jasmine had welcomed Papa into her life with an open heart. She had accepted his viewpoint on everything from river traffic to faith. Of course, she was an adult now. She still respected her father, but she was beginning to see that the world could not be viewed as simply as he had once taught her.

She nodded to a far corner of the ballroom where a knot of dowagers and middle-aged courtiers had gathered. "It looks like Aunt Dahlia is still holding court. No wonder she was so eager for you to have this ball."

"I wonder where Uncle Phillip has gotten off to." Camellia pleated the material of her skirt, her blue gaze fastened on something farther away than their mother's sister. "I for one am glad to see her so animated. Since Grandmother died, she has become more frail somehow. Some days I worry that she will wilt like an unwatered flower."

"I doubt Aunt Dahlia is going to fade away." Lily's voice was practical as always. "She's as strong willed as ever. She may well outlive all of us."

Camellia tilted her head and considered her older sister. "The two of you have always rubbed each other the wrong way. Can you not forgive her for trying to marry you to the wrong man?"

"You can't think I would nurse a grudge like that." Lily's fan swept back and forth with enough speed to raise a breeze. "I forgave her many years ago. But she still expects me to go along with whatever strategy or plan comes to her fevered mind. Last week she told me that Magnolia needed to begin comportment lessons. My daughter is too young to be made to worry about such things. She's only four."

Deciding her two sisters might need someone to play the peacemaker, Jasmine cleared her throat. "And the two of you call me melodramatic?"

Both of her sisters stopped glaring at each other and turned to her. Lily was the first to respond. A smile broke through her frown. She nodded at Jasmine. "You make an excellent point."

Camellia looked as though she'd like to continue discussing the matter, but Jasmine raised an eyebrow and glanced toward the other guests. After a moment her shoulders relaxed. "I should find Jonah. He's supposed to dance with me after this break."

Jasmine and Lily watched her move across the dance floor in search of her husband, her gown barely swaying in spite of all the hoops under it.

"I cannot believe how warm this room is." Lily redoubled the speed of her fan and frowned at Jasmine. "Where is your fan? Has some

21

lovelorn boy stolen it away from you?"

Jasmine's cheeks heated. She had stashed it in a corner of the library earlier, unwilling to hold onto the evidence of her lie to David. "I . . . It's around here somewhere."

Her oldest sister raised her right eyebrow in a mannerism she had picked up from her husband. It conveyed her skepticism quite plainly.

Unwilling to admit the truth, Jasmine pushed herself up from her chair. "I believe the orchestra is ready to begin again." Without another word she escaped Lily's probing gaze, smiling widely at the young man she hoped was coming to collect her for the next dance.

The rest of the evening passed in a blur of mazurkas, waltzes, and polkas. By the time the ballroom emptied out, Jasmine was certain she had danced away at least an inch of her height. Everything hurt—feet, legs, arms—even her head. She could hardly wait to pull the hairpins out, exchange her ball gown for a nightgown, and seek her bed.

Uncle Phillip and Aunt Dahlia led the way as they all headed upstairs for the night. Jasmine yawned and put a hand to her aching head. "Don't expect to see me before noon."

Camellia glanced back over her shoulder at her younger sister. "I'm sure all of us feel the same way."

"*I'm* sure the children will have us up earlier than that." Lily put her hand on Blake's arm.

He laughed, the deep sound echoing in the quiet stairwell. "And I'm sure you'll want me to keep them busy while you get dressed."

"Would you? That would be grand."

Jasmine heard her brother-in-law mumble something but didn't quite catch what he said as she reached her bedroom door. It didn't really matter anyway. Lily and Blake were always carrying on like children.

With impatient fingers, she jerked her hair free from the pins restraining it as a sleepy maid helped her undress. "Thanks for staying up so late, Lynette. Go on to bed now."

The room darkened as the maid left, and Jasmine sighed her relief. She had gotten through the evening even though David Foster's presence had made it a trial. Normally she wouldn't have taken part in every dance, but because she'd told him that she had no dances open, she'd had little choice. A wry smile crossed her face. She supposed she had no one to blame for her aches but her own incautious tongue.

As she drifted to sleep, a Bible verse her father had once taught her floated through her mind. *"In the multitude of words there wanteth not sin: but he that refraineth his lips is wise."* Her last thought was that she was not as wise as she thought. . .according to the Bible anyway.

Chapter Three

I think we should pay a visit to Anna and Jean Luc." Blake Matthews pushed his chair away from the dining table.

"That's a good idea." Lily finished the last bite of her toast and washed it down with a sip of strong, dark coffee. "I noticed they weren't at the ball last night."

She wasn't surprised at the absence of Blake's sister and brother-in-law. They had only come back to Natchez last month, and she had hoped they might attend, even though some sticklers might have raised their eyebrows. Glancing toward her husband, she could tell he was thinking the same thing. So often their minds traveled the same pathways. Lily supposed it was a result of working together so closely. . .and of being married for ten years.

"It would have been a good opportunity to reintroduce them to the people here." Blake tapped a foot on the floor. "But I suppose they were worried about keeping up appearances."

Lily placed her napkin on the table next to her plate. "I tried to tell Anna that no one would think anything amiss if they were seen at a family party. I know they are still in mourning for Jean Luc's father, but that doesn't mean they have to avoid every social gathering."

Aunt Dahlia frowned at Lily's words. "I don't know what this world is coming to. You young people don't have any respect at all for traditions that have been followed for centuries."

"It's a brave new world, Aunt Dahlia." Camellia handed a soft, warm biscuit to Amaryllis, her two-year-old daughter. "We've left the old ways behind."

Lily was surprised at her sister's agreement. In the past Camellia had always been determined to cling to rules and regulations, but her marriage to Jonah had brought about some much-needed changes in her sister's personality. It was a pity the same could not be said for Aunt Dahlia. But she and Uncle Phillip still adhered to the practices that had been in effect prior to the war.

She sent a stern glance to her oldest child, Noah. "You need to practice your sums while we're gone, young man."

Jasmine rushed into the dining room at that point, her expression harried. "Good morning."

She reached across Magnolia and grabbed a piece of dry toast.

"Why don't you sit and break your fast like a real lady?" Disapproval filled Camellia's voice and her face.

"No time." Jasmine stood behind her niece's chair and munched on the toast. "I'm already late."

A harrumph from Aunt Dahlia showed her agreement with Camellia.

Deciding to allow her younger sister the benefit of the doubt, Lily frowned at the other two women before turning a smile to Jasmine. "Where are you off to?"

"The orphanage." Jasmine dusted crumbs from her hands, her bread gone. "We have practice beginning at nine."

Blake pulled out his pocket watch. "It's 8:50. I'm afraid you're going to be late whether you sit and eat or not."

"I know." Jasmine blew them a kiss. "Don't expect me for lunch, Camellia. I'll eat at the orphanage." With that parting shot she left, disappearing before anyone had time to stop her.

"Phillip, don't you agree that girl is allowed far too much freedom?"

Uncle Phillip didn't emerge from his newspaper but gave a grunt that his wife took as agreement.

"I suppose that means Jasmine won't go visiting with us this morning." Lily picked up Benjamin, her baby, and excused herself from the dining room. She was eager to make her escape before Aunt Dahlia started in on one of her diatribes. She knew it would lead to her favorite list of deficiencies since the end of the war.

Like others of her age and social status, her aunt imbued the prewar days with a golden glow that had little to do with reality. If Aunt Dahlia had her way, slavery would be reinstated and Jefferson Davis would still be the president of the Confederacy. No matter what anyone said, she was not likely to change her opinion. Although Lily felt sorry for her, she didn't want to be trapped into either arguing with the older woman or tacitly agreeing with her beliefs.

As she reached the nursery door, Lily heard footsteps coming up the staircase and turned to see who was coming.

Blake appeared at the top of the stairs, their daughter, Magnolia, in his arms and Noah walking as close to his father as possible.

The sight of her family warmed Lily's heart. God had blessed them so.

Her husband's teasing blue gaze met hers. "I can't believe you abandoned me and two of your children to a homily on the waywardness of today's young people."

"Benjamin was growing fussy." Lily stepped into the nursery, depositing her youngest son on his bed while she gathered clean clothes and a fresh diaper. "Besides, you seem to have escaped unscathed."

Blake followed her into the room, handing their daughter over to the nanny, who would watch all of the children. He settled Noah at his desk with a lesson on mathematics while Lily readied Benjamin for his nap in a wicker bassinet. Magnolia and her cousin Amaryllis played with their dolls in one corner of the room under the nanny's indulgent gaze.

Listening to them was almost like traveling back in time to her own childhood, when Lily and her sisters had played together in this very same room. After a few moments, her husband put his arm around her waist and pulled her from the nursery. "How long before we can leave?"

"I just have to put on a cap and get my parasol."

Blake dropped a quick kiss on her cheek. "I'll go get the buggy ready and meet you downstairs."

By the time Lily had gathered her things and stepped out into the warm morning, Blake was sitting in the buggy with the reins in his hands. She climbed up beside him and settled herself as he guided the horse down the lane to the main road.

"I wonder if Jean Luc and Anna will stay in Natchez or if they plan on taking his mother back to Cape Girardeau." Lily glanced at her husband's face. What a boon it would be to have both of their families living in the same town. Of course, given the number of trips they took to deliver people and goods up and down the Mississippi, they were sure to see all of their relatives from time to time. But she rather liked the idea of getting to know Blake's sister better, which was more likely to happen if she and Jean Luc remained in Natchez.

"I hope so." Blake spared her a quick glance before returning his gaze to the road ahead. "I doubt it would do his mother much good to be uprooted from the home she's lived in all these years."

"And Jean Luc could take over his father's shipping business." Lily caught her breath as an idea burst on her with the suddenness of a summer thunderstorm. "Maybe we could even help to make sure he's successful."

"Perhaps."

Lily looked at her husband again, noticing the tightness around his jaw. He could not be worried that Jean Luc was still the malicious person who had once tried to wreck their first boat, the boat that had brought the two of them together. That had been more than ten years ago. In the intervening years, Jean Luc had proved his trustworthiness again and again. Besides, he was the father of Blake's only nephew. "I know you've forgiven him, Blake, but have you put the past behind you?"

"Of course I have." Blake moved the reins to his left hand and put his right hand over hers. "In fact, Jean Luc and I have talked several times over the past few years about the future of river traffic."

His tone of voice was ominous, striking a chord of fear in Lily's heart. "What do you mean?"

Blake's hand squeezed her cold fingers. "You must have noticed how the number of boats has decreased for the past year or so."

"People are just recovering from the war." Lily refused to accept his interpretation of the reduced traffic. Sometimes they might go an afternoon without seeing another boat, but it was unusual. They didn't see as many of the smaller vessels, but that was because the larger boats could navigate better and transport merchandise more economically. "River traffic is going to come back. It has to. It's only been a few years. Think of all the boats we see every time we go to New Orleans."

He pulled back on the horse's reins and turned to give her his full attention. "I know how much you love the river, darling. And I'm sure we can continue to move cargo in *Water Lily*. But you have to realize things are changing. The railroads are a good alternative for a lot of businessmen. More and more bridges will crisscross the river as people out West demand better service. The flaw in our waterways is the difficulty in reaching all destinations. Railroads will always go places that riverboats cannot."

The irony of the situation was not lost on Lily as she listened to Blake explain his logic. Hadn't she just been feeling sorry for Aunt Dahlia because she would not accept the inevitability of change? Was God trying to tell Lily that she should deal with the log in her eye before trying to remove the mote in her aunt's eye? She took a deep, steadying breath. "I'm sure we can make a life for ourselves anywhere, Blake."

"That's my practical Lily." He loosened the reins once more, and the horse picked up speed. "People will always want to seek a better life in new places, and they will need more supplies shipped to them no matter the method of transportation."

Lily bit her lip as she tried to imagine making a home on one of the smoking, belching beasts that threatened her lifestyle. She didn't much like the rumble they made crossing the tall bridges the *Water Lily* glided under. Could she trade gentle breezes and swift-flowing water for hot cinders and soot? Could trains even accommodate a family like their riverboat could?

Yet the idea of visiting new destinations was somewhat intriguing. Perhaps looking into a different mode of transportation was a good idea. With a lift of her chin, she decided that she would first trust God and then her husband and follow. . .no matter the destination.

※

David took a battered envelope from his breast pocket and studied its limp edges. He knew the contents of the note inside. Had memorized the words months earlier when he'd first received the letter originally addressed to his deceased mother.

"What do you have there?" Marguerite Trahan, the assistant at Mercy House Orphanage stepped into the parlor, her dark gaze full of curiosity.

He tucked the letter back into his pocket and turned to the girl who had become his friend when both of them lived here as children. "Nothing of importance."

Marguerite was a sweet young woman, with the dark hair and eyes of her Cajun heritage. Even though she had spent many years on the Mississippi side of the river, her voice still held a hint of an accent. "Is that so, *cher*? Then why the long face?"

David met her stare with one of his own. The air in the parlor thickened as the silence between them lengthened.

She cleared her throat but did not drop her gaze. "You look like a man with a heavy burden."

Part of him yearned to confide in her. More than anyone else in his life, Marguerite understood what it meant to have no family. Perhaps if he talked to her, he could move past the pervading feeling of aloneness that had stalked him for the past months. Not that he felt this bad all the time. Last night's encounter with Jasmine and her sisters had brought back his feelings of inadequacy. A wall stood between him and her family, a wall that he seemed unable to scale. She tilted her head to one side, making him think of a bird. "Does this have to do with that father of yours? Did you find him?"

Her questions pierced him, bringing the grief of loss crashing down on him. He tightened his chin against the tears that threatened. If his father had taught him anything before leaving, it had been that men had to be strong. . .always. David pulled the note from his pocket once more, turning it over in his hands. "I was too late."

Children ran past the doorway, talking and laughing, their voices filling the air as they clattered outside to play in the yard.

Inside the parlor, silence dominated the room. He dragged his gaze from the door to look at Marguerite. He was surprised by the comprehension in her face.

She stepped toward him and placed a gentle hand on his arm. "I'm sorry."

David wondered why it had to be Marguerite who showed him such sympathy. Why not Jasmine? She had known about his father's death, but where was her concern over his loss? His heart twisted. Jasmine was too caught up in her plays and dramas. Playacting was her answer to all of life's questions. Would she never grow up?

"Thanks." David summoned a smile for Marguerite's sake. He wasn't supposed to hurt this badly. Not for a father who hadn't cared anything about him. "It's probably just as well. He was pretty sick when he sent this note. I doubt he would have wanted me to see him that way."

"It might have been easier for you if you could have made your peace with him."

Shamed by his roiling emotions, David wondered what he had expected from his father. He shook off Marguerite's hand and walked to the window, his gaze looking past the children outside as his mind piled up all the reasons he could never have made his peace with the man.

Pa had abandoned him and Ma years ago. Sure, he'd promised he would come back for them as soon as he made a fortune digging for gold. But like so many who had followed the lure of easy riches, he'd failed. And he had failed those who relied on him—the only people in the world who loved him. "All my Pa was ever good for was empty promises."

Marguerite sat down in a narrow chair on the far side of the room. "At least you had a father."

The wistfulness of her words was not lost on him, but David knew there were worse things than not having a father.

"If you could call him that. I had to pay off his debts once I finally tracked down the house he lived in." David heard the hatred in his own voice. It stopped him for a brief instant, but then he realized that he should hate the man. Jeremy Foster had not been a father. Or a husband, for that matter. He'd been a selfish, foolish man who knew nothing about love. "He deserved to die all alone for the pain he caused me and my mother."

Marguerite sighed. "I know he hurt you, David. But you need to forgive him."

He rounded on her then. "Forgive him? Why should I forgive him? His desertion changed my life."

"Yes." She unfolded from the chair, her movements graceful. "But if you don't forgive him, you'll never be free."

"I know that the Bible agrees with you, Marguerite. But God couldn't mean I should just forgive Pa. My mother had to—" He choked, unable to continue for a moment. "She had to make a living in Natchez Under-the-Hill. If not for the Anderson girls—for their acceptance of me—I don't know what would have happened to me." The words were bitter in his throat. Talking about his past was hard, but he wanted Marguerite to understand. He wasn't a bad person. His pa was the villain.

She smiled at him, a world of knowledge and peace in her gaze. "If you don't find a way to forgiveness, it will kill you. Your Pa is already dead. He can't feel your wrath. Who will it hurt if you forgive him?"

The heat trying to consume him ebbed a little. David yearned for the same peace she had found. Was forgiveness the only way to get it?

"I know you're a Christian, David."

"Of course I am." He had never let his parents' poor decisions get in the way of his beliefs. He knew God loved him. He knew Christ had been born a man and died on the cross to save all sinners.

"God gave so much so you and I could spend eternity with Him.

He's your real father. He's the one you can turn to." She smiled at him, a radiant smile that offered promise and hope. "I'll be praying that you let Him show you the way to forgiveness."

He wanted to grasp the promise in her words. But something held him back. Some inner spirit that whispered he shouldn't have to forgive a man who had wronged him to such an extent.

"Why don't you talk to Lily and Blake?" Marguerite's voice seemed to come from far away even though he knew they were still standing in the parlor. "They've been like family to you."

David shook his head. "It's not the same. I know you understand the hope that one day you and your parents can be together again. No matter what they've done, as long as they're out there, you can't abandon them. Lily and her family are special to me, but on some level, I'll always be the discarded kid they felt sorry for. I've never been one of them."

"I think you're wrong, David. They love you. Talk to them. Tell them how you feel. Maybe they'll help you understand what I'm having a hard time communicating to you."

Understanding was not the problem. David understood that his father had been a worthless bum and that he and his mother had paid the price for the man's shiftlessness. While his father had chased the illusion of easy wealth, David had depended on the charity of others for food and shelter. "Lily and Blake took me in. I owe them a debt of gratitude I'll never be able to repay."

She frowned at him. "Then what about Jasmine?"

"What about Jasmine?"

Her laughter was musical. "Come on, David. You're not fooling me. You've always been sweet on that girl."

He lifted a shoulder. "You are a hopeless romantic. Please don't read anything into my association with Jasmine except for a childish infatuation. Jasmine had all the things I did not—wealth, security, and a family who cared for her. She cannot understand my feelings."

A noise at the door took his attention away from Marguerite. His heart climbed into his throat as he saw Jasmine standing there. What had she heard? Did she know they'd been discussing her? Had she heard his confession of infatuation? But that would be no surprise to her. Jasmine had to know how much he adored—*had* adored her. Even as he told himself that the attraction between them was a thing of the past, he knew better. He would always love her, even if she had tired of waiting for him.

"Excuse me, I was looking for Miss Deborah." Her face was frozen, not giving any inkling of her thoughts.

Marguerite stepped between him and the door. "I believe she's in the back parlor, working with some of the older girls on their needlework."

Jasmine nodded, but her gaze was still fastened on him. Were her cheeks paler than when he'd seen her last night, or was it his imagination?

David ran a finger around the collar of his shirt. Why had he given in to the temptation of confiding in someone? "I've got to go. I have business in town."

"Feel free to stop by anytime, David." Marguerite sent a knowing glance his way.

He shook his head. He was not about to confide in Jasmine Anderson. "Tell Miss Deborah I'll come back this afternoon when she's not so busy."

David jammed his bowler on his head and stalked past both women. When would he learn to keep his own counsel? A fine detective he was turning out to be, spilling his guts the first time someone was kind to him. It was a good thing Mr. Bastrup was in Chicago.

David wondered when he would ever learn the harsh lesson that he was all alone. Like always. And he always would be. Except for God, of course. He sent a rueful glance toward the sky. "But God, it sure would be nice to have someone down here to care about me."

Chapter Four

Lily accepted a cup of tea from Anna and balanced it on her knees. "I'm sorry you couldn't come last night."

"We appreciated your invitation, didn't we, Mama Champney?" Anna glanced toward Jean Luc's mother.

Dressed in unrelieved black, the widow was pale and listless. The elder Mrs. Champney's attention was not on her guests but on her lap and the lace handkerchief she was twisting into a tight spiral.

Lily's heart ached for the evidence of the other woman's grief. She would have to remember to say a special prayer for her.

"What?" Mrs. Champney looked up and glanced around the parlor as though she had no idea where she was.

"I said we appreciated the invitation to the ball at Les Fleurs."

"Yes." The older lady's wistful gaze fastened on Lily's face. "Dashiell and I used to have such nice parties."

Unshed tears made Lily clear her throat before answering. "Yes, the whole town talks about the fancy balls and masquerades you've hosted. Not to mention your famous galas on one or another of your boats."

The barest hint of a smile on Mrs. Champney's lips quivered before disappearing. "You're sweet to say so."

The conversation died again as the ladies sipped their tea. Lily glanced around the large parlor that was still swathed in black cloth to mourn Mr. Champney's death. The mirrors and pictures were hidden, as was the outside. She found herself wishing she could pull back the drapes and open the window to let in some sunlight and fresh air. She would rather have gone to walk the garden with her husband and Jean Luc than remain in this dark, stuffy room.

The door opened, and she looked up, hoping her thought had brought her husband back to the parlor. Instead she saw the familiar face of Aunt Tessie, Anna and Blake's aunt. She rose as the lady entered the room, putting down her teacup and moving across the room to offer a hug.

Aunt Tessie never seemed to age. The few wrinkles on her face had more to do with smiles than sagging skin, and her light blue eyes were as sharp as ever. The silver streaks in her hair were a bit more numerous than the last time Lily had seen Aunt Tessie, but they were still outnumbered by light brown strands. Perhaps it was her posture— so straight and tall—that gave her the appearance of a younger lady. Whatever the reason, Lily hoped she would age as gracefully as Aunt Tessie.

"You must tell me all about my great-niece and nephews." Aunt Tessie sat in a chair next to Lily and accepted a cup of tea from Anna. "I imagine Noah has grown several inches since I saw him last."

"Closer to a foot." Lily picked up her tea once more. "Magnolia is not far behind him, and even Benjamin is growing like a weed."

Anna's face lifted with her smile. "I know what you mean. Achille seems to get taller even while he's asleep."

The conversation picked up then as they compared notes and shared stories of their children's accomplishments. Even Mrs. Champney emerged from her miasma long enough to recount a story of the fine mess of fresh fish Jean Luc and his son had caught for dinner a few days earlier.

Lily countered with a story of the large turtle Noah and Magnolia had discovered in an estuary and sneaked aboard the *Water Lily* during a recent trip. Of course the reptile had gotten out of their quarters during a meal and caused enough havoc with the crew that their cook, Jensen, had suggested he could make gumbo with the turtle her children had adopted.

Jean Luc and Blake reentered the room as she was describing Jensen's relief to find that the turtle had "escaped"—with the help of her distressed children—before he had a chance to make good on his threat.

Blake leaned against the fireplace, his gaze darting between his sister and aunt as though he was considering how to broach a difficult topic. He turned down the offer of tea and cookies, patting his flat stomach with a rueful gaze that made even Mrs. Champney smile. "I am most impressed with your son's understanding of the shipping business, ma'am. You must be proud of him."

"Yes." She reached for Jean Luc, who had taken a seat next to her on the sofa, bringing his hand to her cheek. "He's the best parts of his father and has far exceeded our hopes for him."

Jean Luc shrugged, but Lily saw a gleam in his eye that might have been a tear. He brushed a hand across his face before sending a smile toward his mother.

"He and I have been discussing a joint venture that we both believe will strengthen Champney Shipping and ensure that it remains in business for years to come—but perhaps with a new name." Blake pushed away from the mantel and came to stand next to the chair Lily sat in. He put a hand on her shoulder. "A decade ago my wife had the foresight to purchase a boat and chisel out a life for herself and her family on the Mississippi."

Lily looked up at him, her heart nearly exploding with joy. "It was a joint venture."

"Exactly. Partnerships are often successful because one person's strengths can fill gaps made by the other's weaknesses." The look in his blue eyes bathed her in so much approval Lily hardly minded the way he had manipulated her.

"Blake and I have been talking about a partnership I believe would be equally beneficial for both of our families." Jean Luc sat forward, his handsome face eager. His excitement seemed to invade the dark room, holding grief at bay if only for a short time. "The United States is growing by leaps and bounds. Now that the scars of war are healing, people are anxious to make up for lost time. They're building homes and businesses in what used to be uninhabited frontier. Whole new towns are springing up, and with them comes the need for everything from nails to barber chairs."

Lily could feel her stomach turn over as she looked at her husband. Words they had spoken on the way over here flooded into her mind. But perhaps she was jumping to conclusions. She would withhold judgment until she understood exactly what the two men were proposing. "You want us to invest in Champney Shipping?"

Blake shook his head. "We thought it would be better to create a new company—one that will focus on rail transportation instead of the river."

"Rail?" Anna looked confused, her gaze seeking comfort from her husband's face.

Lily put a hand to her chest to calm the pounding of her heart. "Isn't this rather sudden?"

"How long did it take you to decide to purchase the *Hattie Belle*?" Blake's eyes danced as he reminded her of the early days when they had first discovered they each owned part of a large riverboat.

This was different! she wanted to protest, but the words stuck in her throat. She swallowed hard and considered how to answer her husband. "Not. . .long." She didn't want to make the admission, but honesty compelled her to be truthful. "But I knew—"

Jean Luc raised a hand and stopped her sputtering. "The way my father told it, you didn't even know you had a partner until after you bought him out."

"I think it's a splendid idea." Aunt Tessie joined the conversation, making Lily feel like she was the only one resisting the notion. "I've been worried about all of you for years. The river is a harsh place with so many dangers—snags, floods, and storms to name a few. Lily, you and Blake have children who rely on you to care for them. Maybe it's time for you to settle down somewhere and make a permanent home for them. I'm not talking about Les Fleurs. While I'm certain Camellia welcomes your company, you should have an estate of your own."

Lily sat back and nearly overset her teacup. Catching it with one hand, she considered what Aunt Tessie had said. The idea of selling their boat—their home—pained her. She had been raised at Les Fleurs, but she had claimed her adulthood on the riverboat. Besides that, what would her father do? She couldn't imagine him giving up his life on the river. Would she have to choose between her father and her husband?

"Why don't we all give the matter some thought?" Anna's voice was calm and matter-of-fact. She set her teacup on the tray.

Blake nodded. "You're right, Sister. I think it's an option to consider, but we don't have to decide anything today. We have enough business to keep us afloat for some time. In fact, we'll be leaving for New Orleans by the end of the week."

The conversation around her grew more general, but Lily's mind was focused on the idea of buying or building a home. She had no idea where she would even want to live if they sold the *Water Lily*. Natchez might be a place Camellia loved, but for Lily it had been a relief to leave the self-important planters behind. New Orleans? While there was much to commend that city, she didn't relish the idea. Blake's father had settled near Cape Girardeau, Missouri, but Blake had never been interested in living there.

The sound of Anna clapping her hands drew Lily back to the conversation. "You should go with my brother and Lily."

Aunt Tessie's gaze bumped into her own. Lily scrambled for a proper response. She thought they had been talking about the upcoming trip south, hadn't they? "Have you ever been to New Orleans?"

"No." Aunt Tessie lifted her shoulders in a shrug. "I've always wanted to travel, but I never have found the time."

"Do you have room to take on a passenger?" Jean Luc asked.

Lily thought it was a great idea. "Of course we have room for such a pleasant companion, don't we, Blake."

"I don't know." Aunt Tessie glanced toward her niece. "Anna probably needs me to stay here and help with the baby."

"Don't be silly." Anna looked at her husband for confirmation before continuing. "Mama Champney, Jean Luc, and I can handle matters here. You go have a wonderful time."

"We'd love for you to come with us." Blake winked at his aunt. "But don't be surprised if you find yourself washing dishes or setting tables."

"Ignore your nephew." Lily's glare should have burned him to a crisp. She didn't want his aunt to get the wrong idea. "We'd love to have you with us. I won't let him put you to work."

"I wouldn't mind that a bit." Aunt Tessie's eyes were bright with excitement. "I might even get to spend some extra time with my great-nephews and great-niece."

Lily need not have worried that Aunt Tessie would misunderstand her nephew's teasing words. She could feel her irritation draining away.

Jean Luc stood and brushed a hand across his wife's shoulder. "It's settled then. As long as you'll be okay, Aunt Tessie will go with Blake and Lily at the end of the week." He shot a speaking glance toward Blake. "You and I can get together again once you return."

As she and Blake gathered their things and took their leave of the Champneys, Lily couldn't stop her mind from considering once more the idea of giving up life on the river. Could she do it? Should she? What would she really be giving up? While she enjoyed the challenges of life on the river, did she owe it to her children to give them a more normal childhood? The questions swirled inside her mind like an eddying current on the river.

She knew she'd have to spend some time talking to God about what to do. He had led her this far. He would certainly be there to guide her in the future.

ॐ

"I'm worried about your future, Jasmine." Lily watched as her youngest sister picked up a doll she used to play with—one of Magnolia's favorites now—and placed it on a shelf.

The children were playing outside under Camellia's watchful eye, except for Benjamin, who was napping nearby while Lily and Jasmine straightened the nursery.

"By the time I was your age—"

"I know. You were already a successful businesswoman with a boat and crew to manage." Jasmine picked up the toy soldiers that belonged to Noah. "And Camellia was choosing amongst her numerous suitors for the best possible match."

Silence filled the spacious room as Lily considered what to say next. She didn't know how to talk to Jasmine anymore. A part of her longed for bygone days when her sister was a happy-go-lucky girl with a penchant for adventure. "What do you want from me?"

"I want to go to Chicago, or New York, or even San Francisco—anywhere that I can act on a real stage in front of a real audience." A wistful sigh and downcast eyes accompanied Jasmine's answer.

Lily had thought it difficult when Camellia wanted to attend a finishing school in New Orleans during the thorny days preceding the war. That was nothing compared to the idea of sending Jasmine to some far-off city. Nightmare scenarios filled her imagination. "I thought you were happy with the Shakespearean play you and the other young people are putting on for the community. It was your idea. And I am so proud of you for wanting to help the orphanage by donating the proceeds to them. Miss Deborah told me she hopes to purchase a new stove and pay for several other repairs."

Jasmine meandered to the window. "It's fine, but I want to be as famous as 'The Divine Sarah.' And that's not likely to happen here in Natchez, performing in a homemade production to benefit the orphanage."

"I'd say she is more infamous than famous." Lily walked up behind her sister and looked out over the plantation grounds. "What would Aunt Dahlia have to say about a niece who performs on the stage and has the reputation of a Sarah Bernhardt? The poor thing is liable to have a fit of apoplexy."

A choked giggle from Jasmine brought her some hope. If she

could get her sister laughing, maybe they could work together to find a compromise to satisfy Jasmine's need for recognition while keeping her safe from harm.

Lily snapped her fingers as a new idea occurred to her. "What if we plan a trip to Chicago this winter?"

"Do you mean it?" Jasmine swung around, her violet eyes practically glowing with excitement.

"Yes." Lily's excitement built as her vague idea began to take form. "We could ask Camellia and Tamar to go with us, too. We could spend at least a week, maybe even two there."

The excitement disappeared from Jasmine's expressive eyes. "Unless you plan on leaving me behind, that wouldn't be enough time to accomplish anything."

"I'm afraid anything longer is out of the question." Lily frowned at the windowpane. "Maybe we could have David escort us. He would be the perfect one to make sure you were safe if we did have to leave."

"Don't be silly. David Foster doesn't want to be saddled with someone like me."

Lily was surprised at the venom in Jasmine's voice. "What do you mean? That boy has worshipped the ground you walk on since both of you were children. He's pulled you out of more scrapes than I can count."

"Maybe so." Jasmine pulled at the material of her cuff. "But I have it on the best authority that he has no interest in me anymore."

"Who told you that? Some jealous debutante? You should know better than to listen to gossip."

A deep sadness came over Jasmine, and she sighed. "I wasn't listening to gossip, Sissy. He said it himself."

It had been a decade since Jasmine used her pet name for Lily. Aunt Dahlia had forbidden it in public, and Lily thought her sister had outgrown it. Protectiveness was her first response, followed swiftly by betrayal and anger. "I can hardly believe his ingratitude. David has always been welcome in this house and in our lives. For him to say such a mean thing to you is inexcusable. The next time I see him, I'm going to give him a piece of my mind."

Jasmine's eyes widened. "Please don't."

"He deserves much worse. Wait until Blake hears about this."

"You can't say anything to David. He didn't mean to hurt my feelings. He didn't know I was in the room when he said it." Jasmine's chin quivered. "Besides all that, he has a right to his opinion. Everyone has that right. If he has outgrown his feelings for me, I'd rather know it."

Lily pulled her sister into a hug. Jasmine's arms went around her, and the poor thing began crying like her heart was breaking. She rubbed her sister's back in a comforting motion while she wondered how she could have been so wrong.

It had to be a misunderstanding. She had watched David grow up. That man loved Jasmine more than he loved his own life. Sure he'd been away from Natchez for a time, but no one changed that much. And at the ball the other night, he had made a beeline for Jasmine. "Don't worry, sweetheart."

The tears ceased a little later. Jasmine pulled away, sniffed, and began fishing for something.

"What's the matter?"

Jasmine shook her head. "I need a handkerchief."

"Here, use mine." Lily pulled a rumpled square of cloth from her skirt pocket and watched as Jasmine mopped her face with it.

"Thanks." Jasmine tucked the handkerchief into her sleeve. "I'm sorry I fell apart. It was just a shock to hear David describe me as nothing more than a childish infatuation. He said it with such contempt. Like he wished he'd never met me."

Lily brushed a strand of hair back from Jasmine's temple. "The more you tell me, the more I'm inclined to believe something else is going on here. David may be going through something we know nothing about."

"I'll bet Marguerite Trahan knows about it, whatever it is. That's who he was confiding in."

Patting her sister on the shoulder, Lily shook her head. "If you don't want me to talk to him about what he said, I hope you will. He probably has a reasonable explanation. Maybe he's trying to make you jealous. You were a bit cool to him the other night during the ball." The more she thought about it, the more convinced Lily became that David was either put out by Jasmine's refusal to dance or trying to draw her attention.

"I don't think I can."

Lily raised an eyebrow. "If you don't, I will."

That brought Jasmine's chin up. Good. She hoped her sister would confront David. And Lily would be there to comfort her if David really was falling in love with someone else.

As she moved to go outside and collect her other two children so she could get them ready for lunch, Lily wondered why life had to be so complicated. Why couldn't things run as smoothly as they did when the family was on the river? Their biggest problems then were a cranky boiler or passenger. No prickly questions of love or heartbreak.

She could hardly wait to get to New Orleans. Maybe her friends in that city could offer sage advice or some way to redirect Jasmine's energy. She didn't want her sister to continue pining about, dreaming of a future that would only lead to heartbreak and disappointment.

Chapter Five

$\mathcal{J}$asmine peeked out at the audience. Miss Deborah, the lady who had run Mercy House since before Jasmine was born, sat on the front row. Her hair was pulled back in a tight bun, and her kindly face wore a wide smile.

Jasmine didn't even mind seeing Miss Deborah's assistant, Marguerite, occupying the seat next to her. Beyond her were Jean Luc Champney with his wife and mother. David's blond hair was visible on the second row. He sat with Papa, Lily, Camellia, and the rest of her family. Beyond them she could hear the rustle of the audience, but she couldn't make out the faces.

"Are you ready, Cordelia?"

Recognizing her character's name, Jasmine swung around and curtsied to Cedrick Wilson, who was playing King Lear, the title character in Shakespeare's play. A flowing white beard had been glued to his face and obscured everything below his brown eyes. He tugged on the beard with one hand as he waited for her response.

Jasmine glanced down at her own outfit and some of her pre-performance excitement ebbed. Miss Deborah and Tamar had done an excellent job sewing the various costumes for their project. Camellia had not liked the idea of using material taken from the rag bins at Les Fleurs, and Jasmine had wanted to agree with her. She would have loved a fancy costume, complete with flowing robes and a conical hat. But then ever-practical Lily had suggested that the money they would spend on new cloth would do much better going to replace the orphanage roof.

"Buck up, Jasmine." Cedrick's voice teased her. "You don't die until the end of the play."

She raised an eyebrow at him. "I have a lot on my mind."

Cedrick was the handsome younger son of one of the wealthiest plantation owners in Natchez. Jasmine had been flattered when he set aside his philandering tendencies to spend time helping with their production. For a while her family had thought he might be trying to fix his interest with her, but Cedrick had never been anything but a friend. She valued his friendship but knew, as he apparently did, that they had no warmer feelings toward each other.

"I think the whole town is out there." He inclined his head toward the audience.

Jasmine followed his gaze. "What else is there to do in Natchez?"

He raised an eyebrow but didn't answer. He didn't have to. She had spent enough time at the docks to hear about the "entertainments" available at the various inns and gambling saloons.

The voice of the stage manager interrupted their whispered conversation. "Take your places everyone."

As the play began, Cedrick took her hand and squeezed it. Jasmine mouthed the opening words along with the actors playing the parts of the dukes of Kent and Gloucester, George Reed and Tom Hayes. "I've never seen anyone more focused than you, Jasmine. I—"

Other actors joined them, including Ellen Tate and Wendy Jeffers, who were playing King Lear's older daughters, Goneril and Regan.

"Is it time for our entrance?" Ellen asked.

Cedrick nodded and dropped Jasmine's hand. As she followed him and the others onto the stage, Jasmine wished for a moment that he were interested in her. At least Cedrick understood what made her heart pound with anticipation. He didn't try to convince her to let go of her dreams. He would probably even support her desire to leave Natchez. But she didn't have time for romance. She had a career to pursue.

"Love, and be silent." Jasmine's first words were a bit shaky. She needed to forget everything else. She could not fail now, or Lily would never take her seriously. When it came time to speak again, she put everything into the words. They soared over the audience, bringing the reaction she had hoped for and setting up the Bard's tragedy.

The curtain rose and fell, each scene tightening the knot until none of the characters could succeed. From her place off-stage in "prison," Jasmine realized her eyes had adjusted to the dim light in the audience. She could see a few of the women dabbing at their eyes with handkerchiefs, and her heart lifted. This might be a ragtag group of actors and their stage might be nothing more than a raised dais with homemade curtains, but still they were managing to elicit emotion from the audience.

By the time the curtain fell for the final time, Jasmine knew they were a success. Cedrick winked as he took her hand and led her to the center of the stage. They waited as the other actors crowded around them—from the smallest of the children who'd spoken no lines to those who had memorized dozens of speeches over the past weeks—all proud of the work they had done to ensure the orphanage would continue operating.

The curtain rose, and applause began in earnest. Cedrick pulled her with him as he stepped forward. She curtsied while he bowed, wishing he would not be so attentive now. Everyone would think they had an understanding.

Jasmine forced her mouth into a wide smile and concentrated on the future. One day she would perform in front of a real audience. She would stand in front of a heavy curtain made of rich crimson velvet and bow to a full theater of well-educated patrons who had paid hefty prices for the chance to watch her perform.

Instead of enjoying this moment, Jasmine found herself wondering if Lily would ever allow her to follow her own dreams. She wanted more, much more, than what Natchez had to offer. She wanted fame.

She wanted to see her name on a theater marquis, to be feted and adored by people from all over America. From all over the world, actually.

Aunt Dahlia might not approve, but that wouldn't stop Jasmine. She would not be ashamed of her own dreams even if her family didn't support them. Providing entertainment to others was a time-honored tradition. It gave people chances to forget for a while their boring, humdrum lives.

Since she'd been a youngster, Jasmine had found satisfaction in performing for others. Family and friends all told her she was talented. If only Lily would let her go to Chicago or New York—anywhere that would give her a chance to see her dreams come true. Why couldn't anyone else understand that? Was she always to be alone?

❧

David stood back a little as Jasmine's family congratulated her. He wished he understood why she had such a strong hold on his heart in spite of everything. She was beautiful, of course. But he had met beautiful women in both California and Illinois. No one intrigued him like the dark-haired minx who was accepting the compliments of her family with an attitude adopted from British royalty.

Jasmine Anderson was far from perfect. She was headstrong. A grin formed on his lips. He couldn't really blame her for that. None of the Anderson sisters could be described as wallflowers, despite their floral names. Lily was a riverboat owner. Camellia had spent part of the War Between the States nursing soldiers on a riverboat and had been at Vicksburg while it was under siege. He supposed Jasmine was simply following in her older sisters' footsteps.

But did she have to trample on his heart at the same time?

"What did you think of the performance?" Marguerite's voice startled him.

"Impressive." He bowed to her. "Did the orphanage benefit?"

"Oh, yes." Her dark gaze turned toward Jasmine. "Your Jasmine is quite the center of attention this evening."

He could feel heat rising to his face. "I thought I told you there's nothing between us. She's not my Jasmine. . .apparently she never has been."

Marguerite tilted her head. "I know what you said, but I can read the signs for myself. If you're not careful, that girl will tear out your heart and leave you a bitter man."

"I don't think that's any of your concern." He regretted the cold words as soon as they left his mouth.

Marguerite's eyes widened. Then she nodded. "I'm sorry if I overstepped the boundaries of our friendship."

He put out a hand to stop her, but it was too late. Marguerite moved toward Miss Deborah and began gathering the children. He ought to catch up to her. Apologize. But he couldn't bring himself to do it. Marguerite was getting too close to the truth for his comfort.

It was time for him to leave Natchez anyway. He should have headed to New Orleans a day or two ago, but he'd wanted to see the play.

With a disgusted shake of his head, David moved away from the crowd surrounding Jasmine. She would never miss his presence. She had more attention than any of the rest of the cast. Even "King Lear" had not received so many compliments.

Blake Matthews broke free of the crowd and moved toward David. "Lily sent me to invite you to dinner with us at the Bluff."

"Thanks, but I don't—"

"You really expect me to tell Lily you won't come?" Blake put an arm around his shoulder. "Do you know how much discord your refusal will cause?"

David chuckled. "We can't have that." He would rather have returned to his room to brood over his wayward heart, but he didn't want to upset Lily. She'd been so good to him over the years. "I'll get my horse and meet you there."

"Excellent." Blake pulled his arm away and pointed at David. "If you don't show up, I will have to come looking for you."

Both men laughed. David's spirit lifted a bit. If he could keep his distance from the star of the evening, it might be good for him to get out.

He retrieved his rented horse from a nearby stable and rode down Washington Street past stately homes. A dog raced along the length of one iron fence, barking until David and his horse passed the border of the home's lot.

He arrived at the Bluff, a two-story building hunched on the edge of the bluff it was named for, overlooking the rushing waters of the Mississippi. Tethering his horse, he tugged on his neckcloth. Why had he agreed to come? He might have defected if not for the arrival of his hosts.

The restaurant looked as though it was being besieged, as at least a dozen people descended on it from the three carriages. Mrs. Champney was followed by her son, Jean Luc, and her daughter-in-law, Anna. Anna's aunt alit and stood looking up at her escort, Jasmine's father Henrick Anderson. Jasmine's aunt Dahlia and uncle Phillip were the first to disembark from the next carriage, followed by Camellia and her husband, Jonah. The final carriage contained Lily and Blake and Jasmine, who seemed to be still riding high on her success.

David stepped forward to offer her his arm, but she swept past him, her little nose in the air.

Camellia rescued him from embarrassment when she put her hand on his arm. "We can always count on you to be the gentleman, David. I have missed you since you left us for California and Illinois."

Recovering his wits, David smiled and answered the questions she peppered him with. By the time they were all seated, he found himself on Camellia's left hand. Aunt Dahlia sat on his left. He could see Jasmine's dark hair some distance away and drew a breath of relief. At least he would not have to worry about being snubbed again.

"Lily says you are a policeman." Dahlia claimed his attention with her statement.

David shook his head. "I'm more of a detective."

"What's the difference?"

"Policemen are paid by the city. My employer is paid by the people who need his help."

Her husband, Phillip, leaned forward. "So you are a mercenary?"

David supposed it was a fair question. Picking up his fork and spearing an olive, he considered how to answer the man. "Except that I am not a soldier, sir, I guess you can say that is a proper title for what we do."

49

"David's organization is quite famous." Camellia joined the conversation. "He's a Pinkerton."

Both Dahlia and Phillip frowned at him as though they'd never heard of the agency at all. Camellia patted his hand. "I do miss you, though. No one can keep Jasmine in check like you can."

"I don't know about that. Jasmine is high-spirited, but she's always known how to get what she wants." David glanced toward the girl in question.

She threw back her head and laughed at that moment, showing the full length of her white neck.

The waiter standing nearby couldn't take his eyes off her. David wanted to take the fellow out back and explain basic manners. A pain in his hand made him look down. His fork was no longer as straight as it had been.

He looked up and caught Camellia's understanding gaze. "Your sentiments are nothing to be ashamed of, David. Jasmine is too naive to realize her effect on those around her. I'm afraid she is headed for trouble, but she will not listen to us. Perhaps you might have better luck."

Wondering what he could say to Jasmine that might make a difference, David concentrated on the food on his plate. She would never listen to him, and he wasn't sure he wanted to put himself in the position of being ignored or worse. "I'm leaving for New Orleans in the next day or two. I doubt there will be time for me to do much."

Lily, sitting on the opposite side of the table, looked up. "You're going to New Orleans? Then you must go with us. It will be like old times. We'll have such fun reminiscing."

"I thought you were going to Memphis."

Lily shook her head.

Feeling like a butterfly caught in a windstorm, David shrugged. "How can I say no?"

He looked toward the far end of the table once more, and his gaze clashed with Jasmine's. In them he read a challenge. A challenge he was loath to accept.

Chapter Six

"At least we're not carrying many passengers this trip." Jasmine smiled at her nephew Noah. "You won't have as many chores as we used to have when your mama and papa had their first boat."

"Papa says that's bad news." Noah's bright blue gaze, so much like his father's, watched her scrub a greasy spot from one of the dining tables.

"Your papa and your grandpapa are in agreement on that."

The boy frowned. "Do they know about the chores?"

Jasmine laughed. She could understand why her sisters enjoyed having their children around them. "Maybe not."

She moved to another table and bent over it, scrubbing with a strong arm. The smells from the galley made her mouth water. Picking up a fresh tablecloth from the stack she and Noah had brought into the dining room, Jasmine shook it out and spread it over the table with a deft move that came from years of practice.

"Why do you wipe the table if you're going to put a cloth on it, too?" Noah pushed one of the chairs toward the table.

"So everything will be clean."

He frowned as though trying to grasp the concept of cleaning what would not be seen. Jasmine laughed and ruffled his dark hair with her fingers. "You'll understand when you're older."

The familiar words brought a frown to her face. It was exactly what Lily used to say all the time when she was younger. When had she become the responsible one? The grown-up?

"There you are!" Aunt Tessie breezed into the room and pointed at Noah. "I've been looking all over for you, young man. It's time for your mathematics lesson."

Noah cast a desperate look at Jasmine.

In spite of the empathy she felt, all Jasmine could do was shrug. "It won't be so bad."

Noah's shoulders fell. He looked so pitiful.

Aunt Tessie put a hand on his shoulder and smiled at him. "Come along."

Jasmine watched them leave before returning to her work. Noah was growing up so fast. Funny how childhood seemed so endless to the child and so quick to adults.

"This doesn't look like the right activity for a famous actress."

The deep voice sent gooseflesh running up her arms. Jasmine took a deep breath before turning to face David Foster. "You're quite the comedian."

The look on his face made her regret her waspish tone of voice.

"I'm sorry, David. I didn't mean that the way it came out."

A strained smile appeared on his face. "I'm not sure why you're so angry with me."

What could she answer? The truth was too painful. She had missed him much more than he had missed her. "Who said I was angry?"

His gaze challenged her words.

Jasmine lifted her chin, dredging up a measure of self-preservation. She would not be manipulated.

"Your sisters are worried about you."

He only thought she'd been angry with him before. His meddling words made her blood boil. She could feel the fire in her eyes. How dare David presume to speak to her as though they were still as close as they'd been growing up? "What my sisters may or may not think isn't any of your business."

"You're right, of course." He sounded resigned. As though he knew he was in the wrong. The stubborn thrust of his jaw, however, told her how determined he was to continue meddling. "I care about you, Jasmine. I don't want to see you hurt."

She knew she should calm herself, but concentrating on what was wrong between them gave her the excuse to maintain a certain distance from him. It protected her heart. "You don't have to worry about me. I know exactly what I want and how to get it."

David picked up a stack of dinner plates and distributed them on the tables like a dealer would a deck of cards.

So he was not going to say anything? Fine. Two could play at that game. She picked up the salad and dinner forks, placing them to the left of the plates he distributed. As they worked, her ire faded, replaced by their comfortable rhythm. It seemed so natural, so normal. He put one knife and two spoons to the right of each place setting while she folded the linen napkins into neat triangles and set them in the center of each plate.

As Jasmine gathered the leftover implements, David moved to stand near her. "When we were young, I thought you were the most beautiful, most intelligent, most loving person in the world."

"Yes, I heard you telling Marguerite that you've outgrown your childish infatuation." She tried to keep the hurt from her voice.

He put a finger under her chin and lifted her face so that their gazes met. His eyes had not changed. They were as green as a pine thicket. They promised peace and rest and happiness.

Jasmine thought she might melt into a puddle at his feet. She even imagined for a brief instant what it would feel like for their lips to meet. Her eyelids grew heavy. She wanted to lean into him, draw on his strength.

In that instant something changed between them. David was no longer the safe and predictable childhood friend that she loved. He was. . .something much more dangerous.

Her heart galloped like a runaway horse. The feeling was heady, exciting, almost the same feeling she got right before a performance. She could feel herself weakening. . .leaning toward him.

When David stepped back, her heart stopped its furious pace. It seemed to stop beating at all. Jasmine felt it stand still, crack, and shatter into a million pieces, taking with it dreams she'd never before recognized.

"Jasmine, I. . ."

She turned away from him. No matter what his words, she didn't want to hear them. She had to defend herself. "Don't worry, David. You don't have to apologize. It's not as though we're romantically involved. How could we be? You're the brother my sisters and I always wanted, so I suppose I shouldn't be surprised they wanted you to talk to me."

His mouth tightened, and the same eyes that had been so tender a few seconds before spat green sparks toward her. "How can you be so flippant? Do I matter so little to you? Does anything matter to you at all?"

The words nicked her, but Jasmine raised her chin. Let him think what he wanted. Why should she care? When she was famous and had dozens of men begging for her attention, David Foster would see who was right. Then he would be sorry for treating her like a wayward child. She marched out of the dining room without a backward glance, self-righteousness helping her to keep her head high.

&

"Trust God to straighten out your path." Tamar snapped a handful of beans and dropped the pieces into the large pan on her lap. "If you look to Him for guidance, He'll help you succeed."

Jasmine knew the words were true. And they sounded like excellent advice. . .for someone who wanted a conventional life. "You sound like Papa and Lily. But what if God listens to them instead of me? I know they don't want me to be an actress."

Tamar's dark face was dear to her. She had been more a mother than a servant to her and her two sisters. When Lily had secured

Tamar's freedom almost a dozen years earlier, it had been a moment of celebration for all of them. Her marriage to Jensen, a close friend of Blake's, had been as sweet as caramel icing. Now she and Jensen made their home with Lily and Blake on the river, their happiness apparent in their actions and words. "Where did you ever get the idea that God shows favor to one of his children over the other?"

Jasmine shrugged. "Isn't it obvious? Some people are rich. Others have nothing. He shows favor to them, doesn't He? And I know both Papa and Lily are better Christians than I am. So it makes sense that He would listen to—"

Tamar's laugh interrupted her words. "Child, child. You do have the oddest way of looking at life. People are not more or less Christian. We either accept Jesus and His free gift or we do not." She put her pan on the table and reached for Jasmine's hands. "Do you have Jesus in your heart?"

Jasmine remembered the day Papa had led her to Christ. She remembered the incredible lightness she'd experienced when she turned her life over to Him. But since then He'd become less and less a part of her daily routine. "Of course I do." She silenced her conscience with an effort and met Tamar's gaze.

"Then you should know that He places as much importance on your hopes and dreams as He does on those of your sister or your father."

She wanted to believe what Tamar said. But it made no sense. Everyone had a favorite. Camellia was Aunt Dahlia's favorite niece. Grandfather, a man who had spent little time with her, had lavished Lily with his love and attention. Jasmine knew she had been Grandmother's favorite. Grandmother always said she was most like their mother, Rose, even though the portrait of her in the upper hallway at Les Fleurs showed more resemblance to Camellia. Mama's hair had been blond, not dark like Jasmine's. Nor were her eyes as dark. Grandmother had obviously been mistaken in her assessment.

It was time to turn the conversation in a different direction. "Do you think I'm a good actress?"

Tamar sat back and released Jasmine's hands. "God's given you many gifts, like He does all of His children. He'll show you how to use them. . .if you'll let Him." She picked up her pan and began snapping beans once more. "Lily told me you want to go to Chicago."

Irritation blew through Jasmine like a hot wind. Was there no one Lily had not discussed her with? First David and now Tamar. Was she to expect a homily from Blake next? "So the two of you talked about what should be done with me?"

"Your sister wants the best for you."

Click, click, splatter. More beans joined the growing pile in the pan.

Jasmine felt hemmed in on all sides. "Is it so wrong to want to use my God-given talents?"

"Of course not." *Click, click, splatter.* "But maybe you should try to find a way that will ease Lily's worries. She only wants what's best for you."

Frustration pushed Jasmine out of the chair. She walked to the doorway and looked out at the river sliding past them. She wished she could float away on that current, escape her overprotective family. If only they would let her go.

"Could you try for a job in New Orleans?"

The thought had occurred to Jasmine from time to time. New Orleans was a cosmopolitan city with many opportunities. But if she did start to gain notoriety, Lily would drag her back to Natchez, certain some nonexistent disaster was about to befall her. "I don't think that will work."

"I'll pray about it." Tamar sent her a sympathetic smile. "God is certain to see a way that we haven't considered."

Escaping from the galley, Jasmine wondered how Lily had managed to get most everyone on this boat to tell her the same thing. Was it some ploy to convince her to give up her dreams? She glanced up at the sky. Clouds obscured the sun, but its heat made the air sticky and warm, like a damp sponge surrounded her. Wishing for a fan, Jasmine considered going to her room, but the effort seemed too great. She'd have to return there soon enough to change for dinner.

Would God really listen to her? Over the years she'd come to see Him as a white-bearded king sitting on His throne in heaven—

kindly but distant. Wouldn't He be busy with others? People with more pressing needs than hers?

When she had first become a Christian, she'd talked to Him on a daily basis, asking Him to watch over her loved ones and petitioning Him for her heart's desires. But somewhere along the way she had fallen out of the habit of praying every day. And little by little God and Christ and the Bible had become less important to her.

Closing her eyes, Jasmine leaned against the rail. She felt a little silly praying out here in the open. Maybe she should go to her room. Besides, God would probably laugh at her anyway. What could she promise Him in exchange for making her dreams come true?

Her eyes popped open of their own accord, and she took a step back, wiping her hands on her skirt. She would pray this evening, when the time was right.

Chapter Seven

David washed his face and stared into the mirror hanging on the wall. He was so foolish. No amount of water would wash away the words he'd flung at Jasmine earlier. Why had he even thought he could talk to her? Why hadn't he kept his mouth shut? He had enough to worry about with his assignment. He needed to focus on that instead of Jasmine.

For a moment he'd dared dream they might have a future together. That she might return his feelings after all. But she would never see him as anything but the homeless kid she'd rescued. A companion maybe. A brother certainly. But not a man she could love. No matter what he did, no matter what he accomplished, he would never be someone she adored.

When he saw her at dinner, he would be polite. Distant. He wouldn't give her the chance to wound him again.

He picked up a white towel and turned it over in his hands, his gaze tracing the blue curlicues that spelled out *Water Lily*. The towels were finer than what Lily and Blake had supplied back when he traveled with them.

Who had done the handwork? Lily was too busy with running the boat and raising her children, and Camellia never could sew an even line. Had Jasmine's fingers been the ones to stitch the letters into the linen? He could almost see her seated in a rocker next to the fireplace, her midnight-dark hair held back loosely with a ribbon as she leaned over an embroidery hoop.

A smile slipped into place as the scene became more detailed in his imagination. He would be reading a book on the far side of the fireplace. Maybe they would have a child playing on a knotted rug between them—

No! He had to stop this foolishness. Jasmine was following her own path, and it was not one he wished to tread with her. He would purge her from his mind and heart.

With careful movements, he folded the linen cloth and put it next to his washbasin before moving to his bed and reaching for his valise. Digging past his nightclothes and stockings, he felt for the hard edge of his Bible. He sat on the edge of his bed, his fingers finding the ribbon bookmark as he closed his eyes. "Lord, please give me peace about her. Help me follow You wherever You lead." He sat still in the room and let his mind relax as he thought about God. The sounds of the boat and the river faded away as peace filled him. After a period of time, he opened his eyes and began to read.

One verse leaped up at him. *"For I know the thoughts that I think toward you, saith the Lord, thoughts of peace, and not of evil, to give you an expected end."* The ache in his heart faded further. God knew what he needed and would provide it. "Thank You, Lord."

He closed the Bible and left it sitting on the bed as he continued dressing. No matter what happened, he could face life with calm certainty. God had spoken through His Word, a promise that David knew he could claim.

Shrugging into his coat, David checked his appearance one last time, winking at the reflection in the mirror. God had brought him this far. All he had to do now was forego trying to win Jasmine's affections. Like Jehoshaphat had done when the Edomites, the Ammonites, and the Moabites gathered against him, he would allow God to fight his battles for him. This ensured ultimate victory.

The sound of the dinner bell made his stomach rumble. David left his room and strode down the narrow passageway.

Jensen's scarred face was the first one he saw as he entered the dining room. "I wasn't sure you would still be cooking for Lily and Blake."

"Look at you all gone and grown up." The older man might give the appearance of a pirate to a stranger, but David knew his true nature. David held out his right hand, but Jensen ignored the gesture, pulling him into a bear hug instead. "Tell me what you've been doing with yourself."

Feeling like he'd not matured a day as he emerged from the older man's grasp, David shrugged. The boat shifted under his feet, and he automatically adjusted his stance to compensate. "I've been up in Chicago."

Jensen's bushy eyebrows lowered, emphasizing the scar over his left eye. In past years David would have been intimidated by the look indicating skepticism. "Come to the galley when you finish your dinner. I want to hear what's been keeping you so far from the people who care about you."

Not sure if he would have time since he calculated that the *Water Lily* would reach port in a couple of hours, David replied, "I'll do my best." He took a seat at one of the tables as the other diners began to file in.

A bald man with a wide mustache sat to his right, while a younger fellow dressed in the sober suit of a professional businessman sat on his left. The other two chairs at the table were taken by two redheaded females who appeared to be mother and daughter.

The bald man nodded to them and introduced himself as Albert Culbertson. Weldon Brown was the name of the younger man. He also told them he was a photographer and offered his services to them at a reduced rate.

The ladies were Mrs. Bertha Dickinson and her daughter, Adina. As he introduced himself, David noticed that Adina seemed quite taken by the dapper photographer. Her mother also noticed and immediately engaged Mr. Brown in a rigorous interrogation as to his pedigree and prospects.

All conversations stopped when Jasmine and her family arrived. Blake welcomed the guests and asked everyone to bow their heads for the blessing.

He had barely uttered, "Amen," before Mr. Culbertson picked up his napkin and tucked it into his shirt collar. "I hope you ladies have a male relative meeting you at the docks."

Mrs. Dickinson shook her head. "My husband would have come with us, but an unexpected matter detained him. He'll be joining us in a few days, however."

Mr. Culbertson looked grave at this news. "You know how dangerous it is to be unescorted, don't you? Even before the war, women had to be suspicious of strangers, but now that we've been overrun by carpetbaggers and scalawags, it's much worse."

Mr. Brown cleared his throat. "You shouldn't frighten the ladies. I'm certain they'll be safe enough in a New Orleans hotel."

"Which shows how little you know. I've been traveling these waters for years now, and I can tell you this part of the country is a nest for the worst thieves in the country."

Even though the older lady looked frightened, Adina seemed nothing more than curious. "What do you mean?" she asked.

"A long curve just south of Natchez has long been known as Dead Man's Curve because of all the unwary travelers whose bodies have been found there." Enjoying the attention, Mr. Culbertson smoothed his mustache with two fingers. "The innkeepers at Natchez Under-the-Hill offer cheap rates and then murder their guests, tossing them into the river from trapdoors."

The daughter turned to her mother. "I told you we should have stayed at home until Papa could come. No amount of European imports are worth dying over."

"All of that is ancient history." David would rather have kept silent, but he could not bear to see both females so concerned for their safety.

"Most towns have cleaned out the criminal element. You'll be as safe in those places as in your home."

"I don't know where you get your opinion, sir." The mustached storyteller tossed him a disdainful glance. "While those inns may not be murdering helpless souls, bank robbers—probably Confederate deserters for the most part—are very active now. I heard of a robbery across the river from Natchez in Vidalia just a few weeks ago."

David had visited the bank in question as Mr. Bastrup had suggested, so he probably knew more about the robbery than the man beside him. But that didn't mean he could erase the fear in the ladies' faces. Or could he?

"That was far from here. And I've met the sheriff there. He'll probably make an arrest before long."

Mr. Culbertson snickered. "He's more likely to be in league with them. Why else would a gang of robbers be able to get away so easily?"

"Nevertheless, they will be caught." David found the man's foot with his own and stepped on it with some force. "I'm certain these ladies will rest more easily knowing that."

After a grunt and an angry glance that David met with a warning stare, the man took a deep breath and nodded his agreement. "Of course you're right. I apologize. I didn't mean to frighten you."

The ladies exchanged a worried glance. The mother put her fork down on the table and pushed her chair back. "I am feeling a bit out of sorts, Adina. I believe we should retire to our stateroom and rest."

Adina cast a sorrowful glance toward the photographer before nodding her agreement.

David was the first one to stand and bow to them, regret filling his heart because he'd been unable to reassure the ladies. As he watched them make their way around the other tables, his gaze clashed with Jasmine's. He shrugged his shoulders at her frown. Was she so eager to condemn him when she knew nothing about what had just happened?

Before hopelessness could overtake him once more, David took a steadying breath. Hadn't he promised God a little while earlier that he would wait on Him? What had happened to his resolve? He smiled at

Jasmine. Let her think what she wanted, he wouldn't let her boorish behavior upset him.

❧

Walking out onto the deck, David leaned against the rail. A leafy curtain of tall trees gave the illusion that the *Water Lily* traveled through an uninhabited wilderness while showy white magnolia blooms filled the air with their sweet fragrance. During the months he'd spent in Chicago, David had forgotten how green and beautiful the landscape was along the river.

He didn't realize he wasn't alone until a hand clapped him on the shoulder. He turned and looked into Blake's bright blue eyes.

"You look more relaxed than at the restaurant the other night."

"Can you blame me? You didn't have to sit next to Jasmine's aunt Dahlia." David grinned to soften his words.

"I'm sure she had plenty of gossip to share since you haven't seen her for a while." Blake whistled. "It's a wonder your ears still work."

"I know." David pulled on one of his lobes and made a face. "It was touch and go for a while."

"The rest of the family sends their thanks for the pleasant meal." Blake's laughter blended with his.

A splash close to the boat made them look at the muddy brown surface of the river. A ring of concentric circles showed where a fish had broken the surface in its quest for a meal.

As silence enveloped them, Marguerite's advice returned to David. Should he talk to Blake about his feelings? The idea yanked the smile from his lips. What could he say? That he didn't feel like a part of the family? That he'd been naive enough to hope his irresponsible parents might one day get back together and welcome him into a loving home? The very idea of being so candid made his skin crawl.

"Are you doing okay?" Blake's question was hesitant, as though he too wrestled with uncomfortable emotions. "I hated to hear about your father. I know how much you hoped to see him once more."

"I'm fine. It's not like Pa and I were close."

63

Another silence developed, broken by Blake's sigh a few moments later. "Have I ever told you about my own father?"

David shook his head. Even though he'd spent so much time around Blake and the others aboard the *Water Lily*, he'd always thought they led wonderful, nearly perfect lives.

"We were estranged for years. I thought he was wrong in the way he raised me, and I ran away from him as soon as I could. I blamed him for all of my troubles, holding him responsible because I misunderstood him. I was full of bitterness right up until the day I forgave him. Looking back at it now, I wish I hadn't wasted so much time. Forgiving him lifted a huge weight off of me."

How could Blake compare their experiences? "Your situation was different from mine."

"That's true." David could feel Blake's gaze probing his face. "I'm the one who abandoned my father, not the other way around. And I had the chance to talk to my father about the past. I know it's hard, but that doesn't change the fact you still need to forgive your father."

David turned suspicious eyes toward the older man. Had Marguerite blabbed to him about David's reservations? No. Marguerite wouldn't betray his confidence. "Why should I forgive him? If he hadn't run away, my life and my mother's would have been much different."

"Yes, your life would've been different. Whether it would have been better or worse is something we'll never know."

Surprise rocked David. He'd never thought that his life might have been harder if Pa had stayed in Natchez. He'd always been too angry about being deserted.

"But you have a duty to forgive him anyway because you're a Christian." Blake spoke softly, but his words might have been daggers aimed at David's heart.

A sense of betrayal made him defensive. He pushed away the idea that he might be better off because of his father's absence. "It still feels wrong. I shouldn't have to forgive him when he's the one who did wrong. I was only a child. I had no choice."

"I know how hard it seems right now. I struggled with the same sense of unfairness even though I was the one who ran away." Blake's voice roughened. He stopped talking and cleared his throat. "I blamed God. I thought He should have given me a better home, a father who would care for his family's physical needs over their spiritual welfare. I couldn't see that the man who raised me wasn't the problem. I was too busy running away. Even after Lily and I met—after I fell in love with her—I didn't understand how my refusal to face the past affected my future."

David swallowed hard as he listened to Blake's confession. He'd never seen the struggles Blake was describing. He'd always thought Blake and Lily knew how to deal with every challenge. Sure, they'd argued from time to time. Who didn't? "What changed?"

"God called me to Him. He filled my life with Christians and used them to speak to me, to be examples for me." Blake's chuckle held no mirth. "But I was hardheaded. Running away seemed easier than listening to Him. It took losing everything I held dear before I finally surrendered my life to Him."

Taking a deep breath, David turned toward Blake. "And once you did, everything worked out. But that won't happen for me. It's too late. I used to dream my pa would come back to Natchez, get me and Ma, and we'd live together like a real family."

"I'm sorry your dream didn't come true."

David didn't know what he'd expected from Blake. Derision? Disbelief? Certainly not sympathetic understanding. Blake's response gave him the courage to continue. "I think that's why I never quite accepted you and Lily as my family. Don't get me wrong. I know how good you've been to me, how much I owe you."

"You don't owe us anything, David. We may not be your blood relatives, but that doesn't affect our love for you. You're like a younger brother to me. Forget this debt nonsense. You're one of the family."

How could David explain his sense of separateness? "When Ma passed away, I still thought maybe Pa would show up. I thought we could do the kinds of things your family does—work together, rely on each other, love each other without reservation. I even thought we could go fishing and hunting together. Create a family of our own. When I got to California, though, I had to face the truth. Once I buried Pa, I decided to make a break with the past. I walked away from all that you and Lily have done for me."

"Nothing you can say will change my mind." Blake draped an arm over his shoulders. "I know you're not perfect. None of us is. Lily and I are proud of the man you've become. We've watched you and Jasmine grow up together. Lily has even wondered from time to time if the two of you. . ."

David heaved a sigh of resignation. "I don't think that will happen—"

"You don't have to explain anything to me." Blake's voice cut off his protest. "I'm not trying to interfere in your life. I just want you to know how much I care about you and pray for your success. We all miss getting to see you now that you've become a successful Pinkerton detective, but we're thrilled to see you happy with what you're doing with your life."

David wondered why Blake's compliments made him feel so uneasy. He felt like a fraud. The reason he'd made the decision to become a detective was not as straightforward as Blake made it sound. In some ways he thought he might even be doing what Blake had done. He might be using his job to avoid dealing with the past. He circled back to the real question in his mind. "What if I don't know how to forgive my father or how to let go of the past?"

"It will come to you, David." Blake squeezed his shoulders before releasing him. "There's a story in Mark about Jesus telling a father that He could heal his son if the father believed. The father cried out 'Lord, I believe; help thou mine unbelief.' That scripture is important to me because it says that all we have to do is take the first step. Christ will help us cross the bridge. He is the Way."

But what was the first step? How could he forgive a father who was dead? He was alone, an orphan. He was a victim separated from the rest of the world by circumstances beyond his control. And that was the real reason for him to start a new life in Chicago, away from anyone who knew his past.

Blake didn't really understand. No one could. He was as isolated as he'd always been. The only thing David could cling to was the hope of making a difference through his work as a Pinkerton.

⁊❧

Fog, gray and mysterious, wreathed the trees on the west bank of the river as Papa and Blake brought the *Water Lily* up against the dock. The sun was about to make its exit, but people crowded the waterfront. Tall-masted schooners, their sails furled, rubbed against the docks as cargo was loaded into their holds. Beside them, tall smokestacks belched smoky tendrils into the air. Smaller rafts and even a few pirogues bobbed between the larger vessels like tiny fish in a large pond. Looking out at the hustle-bustle, Lily found it easy to discount Blake's opinion that river traffic was on the wane.

Blake's deep voice surprised her. "I know what you're thinking."

Lily felt his arm go around her waist, imparting warmth and strength. She leaned into him, thanking God once again for the life they shared. She glanced sideways at him. "I was wondering if Aunt Tessie can watch Benjamin as well as Noah and Magnolia."

"Is that right? Are you worried about Aunt Tessie or our children?" His eyes, as blue as the sky, teased her. "I would have guessed something different. You aren't looking at all of this activity and discounting the idea that we should get out of the steamship business, are you?"

A blush warmed her cheeks. "How can you know that?"

"You, my dearest wife, are as transparent as a new windowpane, in spite of the fact that muddy water practically runs through your veins." He dropped a light kiss on her lips. "Besides, if I didn't know what your thoughts were after a decade of living and working with you, I'd have to be deaf and blind."

She tried to pretend outrage, but a bubble of laughter in her chest demanded escape. He joined in, and the merriment they shared washed away the fear that had stalked her since he had first mentioned a change in future vocation.

"It does look like shipping is still a thriving business." Lily heard the

67

note of wistfulness in her voice. Was she clinging to something in spite of the evidence? Or was Blake wrong?

"Don't you remember how it was before the war?" His voice was gentle, coaxing her agreement.

Lifting her chin, she nodded. "Business has come back since the war ended, though. Perhaps not quite as much as it was before. But after the heavy toll taken on both people and ships during the war, what do you expect? The ships will return, and we'll be in high cotton again."

He didn't answer her in words, but his silence shouted disagreement. She might have pulled away, but his arm drew her even closer.

They stood like that for several precious moments. Lily knew they both had a lot to do over the next hour or two, but she found herself wishing she could stay right where she was, hoping life would continue as it had for the past decade. They had endured difficulties and hardships like everyone else in the country, but they had survived. Did her husband expect her to simply give up now?

In an effort to breach the silence, she decided to focus on another problem that had been bothering her since they left Natchez. "Jasmine and David still seem to be at odds with each other."

Blake raised an eyebrow but accepted the change of subject. "I don't understand either of them. They were so close before he went off to try to reconcile with his father."

"I know. It's a shame." Lily sighed. "He's lost so much."

Blake nodded. "I talked to him earlier. He's struggling with some tough issues, but he'll figure things out eventually. He's a good man."

She loved that Blake had cared enough to ask David. "At one time I hoped perhaps he and Jasmine would fall in love. They always seemed to get along well together when they were children and up until he went out West. Do you think it's because of his job? His work is dangerous. Maybe he doesn't want to expose Jasmine. Or maybe she's the one who doesn't want to be tied to a lawman."

"I don't know what the problem is, but the two of them will have to work it out on their own." Blake's mouth quirked upward in the crooked smile so dear to her. "I can remember a time or two way back in the past when you and I didn't see eye to eye. Neither of us would have welcomed outside advice on how to run our lives."

"That's true." Lily leaned her head against Blake's shoulder. "But were we ever quite so stiff with each other as they have been on this trip?"

Before he could answer the question, passengers began appearing on deck, coming from their staterooms or one of the two lounges.

With a reluctant sigh, Lily pulled away from her husband. "I left the children with Tamar and Jensen, so I'd better go collect them."

"I thought you were going to ask Aunt Tessie to keep an eye on them for you."

She rolled her eyes. "I told you I'm worried about overloading her."

"I wouldn't concern myself with that. From the amount of time my aunt and your father are spending together, I think you can count on his helping out if she runs into any complications."

Lily halted in midstride and turned to him, her eyes wide. "What are you talking about?"

"I hope you don't mind, but I think Henrick may be smitten with her."

"Of course I don't mind." Lily hugged herself. "I just can't believe you noticed something like that before I did."

He grinned. "One of these days you're going to have to admit that I can see beyond the end of my nose." Without waiting for her reply, he bounded up the stairs to the hurricane deck.

Lily shook her head and set out once again for the galley.

Jasmine met her at the door, Benjamin squirming in her arms. She could see Tamar and Magnolia stirring a pot at the stove. Noah sat on a bench close to them, aimlessly swinging his legs.

Noah jumped up as soon as he saw her. "Mama, will you tell Aunt Jasmine it's time for Bible study."

Smiling at her firstborn, Lily shook her head and took Benjamin from Jasmine. "I'm proud of you for remembering, but we're docked now. I'm afraid we'll have to wait until we get to the Thorntons'."

Jasmine said nothing as Lily gathered her children and began herding them to the stateroom that served as their nursery. When Lily glanced back to see what had caused her sister's uncustomary silence, she realized Jasmine's wide eyes were fixed on something extraordinary. "What is it?"

"A floating theater!" The excitement in Jasmine's voice didn't bode well.

"I don't see any reason for your excitement." Lily looked past the motionless paddlewheel and spotted the gaudy barge decorated with streamers and flags. Lanterns cast a yellow light on the large signs proclaiming the exhibits and dramas available at all hours of the day and night. "Lately, there's always one or another of those boats stopping in Natchez. Most of them are full of drunks and ladies of ill repute."

Jasmine crossed her arms over her chest and tapped her foot on the deck. "I shouldn't be surprised at your attitude. You'll never change—" With a sob she bit off whatever she was going to say and whirled around.

"Wait." Why did her sister have to be so melodramatic about everything? Lily hadn't meant to evoke such a response. She wanted to run after Jasmine, but her children were also clamoring for her attention.

Benjamin patted her cheek with a chubby hand. "Mama?"

Her heart melted as she looked at him. "Yes, sweetheart, I'm listening to you."

Maybe once they were all settled at the Thorntons', she could devote some time to Jasmine's needs. Beginning to wonder if bringing her to New Orleans had been a mistake after all, Lily sighed. Only the good Lord knew what she could do to make Jasmine happy.

Chapter Eight

Jasmine ignored David's hand as she stepped out of the rented carriage. What did she care if no one understood her? She was beginning to think Lily and the rest were conspiring against her. Even Aunt Tessie seemed distant. And Papa had barely said a word to her the whole time they were on the boat. She sailed through the wrought-iron gate and entered the shady courtyard that separated the Thorntons' townhouse from the street.

The door opened, and Mrs. Thornton—*Tante* Charlotte to her and David—stepped onto the veranda, her arms wide and welcoming. "Come let me see you, cher. Let me see how beautiful you have grown since your last visit."

Jasmine began to feel a little better as she allowed Jonah's mother to hug her and draw her inside. "Tante Charlotte, you're the real beauty. You'll have to teach me how to stop aging."

Tante Charlotte laughed and turned to greet the rest of the group. Soon they were all ensconced in the back parlor, a room that seemed as familiar to Jasmine as those of Les Fleurs.

"Lloyd will be home in a few minutes, and we can all go to the dining room to eat." Tante Charlotte had to raise her voice to be heard over the noise of so many conversations occurring simultaneously in the crowed space.

Jasmine had taken a place beside Tante Charlotte on a shorter settee, while Papa and Jensen were perched on the edges of two straight-backed chairs. Aunt Tessie, Tamar, and Lily were seated on the sofa—the latter with Benjamin on her lap. Blake stood behind Lily, one hand on her shoulder, and David stood next to a small round table, claiming that he preferred to stand after spending so much time sitting while aboard the *Water Lily*. Noah and Magnolia sat on stools dragged in from the garden.

"My goodness, I could hear you from outside, Maman." Tante Charlotte's daughter, Sarah, breezed into the parlor, adding more chaos as everyone tried to greet her at once.

"Don't think you can keep all of these guests to yourself." Sarah swept her arm out wide, barely missing a collision with David. "I will take sweet Jasmine and her David to my house."

Jasmine opened her mouth to protest that David did not belong to her or any female, but Sarah rushed on in her usual impetuous manner. "I can also offer rooms to Henrick and Miss Matthews. In fact, I can take the whole family to stay with me."

"I was planning to stay at a hotel." David inserted his statement when Sarah stopped for a quick breath.

"Nonsense." She wagged a finger at him. "You are family. You will not stay in some hotel."

An odd look crossed his face. If Jasmine didn't know better, she would have thought he felt honored to be counted a member of the family. But that was ridiculous. David had practically grown up with them. No matter that they were not blood related, he was one of them.

Whatever he felt was now hidden from view. "You are most generous, but I insist. I have work to do while I'm in New Orleans. I don't want to disturb you with my comings and goings at all hours."

Sarah's smile peeked out. "You will be in our garçonnière, of course. It has a separate entrance, so you may stay out all night or come in as the sun rises. You won't disturb anyone."

"I agree with Sarah. Of course the same is true if you would rather stay here, David. No one will ever know your schedule." Tante Charlotte turned her attention to Sarah, her brow furrowed. "However, I will not allow you to take all of my guests away. I have plenty of room for everyone else."

Sarah looked as though she wanted to argue the point, but she was forestalled when Jensen cleared his throat. "Thank you for your hospitality, but Tamar and I will stay on the *Water Lily* as usual. Someone must meet with the new passengers and keep the boat safe from pickpockets and looters."

Blake exchanged a glance with Jensen. "If you want to stay here, I can hire someone to watch the boat."

Jensen shook his head. "That's our home as much as yours. I don't trust anyone else to protect it like I would."

Sarah clapped her hands to regain everyone's attention. "Who else will come to stay at my home?"

"I promised to help with the children, so I'll need to be wherever they are." Aunt Tessie smiled at Sarah. "It was the main reason I came."

Sarah turned to Papa. "How about you, Henrick? Would you like to share the garçonnière with David?"

He glanced toward the sofa before answering, making Jasmine wonder whose attention he sought. "I think I will remain here, if your parents have room for me."

"It's settled then." Tante Charlotte snapped her fingers for emphasis. "You may have Jasmine and David, but you must bring them to me when I ask."

Sarah agreed and reached a hand out to Jasmine. "Come with me to point out which bags should go with us."

Jasmine could hardly contain her excitement. With Sarah as her hostess, she would be much freer to embrace life. Even though she enjoyed the Thorntons and their home, she could hardly wait to leave.

By the time they had the luggage sorted, Tante Charlotte's husband, *Oncle* Lloyd, had arrived. Even though it had not been that long since Jasmine had seen him, his dark hair did seem to have gained a few more white strands. His hug was as affectionate as ever, and his dark eyes still gleamed with intelligence.

When the greetings were over, Jasmine discovered that Noah and Magnolia had been taken to the nursery on the third floor of the Thorntons' spacious townhouse by one of the maids. Now everyone else was waiting on the two children to return before going in to dinner.

Jasmine remembered the dining room as being spacious, but she wondered if they would all fit at the table.

Oncle Lloyd took his place at the head of the table after helping Tante Charlotte to her seat at the opposite end. The two married couples—Lily and Blake and Tamar and Jensen—took up the left side of the table while the other five—Sarah, Papa, Aunt Tessie, David, and she—squeezed together on the right side of the table.

"I can sit with the children upstairs." Jasmine didn't want to rub elbows with David. Her suggestion caused a stir.

Aunt Tessie, on the other side of David, pushed her chair back. "You stay. I should be the one to go upstairs—"

"No one will be banished to the nursery." Tante Charlotte frowned at them. "We are all family here."

"Bow your heads." Oncle Lloyd's command was stern. No one at the table dared argue. "Lord, we give thanks for the bountiful blessings You shower on us. Thank You for this gathering of family and friends. Please banish the spirit of discontent among us and help us to be ever mindful of Your love for all. Amen."

Feeling properly chastised for bringing the spirit of discontent to the Thorntons' home, Jasmine kept her attention centered on her plate of fresh vegetables and braised beef. Several conversations went on around her.

David handed her a basket filled with crusty rolls, holding onto it a second or two as she reached for it. Was he trying to bait her? She refused to meet his gaze as the silent tug of war ended.

"It's been awhile since you visited with us, David." Tante Charlotte spoke as she took the basket from Jasmine. "Tell me what has been keeping you busy."

Jasmine could see David's hands as he spread butter onto his roll. "I am working in Chicago now, so I don't get to spend as much time in Natchez."

"David has taken a job with the Pinkerton National Detective Agency." Blake's voice was full of encouragement and pride.

"A growing area of the country." Oncle Lloyd joined the conversation from the far end of the table. "Plenty of opportunities open to hardworking young men. I've thought of opening a shipping office up there, but I've never taken the time to go that far north."

"I would be happy to show you around, sir."

Jasmine wondered what kind of home David lived in. Did he rent rooms at a boardinghouse or had he purchased a home of his own? Did he live close to the agency's office or on the outskirts of Chicago? Shame hit her as she realized how little she actually knew about his life anymore. When had they grown so far apart?

"Eli is thinking of closing down the office in Memphis. He believes railroads are the key to the future."

"Is that right? I am surprised to hear that he is ready to abandon the family business." The tension in Lily's voice brought Jasmine's head up.

What was going on here? She saw Blake and her sister exchange a glance.

He covered Lily's hand with his own. "Perhaps after we visit with the attorney here, we should go to Memphis and talk to Eli."

Papa leaned forward. "I find it hard to believe people will exchange their luxurious accommodations on riverboats for smoky, dangerous rides across the country."

"If not for the gold discovered in California, I doubt many would try it." Aunt Tessie spoke with authority. "It's dangerous, too. Thieves and bandits rob trains, taking the passengers' possessions from them by force."

"Mr. Pinkerton has been hired by several of the operators to provide safety." David's voice, so close to her, startled Jasmine.

She glanced sideways at him, suddenly able to see him confronting dangerous men on a trek out West. And able to see him lying face down on a dusty prairie, dead at the hands of a ruthless bandit. Jasmine shuddered.

David must have felt the movement. He looked down at her, concern on his face.

For a moment their differences and arguments faded away. She could see the longing in his eyes. It called to her. Jasmine wanted to comfort him, tell him that everything would be all right. She opened her mouth to find the right words.

But then his expression changed, hardened into a cold mask. He became once more the stranger she didn't understand at all. A man who appeared without warning. A man who had nothing in common with her childhood friend.

Jasmine turned a shoulder on him and gave her attention to Tante Charlotte for the rest of the meal. She would not mourn the friendship they had shared. She and David wanted very different things from life. Very different things.

❧

David woke with the dawn. Rising from his bed, he walked to the window of the Cartiers' apartment and pushed back the curtain.

The city was not fully awake, but wagons carrying milk, cream, and eggs trundled through the streets on their routes, and stumbling revelers picked their way past vegetable vendors. Soon the streets would fill with all manner of carriages and characters—businessmen on important errands, sailors returning to their ships to earn enough for their next shore leaves, and pickpockets looking for easy marks in the rushing, oblivious crowds.

Letting the curtain drop, he thought he had a lot in common with the separate building that was attached to the Cartiers' home. He had no real connection to Jasmine's family, no real connection to any family. He could come and go through life, and no one would take much notice.

A small voice inside whispered that he did matter to Someone. He mattered to God, his Maker. The thought comforted him, gave him the push he needed to get dressed and get on with his mission.

As David left the apartment, he planned a route to take him to the telegraph office and the bank. The smell of freshly baked bread made his stomach growl, so he decided that breakfast was the first stop he would make.

Entering a small café on St. Charles Street, he ordered a baguette and a cup of dark, chicory coffee. The warm, crusty bread calmed his hunger pangs, and the coffee chased away the cobwebs of sleepiness. The warmth of the day was beginning to make itself felt as he left the café and caught a horse-drawn omnibus to Canal Street.

The Daily Telegraph was a large building. Sandwiched between a saddlery and a millinery store, it stood four stories tall. David thanked the driver and disembarked on Canal Street in front of the building. He tugged on his coat to make sure it was not wrinkled and entered with a deep breath.

A slender man with dark hair and hazel eyes stood inside the doorway. "May we be of service?"

David removed his hat and tucked it under his arm. "I need to send a telegraph to Chicago."

"Yes, sir." The employee pointed him to a window on the far side of the large, columned foyer.

Taking his place in line, David considered the most concise way to send his information. He needed to let Mr. Bastrup know he was in New Orleans and would report further progress as he could. By the time he made it to the window, he had the basics worked out. "Good morning."

"What's the message?" The man on the other side had stooped shoulders, a balding head, and deep-set eyes. He looked bored as he listened to David. "Direction?"

"Mr. Homer Bastrup, Pinkerton National Detective Agency, Chicago, Illinois."

Disinterest dropped away, and the telegraph officer straightened his shoulders. "You're a Pinkerton?"

David raised his chin an inch before letting it fall back to a normal position.

"I've never met a Pinkerton before." Avid interest sharpened the man's gaze. He glanced back over his shoulder before leaning closer to David. "Are you on a job?" His question came out in a whisper.

"Didn't you know?" David winked at the man and flashed his badge. "We never sleep."

The telegraph officer guffawed.

After his message was sent, David turned to leave. Several people watched him as he made his way through the lobby. Some even stepped aside to open a path to the front door. David's shoulders itched, and he wondered whether any of the men here were connected to the bank robberies. He hoped not, or his mission would be over before he even got started.

He walked down Canal Street toward the river until he reached Royal Street. Turning right, he left the busyness behind. At the next corner, he found his destination—Citizen's Bank of Louisiana.

The interior of the bank was posh, quiet, designed to invest prospective customers with the assurance that their money would be safe inside. A shiny marble floor gleamed in filtered sunlight. Two counters were strategically placed in the center of the room for customers who wished to fill out paperwork.

David noticed all the details as he strode to the teller window. "I need to speak with your manager, please."

The young man gulped, his Adam's apple moving up and down in his throat. His nose and ears seemed too large for his narrow face. "D— do you have an appointment?"

"No." David pulled his badge out once again and showed it to the boy. "But I think he's expecting me."

Another gulp. "Yes, sir." He closed his cash drawer and disappeared from view.

While he was waiting, David studied what he could see of the area behind the teller windows. The vault looked sturdy enough. The steel door stood open at the moment, but he could see it was at least a foot thick. A large handle and a round dial would lock it closed. Steel bars provided an extra measure of security, essentially enclosing the safe in a jail cell.

"Good morning, sir." A tall man with salt-and-pepper hair and a neatly trimmed mustache approached the counter, the teller a step behind him. "May I help you?"

"I've come from Chicago to investigate your robbery."

Surprise widened the man's eyes. "You're too late. Didn't you know they caught the man?"

David took a step back. "What?"

"That's right. He's moldering in jail right now. I went down there a couple of days ago to identify him." The manager tapped his temple with one finger. "I don't forget a face once I've seen it."

Had he come all this way for nothing? Disappointment was David's first reaction. He shoved it away. Better to focus on the success of the local law enforcement officers. He should be glad for them. But it was a letdown all the same.

"He was arrested for disturbing the peace. When they brought him in, he had one of our bags on him. He denied being involved, but I recognized the scoundrel the moment I saw him."

"He acted alone?"

The manager's chest deflated a little. "No."

David felt a stirring of interest. Perhaps he could still do something here.

The other man thrust his chin out. "He was the ringleader, though. Now that he's in custody, the others will run for the hills."

Wanting to point out to the fellow that Louisiana—especially southern Louisiana—was short on hills, David held his lips together with effort. Citizen's Bank was the customer. He had no right to express his disdain for their manager's shortsightedness. Besides, it would only be his irritation speaking. This was serious business. He needed to keep his emotions at bay and do his job. People he didn't even know were counting on him to follow through.

"Thank you, Mr. . . ."

"Hebert. Émile Hebert."

David dipped his head. "Mr. Hebert, I'm very happy the robber was caught. If you don't mind, I'd like to meet with him before I make my report."

79

Hebert shrugged. "I suppose it will be okay. As long as there's no charge."

"Don't worry. We won't charge you for anything unless you agree."

"In that case, go ahead. It may be a waste of your time, but I suppose you realize that."

A hint of an idea occurred to David. He smiled at the bank manager. "You could be right. I just want to make sure I tie up any loose ends before I make the trip back to Chicago."

He exited the bank with quick steps. His day was going to be longer than he had expected.

Chapter Nine

Camellia Thornton pushed back a lock of hair and leaned over the table where the younger children were copying the alphabet onto their slates. She enjoyed working with the sharecroppers' children, offering them tools that would ensure them brighter futures. One day soon she would begin bringing Amaryllis to the schoolhouse and including her in the lessons she prepared for these children.

Mary, one of her youngest students, caught her tongue between her teeth, her gaze focused on her slate. She glanced up as Camellia walked toward her side of the table. "Am I doing it right, Mrs. Camellia?"

Glancing at the line of letters, Camellia rewarded the child with a bright smile. "You have most of the letters right, but you've mixed up *B* and *D*. It's something I had trouble with when I was your age." She rubbed the bottom of each letter with the heel of her hand and watched as the child wrote them in once more, praising her when she succeeded.

As she went to another side of the table to help twin siblings Abraham and Zipporah, another of the younger children—a boy named Bobby—tugged on Mary's braid. Camellia started to chastise Bobby but stopped when Mary stuck her tongue out at the child and returned her attention to her slate. It might be better to ignore the byplay since Mary didn't seem overly concerned.

Camellia had arranged the children around the table according to their ages, which ranged from five to twelve. The older children often helped her with the younger ones, learning not only the current lesson but also how to pass their knowledge along to others.

She noted a couple of empty chairs and wondered if their parents had insisted the children work today instead of coming to school. Although most of the sharecroppers were grateful to send their children to school, one or two of them balked from time to time, deciding they needed the extra hands with planting or harvesting more than they needed educated children.

"Mrs. Camellia, what is that smell?" Abraham Shasta was a ten-year-old with cheeks the color of mahogany and a heart of gold. He and Zipporah always sat side-by-side in the schoolroom and were inseparable, even when working or playing outside.

Camellia glanced toward the window, surprised to see that the air was hazy. "I don't know."

Zipporah lifted her nose and sniffed. "It smells like a cookstove to me."

This morning when Camellia had walked to the schoolhouse, no clouds had been evident. Had a thunderstorm overtaken the plantation while they studied? She walked away from the children to investigate further.

With each step she took, the air became more pungent. Her heartbeat tripled its speed, threatening to jump out of her chest as she wrenched the door open. Smoke—dense and gray—crept between the gnarled trunks of the oaks surrounding their cabin. It writhed through the upper limbs, ruffling the leaves and obscuring the sky. Her mind screamed the dreaded word as she shut the door with a snap, *Fire!*

What should she do? Where was the fire? Should they run or remain in the cabin? She chewed on her lower lip as she considered the wooden walls of their schoolhouse cabin. If the fire came too close, this place would burn up in a few seconds. She couldn't take any chances with these children's lives at stake.

Maintaining a calm façade to keep from frightening the students, she made up her mind. They would go to the big house and raise the alarm.

An idea came to her, and Camellia clapped her hands for attention. "We're going to have a parade this morning just like the ones on the Fourth of July. Quickly now, I need you to gather your things and form a line."

Concerned faces turned toward her—some black, some white—a fair representation of the families who drew their livelihood from the plantation grounds since she and Jonah had implemented their sharecropping system. "James, you and Charity help Mary and Bobby. I'll hold Dorcas's hand." She pointed Abraham toward his sister. "You and Zipporah will be at the head of the line. Hold hands and march with your knees high like the soldiers do. No running."

The children followed her directions, their voices hushed and their eyes betraying some fear. Praying that the fire was far enough away to ensure their safety rather than running rampant between them and the plantation home, she nodded toward Abraham. "Go. March to the big house."

Dorcas's hand was so small in hers. Would the five-year-old, the youngest of her students, be able to keep up? She was not much older than Amaryllis. Her little legs would not be able to keep up, especially if they had to run for cover. Picking the child up, she settled Dorcas on her hip, glanced around the schoolhouse one last time, and stepped through the doorway.

The heat from the fire was noticeable, but a quick glance around did not reveal the hungry lick of flames. Gray smoke and blackened cinders filled the air, obscuring everything. With her hearing stretched to its limit, she thought she caught the snap and crackle of the fire behind them, on the far side of the cabin. "Follow the path to the big house."

She could barely see Abraham and Zipporah some five yards ahead. James had picked up Mary, but Charity and Bobby were walking hand-in-hand directly in front of her. Dorcas cried against her shoulder as they picked their way down the path. The walk to her home only took a couple of minutes each afternoon, but today the distance seemed to stretch out endlessly ahead of them, as though they were caught in a nightmare. Finally they topped the rise between the big house and the cabin. The smoke had not yet reached this far, and Camellia breathed a sigh of relief as they half-ran, half-marched forward.

When they reached the front lawn, she saw Aunt Dahlia rocking in one of the chairs scattered across the front porch, Amaryllis in her lap. Camellia rushed up the steps toward them. "What's happened?"

"Thank goodness you're safe," Aunt Dahlia's voice squeaked. She cleared her throat before continuing. "Someone came to the house a few minutes ago and said the back field is burning. Jonah and your uncle Phillip have gone to see what can be done."

At least it wasn't harvest time. Perhaps some of the crops would survive. Camellia set Dorcas on her feet. "I have to go help them."

"Don't be ridiculous." Aunt Dahlia stopped rocking. "You mustn't forget you're a lady. Besides, you're needed here. Who do you expect to keep watch over all of these children you insist on coddling?"

"Charity and Zipporah can watch them." Camellia ignored her aunt's complaint and waved the older boys toward her. She loved her aunt, but they seemed to disagree on many things these days, including the necessity of educating the sharecroppers' children. She was beginning to fully understand why Aunt Dahlia and Lily had never gotten along. "I'll go see what I can do to help control the damage."

With an expression as sour as buttermilk, Aunt Dahlia shook her head and began rocking once more. "You grow more like your sister with each passing day."

"Thank you for that compliment." Without waiting for a reply, Camellia turned and headed back the way she had come. When she topped the rise between the house and the woods, her heart launched itself upward into her throat. The schoolhouse cabin was ablaze. If she and the children hadn't left right away, they might be caught in that conflagration now.

She started running toward the springhouse to help with the bucket brigade that she prayed was already channeling water to douse the hungry flames. If they didn't get it stopped soon, her family might lose everything.

❧

Jasmine wandered through the exquisite rooms in the Cartiers' impressive mansion on Prytania Street in the Garden District. She had not seen David since they arrived yesterday evening. He had not joined her and the Cartiers for breakfast, and he had been absent during lunch.

Dr. Cartier, one of the most renowned surgeons in the city, had gone to the hospital to see some patients after lunch. Sarah had told her he would probably not return before nightfall, when they would all go to dinner at a popular restaurant. She had also promised to take Jasmine shopping in an hour or two, as soon as she finished meeting with the housekeeper about menus for the next few days.

All of which meant that Jasmine was bored. She should have stayed in Natchez. In fact, now she couldn't remember why she'd let Lily talk her into coming. The exciting city outside the Cartiers' front door might as well be a thousand miles away for all the good it did her. Could she go for a walk on her own? Do a little shopping? No. Lily had insisted she not be allowed out of the Cartiers' home without an escort.

Jasmine kicked her skirt out in front of her, her feeling of misuse growing with every moment. When would she ever get to do what she wanted to do? She was stuck in a world between—too young to venture forth alone or to be included in whatever business it was that had Lily so distracted and far too old to take part in the childish world of her nephews and niece. She needed a companion. Someone who had similar interests. A partner in adventure. Someone like David Foster.

Where was he when she needed him? Jasmine bit her bottom lip. Dare she send a note to him? Housed in the garçonnière, he had a separate entrance that allowed him privacy. It was an odd arrangement outside of Louisiana but one that many families of either Creole or Cajun heritage adopted, from the wealthy members of society to the middle-class businessmen.

Infused with a sense of purpose, she headed to the back parlor where she thought she'd seen a writing desk. Sarah wouldn't mind if she used a piece of stationery. But as she drew nearer, another problem occurred to Jasmine. What would she say? Could she plead with him to rescue her from inactivity? Would he understand? Come to her rescue? Or would he ignore the note altogether?

Jasmine turned around and walked toward the foyer. She couldn't do it. She would simply have to hold onto her patience a little while longer. Perhaps Sarah would be done before long.

The open door of Dr. Cartier's library drew her attention. She slipped inside, her interest piqued by the walls of floor-to-ceiling bookshelves. They were crammed with every manner of reading material. She moved to the nearest one and began perusing titles. The arrangement seemed to reflect Sarah's haphazard personality more than her staid husband's. Medical books rubbed shoulders with Beadle's dime novels. Classical literature was shelved with books on animal husbandry and at least one tome on popular architectural styles. Shaking her head at the chaotic arrangement, Jasmine selected a dime novel. Aunt Dahlia would have a fit if she knew. But Aunt Dahlia was in Natchez.

She was so engrossed in the description of western frontier life that she didn't hear Sarah calling for her at first. Closing the salmon-colored cover, she slipped the book back onto the shelf and hurried into the hallway.

"There you are." Sarah skipped down the stairs as though she and Magnolia were the same age. Her dress for the afternoon was a bright concoction of white satin under a layer of yellow tulle. Blue organza flowers scattered across the skirt matched the ribbons laced through her cosmopolitan hairstyle. "I have been looking for you all over. Are you ready for our outing? I thought you would enjoy a drive to Place Gravier. It's a park named for Jean Gravier, who donated the land."

Jasmine immediately forgot her woes as excitement filled her. She didn't care where they went as long as she was no longer trapped inside. "Yes, I would adore an outing."

Although Sarah was wearing a dashing hat with a tall crown, she was several inches shorter than Jasmine. But that didn't stop her from patting Jasmine's cheek with a gloved hand. "Poor dear. I've been ignoring you, *non*?"

The older woman clucked her tongue and shook her head, putting her hat in danger of toppling from its lofty heights. "I promise to make it up to you."

Like a leaf caught in a swift current, Jasmine followed Sarah across the foyer. She might have little control over her destination, but it was bound to be an exciting ride.

A cabriolet stood outside the front door, its hood folded back so the two ladies would have a wide view during their drive. Jasmine cast a doubtful glance at her hostess's hat, wondering if it would survive the buffeting of a brisk drive. But as it turned out, she need not have worried. Sarah Cartier might be a whirlwind when it came to her duties as a hostess, but she drove her carriage with all the deliberate speed of a tortoise. Their vehicle crept down the street, earning rude comments from one or two of the drivers stuck behind them. By the time they turned into the park, Jasmine's ears burned with embarrassment.

"I don't know why everyone is in such a hurry." Sarah flourished the whip in her hand but did not direct it toward their horse. "I believe all this rushing about is why people grow ill during warm months. Poor Kenneth is so overworked from April until October that I worry about his health."

Jasmine nodded, her head swiveling back and forth to take in the sights. Ladies and gentlemen strolled about the shady paths of the park or rested on benches. A young girl in a rough cotton shift exhorted gentlemen to purchase flowers from her basket for the women they escorted. A young fellow was being tugged down the path by a large dog on a leash, his arm extended to a degree that made Jasmine wince in sympathy.

A desultory breeze ruffled the leaves on the oak trees and teased Jasmine's collar. "Do you drive here every day?"

"Oh no." Sarah's mouth formed a perfect O when she spoke.

Jasmine wanted to imitate the gesture but managed to restrain herself. She filed away the expression for future use. She had read an article the other day about how the most successful actors studied people to learn how to portray emotions on the stage. She had determined immediately to adopt the habit as she could see the benefits to be derived from it.

"I usually have a coachman drive me to the park, but I wanted to show your pretty face to all of my friends."

An oncoming carriage drew even with them and stopped as the lady inside poked her driver with her parasol. "It's nice to see you this afternoon, Sarah."

"Jasmine, I want you to meet one of my dearest friends, Madame Cécile LeBlanc." Sarah turned to the lady in the other carriage. "Cécile, this is the youngest sister of my brother's wife, Camellia, Miss Jasmine Anderson."

The other lady, dressed in a pink figured silk dress with short sleeves that exposed most of her upper arms, squinted toward Jasmine. "*Enchanté, mademoiselle.*"

Jasmine was glad for Camellia's insistence that she learn a few French phrases for just such social occasions. "*Merci, madame. Comment allez-vous?*"

The other lady nodded her approval. "*Je vais bien.* I am well." She looked at Sarah. "She is indeed beautiful and smart, too. Our poor debutantes will tear their flounces in despair."

Sarah beamed with pride as though she was personally responsible for Jasmine's looks and behavior. "I have told you of their older sister who owns her own steamboat, Mrs. Lily Matthews."

Madame's dark gaze studied Jasmine with interest. "*Oui.*"

"Usually Jasmine stays with my parents when her family is in town, but I insisted she stay with me this time. I hope she will remain with us for a few weeks at least so we can attend some parties. You know how much these young girls enjoy dancing and flirting with handsome young men."

A protest trembled on the tip of her tongue. Camellia was the sister who enjoyed parties. She enjoyed every aspect of the social whirl—from selecting the invitations and hiring the orchestra to sipping lemonade and chatting with the other women about their new gowns. Jasmine could dance, but she got enough of parties at home. And the idea of spending a whole evening at a ball where she would know no one made her shudder. "I'm not certain what Lily's plans are."

"I know." Madame LeBlanc's cocoa-colored eyes sparkled with excitement. "You should bring her to the theater this evening."

This sounded much more promising. Jasmine straightened her spine. "I'd love to see a play."

"But Kenneth and I didn't purchase tickets for this season." Sarah shook her head. "We find it such a crush, and the performances are sometimes too risqué for my tastes. I'm sorry, Jasmine. If I'd thought of it earlier, Kenneth might have been able to procure tickets for us, but I doubt there's time now."

Disappointment filled Jasmine at Sarah's admission. Her smile drooped in spite of her best efforts. A trip to the theater would have been a perfect way to spend the evening.

"I have the solution." Madame LeBlanc waved her hand like the magic wand of a fairy godmother. "Monsieur LeBlanc and I always purchase extra tickets, and we are not attending this evening. I will send them around to you, and then you will not have to disappoint your guest."

"I don't know what to say." Sarah's voice was hesitant. "I will gladly purchase the tickets."

"Don't be silly."

Jasmine's excitement returned full force. Madame LeBlanc's offer was almost too good to be true. Her hopeful gaze met Sarah's.

With a Gallic shrug, her hostess acquiesced. "Thank you, Cécile. You are very thoughtful."

Feeling like she could float on a cloud all the way back to the Cartiers' home, Jasmine turned to Madame LeBlanc. It took her a moment to remember the way to say thank you in French. "Merci *beaucoup*."

"*C'est ne rien*, cher. *Comment adorable*. She is adorable, Sarah." Madame LeBlanc prodded the coachman's back once more to indicate she was ready to leave. As they pulled away, she leaned out of her carriage window. "In fact, I have an idea to arrange a special surprise for your young visitor. She will be *aux anges*."

Jasmine wondered what surprise Sarah's friend was planning. Whatever it was, it could not compare with a night at the theater. Nothing could compare with a treat like that.

Chapter Ten

Les Fleurs

The fire yielded slowly to their efforts. Someone along the line reported that the men had lit a backfire. Camellia knew of the idea to "fight fire with fire" even though it made little sense to her. Would the strategy work, or would it cause even more destruction? She lifted buckets of water until her arms felt wooden and her back ached worse than when she was expecting her child.

The sun had passed its zenith when Jonah appeared, his face so grimy she almost didn't recognize him.

Camellia forgot her aches in the rush to check on him. "Are you okay? Is it over? Was anyone hurt?"

He put an arm around her shoulders and hugged her close. "I'm fine."

Camellia broke free and filled a dipper with water from the spring. Jonah drank greedily before continuing. "We had some scary moments. We lost several cabins, and some of the crops were scorched, but we managed to dig a trench that enclosed the worst of the blaze. The bucket brigade and a backfire did the rest."

As long as he was safe, she didn't much care about the rest of the estate. Crops could be replanted; houses could be rebuilt.

"We need to send for the doctor."

Camellia took a mental inventory of her medical supplies to keep fear at bay. "Where are you hurt?"

His smile reassured her. "I only have a few scrapes, but Amos was burned when a limb fell on him, and I'm sure we'll have some other injuries to sort out before the day is over."

Nahum Shasta walked to where they stood. A brawny man with short-cropped hair, he was Abraham and Zipporah's father and the new foreman. "Jonah, I've got something here you need to see."

"I'll go back to the house and gather some things," Camellia said. "Get anyone who's hurt to come there."

He dropped a quick kiss on her cheek before they separated.

Camellia passed along the information to the women before heading back to the main house. She gathered wheat flour to cover the cleaned burns, needle and thread for any cuts, soap and fresh water, and clean cotton strips for finishing.

Jonah and Nahum brought in the first patient on a litter, and Camellia directed them upstairs to the guest wing.

"Shouldn't you wait for the doctor?" Aunt Dahlia stood at the parlor door. "I don't think it's a good idea to take men like that into the bosom of your family."

Camellia knew what her aunt meant. The man on the stretcher was black. She tried to remember that her aunt had been raised during a different time, but her temper flared. "He risked his life to help put out a fire threatening our home—the very room to which he is being carried. What would you have me do? Leave him on the front lawn?"

"I didn't intend—" The glare Camellia tossed at her stopped Aunt Dahlia midsentence. She fell back a step, her eyes wide.

Trying not to feel guilty for her harsh tone, Camellia sighed. "Please send the doctor up as soon as he arrives."

Aunt Dahlia nodded.

Camellia climbed the steps and found that the men had transferred the patient to the bed.

Nahum dipped his head as she moved toward the center of the room. "Your sheets may not come clean, Mrs. Thornton."

"Don't worry about that." She spared a smile for Nahum before turning to the man on the bed. "We'll have him comfortable in no time."

Jonah and Nahum moved back as she investigated her patient.

His wary eyes watched her with doubt. His chest and arms had been burned. Although not deep, the large area of burned skin concerned her.

Camellia hoped the doctor would arrive soon. She could dress the wounds, but she had no laudanum to ease his pain. "What's your name?"

"Simeon." His skin was the color of café au lait, his eyes hazel.

"Well, Simeon, I want you to relax a little." She reached for the bowl of clean water. "Have you ever been treated by a lady before?"

The frown on his wide brow eased a little. "No, ma'am. 'Cept for my ma when I was a little boy."

"My wife has a lot of experience." Jonah stepped closer. "You're in good hands."

"Yes, sir." His gaze swiveled from Jonah back to her. "I'm sorry 'bout your bed, ma'am."

Camellia made a shushing noise as she continued her work. When she was satisfied that all dirt and debris had been removed, she sprinkled the wounds with flour. Then Jonah and Nahum helped Simeon sit up so she could wrap the cotton bandages around his chest.

The doctor arrived as she was tying the final knot, his black bag held in one hand. Jonah and Nahum left them alone. She held her breath as the doctor inspected her work, prying at the edges of the bandages and grunting as he checked Simeon's pulse and temperature. Finally he glanced up at her over the edge of his oval spectacles. "If you ever wish to work at my practice, Mrs. Thornton, you are more than welcome."

"Thank you, Doctor." She watched as he measured out a dose of laudanum. "It's been awhile since I had to deal with anything more serious than cuts and bruises."

"I know you worked with patients during the war, and you've certainly not lost your touch." He capped his bottle and left it on the dresser. "If he wakes during the night, you can give him one more spoonful." The doctor closed his bag and moved to the door, inclining his head to indicate that Camellia should precede him. "What happened to him?"

Camellia told the doctor about the fire.

He shook his head. "Do you have other patients I should see?"

"I don't know for certain. My aunt may have suffered a fit of apoplexy by now."

He turned his chuckle into a cough. "Never fear, I will check on Miss Dahlia on my way out. I may have a little something to calm over-wrought nerves. Why don't you wash up? You look ready to fall over."

"I concur with your diagnosis." Jonah's voice came from the shadowy hall. Bathed and in a fresh suit, her husband looked much refreshed. "And I intend to see that my wife follows your instructions to the letter."

Shaking her head, Camellia watched as the doctor made his way to the first floor. "I should see to the others before—"

Jonah put a finger over her mouth. "You heard the doctor. You will not be allowed downstairs until you make use of the warm bath waiting in our bedroom."

Recognizing the firm tone in her husband's voice, Camellia nodded. Besides, the idea of washing the grime from her skin sounded blissful. "Are you sure no one else needs to be seen?"

Instead of answering, Jonah swept her into his arms.

"What are you doing?"

"Making sure you follow orders." He stopped long enough to open the door before depositing her on the edge of their bed. "Do you need help undressing?"

Camellia could feel her cheeks heat. "I believe I can manage on my own."

"If you're sure. . ." The look in his eyes was positively wicked.

Fleeing to the dressing screen, Camellia began removing her clothing with racehorse speed. She heard the bedroom door close and giggled. As she climbed into the bathtub, she thanked God for bringing Jonah into her life. He was the only man in the world who could make her laugh on a day like this one.

❧

David was led to the cell by Constable Louis Longineaux. He was young and looked like he needed to gain some weight so he could fill out his uniform—a double-breasted frock coat of a rather garish orange hue and matching trousers. The left lapel of his coat boasted a metal badge in the shape of a star with a crescent surrounding it, the standard emblem of the Metropolitan Police Force.

Ignoring the rude remarks of the prisoners they passed in the dreary hallway, David matched his pace to the young constable's. His nose stung from the noxious odors of waste and filth. As a detective he'd seen the inside of many prisons, but none quite so grimy. The walls were streaked with water and green slime, and decay and hopelessness permeated the air. "Has the prisoner had any visitors?"

"No." The constable stumbled over a loose brick in the floor, setting his ring of keys to jingling before he regained his balance. "I reckon he's a loner. Or maybe none of his friends know what happened to him."

Before he could ask more questions, they reached their destination in a dank corner of the jail. Longineaux rattled his keys and selected one to insert into the lock. "Wake up, Charlie. You got a visitor."

Charles "Charlie" Petrie lay on one of the two cots in the cell, his hands under his head. When he heard the door open, he sat up and swung his legs to the floor.

Several days' growth of a dark beard hid the shape of his chin. His hair was a mess, standing at odd angles around his head and giving him the look of a madman. His eyes reminded David of a cat—almond-shaped and so light a shade of brown they might be called yellow. They glowed in the dim light of the cell, tracking the constable's movements even though the prisoner's head didn't move.

"Whatcha' mean? I got no friends in New Orleans."

David noticed the way he pronounced the city's name. The prisoner said it as two separate words—New Orleenz. A native like Constable Longineaux would have said N'awlins.

"No one said I was a friend." David stepped into the cell and gestured to the constable to lock him in. "You can come back in about half an hour. I should be done by then."

"You sure you'll still be alive?" Petrie's feline gaze skewered him.

David resisted the urge to touch his gun. His holster was empty—a rule enforced with all visitors, even Pinkerton detectives—but he felt secure in his ability to protect himself, even in such close quarters. "I'm not worried."

Longineaux left them alone, and David glanced around the room. It was sparsely furnished—a pair of cots, a chamber pot, and a narrow window so grimy it let in little sunlight. Deciding not to lean against the wall, David sat on the unoccupied cot.

Charlie Petrie didn't say anything, but his gaze bored a hole into David's chest.

Accustomed to anger and belligerence, David took his attitude in stride. He wasn't here to make a new friend, after all. He took a moment to size the other man up before beginning his interrogation. "So you're the man who planned and executed a successful robbery at Citizen's Bank?" He put a hint of disbelief in his voice.

Petrie sneered, his face seeming even more catlike as he wrinkled his nose. "If you say so."

"I'm asking." David took a notebook from his coat pocket. "I have to complete a report. It would help me immensely if you would tell me about the robbery."

Crossing his arms over his chest, Petrie leaned against the wall behind him. "What do you want to know?"

"I don't know." Chewing on the nib of a pencil, David looked up at nothing in particular. He wanted Petrie to think he was a bit of a simpleton. "Why don't you start with the number of men involved in the robbery."

"Just me."

David scratched his head. "Is that right? What about the others who came in with you and held guns on the staff? Are you telling me they were strangers you met on the street as you walked into the bank?"

"Yep. I had me an idea to slip in right quick and empty out the safe.

Those fellows offered to help for a cut of the money." Petrie relaxed as he talked.

"I see." David wrote a couple of words down in his book.

"You could say I've got one of them friendly faces. Folks walk up to me all the time and ask if they can help out."

David let the prisoner continue his story, inserting approving noises here and there to keep him talking.

"Say, what are you writing down in that book about me?"

"Hmmm." David looked up. "Oh, it's nothing much. Kinda boring. My boss likes for me to wrap things up in a nice package so he'll know where to put the file after you're dead."

Petrie's jaw dropped. "What are you talking about?"

"Armed robbery is a serious charge. I was hoping maybe we could talk about a reduced sentence if you knew something to lead me to the others who were at the bank." David shrugged. "But since you didn't know them, and you're not a member of a gang, you really don't know anything I can use."

A crafty look entered the man's yellow eyes. "I might be willing to talk a little more if it would save me from the hangman's noose."

Petrie was an example of the adage "There is no honor among thieves." Few criminals possessed a high moral code. Most of them would be willing to sell their mothers for a jug of whiskey.

"You can talk your head off all the way to the gallows, and it won't make a bit of difference." David closed his notebook and returned it to his pocket. "It's a shame really."

Petrie pushed himself forward, leaning toward David. "You've got to listen to me."

"Why should I?" David stood. "I have enough information for your file. Thank you for your time."

"Wait." Petrie's jaw worked, evidence of the strong emotions passing through him. "What if I was lying? What if I really did know those men? What if I could lead you to them? What if you made a big arrest and got yourself a nice promotion? You'd like that, wouldn't you?"

"Of course I would." David met Petrie's gaze. "But if you were lying then, how can I believe anything you tell me now?"

Petrie rocked back on the cot.

David could practically hear the wheels of the man's brain grinding as he considered his options.

"I don't know much. I ain't been a part of the gang for long. Only since they showed up in New Orleans a few weeks ago."

David's pulse spiked. He'd lost hope that Charlie Petrie might be part of the gang that had been robbing banks up and down the Mississippi River valley. Anyone dumb enough to be caught in a bar with evidence on him didn't seem like much of a mastermind. He had decided that at best Petrie was a junior member of the gang. At worst he would have no connection at all to the robbers David was tracking. He needed to keep his interest well hidden. "So you really don't know anything at all, do you?"

"That's not true." Petrie thrust his chin up, defiance evident in every muscle of his body. Even his beard seemed to bristle with it. "I don't know exactly where they hide out, but I can get a message to them. . . draw them out. Then you can spring your trap."

"I don't know. . . ."

The arrival of Constable Longineaux could not have been better timed. David could see the anxiety in Charlie Petrie's yellow eyes. He would let the man sit for a day or two while he talked with the police chief. Together, they could work out a plan. Something that would stop Charlie Petrie and his gang from ever again preying on innocent people.

Chapter Eleven

Jumping to her feet as the final curtain fell, Jasmine brought her hands together with enthusiasm. She didn't care that none of the others in their box stood. Lily was probably frowning, but it didn't matter. Nothing could undermine her delight in the performance. As the applause of the audience began to die down, she returned to her front-row seat. "I wish it wasn't over."

Sarah leaned toward her. "Kenneth and I are enjoying watching you enjoy the play. You're a breath of fresh air. I had almost forgotten how much fun the theater can be."

Jasmine felt a bit like a brown sparrow sitting next to a peacock. When she first walked downstairs this evening, she had been more than satisfied with her navy blue frock. Six flounces edged in bias-cut lace decorated the skirt. The bodice was unadorned except for a single row of buttons, a narrow collar, and a rosette of the same silk faille as her dress. Her jewelry was a single strand of matching pearls, and her hair had been pulled back in a simple style that allowed soft ringlets to touch her shoulders.

But Sarah's dress put hers to shame. It might have been shipped directly from Paris. Forest green in color, the silk gown nipped in her waist and exposed her dimpled shoulders. The flounce was caught up high on the skirt and cascaded toward the floor in elegant folds. A diamond collar sparkled around her neck, complementing the glittering earbobs that dripped from her ears. She looked like a plate from a fashion magazine.

Sarah touched Jasmine's elbow with the tip of her fan. "Would you like to go backstage to meet Miss Barlow?"

Jasmine's jaw dropped. She couldn't imagine anything any more thrilling.

Lily leaned forward from her seat on the second row. "You'd better close your mouth before an insect flies into it." Her whisper fell into one of those sudden silences that sometimes happens even in large crowds.

The people in the next box glanced in Jasmine's direction as a result of her sister's warning. She heard a chuckle from Blake behind her and saw the smile on Kenneth's face. A tide of hot blood stung her cheeks. Wanting to bring her hands up to hide her embarrassment, Jasmine trained her gaze on the floor. She wished Lily and Blake had stayed at the Thorntons' house tonight. The outing would be much more pleasurable without her sister's constant poking and prodding.

Sarah came to her rescue. "Don't be so hard on the girl." Her dress rustled as she stood and looped her arm through Jasmine's. "Madame LeBlanc arranged it for you, but if you don't wish to go, I will understand."

"Oh, no." Jasmine bit her lip. "I mean, yes, please. I would like that above all things." The very idea of meeting one of the talented people she'd just seen on the stage made her heart race. She lifted her free hand to check her hair and realized it was shaking. Hoping no one else had seen it, she allowed her arm to drop back to her side. This was the most exciting moment of her life. But she didn't have to advertise that fact to her naysayer sister.

"Good." Sarah turned to Kenneth. "Why don't you take Lily and Blake outside to the carriage? We won't be long."

"Actually, Lily and I have decided to go back to the Thorntons' alone instead of making you drive back to the French Quarter to drop us off."

Kenneth looked toward his wife, a frown on his normally calm face. "Aren't we going to Bonhomie for dinner?"

Jasmine could see her dream of visiting the backstage area slipping between her fingers. Life was so unfair. Why did Lily have to spoil things?

"I hope you won't change your plans because of us." Lily hid a yawn behind her fan. "I am so tired this evening. I suppose I'm getting too old for all of this excitement."

"Jasmine may have a conniption if she doesn't get to visit with that actress." Blake smiled to remove the sting from his words.

Dr. Cartier's frown deepened until everyone laughed. He was so serious—an odd spouse for someone as animated as Sarah.

Holding her breath, Jasmine looked at Sarah, who leaned toward her husband and whispered something in his ear.

Kenneth nodded. "We insist you take the carriage home. I will arrange for a cab while the ladies are visiting."

"That makes no sense." Blake settled his wife's cloak around her shoulders. "I can get a cab for Lily and me."

Kenneth and Sarah exchanged a glance. She lifted her shoulders, and he nodded before turning to Blake. "I'd be most happy to take you home while the ladies are visiting the actors backstage."

Blake's refusal was polite but resolute. By the time Sarah's husband agreed, Jasmine wanted to scream her frustration. "Can we go now?"

Laughing at Jasmine's obvious fervor, Sarah nodded and led the way out of the box. They were immediately caught up in throngs of laughing, chattering people who were making their way toward the building exits. By the time they made it to the relative quiet of the dressing rooms located in the back of the theater, Jasmine felt bruised by the effort. But she would have turned around and done it again if necessary.

Sarah explained to one of the workers that they were supposed to meet Miss Barlow in her dressing room. The man looked them over with a raised eyebrow before directing them down a hallway.

Several young men crowded around one of the doorways, jostling with good-natured rivalry in their attempts to gain entry into one of the dressing rooms. As they drew closer, Jasmine realized it must be Miss Barlow's room. She had never imagined such a throng all seeking the same goal. Would they be able to see the actress, after all?

"May I be of service to you young ladies?" A tall figure separated from one of the shadowy corners of the hallway.

When he came fully into view, Jasmine thought she might faint. She recognized him—the actor who portrayed the hero, Vance Hargrove. He was even more handsome up close than he'd been on the stage.

Sarah seemed unfazed by his good looks or fame as she nodded and once again explained their objective.

Mr. Hargrove bowed. "She is inundated for the moment, but perhaps you ladies would care to join me for dinner. We can return here in an hour or so once her admirers have cleared out. I'm certain Miss Barlow would be delighted to spend time visiting with such charming ladies."

Sarah shook her head. "I'm afra—"

The opportunity of a lifetime was within her grasp. Unable to let it slip past, Jasmine interrupted Sarah's response. "Perhaps you could join us for dinner instead, Mr. Hargrove. I would love to ask some questions about the theater." Fear struck as she wondered what had possessed her to be so forward. What would Mr. Hargrove think of her?

A smile appeared on the man's handsome face, lending him a worldly look. "Are you perhaps an aspiring actress, Miss. . . ?" He held onto the last syllable, inviting her to offer her name.

"Jasmine. Jasmine Anderson." She curtsied as gracefully as possible in the narrow confines of the hallway.

Mr. Hargrove took her hand in his and brought it to his lips. As he placed a lingering kiss on her knuckles, his soulful gaze seemed to consume her. "What a lovely name for a lovely girl."

He turned to Sarah. "And this gorgeous young creature must be your sister."

A sharp pang ate at Jasmine's heart as Mr. Hargrove took Sarah's hand and kissed it with the same lingering attention.

But Sarah didn't seem to mind. She fluttered her eyelashes at the man as he straightened. "You are quite the flatterer, are you not, Monsieur Hargrove?"

He put a hand to his chest and staggered back a step. "You wound me, mademoiselle. If I cannot remark on beauty where I see it, what use is this tongue?"

Sarah laughed. "How would you earn wages without it?"

"This is very true." He winked at her before turning his attention back to Jasmine. "If you can convince your sister to include me in your family party, I would be most delighted to join you."

Jasmine's pang intensified. She wished for a moment she'd paid more attention to Camellia's advice about learning the art of flirtation. But she had never needed it before this evening. Could she even flutter her eyelashes? "I'm sure Mrs. Cartier wouldn't mind."

From the odd expression on the actor's face, Jasmine's attempt to flutter was not going well. She closed her eyes for a brief moment as she realized how gauche she must appear to him. When she opened them, he had recovered his aplomb. He bowed to her and offered his arm. . .to Sarah. Didn't he hear her say that Sarah was a married lady? Jasmine trudged behind them and wondered how she might regain Mr. Hargrove's attention.

"My heart is broken to learn that some other man has stolen your affections. Dare I hope that your family forced you into a marriage with a doddering old fool who is at the point of demise?" His voice was pitched low, but Jasmine had no trouble overhearing him.

Sarah giggled and rapped his hand with her fan. "You are a rascal. Dr. Cartier won my heart a decade ago."

"He is in poor health, though?"

"My husband is in the prime of his life."

Mr. Hargrove shook his head. "Then I am doomed to worship you from afar."

Jasmine rolled her eyes. By the time they found Kenneth and performed the introductions, she was wishing she'd not been so impetuous.

The drive to the restaurant changed her opinion slightly as Mr.

Hargrove recounted several humorous stories of past performances. He accompanied his tales with admiring glances in her direction. By the time the coachman pulled up, she found herself in better humor.

The men climbed out first and turned to offer their assistance to the ladies. Sarah accepted her husband's arm. Jasmine had to wait a moment before Mr. Hargrove reached inside for her hand, so by the time her feet touched the ground, the Cartiers were almost at the entrance.

Instead of releasing Jasmine's hand, Mr. Hargrove tucked it into the crook of his arm. He leaned over so that his mouth was close to her ear. "I trust you understand that I must appease your chaperones if I am to have access to your company."

She didn't know if she should be relieved or repelled by his explanation. "Sarah is very beautiful and accomplished."

"But she lacks a very special quality that you have in abundance." His eyes shone in the light of a nearby lantern.

Jasmine felt the blood rushing upward to stain her cheeks and hoped he could not see it. Prying her tongue from the roof of her mouth, she swallowed hard. "Wh–what is that?"

"Innocence." His smile made her heart stutter. She could hardly believe such a handsome, sophisticated man found anything interesting about her at all.

He found her lack of experience a good thing? Jasmine could hardly believe he wouldn't prefer a female who could match his own qualities. He was so suave, so comfortable in social situations. Perhaps he was teasing her? But a glance at his face showed nothing but admiration. She didn't know how to answer him.

The atmosphere inside was conducive to a romantic mood. Small round tables covered with white linen were scattered between vine-wrapped white columns of varying heights. Large potted ferns and tropical trees gave the illusion of privacy while kerosene lamps turned low made each table an intimate island. Jasmine felt as though she'd left America altogether and been magically transported to a romantic Greek ruin.

A waiter dressed in black formal wear led them to a table and gave menus to the gentlemen.

After glancing at the restaurant's offerings, Mr. Hargrove leaned toward her. "I don't know anything about your tastes, Miss Anderson. Do you wish to order for yourself?"

Jasmine didn't much care what food was brought to the table as long as she was in his heady company. The only thing that would make the evening better would be if she and the actor were dining alone. "I trust you to make a proper selection, Mr. Hargrove."

"I don't know how proper my selection will be if you are involved." His heated look set butterflies loose in her stomach. "It would give me great pleasure if you would use my Christian name, Vance."

Kenneth cleared his throat and gave a tiny shake of his head before handing his menu back to the waiter. "I'm sure we'll all enjoy the braised lamb."

Taking the reprimand in stride, Vance smiled at his host. "I was telling your wife earlier that you're a very lucky gentleman."

"Why is that?" The frown on Kenneth's face did not bode well for the rest of the evening.

"Because you snatched up Mrs. Cartier before any of the other men in New Orleans could. I am sure you're the envy of everyone you know."

Sarah beamed at both men and put her hand over her husband's. "I'm the lucky one."

Kenneth sat back, his features easing a tad.

Jasmine was relieved. She listened to the two men discuss politics and the general state of the country, Sarah tossing in a witty comment now and then. The meal came, but she found herself unable to consume much. The butterflies still fluttering inside her stomach forbade her. She played with her fork, picked at a loose thread on her napkin, and managed to swallow a few sips of water. If tonight was a preview of what New Orleans had to offer, perhaps she should reconsider staying here.

❧

A black police officer studied David's badge, a furrow between his brows. "Didn't I see you here yesterday?"

David held out his right hand. "That's right. My name's David Foster. I'm investigating the Citizen's Bank robbery."

"Levi Campbell." The officer's grasp was firm. "The chief's down at the mayor's office, but Lieutenant Moreau might be able to see you."

It was a place to start. David knew he needed to enlist the support of the department if his plan was to succeed. Putting his badge into his coat pocket, he smiled at Officer Campbell. "Lead the way."

The constable who'd escorted him the day before sat at one of the wooden desks in the main room of the police station. A look of concern crossed his features as he recognized David. "Is something wrong?"

David wracked his memory for the man's name. French. Long. That was it! Longineaux. "Morning, Constable Longineaux."

A look of surprise and appreciation replaced his concern.

Before he could say anything, Officer Campbell blew out a breath to show his exasperation. "Pinkerton here wants to see the chief."

"Does it have something to do with the robbery?"

" 'A course it does." Campbell answered for him. "That's what he supposed to be investigating."

Longineaux sent a glare toward his fellow officer and turned back to his desk. "He's gone. I doubt he'll be back before dinner."

"I know that." The black man's answer was clipped and full of disdain. "I'm taking him to Lieutenant Moreau's office."

As they moved forward, David maintained an air of neutrality. He didn't want to get caught up in any local politics. He was supposed to work with local law enforcement, not take sides in their squabbles.

Turning into a hallway, they left the central office behind. David counted two doors on the left and one on the right before Officer Campbell stopped and rapped smartly on an unmarked entrance.

Someone on the other side barked out a command to enter.

Campbell glanced at him, his brown eyes cool. "Wait out here." He turned the knob and disappeared. After a moment the door opened again, and Campbell waved him inside.

Lieutenant Moreau was a short man with dark skin that hinted at mixed ancestry. His hair was as black as Jasmine's, and his eyes were a deep brown. He waved a hand toward a wooden chair and leaned back. "What brings you down to New Orleans?"

"The robbery two weeks ago at Citizen's Bank." David wondered how many times he would have to describe his mission. "We think it may be connected to a string of robberies that started in Chicago a couple of months ago."

Moreau moved a stack of papers to one side of his desk. "What makes you think the man we arrested has anything to do with your robberies?"

"In Chicago the thieves seemed to know the exact time to strike. They don't ever shoot anyone. They empty the safe, fire off a couple of shots into the air, and escape. Sound familiar?"

He could tell he had the lieutenant's attention. "Very."

"They've hit a couple of other locations on their way down here. My captain thinks they may be headed for Mexico next. We want to stop them before they get out of the country."

"And you think our prisoner can help you?" Moreau didn't sound convinced. "Do you want some of my men to interrogate him?"

David shook his head. "I don't think he's the type to be intimidated. But I think he'd do anything to save his own skin."

"I don't know why you think you could trust him to be honest with you." Moreau's eyes narrowed. "He's more likely to get you killed by giving you the wrong direction or sending a message to warn his friends."

Inspiration dawned on David with the other man's words. "That's it! He can send a message."

Moreau's eyebrows climbed toward his hairline. "You want him to warn his cohorts?"

David shook his head. "I want him to draw them out, get them to meet him. Didn't you catch him with a sizeable amount of money on him?"

"It's in the evidence room." Moreau rubbed his chin as he considered David's suggestion. "But I still don't see how you plan to work this."

"The one we're really after is not someone who actually carried out the robbery. The robbers are nothing more than puppets. Half an hour with Petrie convinced me he doesn't have the wit to execute one robbery with such precision, much less ten."

"Ten?" Moreau whistled. "They must be the luckiest group of men in existence."

"No one has that kind of luck. It takes careful planning and inside information to pull off that many crimes without a hitch. I believe a mastermind is behind them. He's the one I want."

"I see. But how do you plan to get Petrie to convince him to show his face?"

"Blackmail." David allowed a small smile on his lips. "I'll put a reward notice in the newspaper, and our friend can threaten that he's going to claim it if his boss doesn't take him back into the fold."

"What if the boss isn't the only one who shows up? I know Pinkertons are well trained, but I don't think you can take custody of the whole gang."

David knew he would need the support of the police department, but he wanted to lead the mission. "If you can supply me with a couple of men at the right time, I can manage."

Moreau frowned at him. "What about Petrie? Are you sure he won't betray you as soon as his friends show up?"

"I doubt he would want to get caught in the crossfire. He knows he'd be the first to die. And Mr. Petrie has a driving desire to live."

The lieutenant's face relaxed. "If you get Petrie to go along, I'll make sure you have what you need." He stood and held out his right hand.

David took it, his smile widening. "Thank you, sir."

He left the office and went to find the constable. He was anxious to set his plan in motion.

Petrie was less than enthusiastic about the plan. "I don't know who calls the shots. He sends us written instructions. I've never seen him, and I sure don't know how to send him a note."

"There has to be a way." David thought hard. "How do you get the money to him?"

"He tells us where to drop it off."

That wouldn't work. David considered a few schemes, each too unwieldy or unbelievable. Finally it came to him. "We're working at this too hard. All I have to do is tell the newspaper that you've turned over a new leaf since escaping the hangman's noose. You plan to tell us everything we'll need to arrest your leader. That will bring him out into the open."

"You're forgetting that I don't know what he looks like. I could walk past him on the street and never realize it. He could shoot me before I said a word."

"He'll want to know how much you've already told us before killing you. Once he shows himself, we'll take him down." David grew more excited as he talked. If he caught the man who was the head of the outfit, it wouldn't take long before they had all of the robbers in custody. He could practically hear Mr. Bastrup's accolades already.

Chapter Twelve

I knew your plan for saving Les Fleurs was liable to get us all murdered in our beds." Aunt Dahlia glanced across the dining room table at her husband for support.

Uncle Phillip's grimace was exaggerated by a singed mark on his forehead. Proof of his efforts to save Les Fleurs. "All's well that ends well, Dahlia."

Although her husband's defection must have been a blow to Aunt Dahlia's esteem, she was not likely to be silenced by it. Like the other women in the family, she had a strong personality and boundless self-assurance.

With a sniff, she turned from Uncle Phillip to glare at Jonah. "Before you married Camellia, she was a good girl who understood how things should be."

"Aunt Dahlia, don't try to blame Jonah." Camellia kept her voice low even though she wanted to spring to her husband's defense. "If we hadn't done something, we would have lost Les Fleurs for taxes. The sharecropping system Jonah put in place saved us. We rent the land, and our tenants help us with the work. Everyone prospers."

"I don't understand why we couldn't keep selling our cotton to those Europeans who have always been so eager for it. You can't convince me that the Yankees aren't putting a great deal of profit into their own pockets."

Camellia refused to be baited. Conspiratorial Yankees, greedy tax collectors, and uppity former slaves—these were the things that vexed Aunt Dahlia the most. As well as what she viewed as Camellia's foolish decision to marry a Yankee sympathizer at the end of the war.

"Jasper Calhoun went to Natchez Under-the-Hill last night to celebrate the demise of Les Fleurs." Jonah continued the story he'd already begun. "He bragged about the fire to anyone who would listen."

"Why would he do such a thing?" Nausea threatened to overwhelm Camellia as she considered how narrowly they had avoided disaster. "Jasper brought his family here for the Christmas celebration last year like all the other workers. He's worked here for most of the past five years. Did he hate us all that time?"

Jonah's dark gaze showed empathy for her pain. "Apparently, he's felt ill-used for quite some time. Then everything came to a head with our decision to appoint a new overseer to replace Mr. Smithson."

"But Nahum got that job." Camellia had agreed with her husband's choice of the hardworking, honest man. Like the Bible parable of the men given talents, Nahum had taken what he had and increased its worth. Both he and Jasper had been among their first sharecroppers but the differences between them were marked.

Nahum's home was one of the prettiest on the grounds—the yard was always well-kept, and his house received a fresh coat of whitewash every year. His pride was obvious in the way he took care of his home.

The windows at Jasper's cabin were stuffed with rags, his yard had more weeds than grass, and his field had one of the lowest yields, if not the lowest, each year. Furthermore, he never allowed his children to attend classes at her school, showing his lack of concern for their futures. With all that, why would he think he could handle more responsibility?

"Some people refuse to see the facts before them." Jonah sighed. "He seems to have gotten it into his head that he would receive the promotion based solely on the fact that Nahum is black and he's white."

"I have no patience for that kind of attitude." Camellia straightened her back and glanced at her aunt, whose gaze dropped to the table between them. "The true worth of a person has nothing to do with the color of his or her skin."

Jonah cleared his throat. "I spoke with the sheriff earlier this morning. He rode out here to find out what happened, and he's promised to locate Jasper and take him in for questioning."

"Do you really think he'll tell the sheriff the truth?" She was unable to keep the skepticism out of her voice. Bragging about his misdeeds under the influence of alcohol was one thing. Confessing to the law in the cold, sober light of day would be different.

Jonah's mouth quirked upward. "I think the sheriff has the expertise to separate truth from lies. I imagine Jasper will have to answer for what he's done."

"I'm sure your husband is right." Uncle Phillip exchanged a glance with Jonah. "Jasper Calhoun will be going to jail for a long time."

Camellia was glad to see evidence of the affection between the two men. Of course, men seemed to rub along better in most circumstances than women. If only she could convince Aunt Dahlia to let go of her prejudices long enough to give Jonah a chance. . . . What would it take for the older woman to do so? Prayer was the only option. She prayed for their family every day. And for everyone on the plantation, including the treacherous Jasper Calhoun. Camellia's mind wandered in another direction. "What about his poor wife and children? How will they manage without him?"

"With a little help from us, they may be better off than when he was living there." Jonah pulled out his pocket watch and flipped it open. "I'd better get back to work. We still have a lot of cleanup to do from the fire."

Putting down her napkin, Camellia rose at the same time as her husband. "I've moved the classroom to the back porch for the time being."

"That's probably a good idea." Jonah kissed her on the cheek. "It may take us a week or more to rebuild your schoolhouse. But when we do, it should be better than before."

"Which wouldn't take much." Camellia thought back to their decision to use the old cabin and shuddered. Imagining a large room with generous windows and a separate desk for each of her students, she shooed her husband out of the room and headed to the back of the plantation home.

She was so thankful to be married to Jonah Thornton, a man with an abiding love for Christ and a shared vision for what their life should be. No matter what men like Jasper Calhoun tried to do to stop them, they would always rise again, secure in God's promises for their future.

꧁

Jasmine's heart felt like it was going to burst...into blooming flowers or flocks of songbirds. She'd never been happier in her life. The butterflies that had taken wing last night danced about every time she thought of Vance. Was this love? If so, she never wanted it to end.

A giggle escaped her lips. She was happier than she'd ever been... all because of Vance Hargrove. He was handsome and interesting and knew everything there was to know about the world of acting. Had a girl ever been more blessed than she?

Everything was perfect. The sun was bright outside, and she and Sarah had entertained a steady stream of morning visitors. Vance had not been one of them, but he'd probably been involved in rehearsals. He would come see her this afternoon. And he was going to take her to Lake Pontchartrain tonight. Her life was perfect.

"I can't wait to tell Maman and Lily about your new beau." Sarah appeared at the parlor door in a dark brown riding dress cut to resemble a military uniform. The matching hat was smaller than the one she'd worn to the park the day before. Perched at a jaunty angle, it had a curled brim and a veil. "Once we've told them all about Mr. Hargrove, we'll all go shopping together. I've heard of a charming new dress shop in the French Quarter I'm dying to visit."

Jasmine's eyes grew rounder. She wondered how many trunks

of clothing Sarah owned. She had always thought of Camellia as a clotheshorse, but her sister practically dressed as a Quaker in comparison to her wealthy hostess. "What about your afternoon visitors?"

Sarah fixed her with a knowing look. "Never fear, cher. We will be back in plenty of time to see your beau. Now get your parasol and let's go."

The journey to the Thorntons' home was a repeat of the drive to the park. Staid. Jasmine was beginning to grow inured to the yells of the other drivers as they sought to pass the cabriolet. At least the roof had not been let down, and therefore she could lean back and avoid their angry glares. By the time they arrived, her excitement had dwindled some. But she was sure it would return once she saw Vance again.

She could hear the excited voices of Noah and Magnolia as they entered the townhouse. After surrendering hat and gloves to the Thorntons' butler, she followed Sarah to the front parlor. Blake rose from his seat, and the conversation between Lily and Tante Charlotte halted in the wake of their arrival.

Magnolia, who had been playing with her brother, stood and ran to them, throwing her arms around Jasmine's skirts. "I'm so glad you found us."

Blake chuckled. "We may have another actress in the family."

"I hope not." Lily's mouth straightened into a tight line. "One is more than enough."

The words were like a stab wound to her abdomen. Jasmine hid her pain by dropping a kiss on Magnolia's head, focusing her attention on her beautiful niece. "I'm glad I did, too."

Magnolia let go of her legs and rejoined Noah on the floor.

Why was her sister so critical of the one thing she wanted to do? Why couldn't she be a little more understanding and supportive of Jasmine's dreams? Her life on a riverboat had not followed a traditional path. Why did she have to be so judgmental when it came to what Jasmine wanted?

"Lily tells me you had a wonderful time at the performance last night." Tante Charlotte rose and moved toward her. "Let's go to the dining room and you can tell us all about it over luncheon."

Lily stood and beckoned to Noah and Magnolia. "I'll get the children settled upstairs, check on Benjamin to make sure he is still napping, and join you in a minute."

Jasmine counted only five place settings as they entered the dining room. "Where is everyone?"

"Oncle Lloyd has taken your papa and Miss Matthews on a tour of the shipping office." Tante Charlotte took her place at the table. "They are not supposed to return until later."

Blake pulled out both Sarah's and Jasmine's chairs. "I couldn't convince Jensen and Tamar to remain, either. He insists the *Water Lily* is not secure if he isn't there."

Sarah reached for her napkin as Blake went to the opposite side of the table. "He is a good friend."

"So tell us about your evening." Tante Charlotte reached for a large bowl of fresh fruit in front of her plate.

Jasmine took a deep breath, thankful for Sarah's encouraging glance. "It was magical, stupendous, better than I have ever enjoyed in my life."

"Our Jasmine has caught the eye of a very distinguished gentleman."

Lily walked into the room at that moment. "Whom did you meet?"

"His name is Vance Hargrove." Jasmine saw the glance her sister and brother-in-law exchanged. Her chin went up.

"I see." Lily's disapproval was back in full measure. But then it had probably never gone away.

Sarah handed her the bowl of fruit, and Jasmine spooned some berries onto her plate before passing the food to Blake. Had anyone ever been so misused? So poorly understood? The only sympathetic expressions she saw in the room did not come from her family.

"Mr. Hargrove joined us for dinner." Sarah's glance was warm and reassuring. "Kenneth and I were both impressed with his wit and charm."

"Where did you meet this debonair gentleman?" Suspicion filled Lily's words. "At the restaurant? Is he a friend of the family?"

Jasmine's stomach tensed. She knew her sister would not like the answer to her questions. "At the theater."

Sarah waved a hand in the air. "We met him when I took Jasmine backstage. A crush of visitors prevented us from meeting Miss Barlow, but Mr. Hargrove came to our rescue. I believe he is above reproach."

"I see." Lily didn't sound reassured by Sarah's recommendation.

Sarah turned her gaze on Jasmine. "Now is the time to ask your sister for permission."

Jasmine could feel the concerted stare of everyone at the table. She lifted her chin. "We've made plans to visit Lake Pontchartrain this evening."

Now Blake looked as stern as his wife. "Alone?"

"I don't like the sound of that, Jasmine." Lily put her fork down. "You cannot go to dinner alone with him. . .at least not until I've met him."

She should have known her sister would be this way. Lily didn't want her to have any tiny bit of freedom. She wanted to make Jasmine into a replica of herself. Anger boiled through her blood. "I'm a grown woman, and I can decide how to spend my evening."

"You may be, Jasmine, but you're far from mature." Lily pushed back from the table. "I blame myself for coddling you too much over the years. Perhaps I should have sent you to a finishing school like the one Camellia attended."

"I don't need a school. I need to be treated like an adult." Jasmine could see the frozen expressions on Tante Charlotte's and Sarah's faces. She regretted airing her grievances in front of them, but Lily had started this. She would not back down.

Tears stung her eyes, but Jasmine refused to give in to them. Her sister would use them as an example of her naïveté. Gritting her teeth, she glared across the table. "I'm practically a prisoner in my own home. My desires don't matter at all. I don't know why I'm even surprised by you, Lily. You never want me to have any fun or to experience true freedom."

"Be that as it may, I am still your sister. As long as you live with me, you will do as I say." Lily's voice was shaking. "I forbid you to go out with this Vance Hargrove tonight."

Thrusting her chair away from the table, Jasmine stood.

"Where do you think you're going?"

Jasmine directed her words toward Tante Charlotte. "Please excuse me, I don't feel well." Without waiting for a reply, she spun and marched from the room, her head high and her shoulders back. She had no idea where to go, but she knew she couldn't remain in the dining room. Not until Lily could be more reasonable.

❧

"Was I wrong?" Lily folded her French silk scarf and laid it in the trunk she shared with Blake. She'd worn it last night to the theater and wouldn't need to use it again while they were in New Orleans. "Am I being unreasonable to want to meet this strange man before I trust my sister with him?"

Blake sighed. "No, not wrong. . .but you might have waited until you were alone with Jasmine before you told her how you felt."

Lily's first reaction to his words was betrayal, but her conscience prodded her to listen to him. Blake was right. She should have pinned a smile on her face while Jasmine described her evening. Telling her sister her concerns could have come later. While she considered the Thorntons to be family, they were not actually relatives. She should not have aired her concerns in front of them. Would she ever learn to control her tongue?

"I've ruined everything."

Her husband's blue gaze chided her for the passionate statement. "This is not the first or the last argument you'll have with Jasmine. The two of you want very different things out of life. You want her to settle down close to you and raise a family with someone like David Foster. Jasmine wants to see something of the world. She craves excitement and adventure—the very things you are denying her. She feels trapped here."

"Trapped? She can rant all she wants about freedom. Her family makes fewer demands on her than most young ladies."

"That doesn't matter." Blake pushed away from the mantel and moved toward her. "All your sister can see is the restrictions we've placed on her. I think I understand some of Jasmine's actions better than you do. I felt much like she does when I was young."

Lily put a hand to her forehead. "She *is* young. And naive. She understands so little about the ways of the world. I don't think I was ever as young as she is. Dealing with her sometimes makes me feel like I'm a hundred years old."

"I don't know about that." Catching her hand, Blake raised it to his lips. "You're well preserved for a centenarian."

She appreciated her husband's attempt to make her smile, but she couldn't make room for his levity. Not when she was so upset over the argument with Jasmine. "Why can't Jasmine understand that I have her best interests at heart? Can't she see that we're trying to protect her?"

"I doubt it." Blake's face sobered. "How did you feel when your relatives told you what to do?"

"That was different. They wanted me to marry a man twice my age." Lily ignored the petulant tone of her own words. Couldn't Blake see the truth? "I'm not trying to push her out into the world before she's ready."

"Maybe she's ready."

The world seemed to move under Lily's feet. She sat down hard on the edge of the bed, reaching for the headboard to keep from falling over. Jasmine was not ready. At the rate she was going, she wouldn't be ready for several years yet. What did Blake expect her to do? Stand by silently and watch her sister ruin her life? That's exactly what would happen if she let Jasmine have her way. Her plans for the evening were a perfect example. She spared not a thought for her own safety, blithely planning to go to some unnamed location with a man she had just met.

Blake took her hands and chafed them. "Are you okay?"

"Do you really think she's ready?" Lily searched his eyes for the truth.

"I only know that everyone in the family—from your father to Camellia—has given Jasmine the foundation she needs to succeed. And we'll be here to love her no matter what else happens to her." He placed a soft kiss on her cheek. "Once she's tested her wings, she'll have a better perspective."

"I don't want her to get hurt."

"Everyone gets hurt, Lily. That's the way of this world. You can't be there for her at every turn. You're going to have to trust God to watch out for her."

Peace slipped into the room with his words, giving her a little protection from the fear that nipped her. Blake pulled her up from the bed and drew her into his embrace. His heartbeat sounded beneath her ear, its rhythmic beating as slow and steady as the thrum of a paddlewheel. Lily felt the prickles of worry ebbing even further as she stood within the circle of his arms. She closed her eyes and thanked God silently for linking their lives.

Blake was right. What had happened to her faith in the Lord's provision? She would give Jasmine the freedom she craved. She would even let her sister go out with Vance Hargrove once she made sure he understood the consequences of stepping out of line.

A knock at the door separated them. Blake sent her a reassuring smile before he went to answer it. Lily took a deep breath and prayed for the right words to use with Jasmine. She would have to apologize first. And no matter how hard it was, she would have to allow Jasmine to make her own mistakes. She would be a support to her sister's dreams instead of an obstacle.

Lily's heart fell as she realized Jasmine was not their visitor.

Sarah was the one standing in the doorway, a guilty expression on her face. "I'm so sorry for causing this trouble."

Blake performed a shallow bow. "I believe I'll check on the children and allow the two of you a little privacy."

He disappeared into the hallway as Sarah advanced into the room. Lily felt some of the peace leave with him.

Putting on a polite expression, she focused on Sarah. "It's not your fault. Jasmine and I have been feuding with great regularity over the past months."

Unshed tears moistened Sarah's eyes. "But this latest argument is my fault, and I've come to see how I can mend it."

"I'm the one who will have to do that." Lily perched on the edge of the bed again. "But you can tell me about this Hargrove character. Do you trust him? Is he from New Orleans? Do you know his family?"

"Yes. No. And no." Sarah sat beside her and sniffed. "His manners are exquisite. I would trust my own daughter with him."

Lily was still uncertain, despite Sarah's assurances. She needed to know more than what kind of manners he had learned. What sort of man was he? Could he be trusted to treat her sister with respect?

"I believe he said that he came from New York." Sarah's eyes narrowed as she thought. "At least he said he performed in New York. He's even spent some time in Europe. I remember your sister asking if he had ever met the divine Sarah Bernhardt. . ."

A woman of dubious reputation herself. Lily kept her opinion to herself as Sarah continued prattling on about Hargrove's exploits. If the man had done half the things he claimed, he would have to be more than thirty years old. What interest would a man of that age see in her sister? Lily shuddered as she considered the possible answers.

"Wouldn't that fix everything?" Sarah's question hung in the air between them.

Lily scrambled to recall what suggestion the other woman had made. Something about dinner tonight. Comprehension dawned. Sarah had suggested they go out to dinner together and invite Mr. Hargrove to join them. That way she could meet the man and judge for herself if he was an appropriate escort for her sister. "You're right." Lily smiled at her. "At least, I'm not sure that it will fix *everything* between Jasmine and me, but it will go a long way toward healing this latest breach."

Sarah's hug was scented with a floral fragrance that made Lily's nose itch. "I had hoped we could go shopping, but this is more important. I'll collect your sister right away. We'll go back home and word an invitation to him." She stood and swept toward the door. "I'm sure he'll agree. And then you can see for yourself what a nice man he is."

Lily sneezed twice in swift succession.

The sound turned Sarah around. "I hope you're not catching a cold. That would unravel all of our plans."

Holding a finger under her nose to avoid another sneeze, Lily shook her head. "Don't worry. I'm sure it's only temporary. I never get sick."

She went to the trunk and drew out her silk scarf. It seemed she would need it again after all.

Chapter Thirteen

Vance Hargrove was standing in the Cartiers' foyer when Jasmine and Sarah returned. Jasmine's breath caught when she saw the large bouquet he had in his hand. Blood red roses and parchment-hued lilies nodded as he swept a bow. "I was so cast down to learn that you were out, Miss Anderson. I had thought to leave this little token with your butler, but now I do not have to deny myself the pleasure of giving them to you myself."

Jasmine thought she might swoon with the pleasure of the moment. The recent scene at the Thorntons' house faded as she once again looked into Mr. Hargrove's coffee-colored gaze.

He offered the flowers to her.

"They're beautiful." Jasmine buried her nose in them, enjoying the sweet aroma.

Mr. Hargrove put a hand on his chest. "They're not half as lovely as you are. But alas, they were the prettiest blooms in the shop."

Sarah sighed. "Will you give us a moment, Mr. Hargrove? Jasmine and I need to freshen up a bit. You can make yourself comfortable in the music room while you wait."

"Of course." He kept his hand on his chest. "I would wait twice—no thrice—as long for your company."

Jasmine floated up the stairs behind Sarah. She put the flowers in her water pitcher for the time being, pulled off her hat and gloves, and sat down in front of her mirror. Her mouth was slightly parted, and her eyes glowed with pleasure. At least her coiffure was not windblown from the drive. She pinched her cheeks and checked her collar to make certain it was still pristine. The dress she had worn to lunch would have to suffice as she had not brought an extensive wardrobe with her.

Putting a hand on her stomach to still the fluttery feelings that had returned, she rose and walked to the bureau that held her pitcher and basin. Should she take the flowers with her so one of Sarah's maids could put them in a vase? Already the heady fragrance filled her bedroom. Deciding to leave the flowers where they were for the moment, she went in search of a fan. If Mr. Hargrove continued his compliments she was sure to need it.

Wondering why Sarah had instructed their guest to go to the music room instead of the parlor where she usually entertained visitors, Jasmine slipped down the stairs. She could hear the *plink* of a piano chord and wished she knew how to play. Perhaps Mr. Hargrove did. Of course singing was another accomplishment she lacked. Which meant she would never get any parts in operettas or other productions requiring singing.

She peeked into the room to see if Sarah had arrived before her, but the room was empty except for the tall man towering over the keyboard. With a deep breath, she swept into the room, her skirts rustling around her. "Thank you for waiting, Mr. Hargrove."

He spun around, and a wide smile broke out on his face. "That didn't take long. Dare I hope you are as anxious for my company as I am for yours?"

Why had she pinched her cheeks? They were bound to be flaming at the moment.

Sarah swept into the room before Jasmine could come up with an answer to his daring question. "Mr. Hargrove, I know you and Jasmine made plans to visit the beach at Pontchartrain this evening, but I have an alternative invitation for you."

Jasmine could not have been more surprised if Sarah had pulled out a pistol and aimed it at her heart. This was the first she'd heard of a new arrangement. Lily might have forbidden her outing, but as an adult Jasmine could arrange her time according to her own desires.

"Jasmine's sister was so upset she didn't get a chance to meet you last night." Sarah's laugh tinkled. "She saw you on the stage, and I believe she was a bit jealous that we got to share a meal with you while she was stuck at dinner with my parents."

At least Sarah had come up with a good excuse to give the man. But Jasmine knew the real reason for the suggestion. Lily was determined to control her life.

"I. . .of course I would be delighted." Vance looked confused. And why not? He was probably not familiar with meddling relatives.

She wouldn't have thought it was possible for anyone to extract the pleasure from her visit with Vance. Her lips thinned. If she got a chance to talk to Vance alone before he left, she would tell him that they need not change their plans. Or maybe she could send a note to the theater. She would make some excuse to Sarah and Kenneth and send them off to dinner with her sister. As long as Vance didn't arrive before they departed, the two of them could still go to Pontchartrain together. Alone.

"Excellent." Sarah looked pleased with herself. Her smile encompassed both Jasmine and Vance. "And now, if you don't mind, I am going to the parlor. I'm expecting a few of my friends to drop by for tea."

Masking her surprise, Jasmine nodded. She had never thought the opportunity to talk to Vance alone would be so easy.

Sarah paused at the doorway. "Make sure you don't close this door. I would hate for Lily to think I wasn't being careful of your reputation."

Jasmine's cheeks flushed again. She opened her fan and used it to cool her face. Her gaze met Vance's. Was he laughing at her? Her family?

The room was furnished with half-a-dozen straight-backed chairs, arranged in rows for musical evenings. Choosing one on the front row, she sank into it, her fan fluttering fast enough to lift her collar. "I. . .I'm sorry about—"

"Don't apologize." He sat next to her, his voice pitched low. "I think you've seen that I know how to make myself popular with chaperones."

Jasmine doubted her sister would be won over by a few compliments. Besides, she didn't intend to remain under Lily's thumb any longer. She would be free no matter what it took. "You don't have to do that. I'd much rather spend the evening alone with you."

Vance took her hands in his own, pulling her fan away and placing it on the chair behind him. "I would like that, too, but I don't want to cause you any trouble."

"What is going on in here?" David's voice caused Jasmine to jump.

Vance dropped his grip on her hands and stood to face the man at the door, the man whose eyes blazed green lightning.

Something must be wrong with Jasmine's heart. It felt like a frightened bird trying to escape a hunter's noose. She lifted her chin and willed it to slow down. She had done nothing wrong. Her eyes narrowed. Was Lily behind David's appearance, too? It would make sense as she had seen nothing of him for the past day and a half. Her chin went up another notch. Would she ever be free of chaperones?

※

David could hardly believe he'd walked in on Jasmine making eyes at some stranger. Had she lost her mind? She glared at him like he was the one in the wrong, but he refused to accept any blame. He had not closeted himself with an unmarried lady. Which led him to another question. Where was Sarah Cartier?

"I suppose this is another of your swains?" The stranger's question interrupted their staring match.

"What?" Jasmine looked as though she'd forgotten he was in the room.

"Not at all." It was one of those moments when David knew exactly what to say. He smiled at Jasmine, causing her eyes to narrow in suspicion. But she need not worry. She was the one who had suggested their relationship after all. "Jasmine is my sister."

He felt the twin pricks of their stares. Jasmine looked as though he had slapped her. Then guilt entered her expression. It was too late for that. And posing as her brother would scare off the man he'd found her with. The man who shouldn't be alone with her.

"Indeed?" The stranger infused a large measure of disbelief into the two syllables.

Jasmine briefly closed her eyes. All the color had drained from her cheeks. For a moment David almost recanted. But then she opened her eyes. The deep purple in them seemed sad, mournful even.

"David, this is Mr. Hargrove. Mr. Vance Hargrove." The way she said the man's name made it obvious she thought David should know him.

Unable to put any significance on the name, David gave a brief nod.

"It's a pleasure to make your acquaintance, Mr. Anderson." Hargrove offered his hand, and David shook it, barely managing to suppress the urge to wipe his hand on his trousers afterward.

"Mr. Hargrove is a famous actor here in New Orleans." Jasmine recovered her composure and cast an admiring glance in his direction. "He is the star of a current production."

Which explained Jasmine's fascination with the man. David ignored Hargrove. "Where is your chaperone?"

Another wave of red darkened her cheeks. "Sarah is in the parlor."

"Does she know you're in here with. . .him?" David couldn't bring himself to repeat the man's name. He didn't like Vance Hargrove. He didn't like the shiftiness in his eyes or the wet gleam of his pomaded hair. He didn't like his voice or his clothes. But the thing he didn't like the most was the admiring glances he was exchanging with Jasmine. Something was not right. It made David itch to pull Jasmine out of the music room—get her to a safe place and convince her to avoid any future dealings with the actor.

"Of course she does." Jasmine sniffed. "Not that it's any of your business, but Sarah left a few moments ago and told us to leave the door open."

"I see." David walked to the piano and sat on the stool, resting his arm across the keys. Sarah might trust Hargrove to act the gentleman, but he didn't. Looking at the man put him in mind of a snake. A snake on the hunt for prey.

"Are you enjoying your visit to New Orleans?" Hargrove directed the question toward him.

"David is working." Jasmine answered the question for him.

"Yes," he interrupted her. "I'm working my way through every bar and card game in town."

"I suppose that's why you didn't join your sister at the theater last night."

David hid a yawn behind his hand. "I had more than one reason to choose other entertainment."

An understanding smile curved Hargrove's lips. "Have you enjoyed much success?"

"Not yet." He winked at the man. "But I'm sure my luck is about to change."

Jasmine was wearing a frown as her gaze bounced between him and Hargrove. At least she didn't challenge him. She had enough sense to know he had a reason for his falsehood.

Hargrove bowed to Jasmine. "I do have an appointment this afternoon, but I'll see you this evening."

David felt the hair on the back of his neck rising. He didn't like the idea of the two of them spending any time together.

The actor turned to David. "It was a pleasure to meet another member of Jasmine's family. I'm looking forward to meeting your other sister this evening."

This sounded much better. David allowed a little smile to relax the muscles of his face. Lily and Blake would put an end to the man's pretensions. "I'm sure you'll have a wonderful time."

Jasmine stood. "Let me show you the way to the front door."

Having risen when his "sister" did, David made as if to accompany them. Jasmine's warning glare stopped him, however. "I need to talk to you after you see Mr. Hargrove out."

She nodded and reached for the arm the actor presented. "I'll be right back."

David returned to the stool and tapped an impatient rhythm on the wooden top of the piano as he waited for her.

It took several long moments, but she finally reappeared, her cheeks suspiciously red. "Why did you lie to Vance about who you are?"

"Because you were about to tell him I'm a Pinkerton detective."

"At least it's the truth." She lifted that chin of hers again.

He pushed a hand through his hair. "I don't need everyone in town to know my business."

"But the Thorntons and Cartiers know. And Papa. And Aunt Tessie. Jensen and Tamar, too." She ticked off the names on her fingers as she listed them.

"They are all either family or close friends."

"Well, Vance is a close friend of mine."

"A close friend? How well do you even know him? Where is he from? How long has he been in New Orleans? Does he have family here? You don't know anything about him except that he's an actor."

"I can tell what kind of man Vance is by looking in his eyes and listening to him."

David couldn't believe how foolish she was being. Jasmine couldn't really think she knew Vance well enough to consider him a trusted friend. "We aren't children anymore. You seem to think life is nothing but a game, a theatrical production that will end after all the lines are spoken. But it's not. People aren't always what they seem."

"Vance Hargrove is." She turned on her heel and stomped toward the door.

"Be careful with that man." David raised his voice so she could hear him even in the hallway. "I don't want to have to pull you out of any scrapes."

"Don't worry." Her voice floated back to him. "You're the last one I would call on, dear brother."

His elbow slipped off the piano, hitting several keys and producing a discordant noise that made him wince. He supposed he would have to allow her the last word. His threat had been an empty one, and she probably knew it. David would always come to her rescue. Whether she returned his affection or not, he would always be there for her.

Chapter Fourteen

Lily winced as her amethyst earbob clamped down on the tender portion of her earlobe. She didn't like having to wear jewelry. It pinched and poked. But the jewelry was a gift from her husband. And they matched her lavender dress. She settled the matching piece on her other ear. She would make the sacrifice for his sake.

"What do you think I should say to Jasmine?" She glanced at his reflection in the mirror above the bureau.

Blake pulled his suspenders over his shoulders and attached them to the high waist of his trousers. "Dwell on the things you have in common instead of your differences. Let love guide you instead of your mothering instinct."

She leaned her head to one side as she considered the advice. "I want her to have a good time this evening."

"Then we should be taking her back to the theater instead of to dinner."

Lily walked to the bed and picked up her husband's black frock coat. "But we went to the theater last night."

He slid one arm into a sleeve before turning slightly to reach for the other one. As soon as the material was on his shoulders, Lily reached up and smoothed it. "I doubt Jasmine would complain if we returned every night while we're in New Orleans. Your sister loves the theater. She has ever since she was a child, and I don't look for her to change anytime soon."

A part of Lily dreaded the evening. But she needed to talk to Jasmine and reassure her that she would be more reasonable. She didn't want to drive her sister away. She wanted to avoid the type of division that Blake and his father had experienced. Spending the afternoon praying had helped, but Lily wondered if she would be able to maintain her calm.

"It's going to be okay, Lily." Blake put his hands on her shoulders and leaned over to kiss her.

Lily melted into his embrace, letting her fears go. She clung to him, wanting to remain in his arms a little longer before facing the people waiting for them in the parlor.

Blake hugged her tight before letting go and offering his arm. "You are looking very lovely this evening, Mrs. Matthews."

"Thank you, Mr. Matthews." Lily accepted his compliment with a smile. "You look very handsome yourself."

His tender look buoyed her. Blake believed in her. She sent a silent plea to heaven that his faith was not misplaced. And for patience and wisdom in dealing with Jasmine.

They negotiated the stairs side by side and entered the parlor together. Kenneth stood, and Sarah looked up as they entered. Lily glanced around the room, her face tightening into a frown. "Where is Jasmine?"

"Don't worry, dearest." Sarah stood and rushed across the room, her satin dress rustling in the quiet room. "Your sister wasn't feeling well this evening. I'm sure it had nothing to do with that little tiff between you. She had several visitors this morning and then again this afternoon."

Lily wanted to forget their plans for the evening and rush over to the Cartiers' home to check on her sister. She turned to Sarah's husband. "Did you see her? Is she coming down with something?"

Kenneth shook his head. "She had no fever, only a few nebulous complaints. I'm sure it's nothing that a restful night's sleep won't cure."

"I shouldn't have forbidden her to see that man." Despair laced her words. No matter what Sarah thought, it had to be the argument that had prevented Jasmine from coming. Her sister didn't want to be around her. The thought pained her. Where had she gone wrong? And how could she make it right?

Sarah put an arm around her waist and drew her toward the sofa. "That's not it at all, Lily."

"It has to be." Lily sat down and put her face in her hands.

"No." Sarah touched her arm. "Mr. Hargrove was coming to dinner with us until I sent him a message that your sister was not feeling well."

Lily lifted her head.

"He was at my home when we returned this afternoon. He's such a gentleman. I can understand why Jasmine would find him attractive. He presented her with a beautiful bouquet. And he is so handsome, so polished. When I invited him to dinner as you and I discussed, he accepted most graciously. Both he and Jasmine seemed pleased by the idea."

The information from Sarah set her head spinning. "Then I wonder why Jasmine decided not to come?"

"It is evident that you don't need to worry so." Blake offered his reassurance from the other side of the sofa. "If Jasmine was as smitten with him as you thought, she would have joined us, no matter how she felt."

Her husband's thoughts matched hers. Jasmine was as determined as any member of the Anderson family. No headache would have prevented her if she really wanted to see this Hargrove fellow.

Was Kenneth wrong? Was Jasmine sicker than he realized? That made no sense. Sarah's husband was a renowned doctor. He would recognize any symptoms.

The temptation to excuse herself and go across town to check on her sister was strong. Lily glanced around the room, her mind considering and discarding half-a-dozen excuses. But in the end, she realized she had only one course to follow. She couldn't wreck all their plans to go and check on Jasmine tonight. Holding onto an image of Jasmine sitting in bed, a cap on her head and a book leaned against her knees, Lily stood. "Shall we get going?"

Blake's gaze met hers, and he sent her an approving smile. The dread that had been building in her chest eased some. Jasmine was safe. And the two of them might do better with a little more breathing time.

This was a first step in allowing her sister to make her own decisions, an olive branch of good intentions. Perhaps it would help heal the breach between them.

❧

The *Smoky Mary* was well named. Thick billows of gray smoke blew past them as the train picked up speed. But Jasmine could endure a little discomfort on her adventure. The *Water Lily's* twin smokestacks were almost as obnoxious at times.

She still couldn't believe how easy it had been to slip away from the Cartiers' home. When Vance had called for her, after the departure of her host and hostess, Jasmine had blithely told the servants that she was going out.

The butler had not looked pleased, but he had not said anything. What could he say? He was not her father or any other relative. She was free. Finally free.

"I'm glad you managed to keep our assignation." Vance shared the narrow bench with her, his knee a bare inch from hers.

She giggled and fluttered her lashes at him. She'd practiced the move in front of her mirror all afternoon while she pretended illness. Apparently her hard work paid off. His scorching glance made her feel heady. And powerful. Maybe he wouldn't think her so innocent now.

When he put his arm on the bench behind her head, however, Jasmine gulped. She didn't want him to think she had no morals. Leaning forward, she pretended interest in the passing scenery. "How long before we arrive?"

He must have understood the message because Vance withdrew his arm. "Our destination is less than five miles away."

Relief coursed through her. He was too much a gentleman to make her uncomfortable. "How did you come to be in New Orleans?"

"I suppose you could say it is Tabitha Barlow's fault." He rubbed his hand on his pants leg. "She and I were performing in Dickens's play *No Thoroughfare*. Are you familiar with it?"

"Yes. I've read it, anyway. But I've never seen it performed."

"We were receiving wonderful reviews, but then the theater owner closed us down three months ago." Vance sent a winning smile in her direction. "So we came here. Tabitha has performed in the city in the past, so she had plenty of contacts."

A pang of jealousy drowned Jasmine's butterflies. Did Vance love Miss Barlow? He had been waiting in the hallway outside her door when she first met him. "Are you m—married to her?"

His laughter rang out, turning heads of some of the other passengers. "No, dearest Jasmine. We are friends, of course, and business associates. Once you begin working in the arts, you will understand how it works."

She opened her fan with a snap and used it to cool her cheeks. Jasmine felt like an adolescent schoolgirl. Vance must think her ignorant. She was afraid to say anything else and reveal to him her lack of knowledge.

Vance leaned forward to get her attention. "I believe I should be offended. Do you really think me such a scoundrel that I would pursue a lady while my wife pined for me at home?"

Jasmine's hand redoubled the speed of her fan. "No, that's not. . . I mean I just thought. . . I—"

"Don't." His dark eyes sparkled in the fading light. "I was only teasing you a little. I'm sorry. I didn't mean to upset you, Jasmine."

She let her fan drift to her lap as she stared into Vance's eyes, noticing for the first time the dark band of black that outlined his pupils. His smile disappeared. Why would his serious face cause her heart to stutter? Jasmine swallowed hard as she lost all sense of her surroundings. Vance Hargrove was the most exciting, most mature man she'd ever known. He made her feel both desirable and gauche at the same time.

The train lurched to a stop, breaking the spell between them. Vance stood and offered her his hand. "For the rest of the evening I'll do better, Jasmine. I promise not to tease or scare you anymore."

She managed a smile and put her hand in his. But she was beginning to wonder if she was completely out of her depth. They disembarked from the train, and she looked around. The town of Milneburg was not what she'd expected. In a way it reminded her of river towns. The waterfront was crowded with boats and rickety buildings. Even the water seemed filled with houses, suspended on long lines of piers. One two-story house had a wide porch on all four sides and a smaller guesthouse behind it.

Even though the sun had set, dozens of people walked on the lantern-strewn paths, some showing the effects of alcohol. Somewhere in the distance, a horn played a lively tune she didn't recognize.

The spirit of adventure which had begun their evening together returned to Jasmine. She intercepted an appreciative glance from one of the women walking past, and a secret sparkle coursed through her. She knew jealousy when she saw it.

"Do you like seafood?"

Jasmine wrinkled her nose. "We eat a lot of fish on my sister's boat."

"Ah." He changed direction, guiding her away from a huge white gazebo with exotic-looking parapets on top. "Then I believe we'll need to avoid the music pavilion."

As they left the crowds behind, the sound of frogs and crickets filled the air. Jasmine's footsteps slowed. "Where are we going?"

"Don't you trust me, little Jasmine?" He stopped and looked down at her. "I would tell you that I'm taking you to a pirate's hidden treasure, but I promised not to tease you. I know of an intimate little café I think you'll like."

Jasmine studied his face and tried to decide if he was being serious. Taking a deep breath, she nodded. " 'Lay on, Macduff.' "

His chuckle was so attractive. Unpretentious and open. Exactly like Vance's personality. " 'Hold! Enough!' "

She was pleased that he recognized her quote from Macbeth. It was something no one in her family would have done. No matter how many times she read to them from the classic plays of Shakespeare, they didn't understand. She was finally in the company of someone who did. And it felt like coming home.

Chapter Fifteen

Andrew Jackson held his seat on the rearing bronze horse, one of his hands loose on the reins, while the military hero held a "fore and aft" hat aloft in the other. When he had looked at the statue earlier in the day, David had thought Andrew looked calm and in control. The way David wanted to feel. But he knew many things could go wrong with his plan to discover who controlled the ring of successful bank robbers. Like the Union general who had added an inscription during the occupation of New Orleans, he believed he had a responsibility to uphold the law of the land. The words General Benjamin Butler had ordered were simple but profound—THE UNION MUST AND SHALL BE PRESERVED.

A hissing sound made him look at the constable crouched a few feet away behind a palm tree. "What time is it?"

"Five minutes later than the last time you asked." David kept his voice low. If the informant heard them, he would realize what was happening and disappear. They would not get the information they needed or an additional arrest. "He'll be here soon."

Gas lamps cast a sickly glow on Petrie's face as he leaned against the cast-iron fence surrounding the statue. David hoped he would remember their instructions. He would tell the man he was meeting that the police were about to close in on the ringleader because their group harbored a traitor. He would claim to know the informant's name but refuse to give it to his cohort in case the man was working with the snitch. Once he had the leader's name, Petrie would raise his right hand and place it on his head as a signal for David and the constable to rush in and make their arrest.

David shifted his position and let his mind wander to earlier, more pleasant visits to Jackson Square. He and Jasmine had explored the area many times during visits to the city. They had chased each other around the palm trees and bushes on the outside borders of the square. Tonight that same greenery was providing cover for himself and Constable Longineaux as they waited for Charlie Petrie's contact to arrive.

A shadow separated from the alley between St. Louis Cathedral and the Cabildo. David's heart rate increased. This might be it. He put a finger over his lips to warn Longineaux and bent his head in the direction of the cathedral.

Petrie must have heard footsteps even though the statue blocked his view of the man approaching. He glanced over his shoulder once toward the position where David and the constable waited, pushed away from the fence, and stood with his feet planted wide.

Filtering out the sounds of gaiety coming from the Café du Monde on the river side of the square, David stretched his hearing as far as he could manage. They were too far away. He couldn't hear a single word.

He raised his hand to tell Longineaux to stay here and slowly rose to avoid making any noise. The lawn between him and the two men didn't offer any hiding places, but it was dark enough that he should be able to avoid detection. David took a step onto the grass, moving with deliberate, quiet precision. He listened intently, but the men were whispering. Was Petrie betraying them?

It was a risk he'd convinced Lieutenant Moreau to take. Petrie could run, but he had to know he would be caught. Too many people knew what he looked like. During the trial, someone had taken a photograph of him that had appeared in the *Picayune*. He wouldn't get far.

He hoped Petrie would remember what he'd been told. The only way for him to avoid the noose was to give them the leader of his gang—not just the other members.

A carriage drove down the street, and David dropped to the ground. He didn't want the coachman's lamp to expose his position. Dirt clogged his mouth and nose, making him want to sneeze. He rolled over on his back and clamped a hand across his face until the need passed.

"You'd better be telling me the truth—" The phrase caught his attention. It sounded like their plan was working.

Petrie was talking now, his mumbled words defying translation. David turned over again and crawled forward. Just a few more feet and he should be able to hear everything.

A sound made him look back over his shoulder. What he saw brought his heart up into his throat. Longineaux had left his hiding place. Wanting to blister the man's ears for not following orders, David waited as he crept forward in a crouch.

Disaster struck with the suddenness of a lightning bolt. Longineaux tripped over some unseen obstacle and fell forward. With a loud *thud*.

"Who is that?" The shadowy figure shouted the question as he lunged toward Petrie. "What have you done? You're the filthy traitor."

Petrie staggered backward two steps as David got to his feet and made a dash toward them, his focus on the unknown crook. Out of the corner of his eye, he saw Petrie grab his stomach and fall to his knees, but he kept his attention on the other man.

David pulled his Smith and Wesson revolver and aimed it. The chance of hitting the man at this distance was slim, but he had to try. He planted his feet and held the weapon in both hands, drawing the hammer back and squeezing the trigger in one fluid motion. The loud report was followed by a grunt. His target staggered but kept moving forward. Before David could fire again, he was gone, swallowed up by the shadows of Orleans Alley.

"Foster, come back." The constable's voice sounded frightened. "You can't go into that alley alone."

He took a couple of strides forward before stopping. Longineaux was right. He trotted back to the center of the square, his jaw clenched. Petrie was on his back, groaning. A dark shadow spread over his shirt and onto the ground. Blood. A lot of blood.

David breathed a prayer for the man's soul as he dropped to his knees and pulled Petrie's hand away from his stomach. It was bad. He stripped off his coat and used it to try and staunch the blood.

"I'm sorry." Longineaux stood over them, wringing his hands. "It's my fault."

"We'll deal with that later." David bit out the words as he applied pressure on the wound. "For now you need to get help before he dies."

He didn't look up as Longineaux ran toward Levee Street. Even as he prayed for God to spare Petrie's life, he had the feeling the stab wounds were fatal. Even if a surgeon of Kenneth Cartier's caliber were kneeling next to him, it might be too late to save Charlie Petrie's life.

"How bad?" Petrie choked out the question between painful gasps.

David ignored his intuition and summoned a smile. "You're doing fine. Save your strength for when the doctor arrives."

Seconds ticked by and still no one came. Blood oozed around the fabric of his coat, filling the air with the scent of copper. David pushed harder, trying to stem the flow.

Petrie groaned and put a hand over David's. "O–O. . .fee—" A dry cough cut off his groan.

David's sympathy rose. He wished he could ease the dying man's pain. "I'm sorry, I didn't bring a canteen."

Petrie shook his head, coughed again. His eyes opened wide, and he reached up with one blood-smeared hand, his fingers catching David's shirt collar and dragging him closer. "Ophelia."

"What?" David could make no sense of the word. Why would Petrie mention a woman's name? He leaned an inch closer, hoping for more details. . .a last name. . .anything.

The hand on his collar went slack, and David sat back. Looking down he realized his question was futile. Petrie's eyes stared sightlessly at the sky. He was dead.

⊱

Jasmine wondered if Vance would try to kiss her before returning her to the Cartiers' home. And would she allow him such liberties or risk being considered too provincial? But she couldn't allow him to kiss her. Yet the thought of his lips pressing against hers made her stomach attempt a somersault.

Pirate's Cove, the cozy restaurant he had chosen for their dinner, was conducive to a romantic rendezvous. Most of the couples sat next to each other instead of on opposite sides of their tables. This arrangement led them to all sorts of risqué behavior, from eating off of their partner's forks to nuzzling each other's necks. She was glad Vance sat across from her, even though his dark gaze had more than once made her breath catch.

Vance picked up the wine bottle he'd ordered and poured an additional amount in his goblet. "Would you care for some more?"

Jasmine shook her head. She had tried a sip but could not imagine why someone would choose to drink such a nasty-tasting beverage. "No thank you."

He leaned back and raised a hand to summon a waiter. "We are finished with our meal."

"I hate for the evening to end." Jasmine watched as their plates were whisked away.

A burning gaze from Vance threatened to consume her. "Perhaps we can return on Friday. I could rent a camp and let you experience the coolness of a bath in the lake."

Jasmine tried to hide her shock. Sharing a meal with him was risky enough for her reputation. What he was proposing now sounded scandalous. If any members of her family heard him, they would definitely forbid any further contact.

"I—my sister is planning to return to Natchez soon."

His facial muscles drooped. "So soon? I thought you would remain in New Orleans for a while."

The disappointment in his voice resettled her composure. She must have misunderstood Vance's intent. He cared for her. Was he falling in love with her? The idea took root in her mind. They would share the limelight and fame, acting together as they traveled all over the United States and perhaps to Europe. They could even form their own troupe.

"I wish I could stay here, but I doubt Lily will allow it." She grimaced at the memory of the angry words she had tossed at her sister earlier in the day. Jasmine raised her chin. It was really Lily's fault. Lily was not her mother. She needed to realize that Jasmine was a grown woman and could make her own decisions.

Vance dropped several bills on the table and stood. "When will you leave?"

"Far too soon." She pushed back her chair and headed for the entrance.

Instead of offering his arm, Vance placed his hand at the small of her back. "Even if you could remain several weeks, it wouldn't be enough time to suit me."

Gooseflesh erupted on Jasmine's arms. She was simultaneously freezing and burning. If this was what love felt like, she understood why her sisters had married. She wanted to spend all of her time with Vance. The thought of being separated from him was like a dagger to the heart.

They walked back to the train station and waited. "Thank you for bringing me here, Vance. It's been a wonderful evening."

"It is my pleasure." His gaze spoke volumes to her, promising constancy and passion, a love to last for all of eternity. "I've been the envy of every man within the resort."

Perhaps she would let him kiss her after all.

They boarded the train, sitting even closer than they had on the trip to the lake. His knee pressed against hers. His arm, warm and muscular, slipped across the back of the seat. This time she didn't lean forward.

He leaned close and whispered in her ear. "Jasmine, I have a confession to make."

Her breath caught. Was he about to declare his love?

"I cannot bear the thought of separation."

Jasmine shivered when he pulled his arm from the back of the seat. But then he took possession of her hands, capturing them with his long fingers. "I wasn't going to tell you this, but I, too, am leaving New Orleans, although not as quickly as you."

Her heart fell, and she began to breathe again.

"Then why did you suggest we spend more time together?" Jasmine tried to pull her hands free, but Vance tightened his grasp.

"Please let me explain. I am not hiding anything from you, Jasmine. I didn't tell you my plans earlier because I thought we would have more time together. I know how young and innocent you are, and I don't want to frighten you."

She lifted her chin. "I'm not a child."

He smiled at her words. "And I am most grateful for that fact. What I feel toward you would not be appropriate if you were."

Jasmine stopped trying to pull away. "Oh!" A fleeting memory of Sarah's round mouth occurred to her. She hoped she looked as graceful.

"Tabitha. . .Miss Barlow. . .and I have received contracts to join a troupe on one of the showboats. I have not decided for sure, but I think it would be fun to cruise up and down the river for a while. The crowds every night would be different, and we would get to see so much more of the countryside than the view from the windows of a stagecoach."

"So you are going to join this troupe?" Her mind whirled. A showboat. What she would give to accompany him. It would be such a wonderful experience.

He nodded. "I think there might be room for one more."

The meaning of his words burst upon her like an explosion of fireworks on the Fourth of July. He wanted her to come with him. He didn't want to be separated from her any more than she did from him. No meddling family to chastise her. No rules to follow. Just her and Vance and crowds of adoring theatergoers. "Do you really mean it?"

He squeezed her hands and lifted them to shower kisses on her knuckles. "Of course I mean it. You would be perfect. Your fresh face and knowledge of the classics would be perfect."

Jasmine's toes curled in her shoes. She would do it. She would talk to Lily and Blake, tell them about this wonderful opportunity, and—A door slammed in her mind. When had Lily ever understood her dreams? "I can't."

Vance raised his head and stared into her eyes. "What do you mean?" He dropped her hands and shifted away from her. "Have I misread your feelings? Are you toying with me?"

She reached for his hand. "No, of course not. I. . .I think I may be falling in love with you."

He turned back to her, confusion bringing a frown to his handsome face. "Then why?"

"It's my family. They don't understand me. Lily is determined to ruin my life."

"I see." Vance's sorrowful tones wrung her heart. "Your feelings for them are stronger than your feelings for me."

Jasmine put a hand on his arm. "That's not it at all. Please believe me when I say I want to join you more than anything."

"Then you must change your mind." He ran a finger down the side of her face. "You must find a way to join me on the showboat. It would break my heart to think of never seeing you again."

The train lurched to a stop before she could answer him. Jasmine gathered her things and tried to keep the tears out of her eyes. She had to find a way to convince Lily to let her follow her heart.

"Didn't you say that your family is returning to Natchez?"

Jasmine nodded, her throat too clogged to allow speech.

Vance snapped his fingers. "That is the answer then. The *Ophelia* won't leave New Orleans for a week or so, but I know we'll be stopping in Vicksburg by the end of the month. That is not far from Natchez. You can convince your family and join us there."

She didn't want to tell him she doubted Lily would ever change her mind.

They walked back to the Cartiers' home in silence as she tried to imagine a future without Vance Hargrove. It was inconceivable. And yet no less so than getting Lily's blessing on her becoming Mrs. Vance Hargrove.

Chapter Sixteen

David kicked the leg of a chair, sending it tumbling to the floor. "Think, man. Petrie used his dying breath to give us that name. It had to be important to him."

Constable Longineaux jumped in response, making David feel like a jerk. He shouldn't take out his frustration on the police officer, but it was hard not to. The man who had escaped would certainly warn the others. They would lose any chance of catching them. The ringleader might even go into hiding or flee to Europe. It wouldn't be the first time a criminal escaped the arm of the law by leaving the United States.

"Let's start again." David took a deep breath, righted the chair, and dropped into it. "Ophelia is a woman's name. She could be a mother or sister or even a girlfriend."

"I'll make the rounds in the French Quarter and ask if anyone has heard of Ophelia Petrie." Longineaux rubbed the stubble on his cheeks.

Neither of them had found time to return to their homes and shave. Or sleep. David had spent several hours making out reports—one for the local lieutenant and a second for Mr. Bastrup in Chicago. They had been difficult to finish. He placed the blame for the failure on himself.

It didn't matter what had spooked the man Petrie was meeting. When the mission failed, it was his responsibility.

Longineaux had spent his time taking care of Petrie's body, making sure it got to the morgue and was scheduled for quick burial at Pauper's Graveyard. Maybe they should put an advertisement about the burial in the *Picayune* and watch to see if anyone showed up to mourn Charlie Petrie.

"Charlie wasn't a local boy. His family probably doesn't live here, either. But it's worth making further inquiries." David looked at the next item on their list. "Shakespeare. The play *Hamlet* has a character named Ophelia. Maybe the ringleader is an actor."

"I didn't get the idea Petrie was an educated man. Do you think he would even know who Shakespeare was?"

Longineaux's question was valid, but David didn't want to make any hasty assumptions. The best police work came from following every possible avenue until it either ended or led to the culprits.

His mind conjured an image of Vance Hargrove. Wouldn't it be great if he was somehow involved? That would get the man away from Jasmine. He shook his head. Just because he didn't like Vance or the way he looked at Jasmine didn't mean the man was a criminal. David had to stay focused on this case if he was going to catch a killer. "I still think I'll check the local theaters and see if anyone is showing *Hamlet*. Petrie might have been trying to tell us to look for someone involved in the production."

"We could put an advertisement in the paper. Offer a reward for information leading to Ophelia Petrie."

"That's a good idea." David yawned, shaking his head to clear it of the cobwebs spun by his lack of sleep. "But we'd better send it to more than the local papers."

"I don't think Petrie was from back East." Longineaux stared out the window.

David followed his gaze. The sun was up. What had happened to the night? "Agreed. He had a drawl, just not the extra twang to indicate a lifetime here."

Longineaux looked down at the paper on his desk and started writing. "So Mississippi, Alabama, Georgia."

"Yes, and you may as well include Tennessee and Kentucky, too."

"Florida?"

David shook his head. "Let's see what we get first."

"I hope our luck changes." Longineaux drummed his pencil on his desk, an indication of either exhaustion or nervousness. "I'm sorry about last night. I should have remembered how clumsy I am."

The taps of the pencil threatened to get under David's skin. But he had to hold onto his temper. "It wasn't your fault. We both wanted to hear what was being said. Jackson Square simply doesn't offer enough cover closer to the statue. That's probably why the man chose it in the first place." He hesitated, choosing his words carefully. "You may have saved my life last night when you told me not to chase him. I made a note of it in my reports."

The praise brought a look of wonder to the other man's face. He cleared his throat. "Thank you."

"Let's get to work." David stood.

Longineaux's jaw dropped. "You can't go onto the street looking like that. People will either think you're a victim or a murderer."

David looked down and realized the man was right. Splatters of blood smeared across his shirt. He'd already tossed out his coat. He knew the blood would never come out of it. "I'll run by my apartment and pick up some fresh clothes."

"You need more than clean shirts." Lieutenant Moreau leaned against the office doorjamb. "Both of you need a couple of hours of sleep."

Longineaux jumped out of his chair and saluted. "But they could get aw—"

"Do you really think you could hold your own if you ran into those men right now?" Moreau shook his head. "All you'd manage to do is get yourselves killed."

Another yawn threatened to crack David's jaw. Maybe the lieutenant was right. While he wanted desperately to catch the gang, they needed to be smart about it. Deliberate action would win out over speed. "What time is it now?"

Moreau pulled out his watch. "Seven thirty."

David glanced out the window again. "Let's meet at the Café du Monde at noon. We can start there and work our way into the surrounding neighborhood."

Longineaux's red-rimmed eyes showed relief. "If you think that would be best."

"Don't forget to leave that report on my desk on your way out." Moreau sauntered down the hall.

Picking up the sheets of paper, David glanced through them once more. He wished he could give a better description of the man who had murdered Petrie. Or something else to prove that he hadn't completely botched this job. But nothing came to his mind.

With a sigh he followed Longineaux down the hall. Maybe this afternoon they would turn up a new lead to follow. If he could only figure out who Ophelia was. And what the name had to do with bank robberies.

◈

For once Lily found her father alone in the library. Since their arrival in New Orleans, he'd been spending a lot of his free time with Aunt Tessie. Practically living in her apron pocket.

He glanced up as she entered and put down the newspaper he'd been reading.

"Am I disturbing you, Papa?"

"Of course not." He rose to give her a tight hug. "You know I'm always available to talk to my daughters."

Lily clung to him for several long minutes, burying her face into his shoulder and breathing in the scent of river that always clung to him.

"Is something wrong?"

She forced herself to let go of him. "I don't know." Tears welled up at the corners of her eyes. "It's just. . .I'm worried about Jasmine."

The words were hard to utter, especially to this man whom she had once blamed for walking away from his parental responsibilities. What irony to once again admit that she needed his help. Since returning to their lives, Papa had allowed her to continue mothering his younger daughters. He had always been ready to dispense advice, however. Advice that had been valuable and effective in the spiritual, social, and educational development of both of her sisters.

He perched on the arm of Mr. Thornton's leather sofa. "I heard the two of you had an argument."

"I said some awful things to her—embarrassed her in front of everyone here." Lily paced across the room, her hands locked behind her back. When Jasmine had not come with the Cartiers last night, she had wanted to go talk with her sister. Apologize for her thoughtlessness if not for her decision. Maybe she should have.

"You've done an excellent job with both of your sisters, Lily. One thing you may not have thought about is how she's feeling. I'm sure Jasmine is as upset as you."

She didn't feel like she deserved Papa's praise or his sympathy. She was a failure. How had she ever thought she was up to the task of setting her sister's feet on the right path? Hadn't she learned yet that she didn't have all the answers? A little voice inside Lily's head whispered that she had more answers than Jasmine.

"Why don't you send her a note and explain how you feel and why you said what you did?" Papa's voice drowned out the internal voice. "You could invite her to go shopping. Jasmine may not love new clothing as much as Camellia, but she'd probably love to pick out some new gewgaw that she can't find at home."

Lily considered his advice. "It might work."

"But?"

She stopped pacing and looked at him. "I told her not to go on an outing alone with this actor that she met at the theater. At least not until after Blake and I meet him. Do you think I'm being unreasonable? I know she's an adult, Papa. But you know how naive Jasmine can be. She always believes the best of everyone. He could be a scoundrel, and she wouldn't see it until it's too late."

"You can't protect your sister forever. All you can do is give her the moral foundation to make the best decisions possible. Give her the tools she needs. God will handle the rest."

Lily began pacing again. "But what if she ruins her life? Who will I blame if she's carried off by some Lothario with a suave manner and a lack of morals?"

Papa's chuckle should have soothed her raw nerves. "I can't help but think of Jesus' parable of the prodigal son. Sometimes our children have to be allowed to fail. They have to be freed even if the result is disastrous."

"You think I shouldn't give her advice?"

"If she's not willing to hear it, what good will your advice do her?"

Lily chewed on the inside of her cheek. But she had to try, didn't she? She loved Jasmine. Who better to advise her?

"When everyone told you not to purchase a riverboat, did you listen? Did you follow the counsel of those who were older and wiser? They probably thought you were being naive."

"But I was—"

The shake of his head stopped her words. "You were younger than Jasmine is now. And you knew next to nothing about moving cargo on the river. You were naive. If not for God's provision, you would have failed. You might have even died on the river."

She stared at him, knowing how much the words must have cost him. He was right. Her own mother had died on the river in spite of everything. Looking back at those days, she saw her family in a new light.

Papa stood, putting a hand on her shoulder. "I know how much it must frighten you to think that your sister may be hurt. It's a fear every parent must face."

"So I should let her go her own way? Give her the freedom to fail?"

He squeezed her shoulder and nodded. "God has given us that same freedom. Think of how He must feel when He knows that we will yield to temptation. Some of us will pay the highest price for that—an eternity separated from His presence. Yet He knows how important it is not to compel us. He stands ready like the father in the parable to welcome us home. But He'll never stop us from leaving."

A tear slipped down Lily's cheek, and she flicked it away with an impatient finger. She didn't know if she was strong enough to let Jasmine go. Everything in her cried out against the idea. "Isn't there another way?"

He shook his head, his own eyes moist.

Before he could say anything else, the library door opened, and Aunt Tessie stepped inside, her attention focused on the glove she was putting on. "Henrick, are you—" Her question came to an abrupt halt as she looked up and realized Lily was in the library. "I'm sorry. I'm interrupting."

"No, don't go." Lily sniffed to keep her tears at bay. "Papa and I are finished talking."

Aunt Tessie looked from her to her father, an unspoken question apparent in the arch of her eyebrows.

Papa cleared his throat and nodded. "I'll be ready in a few moments."

The unspoken conversation between the two of them made Lily want to giggle. It was a relief from the heavy burden of guilt she'd been carrying.

"I'll just go see if Charlotte has—um—has finished that list." Aunt Tessie disappeared into the hallway, her discomfort obvious.

Lily turned to her father. Was he blushing? She knew she was grinning. "Papa, I'm so happy for you. Tessie is a wonderful lady."

His eyes opened wide, and he blew out a relieved sigh. "You don't need to send out invitations yet, but I have to admit being in her company does my heart good. I wasn't sure if you girls would be upset."

"Upset?" Laughter filled her, lifting Lily's spirits. "I think this is the most exciting thing that's happened to us in a long time."

"You don't think I'm being foolish?" His brown gaze begged for reassurance.

"Not at all." Lily put her arms around him and hugged him hard. "I think Tessie is one lucky lady to have snagged the attention of such a fine Christian man."

"And I think I'm blessed to have the love of such an understanding daughter." He dropped a kiss on her cheek before taking a step back. "Now you quit worrying so much about making Jasmine's decisions for her. You and she are alike in many ways. She's going to be all right in spite of what you may think."

Lily watched him walk toward the door, his step jaunty. Wondering how the father of the prodigal son had managed for all those years that his child was away from home, she shivered. She hoped she would never have to find out for herself.

⁂

Jasmine stood at the rail as the *Water Lily* pulled away from the dock. How could the day be so beautiful when her heart was being torn in two?

She hadn't been at home with Sarah yesterday when Vance called on her, because Lily had shown up and insisted they go shopping together. It made no sense at all. Unless Lily had some ulterior motive. But she couldn't have known when Vance would come. It was all too confusing.

When Lily first showed up unannounced at Sarah's house, Jasmine had been afraid her deception had been uncovered. Certain that Lily had somehow found out about her evening with Vance, Jasmine had braced herself for a homily on deceit and ruination. What she'd gotten instead was an invitation to go shopping. Shopping? Something Lily abhorred. It made no sense.

"Are you looking forward to seeing Eli and Renée's boys again?"

Caught off guard by Lily's unexpected presence on the deck, Jasmine shrugged. Her sister was usually far too busy taking care of passengers during departure. She kept her gaze on the muddy surface of the river. Now was not the time to tell Lily she wasn't going to Memphis. "Remington is nice enough when he's not plotting some prank. As for Brandon and Cameron, they've never shown much interest in me."

Lily smiled. "They have matured greatly since they last saw you. I predict that they'll buzz around you like honeybees gathering nectar when they realize what a beautiful young lady you are."

Flattery was not something Lily excelled at. She sounded too bright.

The forced cheerfulness didn't sound at all convincing. Jasmine suspected she was trying to make amends because of the way she'd embarrassed her at the Thorntons' earlier in the week. Jasmine was ready to forgive her sister's boorish behavior. . .*if* Lily vowed to be more circumspect.

The horn sounded above them as Papa guided the paddlewheeler around a sharp curve.

Jasmine cast about for a different topic—one that would not concern her or her plans. She didn't want Lily to figure out what she planned to do.

"Did you give the children the toys we found yesterday?"

"Yes. They were excited. Benjamin loved the silver rattle you picked out."

Besides the toys for all of the children, they had purchased a lovely straw hat for Camellia, a magnifying glass to help Uncle Phillip read his newspaper, and a lacy shawl in shades of brown and coral for Aunt Dahlia. Jonah was getting a fancy stereoscope and several stereographic images of boats and trains.

"I'm sorry I didn't get to meet your friend Mr. Hargrove." Lily seemed determined to bring up uncomfortable topics.

Jasmine didn't know if she was sorry or not. If Lily had actually met him, she might have agreed that he was everything both she and Sarah had claimed. But then again, she might just as well have taken an instant dislike to him. This way Jasmine didn't have to defend her interest in him. "Perhaps he'll come to Natchez someday, and you can meet him then."

Lily's gaze swept her. "Did he tell you he was coming to visit?"

"No." Jasmine could not meet her sister's gaze. "You're probably right. I'll never see him again."

Silence enveloped them. Jasmine wanted to look up, but she didn't dare. Lily might not know everything, but she had an uncanny knack for discerning untruths. Not that Jasmine believed Vance would come to Les Fleurs without an invitation. He didn't need to. She was going to go to him, get a job on the *Ophelia*, and reach for her dreams.

"I'm sorry." Lily's hand covered her own. "I've been thinking about that trip to Chicago. The one you and I discussed back at Les Fleurs."

"You don't have to worry about that." Jasmine pulled her hand free. "I don't know if I even want to go to Chicago anymore."

"Really? I thought that was your heart's desire. What's happened to change your mind?"

Jasmine wished her sister would go away. "Nothing. I just realized that the big city is not as romantic as I'd once thought."

"Is it that man?" Lily grabbed her shoulders and pulled Jasmine around to face her. Her brown eyes were full of fire. "Did he hurt you?"

"Of course not." Exasperation lent sincerity to her words. At least she could be truthful about this. "Vance was a perfect gentleman."

Lily continued to search her face. "Something happened. You've been pining for the chance to move to Chicago for more than a year. You couldn't have changed so completely in less than a week." An odd look entered her eyes, driving out the anger and replacing it with sympathy. "Is it David? I know that you care about him, Jasmine, in spite of what you tell me. It's written all over your face."

David? Lily thought she was heartbroken because David was not returning with them? She opened her mouth to correct her sister's misunderstanding but snapped it closed again as she realized this might be the perfect way to avoid Lily's interference. Drawing on her experience playing the misunderstood daughter of King Lear, she hung her head. "I—he is nothing to me at all."

"Oh, dear." Lily drew her close and rubbed her back. "I'm so sorry, Jasmine."

As she stood within the circle of her sister's arms, Jasmine ignored the prick of her conscience. It was Lily's fault that she was driven to deception. If she told her sister the truth, Lily would drag her off to Memphis or some other bleak, depressing location and never let her out of her sight.

Her way would be better for both of them. For everyone in the family. She would disappear from their lives until one day when they would learn of her stunning success in the theatrical world. Then they would understand why she had left home in the first place.

Chapter Seventeen

The hired carriage rocked as it hit a rough spot on the dirt road leading out of Natchez. With practiced ease, Jasmine grabbed the hand loop above her head to keep from being jostled about.

Lily swayed with the movement, her arm around her drowsy youngest son. "I'm glad Papa took Aunt Tessie home."

"Mommy, Noah's touching me." Magnolia pushed at her brother's arm as she made the complaint.

Jasmine hid a grin as she listened to Lily dispensing justice to her nephew and niece. Had she ever been that young? She didn't remember arguing with David in the same way. Of course, Lily wasn't her mother. . .and he certainly wasn't her brother.

She felt a greater kinship with Benjamin, wondering if he would chafe against being the youngest. Jasmine knew firsthand how it felt. She was ready to be treated like a grown woman, receiving respect from her family even if they couldn't give her enthusiastic support. If everything proceeded according to plan, they would have to respect her. They wouldn't have any other choice. She would be out in the world, making her own way and excelling in her chosen profession.

A thrill of anticipation swelled within her. Maybe she would marry the handsome Vance Hargrove. . .if no one better came along. After all, once she became a famous actress, dozens of men would want her by their sides. . .maybe hundreds. She could choose a husband from among them.

The carriage slowed and turned off the road.

Jasmine leaned forward for a glimpse of Les Fleurs, her breath catching at the unexpected sight. "Look, there's been a fire!"

Her exclamation stopped the children's squabbling, and they leaned forward to see the blackened field. She heard hoofbeats as Blake, who was escorting them on horseback, spurred his mount forward.

Lily held Benjamin's head as she surveyed the damage. "I wonder what happened. Can you see the house?"

"Not yet." Out of the corner of her eye, Jasmine saw Magnolia reach for her brother's hand. The sight warmed her heart, reminding her once again of the close relationship she, Lily, and Camellia had once enjoyed. A part of her missed those days. They rarely—if ever—saw eye to eye anymore.

Blake returned, leaning down to report what he'd seen. "It looks like the only damage was to a couple of the cabins on the other side of the fields."

Benjamin woke and pulled on his mother's shoulder. Lily returned her attention to him.

Jasmine, along with Noah and Magnolia, continued peering out of the window. She hoped no one had been hurt.

Camellia and Aunt Dahlia stood on the front porch, waving their handkerchiefs. They must have heard the carriage coming.

Blake dismounted to open the door for them. Noah and Magnolia tumbled out first and went running up the steps to be welcomed by the two ladies as Blake took Benjamin. He set his youngest child on the ground and watched him run, as only a toddler can, toward the steps before helping Lily and Jasmine alight.

As she climbed the stairs ahead of Lily and Blake, Jasmine looked for any signs of strain in Camellia's face, breathing a sigh of relief when she saw none. In spite of the damage they had seen on the drive to the plantation, everything must be under control.

"Why don't you go inside and see if the cook has any treats left from our tea this morning?" Camellia held the door open and watched as Noah, Magnolia, and Benjamin ran to do her bidding.

"What happened?" Blake asked the question as soon as the children were out of sight.

"We were all nearly burned alive." Aunt Dahlia dabbed at her eyes with her handkerchief, even though Jasmine couldn't see any evidence of tears. "I thank the good Lord we weren't killed while we slept."

"Aunt Dahlia, you know the fire started well after we were up and about." Camellia hugged Jasmine first and then Lily. "Besides, the house was never in any danger."

Aunt Dahlia heaved a loud sigh. "I blame Jonah for bringing this on us."

Jasmine could not believe what her aunt was saying. Aunt Dahlia had never liked Jonah because he fought with the North during the war, but surely she could not believe he would purposely try to burn down their home.

"Aunt Dahlia," Lily and Camellia admonished in unison.

"Well, I do." Aunt Dahlia sniffed and turned to go inside. "You young people don't know as much as you think. Whenever someone tries to change the natural order of things, we all have to suffer the consequences."

Blake shook his head and turned to face Camellia. "Tell us what happened."

"I know you remember Jasper Calhoun." She waited for Blake's nod. "He set fire to the woods out of spite when Jonah didn't choose him as overseer."

"Why don't you sit down and tell us all about it? Don't leave out any details." Lily moved to one of three rockers to the right of the front door, arranging her skirts as she settled against the wooden seat.

Blake glanced toward the front door. "Where's Jonah?"

Camellia waved her hand toward the burned woods. "He and a few of the others are finishing up the repairs to the schoolhouse. It received the most damage, but I hope to hold class there again tomorrow."

Camellia and Jasmine sat in the empty rockers as Blake went in search of his brother-in-law. As succinctly as she could, Camellia described the fire and how narrowly she and the children had avoided the danger. "Besides minor scrapes and cuts, only one man was seriously injured. The doctor came to help treat him, and I'm thankful to say he is already back on his feet."

"Praise God no one was killed." Reverence filled Lily's words.

Camellia nodded. "Yes, He was definitely watching out for our welfare."

Jasmine was thankful to hear that the damage had been no worse, but she thought her sisters should also recognize the hard work of the men, women, and children who had risked their lives to fight the flames. Not that God had not been with them, but without the others, the plantation might have burned to the ground. But now was not the time to express her thoughts. She forced her lips into an agreeable smile.

"Let's talk about something else." Camellia looked at her. "Did you and David settle your differences, or are you still spatting?"

Lily cleared her throat and shook her head. "Blake and I were planning to make a trip up to Memphis right away, but I think we'd better stick around a few days to help you out."

While she was thankful to Lily for intervening, irritation pressed Jasmine's lips into a straight line. Why was everyone so interested in her relationship with David? He was her past. The theater was her future.

"Don't be ridiculous. I won't hear of such a thing. Jonah and I have everything in hand. Please don't change your plans. As you pointed out, we have so much to be thankful for."

Jasmine thought it would be good to add a little reinforcement. If Lily and Blake didn't leave, it might wreck her plans. Besides that, Lily needed to get past the idea that her sisters were helpless. Jasmine had no doubt Jonah and Camellia would do fine without Lily directing the repairs. "Didn't you say you need to talk to Eli Thornton about the railroad business?"

"That's true. He and Renée will know all the pitfalls of changing over from river to rail transportation. Now that so many people are moving westward, it seems we're going to have to consider the possibility of leaving the river." Lily stopped and frowned. "But family is more important than business."

"I agree, Sister. And if it were necessary, I would beg you and Blake to remain here a few days. But we're coping. You should go."

Jasmine held her breath as she watched the emotions crossing Lily's face.

"Are you going, too, Jasmine?"

Grateful for the chance to put her plans in motion, Jasmine stretched out her arms and yawned. "I don't think so." She looked at Lily, summoning all the pathos she could manage. "I'm really tired. Would you mind if I stayed here with Camellia?"

Lily shot her a concerned look. "Are you sick?"

"Not at all. Sarah was such a whirlwind of activity. I need a little time to recover from all that gadding about. I love staying with her, but it does wear me out."

"I know what you mean." Lily's expression turned to one of sympathy.

"So it's settled." Camellia headed for the door. "Jasmine is staying, and everyone else is leaving in the morning."

"I suppose so." Lily's nod eased the tension in Jasmine's shoulders. "Did you leave anything on the *Water Lily* that we need to send back before we leave?"

Without hesitation, Jasmine shook her head. "I have plenty of clothes here."

Camellia stopped and turned to her sister. "Are you planning to stop in Vicksburg?"

Jasmine's heartbeat tripled. Why would Camellia ask about Vicksburg?

"No, why? Do you need something from there?"

"Oh no. It's nothing. I was going to send a reply to a letter from Jane Baxter, but it can wait."

Jasmine's shoulders tensed again. She didn't want Lily and Blake to stop in the port that was her destination. If they saw her in Vicksburg, her bid for freedom would end before it began.

"It wouldn't be any trouble to stop." Lily stood. "We could send it by messenger to that bank where her husband works."

"Don't worry about it, Lily. I probably need more than one evening to write the letter anyway. I want to tell her all about the fire and that wicked Jasper Calhoun." Camellia shook her head. "Now that I think about it, I'm sure it wouldn't work."

Jasmine breathed a sigh of relief as she followed her sisters inside. For a moment she'd thought she would have to wait another day to avoid running into her oldest sister on the dock at Vicksburg. She also didn't want Lily to see either the *Ophelia* or Vance. Her sister didn't need any clues about her possible whereabouts.

❦

Camellia was leaving for the schoolhouse when Jasmine finally made her appearance in the front parlor. "You really must be exhausted. Do you feel all right?"

"Yes." The dark circles under Jasmine's eyes belied her answer.

"Are you sure you're not sick?"

"I—am—certain," Jasmine stated emphatically. "Don't try to act like Lily. One of the main reasons I didn't want to go with them to Memphis is because she's always hovering. I'm a grown woman. I can take care of myself."

"I'm sorry." Camellia could hear the exasperation in her own voice and knew some of it was directed at herself. It wasn't that long ago she'd felt the same way Jasmine did. Was she becoming as domineering as their older sister was at times? "I'll try to do better."

Jasmine looked contrite. "I'm sorry, too. I didn't sleep well."

"I was going to ask if you wanted to go with me to the schoolhouse, but maybe it would be better if you stay here and try to get some rest instead." Did she still sound like she was trying to manage Jasmine's life? "Or whatever you want to do."

Camellia's mouth dropped open as her sister darted across the parlor and threw her arms around her. She wanted to ask what was wrong now, but she was afraid to. Afraid she'd be accused of hovering. She returned Jasmine's hug. "I love you."

Was that a sniff? Was Jasmine crying? When Camellia pulled back, her sister's violet eyes were dry, so she decided it must have been her imagination. She searched Jasmine's face for some hint of what had her acting so oddly. "I got a new copy of *Godey's* last week. Would you like to read it?" It was the only thing she could think of to offer.

"No, thank you. I think I'm going to visit Miss Deborah at the orphanage, and I also plan to stop by to see Jean Luc and Anna." Jasmine's smile didn't seem as perky as usual, but Camellia put it down to her sleepless night.

"I could hardly believe it when Lily told me about Tessie and Papa."

"Are you upset?"

Camellia shook her head. "Of course not. Tessie's a wonderful woman. She taught me everything I know about medicine and healing. If not for her, I might never have learned how to be a proper nurse. If Papa's happy, I am, too."

"It seems a little odd to me." Jasmine wrinkled her nose. "They're so old."

Laughter bubbled up from Camellia. "Did you think romance was limited to the young?"

"Of course not. I was just surprised because it's Papa. I guess I thought he was still in love with Mama."

Camellia picked up her bonnet and walked to the window. "Mama will always have a special place in Papa's heart. But he has a right to seize happiness if he can find it with Aunt Tessie."

"I suppose."

Tying a large bow under her chin, Camellia glanced in the window to check her appearance. "Maybe we'll have a wedding for Christmas."

Jasmine shrugged.

Camellia supposed her sister was still trying to get used to the idea of "old people" falling in love. "I have to go, dearest. I'm taking a lunch to share with the children since it's going to be a long day." She turned to find Jasmine studying the newspaper. "I'll see you sometime this afternoon."

"Don't worry if I'm not back when you return." Jasmine glanced up. "I may stay in town for a while."

Camellia pointed a finger at her. "If you go shopping without me, my feelings are going to be hurt." The laugh her comment brought eased Camellia's concern. She breezed out of the room with a kiss and a wave.

She enjoyed the walk to the schoolhouse in spite of the scorched ground from last week's fire. Wondering which of the children would be in attendance this morning, she opened the front door and sniffed. The mint she'd gathered yesterday morning and left inside had done the trick, replacing the pungent smells with freshness. No hint of smoke remained inside the room. Thanking God once more that Jasper Calhoun had not done any more damage, she checked the children's slates while she waited for her students to arrive.

The morning was a busy one as always. Camellia loved the bright eyes and eager minds of her pupils. Their week-long separation made the day even more special than normal. The hours flew by, and by the time she sent them to their homes, the shadows outside were beginning to lengthen.

Arriving home, Camellia pulled off her bonnet and let it dangle from one hand as she went in search of her aunt and her sister. Because it was the first room off the main entrance, she stopped to see if they were in the library. "Jasmine? Aunt Dahlia?" No one answered, which was not surprising. Jasmine had already read most everything inside, and their aunt probably never would. Moving to the parlor, she checked for the two women, growing a little concerned when she found the room empty.

They weren't on the porch or she would have seen them coming in. Had they gone to the dining room? Concern prickled across her skin when they didn't turn up there either. Before she could descend into a full panic, however, footsteps descending the main stairwell brought her into the foyer.

Aunt Dahlia steadied herself on the handrail as she negotiated the stairs. "Did you call me?"

Nodding, Camellia smiled. "Is Jasmine upstairs?" Her sister must have returned to her bedroom for a nap before dinner.

"I haven't seen her at all today." Aunt Dahlia reached the bottom step before continuing. "Didn't she leave with Lily and Blake?"

Camellia's heart clenched before she remembered that Jasmine had warned her she might not be back on time. She glanced out the window. It would grow dark soon. "No, she didn't go with them. She had some errands to run. I'm sure she'll be back soon."

"Someone needs to put a rein on that girl. She's allowed far too much freedom."

"According to what Lily told me, Jasmine would definitely not agree with you." Camellia gave her aunt a peck on the cheek. "I've got to go meet with the cook about the menu before I go upstairs, change for dinner, and check on Amaryllis."

"I'll send Jasmine up to you if I see her before you're done." Aunt Dahlia's sigh was filled with disapproval.

She opened her mouth to continue, but Camellia cut off her words with another kiss. "Thank you."

Aunt Dahlia entered the parlor as Camellia headed to the back of the house, her mind full of all that needed to be done prior to dinner.

When she finally made it back to the parlor, the lanterns had been lit. She entered the room and looked around expectantly.

Aunt Dahlia put down her needlework. "If you're looking for your sister, you're going to be disappointed. She's not returned."

A frisson skittered down Camellia's back. She was going to talk to Jasmine about being more considerate. It was fine to stay for dinner with friends, but she should at least send a message so her family wouldn't worry.

Jonah walked into the parlor, already dressed for dinner. "You look worried."

"I'm more irritated than anything." Camellia told him about Jasmine's absence. "Would you mind taking me over to the Champney's?

I know she must have decided to have dinner with them, but I'd feel better if I knew for certain she's okay."

Jonah rubbed his chin with one hand. "Do you really think that's necessary?"

"Probably not, but I hate to think of her riding her horse back home in the dark."

He dropped his hand and nodded. "Okay."

Camellia hadn't realized how tense she was until her husband agreed. "Thank you."

His smile warmed her heart. "Go get your cloak. I'll have the carriage brought around."

Aunt Dahlia was shaking her head, but Camellia knew she had the most wonderful husband in the world.

Chapter Eighteen

 Jasmine was ready to get off the *Evangeline* long before it docked at Vicksburg. She had purchased the cheapest ticket she could manage— an outside ride on the hurricane deck between the paddlewheel and the pilothouse. Several immigrant families huddled together and watched her with suspicion in their eyes. She tried smiling at some of the children, but their mothers gathered them closer and chided them in a guttural language she had never heard, apparently reminding them to steer clear of strangers.

Someone stepped into the pilothouse, and she caught her breath as a desire to see her father overwhelmed her. But that was silly. If Papa were here she wouldn't be on her way to meet Vance.

Wishing she had brought more than a shawl as protection from the damp wind, Jasmine set her chin and focused on the future. They should reach Vicksburg within the hour. She hoped it wouldn't be too hard to find Vance. Jasmine couldn't wait to see him. Would he be as thrilled as she? What role did he have in mind for her? She knew she would excel even if she only got to appear in a minor part for now.

It wouldn't take her long to rise to the rank of someone like Miss

Barlow. She might not have much experience as a professional actress, but Jasmine had been performing for family and friends since she was old enough to memorize lines. Everyone raved about her acting abilities. And it was due to her efforts that the orphanage could hire workers to replace the roof.

In spite of his parents' warnings, one of the immigrant children moved cautiously closer. Jasmine wished the little boy wasn't afraid of her. She would love to talk to him, find out where his family was headed and maybe even offer some pointers to his parents about dangers on the river. It would be so nice to help them like she had the orphanage. One day perhaps she would have enough money to fund an organization to help those in need. The idea warmed Jasmine better than her thickest shawl would have done. She would do it. . .as soon as she was famous enough.

They docked with little trouble, and she disembarked with her bag held firmly in one hand. As soon as she reached the other end of the gangplank, she began looking for the *Ophelia*. Her heart pounded when she spotted the long, two-story barge floating in front of a shorter tugboat called the *Miss Polly*. This was it. The beginning of the rest of her life. Raising her chin and tightening her hold on her portmanteau, Jasmine marched across the gangplank and stepped onto the *Ophelia's* deck.

"Sorry, ma'am." A wiry man with a narrow face stopped her. "The next show won't start until seven o'clock. You can come back around five to purchase a ticket, but the doors won't open until a quarter to seven."

"I'm not—" Unhappy with the shaky sound of her voice, Jasmine halted her words and took a deep breath. "I'm here to see Mr. Vance Hargrove."

His face grew thoughtful. "You'll find him inside, but if you don't mind my saying so, you ought to turn yourself around and go home before he ruins your life."

"That's enough, Arnold. Are you already finished with the repairs to the backdrop?"

Jasmine recognized Vance's voice before he finished speaking. She turned, and there he was, as tall and handsome as she remembered. And his attractive smile made her knees weak. She thought she might die of happiness then and there. "Vance."

He swept her a deep bow, every inch the gentleman she remembered. "I wasn't sure you would come."

"I couldn't stay away." She blushed at the confession.

"Here, let me help you with that bag." He reached for her portmanteau. "How did you convince your family to let you come?"

Should she tell him the truth? She couldn't. He would think her a baby. And he might balk at accepting a runaway on board. "It wasn't hard. They accepted my decision and let me go." The lies tripped off her tongue without effort—almost like she was already playing a role.

His dark gaze searched her face for a moment as though testing her veracity.

Jasmine lifted her chin and stared back. Let him think what he might. She could be as imperious as Cleopatra.

He nodded and held the door open for her. "Come inside."

Jasmine stepped past him and came to a halt, her mouth dropping open. She had never seen anything so beautiful in her life. The main cabin was long, with a stage taking up the back third of the space. In front of the stage was seating for at least a hundred people. A red rope cordoned off the long padded benches. She supposed its purpose was to prevent anyone from sneaking in without purchasing a ticket. "It's beautiful."

"Wait until they light the candles this evening." He pointed out the numerous gold leaf sconces, each holding three candles. "Do you see the mirrors they're mounted on? They magnify the light until it's nearly as bright as noon inside."

The boat had been appointed to cater to rich customers. Thick carpet cradled her feet, the seating was softened by deep cushions, and an ornate chandelier hung above her head, holding what appeared to be hundreds more lights. "You must love performing in here."

"As will you." He held the red rope high so she could pass under it. Taking the lead, he stepped past her and walked up a set of steps onto the stage, waving to two men who were painting a backdrop off to one side of the stage. "I want you to meet someone special."

The rich red velvet curtain moved, and a beautiful woman stepped onto the stage.

Jasmine caught her breath. She had never dreamed she might be near enough to touch someone she so deeply admired.

"Vance? Are you ready to go over that scene now?" Tabitha Barlow asked.

"In a moment." He set down Jasmine's bag and reached for her hand. "We have a new recruit. A young lady I know you'll enjoy meeting."

The actress's gaze narrowed as Jasmine dropped a curtsy. "Really, Vance. Are you up to your old tricks again?"

Jasmine didn't pay much attention to Miss Barlow's words. She was too intent on trying to think of what to say to her. Why hadn't she thought of this? Her mind scrambled through reams of lines and came up empty. Only three words came to her. "I know you."

Miss Barlow's face lost its bored expression. She smiled at Jasmine and beckoned for her to come closer. "You do?"

"Yes, ma'am. You were playing the part of Laurette in *Richard Coeur-de-lion* in New Orleans. I remember it like yesterday. I was only nine at the time, but you inspired me to become an actress."

The smile drooped, and her eyes iced over as at least one of the workmen snickered. Miss Barlow looked past her to Vance. "Get her out of here this instant."

Before she could quite understand what she had said to upset the actress, Vance had grabbed her arm and dragged Jasmine off the stage. He hustled her into a narrow corridor and looked around. "Clem, come here."

She was surprised when the person who answered his summons was a slender girl not much older than she with a line of brown bangs across her forehead and a distracted look in her hazel eyes. "Clem?"

"Clem McCoy." The girl held a pincushion in one hand and a measuring tape in the other. "My real name is Clementine—it means 'merciful.' But everyone here calls me Clem."

"See that Jasmine gets settled." Vance turned to her, taking her hand to drop a kiss on her wrist. "I'll be in rehearsal this afternoon, but we'll talk after the play is over."

Jasmine's skin tingled where his lips had touched it. She wanted to ask him about the confrontation with Miss Barlow. Did the older woman misunderstand her intent to offer a compliment or was she simply too shy to appreciate such adoration?

"Come along." Clem walked down the hall, her gown swaying with each step.

Picking up her bag, Jasmine followed.

"You can share my room for now." Clem pushed a door open. "But I can't stand a mess, so make sure you pick up after yourself."

The room was barely large enough for the pair of single beds inside. A small dressing table took up one corner of the windowless space, its mirror the only brightness in the room.

"Thank you." Jasmine dropped the portmanteau on the floor and sank onto the mattress. So far, life in the theater was more confusing than exciting.

❧

Jonah turned into the Champneys' drive, and the warm light spilling from the windows encouraged Camellia to believe they would find Jasmine inside. But if Jean Luc and Anna had invited her to dinner, why hadn't they sent a note to Les Fleurs? The question pricked her concern, making Camellia more anxious than she should have been. Something wasn't right. She tapped her foot on the floor of the carriage as Jonah came around to help her down. His hand at her waist steadied her as they climbed the steps to the front door.

Leaning past her, Jonah lifted the knocker and rapped it smartly. The seconds crept by as she waited for someone to answer her husband's summons.

The door finally creaked open, and Camellia summoned a shaky smile, knowing how odd their presence must seem to the butler at this hour.

Jonah inclined his head. "We need to speak to Mr. or Mrs. Champney."

Camellia was right on his heels as the butler announced them. "Is Jasmine here with you?"

Aunt Tessie, Anna, and Mrs. Champney were sitting in the parlor. Anna and Aunt Tessie came to their feet.

Aunt Tessie spoke first. "I haven't seen Jasmine since the *Water Lily* landed yesterday."

Was it only yesterday? That carefree time seemed an eon ago. Camellia's knees turned to water. She was more frightened than when she'd been leading the children away from the fire at Les Fleurs. More frightened than when the Yankee army surrounded Vicksburg and shelled the city.

"What's happened?" Anna stepped forward, a concerned look on her face.

Camellia turned away to control her tears while Jonah filled them in briefly.

"What can we do to help?" The question came from Mrs. Champney, still seated on the sofa.

Camellia gave her the only answer she could. "Pray."

They were out of the house and back into the carriage with a minimum of fuss. Jonah whipped up the horses, and she followed her own advice as they headed to town.

"What if she's not here?" Camellia looked at her husband's profile. She wanted him to tell her everything was going to be okay, but not unless he really thought it would be. Empty promises would be worse than silence. She didn't need false hope.

"Don't borrow trouble." He put his free arm around her. "We'll find her in town, Camellia."

Why was it getting so dark? They needed light to check the byways for signs of an accident. She searched her memory for the time of the month and came up empty. "Will the moon be full tonight?"

Jonah spared her a glance. "No, but we'll be able to see well enough."

As he drove the carriage, she looked for any evidence of an accident.

Fear, dark as midnight, stalked her. She had managed to hold onto hope that nothing was wrong until learning that Jasmine had not visited the Champneys. Now that hope was gone. Something had happened to her sister.

What if she'd been abducted? They hadn't seen any bushwhackers in the area for more than a year, but what if one had been crossing their land this morning? Tears sprang to her eyes as fear swelled.

The hooves of the horses barely touched the ground as they rushed toward the orphanage. The rhythm normally soothed her, but this evening the sound only increased her anxiety.

Hope burst on her with the force of a lightning bolt when she saw Jasmine's horse tethered in front of the orphanage. "That's Juliet, isn't it?"

Jonah grinned at her. "I told you we'd find her."

Camellia climbed down before the carriage came to a full standstill, running toward the orphanage without a thought for her dress or her dignity. She pushed the front door open before Jonah caught up with her. "Jasmine!" She shouted the name as loudly as she could manage.

Jonah came through the front door as Miss Deborah entered the foyer from the back of the house. "Camellia, Jonah, welcome."

"Where is Jasmine?" Jonah sounded as impatient as she felt.

"Jasmine?" The confusion on Miss Deborah's face frightened Camellia, brought the fear roaring back. Miss Deborah had to know where Jasmine was. Anything else was impossible.

"Her horse is out front. Where is she?"

The puzzlement on the other lady's face deepened into a frown. "What horse?"

Jonah stepped aside so she could look down the walk through the open doorway.

Miss Deborah shook her head. "I'm sorry, Camellia. It may be Jasmine's horse, but she hasn't been here all day."

"Are you certain?"

"I saw her." Marguerite appeared from the same area of the house where Miss Deborah had been. "I thought she was acting a bit strange. She told me she was leaving her horse here and would send someone to retrieve it tomorrow. I assumed she had gotten a ride back to Les Fleurs."

What was her sister doing? Camellia wracked her brain for an answer that made sense but came up with nothing. "Is that all she said?"

Marguerite nodded. "I'm sorry."

"It's not your fault." Jonah put an arm around Camellia.

Miss Deborah wrung her hands. "What can we do? Do you want me to send someone to make inquiries downtown?"

This couldn't be happening. Camellia wanted to wake up and discover she'd been having a nightmare. But the rough texture of her husband's coat against her cheek told her this was no dream.

As Jonah explained what little they knew, she thought back to the morning. Had Jasmine been planning to disappear then? Or had she been forced to leave her horse behind by some heartless kidnapper?

Camellia couldn't feel her legs beneath her as Jonah half-carried her back to the gate. She sat with her hands in her lap, her gaze locked on nothing, as he tethered Juliet to the carriage.

"What do we do now?" She asked the question as he climbed onto the bench and turned their vehicle back the way they had come.

His jaw was tight as Jonah shook his head. "It's beginning to look like your sister has run away."

"Why would she do such a thing?"

"I have no idea. But then again I don't understand why ladies act the way they do more than half the time." He blew out a long sigh. "Think, Camellia. Did Jasmine say anything odd this morning? A hint of what she was planning?"

"We talked about Papa and Aunt Tessie." Camellia remembered her sister's reaction to the affection between them. "And she said she didn't sleep well last night. I remember thinking that she looked tired."

"Was she upset?"

Camellia didn't want to admit that Jasmine had been angry with her, but she knew she had to put her own feelings aside. She gave him a reluctant nod. "She thought I was being too controlling. She even accused me of being too much like Lily."

"None of you can be called mealy-mouthed."

A sob caught in her throat. "It's my fault, Jonah. All my fault. Lily is never going to forgive me for not taking better care of Jasmine. And I don't blame her."

"Shhh." His arm tightened around her once more. "It's not your fault, Camellia."

Hot tears bathed her cheeks. She wished his reassurances didn't sound so hollow. She had failed both of her sisters. Camellia had known Jasmine was acting strange this morning, but she'd been too focused on her schedule for the day. Instead of rushing off to teach the children, she should have stayed with Jasmine. She had made a terrible, thoughtless mistake. A mistake she would regret for the rest of her life. "What are we going to do, Jonah?"

"If she's run away, we need to try to find her." Jonah's voice sounded determined. "But even if we know where she is, we may not be able to compel her to return to Les Fleurs. She is twenty years old."

His warning brought her no relief. She wished for Lily's calm presence. Then the responsibility wouldn't be all on her shoulders. The thought was a revelation. Even in the midst of her fear, she gained a new respect for her older sister. Who could Lily turn to when life—in the form of her younger sisters—threatened to overwhelm her? Camellia felt shame at the knowledge that she had been as hard to handle at eighteen as Jasmine was now.

"What about asking David Foster to look for her?"

She sat up straighter and considered Jonah's question. David was the perfect answer. In spite of the differences that had sprung up between him and Jasmine, he would be concerned for her welfare. And he was a detective. If anyone could find her, it would be a Pinkerton man. Perhaps he could reason with her once he found Jasmine and convince her to come home. "Is he still in New Orleans?"

"I think so." Jonah turned the carriage onto their private drive. "We need to make sure Uncle Phillip didn't find her hiding out somewhere on the grounds first. But if she really is missing, we can send a telegram to David the first thing in the morning."

Uncle Phillip stood at the front door as they pulled up, his face drawn. One glance told the story. The last vestige of hope drained from Camellia. Feeling older than her aunt and uncle, she dragged herself out of the carriage.

"Mommy, Mommy." Amaryllis ran onto the porch, her sweet face puckered with worry.

"It's okay, Amaryllis. Mommy's here." Camellia held out her hands to her daughter, gathering her close and burying her face against Amaryllis's soft neck. Even though she felt unworthy of the love flowing from the little girl, it buoyed her spirits a little.

She felt Jonah's arms encircling both of them. "We'll get through this, Camellia." His whispered words were another pinprick of light piercing the darkness of her fear. "God is watching out for Jasmine tonight even though we cannot."

She prayed he was right.

Chapter Nineteen

David held out his left hand to the young constable who'd been such a help in his search for leads. "It's been a pleasure working with you, Constable Longineaux."

Longineaux grabbed his hand and pumped it once. "I'm sorry the leads didn't pan out, but I know you'll catch the thieves soon. I only wish I could be there when you do."

"If you get any response from those advertisements—"

"You'll be the first to know." The constable scraped his foot on the floor. "Who knows, maybe one of these days I'll come up to Chicago and see your Pinkerton operation."

"I'd like that." David left the busy police office, squinting at the sunlight as he considered what to do next. He could rent a horse from the nearby livery stable, but it wasn't that far to the docks. A walk might clear his head.

The sights around him faded as David once again went through the events at Jackson Square. What had Petrie been trying to tell him? He shook his head in frustration. He had run into an impenetrable wall here. It was time to leave.

The New Orleans Police Department had shelved their case when no new robberies occurred. As Lieutenant Moreau had told him earlier that morning, they didn't have time or the manpower to chase all over the country looking for a needle in a haystack.

It didn't take David long to find a riverboat heading north. After purchasing a ticket, he walked to the Cartiers' home. Packing his belongings, he descended the staircase that was his private entrance and walked across the porch to the main entrance of the house. The Cartiers' butler answered his knock and led him to the parlor.

Sarah had been reading a novel but put it down to greet him. "I'm so glad to see you, David. How is your work progressing?"

He sat in a dainty whitewashed chair and shook his head. "I've exhausted every avenue I can think of. It's time to admit defeat. I came by to thank you and Dr. Cartier for your hospitality. You've been very gracious hosts, never complaining about my odd hours or the amount of time I dedicate to my work."

"That reminds me." She snapped her fingers and jumped up from the sofa. "You received two telegrams this morning."

David stood when she did and waited while she went through a stack of invitations on the Queen Anne desk in one corner of the parlor.

"Here they are." Sarah turned with a triumphant smile and handed him the envelopes.

He opened the top one and read the message inside.

ROBBERY PLANTER'S BANK VICKSBURG *Stop* INVESTIGATE CONNECTION
PINKERTON DETECTIVE AGENCY

The information galvanized him. "It's from my headquarters. There's been another robbery, this time in Vicksburg." He would have to make sure the riverboat captain was planning to make a stop in that city. "Maybe I'll catch them there."

Sarah's head nodded, but her concerned gaze studied him. "You're so brave, David. I cannot imagine facing such danger. But open the other telegram. Maybe it says that the thieves were already arrested."

Even though he doubted such an eventuality, David nodded. His eyes widened as he saw the name on the envelope. "It's from Camellia and Jonah."

As he read the note, irritation and disbelief filled him. "Jasmine has done it now. It seems she's run away from home. Your brother and Camellia want me to help find her."

"That poor child." Sarah grabbed his arm. "You must help look for her."

"She's not a child." He looked down at Sarah's troubled expression. What did they think he could do? And what about his job? What about the people who suffered loss and hardship because their money had been stolen? Was he supposed to ignore their needs to go running after a spoiled brat? "Besides, I have no idea where she would go."

"But you know Jasmine better than anyone." Sarah loosened her grip and stepped back as though she could read his thoughts. "You cannot ignore her family's plea."

She had hit on the real problem. He owed a debt to Lily and both of her sisters. "If the boat I'm on stops over in Natchez, I'll make a quick trip to the plantation and find out exactly what's happened. Maybe I can suggest another detective they can hire to look for her."

Even though Sarah didn't say it, he could tell she wasn't happy with his answer. David didn't know what else to do, though. He couldn't— wouldn't—ignore his employer's instructions.

Besides, he'd already wasted enough time trying to curb Jasmine's headstrong personality. Perhaps if she found out what life was really like away from the protection of her family, Jasmine would grow up. Maybe she would finally learn to listen to others who knew more about the world. It wasn't all kittens and compliments. After a week or two of battling greed and disinterest, she would probably be eager to return to her family.

He bowed to Sarah. "Thank you again for your hospitality, Mrs. Cartier. I'll mention to Jonah your concern over Jasmine's welfare and ask him to send you a note once she returns to Les Fleurs."

"Thank you." She pulled herself to her full height and nodded regally. "I hope we'll see you again soon."

David left her standing in the center of the parlor, her chin high and her eyes moist with unshed tears. He could strangle Jasmine himself for causing so much worry. The girl never thought of anyone but herself.

He passed the music room and remembered the way she'd made sheep eyes at that self-absorbed actor. Jasmine had less sense than the sheep she imitated. She had no business leaving the shelter of her home and family.

But then he imagined her scared and alone, adrift in a sea of cruelty and violence. A fierce protectiveness smothered his irritation. Where could she be? Had she gone to Chicago or New York or somewhere else in her search for fame and glory? She needed a keeper, someone who would control her wild tendencies. He wished he had the time to expend on finding her. He would make sure Jasmine was okay. Then he would drag her back home and dare her to ever leave again.

ॐ

Working aboard the showboat was not as glamorous as Jasmine had imagined. Clem was sweet, and it was exciting to watch from the wings as Vance and the other actors performed *Romeo and Juliet* the night before. Talking to the male lead was another matter entirely. With two performances daily, the whole crew was busy with their various chores.

"Aren't you done polishing those sconces?"

Miss Barlow's querulous voice startled her, and Jasmine nearly fell from the ladder she was perched on.

"Be careful." The actress stepped back, entangled her shoe in the hem of her dress, and cried out. Before she could fall, however, Vance rushed forward and caught her.

"I'm sorry." Jasmine gritted her teeth as jealousy washed through her. Miss Barlow seemed to command all of Vance's time.

Standing with an arm around his co-star, Vance sent her a wink. "Leave the girl alone, Tabitha. She'll finish the sconces as soon as she can."

"Well, I don't know how we're supposed to practice when I can hardly see my hand in front of my face."

Jasmine had to agree with her that it was difficult to see without the candlelight. That must be why Miss Barlow's titian-colored hair seemed to be a different shade than she remembered.

The outer door opened, and sunlight spilled into the room. Angelica Fenwick, the second female lead and understudy for Miss Barlow, strolled in.

The older actress rounded on her. "I'm glad you found time to join us this morning. Your portrayal of Juliet's nurse was lackluster yesterday evening."

Miss Fenwick was as blond as Camellia but much more rounded. Her dimpled elbows and generous chest almost made her seem plump. Jasmine knew from talking to Clem that Miss Fenwick played the secondary parts, the parts that often had the better lines. She'd also warned Jasmine about the constant tension between the two actresses.

"That's not what Rafe said." Miss Fenwick's New England accent was evident in her clipped syllables. "And the audience didn't seem to mind."

"Rafe's opinion doesn't count for anything. Everybody knows he's in love with you." Miss Barlow pouted at Vance. "I don't know why I put up with this trumpery, two-bit operation."

Vance chuckled and released Miss Barlow. "Our generous salaries might be one of the reasons."

She swept down the central aisle, her irritation evident in the swish of her skirts.

"I don't know what you're looking at." Miss Fenwick sniffed as she looked toward Jasmine. "You may be new here, but that's no excuse for inefficiency."

Jasmine returned to her task with renewed energy. Miss Fenwick and Miss Barlow were still squabbling as she removed the last nub and replaced it with a fresh candle. Taking the tinderbox, she started lighting the central candle in each sconce as the manager had instructed.

Rafe Griffin, dressed in a purple doublet, made an appearance a few minutes later. Jasmine supposed he was handsome. His eyes were large and dark, his brow wide, and a pair of dimples bracketed his mouth when he smiled. But he wasn't nearly as handsome as Vance, at least to her. Standing close to her ladder, he showed his dimples. "You must be the new girl Clem was telling me about."

"I was about to send someone out looking for you, Rafe." Miss Fenwick addressed the actor, but her pale eyes shot daggers at Jasmine.

Jasmine wanted to sigh. She had not been here for two full days, and she'd already managed to earn the dislike of both the female leads. What had she done wrong?

Rafe pointed at a spot on his doublet sleeve. "Clem was mending my costume."

Harmon Easley, the owner and manager of the *Ophelia*, entered the stage from the wings. He was a burly man with beefy arms, a round belly, and bowed legs. "What's going on out here? Why aren't y'all practicing? Do I need to advertise for new actors?" He smoothed his mustache with a finger. "Or maybe I should turn this into a circus boat. I don't imagine animals would give me any more trouble than the lot of you."

Properly chastised, the foursome took their places on stage. Jasmine could tell the other members of the cast were waiting backstage from the occasional movements of the curtain. They were the stock company, the actors who filled in the minor parts for much lower pay.

"We'll begin with this week's farce, *Fish Out of Water*." Mr. Easley crossed his arms over his chest. "Places everyone."

As the one-act play began, Jasmine slipped into one of the empty seats, her heart thumping as they began. How she wished to join them onstage.

Someone sat down beside her, and she turned to see Clem's brown hair and plain garb. "If Mr. Easley finds you sitting here doing nothing, he'll sack you for sure."

Jasmine nodded, and the two of them slipped out.

"Here." Clem led her downstairs to the area where the props were stored. "I have to make some alterations to Lady Montague's dress. The girl playing that part was tripping all over the hem last night. It's a wonder she didn't fall and break her neck."

"Do you ever act?"

"No." Clem folded the material at the bottom of the skirt and pinned it in place. "Not for a long time. I tried it when I first started working in this business, but I didn't want to deal with the petty quarrels and backbiting. And the men who see you on stage get funny ideas about a girl's morals."

Jasmine remembered that the first night she'd met Vance the men had crowded around Miss Barlow's door, wanting to take her to dinner. That didn't sound bad to her. Bickering with her coactors, though, was not a pleasant idea. Perhaps she could find ways to accommodate the needs of the other actors by giving them sufficient respect. In her experience it was the best way to avoid confrontation. She sighed at the realization that she had not made a promising start. "I seem to have a talent for making people angry. Both Miss Barlow and Miss Fenwick have given me tongue-lashings."

"Miss Barlow isn't so bad. I've learned as long as you don't get in her way she's happy to ignore you."

Clem's advice didn't make much sense. She'd only been trying to compliment Miss Barlow when they were first introduced. For her troubles, she'd received a sharp word and been sent to her room like a young child. Even Lily hadn't done that to her in years. "I'm beginning to think you only see the good in people."

Clem shook out the skirt and eyed it carefully. "You need to give Miss Fenwick a wide berth. She'll scratch your eyes out if she thinks you'll get in her way, especially with Rafe. She doesn't like it if he even looks at another girl. Give him a wide berth, and she'll leave you alone."

"What about Mr. Hargrove?" Jasmine's heartbeat increased, and a blush darkened her cheeks. Even thinking about him made her quiver.

"He's a ladies' man." Clem put away her supplies before turning back to Jasmine. "But I can see you already know that."

"He's the one who first told me about the *Ophelia* and said I should meet the boat here."

"So he got you a job. I wondered about that. Mr. Hargrove must be sweet on you. But be careful. He and Miss Barlow have been friends forever."

"They're not. . .in love?"

"I don't think so. Maybe once a long time ago. They're mostly friends now, although she does like to keep him close by."

Jasmine clasped her hands in front of her, her worries easing. Vance must be in love with her. He'd spoken to the manager about her, made sure she would have a job on board. And to think she'd been miffed because he had not sought her company after the performance last night. He'd been doing something much more important—making sure she would have a reason to stay near. She was certain he'd seek her out as soon as he could.

Chapter Twenty

David lost a whole day because the boat he'd been planning to take north was not making a stop in Natchez. He cashed in his ticket and went looking for another berth. The docks were full of steamers, but many of them did not want to stop before getting farther north on the river. Finally he found a captain who agreed to make a short stop in Natchez before continuing. The only catch was that he would not leave that afternoon. He purchased the ticket, stowed his gear, and settled in for a long night. By the time the sun rose, he was more than ready to be active again.

Pent-up energy had him threading his way around the cargo of barrels and boxes as the side-wheeler pushed its way against the strong current. Memories of trips on the *Water Lily* clamored for David's attention, growing more distinct with each mile traveled.

A flock of pelicans turned the sky pink above the boat, reminding him of the time Jasmine had decided to capture one for a pet. He'd had to rescue her from the swamp and drag her back to the *Water Lily* before she became a tasty meal for a passing alligator. She had pouted for days until her father helped him carve one from a piece of walnut. He still remembered the look on her face when he presented it to her. He'd felt like he was ten feet tall.

That was the day he'd known his heart belonged to Jasmine Anderson. He had hidden the knowledge from her, feeling he didn't deserve her love. She was from a wealthy family while he had no family to speak of—only a downtrodden ma and a gold-hungry pa. Jasmine and her sisters had taken him in, given him a glimpse of what life could be like. He probably wouldn't be a Christian if he hadn't spent so many afternoons talking to Jasmine's father about Jesus and the Bible.

But even now he felt separated from them, his face pressed against an impenetrable window. Like the rich man in the Bible who could only see heaven from across a chasm, he was doomed to live out his life yearning for what could never be his. The kindness Jasmine's family offered him was more akin to affection for a pet. And now, even though he had a good job and an honorable purpose, if one of the Anderson sisters called, he came running like an obedient puppy.

They sailed past Dead Man's Curve and docked next to a timber barge at Natchez Under-the-Hill.

"Be back by three or we'll leave you." The captain's warning rang in his ears as he left the boat.

David waved at the man. "I'll be back." Finding a horse to rent, he headed for Les Fleurs. He noticed the charred ground on his way in and wondered if Jasmine had caused that disaster before running away.

Camellia met him at the front door, her hair an uncontrolled mass of curls around her face. The frightened look in her blue eyes told him how concerned she was about Jasmine. "Thank you for coming." She sat in one of the rockers and motioned for him to sit next to her.

David shook his head. He would rather stand. "I don't have long, so why don't you tell me what happened." David braced himself. As Camellia told him about the day Jasmine disappeared, he asked a few pertinent questions. The more he heard, the more his exasperation overcame his concern for Jasmine's safety. She didn't take time to think how her selfish actions would affect others. When would she ever grow up? He paced the length of the front porch. "Have you had any word since she left?"

Camellia shook her head. "I feel so guilty for what I said to her. If only I'd been more understanding or less caught up in my own needs..."

David didn't hide his snort of disgust. "You didn't do anything wrong, Camellia. Jasmine has no excuse for causing you all this worry. What did Lily say?"

"She doesn't know." The confession was a bare whisper.

"You have to tell her." David sat next to Camellia and took her hands in his own. "Don't worry about her response. Lily isn't unreasonable. She'll understand you had no control over your little sister. Besides, she loves both of you. She won't blame you any more than I do, but she may have an idea of where Jasmine would go. And she can check for any word of her up and down the river. A lot of people know Lily and Blake. Contacting all of them and warning them to watch for Jasmine may be the easiest way of locating her."

Camellia nodded. "I—I just don't know what to say to her."

"I know it's hard, but you can do it."

She surprised him when she pulled her hands free and stood. Even more so when she wrapped her arms around him in a fierce hug. "I'm glad you came. I know you'll find her if anyone can."

Her words caged him as securely as a prison cell. Before the door could lock him in, he pulled away from her. He was determined to keep his wits about him in spite of the warring desires in his heart. "I don't have much time to devote to the search, Camellia. As soon as I leave here, I'm going to investigate a robbery at Planter's Bank in Vicksburg."

She gasped, and the blood drained from her face. "Oh no. My friend Jane is married to an officer of that bank, Harold Baxter. Please tell me no one was hurt."

"I wish I could." David hoped her connection to the man at the bank would help Camellia understand why he couldn't devote all his time to finding Jasmine. He had to keep his priorities in order. "I don't know any details yet. But I'll make it a point to visit your friend and ask her to send you a note telling you more about the robbery."

Camellia nodded slowly. Her blue eyes shone like glass. "I'm so proud of you, David. I wish you and Jas—"

"I really have to get going." David cut her off before she could finish what she'd been about to say. No one wished for a match more than he. But Jasmine had other ideas about what to do with her life, and he had to respect her decision. . .no matter how ridiculous it was. "Either Mrs. Baxter or I will be in touch soon."

"I'll pray for both of you."

David returned to his rented nag and rode back to Natchez Under-the-Hill, relieved to see that the captain had honored their agreement. He'd already lost enough time. He wanted to find and arrest the bank robbers and return to Chicago. He would refuse any new assignment in the lower Mississippi Valley. Spending time close to the Anderson girls was tearing his world apart. He felt like a ship foundering among the hidden snags of loyalty and devotion. One day he was liable to wash up on a sandbar—broken and abandoned by both the job he felt called to do and the woman he adored.

෨ෑ

"You're going to play the part of Lady Montague." Vance Hargrove acted as though he offered her the moon.

Jasmine balanced on a stool, the gold skirt of Miss Barlow's ballroom costume spread around her. She had been reattaching the flounce when Vance found her, a tedious task that Clem said was needed on a daily basis.

She put down the needle and tried to summon a gracious smile for his sake. But it was beyond her acting ability to hide her disappointment. Her first appearance on a real stage would be as Vance's mother. And she knew *Romeo and Juliet* well enough to know that she would only have a line or two.

"Aren't you excited?" The light in his dark eyes dimmed. He glanced around the prop room, his gaze searching for an ally. "Clem, tell Jasmine what a big break this is. She'll be onstage."

"This is a big break, Jasmine. You'll be onstage." Clem parroted the words from the other side of the costume trunk.

Jasmine hid a grin at her friend's lack of intonation.

"I see how it is." A frown marred Vance's handsome face. "You think you're above such a small part. I suppose you think you should take Miss Barlow's place as Juliet."

"I'm excited, Vance." She tried to convey an enthusiasm for the breadcrumb he offered.

"I worked hard to get Mr. and Mrs. Easley to give you this chance." His mouth turned down.

Her heart sank at the disappointment on his face. Vance was being sweet and thoughtful. She had no right to trample on his kindness. "I'm sorry. I suppose it's a little overwhelming to think of going onstage so soon."

She ignored Clem's grunt. Clem had little respect for any of the actors. She was constantly pointing out to Jasmine the advantages of working with the production instead of reaching for fame as an actress. She might be right, but Jasmine wanted the adulation of the audience. She wanted to be sought after. She wanted her name on the playbills passed out in the town as advertisement.

Vance took her arm and pulled her off the stool. "Come with me."

"What happened to the actress who was supposed to be playing Lady Montague?" Jasmine asked the question as they left the lower floor of the barge.

Vance led the way, his long legs taking the steps two at a time. "She's too drunk to stand up. Mrs. Easley told her to get off the boat. So see, this is the perfect chance for you to be able to perform regularly."

Jasmine tried to hide her surprise. A drunk actress? She'd never dreamed of rubbing elbows with women who drank alcohol. Maybe that's why Lily had been so worried about her. But her oldest sister should know she would never do such a thing.

Vance halted suddenly and turned to face her. "Things have been hectic, but I want you to know how often I think of you, Jasmine. This is your chance, you know. Once you get on that stage, I know you'll be on your way to stardom."

Her bruised heart healed a little from the warmth of his words. "Thank you." She could swallow her disappointment. Vance was doing what he could. Maybe when they left Vicksburg, he would be able to spare some time for her. Maybe then—

Her thoughts ended abruptly when Vance gripped her arms and yanked her off balance. She fell against his chest with an audible *oomph*, and before she realized what was happening, his lips covered hers. Shock kept her still for an instant, and he took full advantage, slathering her face with his wet, soft mouth. It was like being kissed by a fish. Her mind and her body reacted violently to his assault. Twisting and pushing, she forced her elbow into his stomach, gaining her freedom when he stepped back.

"Mr. Hargrove." Jasmine put all the disdain she could manage into the two words, raising her hand to wipe the disgusting wetness from her mouth.

"I thought you felt the same for me as I do for you, Jasmine." He tried once again to pull her close.

This time she was prepared. She stiffened her arms and shook her head. "I hold you in high esteem. . .but I'm not some fancy woman you met in a tavern."

"Of course not." He dropped his grip on her and hung his head. "Don't you know how I feel about you? Don't you know how your beauty—your radiant innocence—drives me mad? 'Come live with me and be my love, And we will all the pleasures prove.'"

Christopher Marlowe's poem was one she had loved as a young girl, thinking it the height of romance. But he needed to understand that she wasn't about to let him ruin her.

Borrowing from the same poem, she answered him. "'I don't need beds of roses or a cap and kirtle.'" With her nose in the air, she pushed past him to the stage door. Fame was awaiting her.

"Take your place upstage, Lady Montague." Mr. Easley's words were accompanied with a lift of his chin.

She scampered toward the back of the stage, thankful that she knew enough to understand his direction. Two other actors were center stage after the fight scene between the two families. Listening intently, she stepped forward as Benvolio ended his speech. Her heart pounded. "O, where is Romeo? Saw you him today? Right glad I am he was not at this fray." The words flowed out of her mouth with exactly the right emphasis and tone.

As Benvolio answered her question, a movement to her right caught her attention. Vance blew her a kiss just before he stepped onto the stage.

A moment more, and it was over. Lord Montague called her away, and they walked off the stage. "Well done." The older man, Stan Mitchum, one of the stock actors who played the smaller parts, sent her a smile. "You're a natural, honey."

The praise made her glow. Clem found her and dragged her back to the prop room so her costume could be altered. Then it was time to grab a bite to eat and get dressed for the performance.

As soon as the farce ended, Jasmine took her place behind the curtain. The chorus—two women—were already on stage and would soon introduce the audience to the blood feud between the Montagues and the Capulets. Miss Barlow, dressed in the resplendent gold ball gown with its newly attached flounce, stood nearby.

Between them, the men rushed forward, their swords raised. It seemed only a moment later that Lord Montague whisked her onto the stage. She faltered for a moment when she saw the number of people in the audience. It seemed every seat was taken. Mesmerized by the reality, she missed her cue and silence filled the stage.

"Hold me not," Lord Montague shook the arm that she had barely managed to retain her hold on. "Let me go."

Jasmine's gasp was loud as she realized what had happened. "Thou shalt not stir a foot to seek a foe." At least her gasp fit the part of a distressed Lady Montague concerned for her husband's welfare.

The scene played out without further incident. Vance, looking handsome in a crimson doublet and hose, winked at her as he returned to the stage.

She was in heaven as she exited and took the opportunity to glance once more toward the audience. What she saw made her heart drop to her toes. Jane Baxter, Camellia's best friend from the finishing school in New Orleans, was seated in the front row.

Had Camellia's friend recognized her? Jasmine tried to tell herself it wasn't possible. The heavy stage paint they wore disguised her features. And Jane wouldn't expect to see her here. As Jasmine stripped off her costume and returned to helping Clem with the other actors' costume changes, she decided Jane could not have recognized her. She was safe for now.

"What did you think?" Clem's curious voice gave Jasmine something else to concentrate on besides her fears.

"It was wonderful. I was born to be an actress. It was a small part, but the audience liked me."

"I heard you flubbed your first line." Miss Fenwick appeared in the doorway. "Do you have my green dress ready?"

Clem shook her head. "It'll be in your room by the third act."

"I'll not be pushed aside for Vance's latest trinket." Miss Fenwick glared in Jasmine's direction. "If she can't have my clothes ready on time, she'll have to give up acting. She wasn't hired for that purpose anyway."

"If you would stay away from those French pastries, we wouldn't have to keep letting out your dress." Clem shook a finger at the actress. "Go away before I tell Mrs. Easley that Jasmine should study for your role."

Miss Fenwick's mouth opened and closed several times, but apparently she didn't know what to say unless the words were scripted for her. Her face turned an ugly shade of red, and she turned on her heel.

Jasmine met Clem's gaze, and a giggle forced its way past her throat. Soon they were both laughing, tears streaming from their eyes.

Clem sobered first. "We'd better get back to work, or Miss Angelica Fenwick will have a real reason to complain. I don't want to lose the best friend I've had in years."

Grabbing her needle and scissors, Jasmine nodded and looked around at the pile of material. "How long will we stay in Vicksburg?"

"We have to perform in Memphis on Thursday, so we'll probably leave tomorrow after the early show."

Jasmine was relieved. Perhaps Jane had not recognized her tonight, but if she ran into the woman in town or if Jane attended another performance, she would be caught. The sooner the *Ophelia* left Vicksburg, the more likely she could remain hidden.

Chapter Twenty-one

"Did you see any of their faces, Mr. Baxter?" David asked the bank manager, even though he thought he already knew the answer.

A slight man with hair as white as a field of ripe cotton, Mr. Harold Baxter exuded an air of quiet competence. His hair must have grayed prematurely, because he looked only a few years older than David. He carried himself well in spite of the empty sleeve of his jacket. David wondered if he had lost his arm during the war and which side he might have fought for.

"Please call me Harry. That's what everyone around here calls me. Some of my fellow employees don't even know that my given name is Harold."

"All right, Harry. Now, about their faces?"

"The lower parts were hidden behind handkerchiefs." Harry frowned. "But they seemed to know exactly where to go, as if they already knew the layout of the bank."

"We think they spend some time in town, slipping in and out of the area while they learn what they need to know. Hours of operation, security, and the number of employees to name a few."

"You think I've seen them before?"

"It's quite likely." It was the only theory David could imagine. The bank robberies were too smooth. He had first believed they might have inside help from someone who worked for the bank, but these robbers had struck banks from Chicago to New Orleans. No one could have acquaintances associated with that many banks. What was the connection? The elusive "Ophelia" was the most obvious answer. He closed his notebook and stood. "Please think about the past few days carefully. Any new customers? Or perhaps your tellers might remember someone who has been hanging out in your lobby for the last week or so. Any little detail to help me catch these men."

"I'll be glad to, Detective." The other man stood and walked around his desk. "I want you to catch those scoundrels as much as you do."

"Thank you." He hesitated before going to the door. "I do have something else I wanted to mention to you, Harry. It's about your wife, Jane, and a friend of hers."

"Oh?"

David cleared his throat. "Yes. Camellia Thornton is a close friend of mine, and she was concerned about you and Jane when she learned of the bank robbery. I wish you would ask your wife to send her a note. I would send word, but I know she'll want to hear confirmation directly from Mrs. Baxter."

"You're a friend of Camellia's?" Baxter's face was warmer than it had been during their interview. "I insist you join us for dinner this evening. Jane will skin me alive if she discovers a friend of her old schoolmate is eating alone."

"Thank you, but I'm afraid I have work to do."

"I understand that, but you must find time to eat. . .if not tonight then another evening." Harry clapped him on the shoulder.

Realizing he couldn't refuse without sounding churlish, David inclined his head. "Thank you, another night would be better."

"Good. How about this Thursday? That should give you time to wrap up the most pressing of your business."

After receiving directions to the Baxters' home, David left. He had a lot of ground to cover.

Over the next several days, David met with the police, who had no additional information, and spent hours interviewing the proprietors and patrons of businesses close to the bank. No one had heard of Ophelia, and no one had noticed any strangers hanging about. How did these men manage to hide in plain sight? What magic did they use to pass freely through the town and escape notice? It was frustrating to find no evidence. . .again.

David was beginning to doubt his ability as a detective. He should be able to pick up the trail of at least one of them. So far, the only mistake they'd made was letting Charlie Petrie get caught. And they'd remedied that by killing him.

On Thursday evening, he returned to the hotel, pulling his extra coat from his bag and smoothing it with a damp cloth. He hoped it would pass muster tonight. Jane and her husband were obviously as wealthy as Jasmine's family.

Since the address was not too far from the hotel, he decided to walk. David wanted to turn away when he arrived at the Baxters' home, a graceful three-story mansion that was the largest house on the street. But it was too late. David stiffened his shoulders and climbed the front steps. The porch provided a panoramic view of the Mississippi River, and a cool, steady breeze teased his coattails as he waited at the front door.

A butler ushered him inside, took his card, and guided him to the main parlor. "Detective David Foster."

After the announcement, the man stood aside, and David entered the parlor. The room looked like a garden brought indoors. Images of roses graced the wallpaper, the curtains, and the rug at his feet. A large vase on the table in the center of the room was filled with fresh roses, their fragrance filling the air.

He saw Harry first, and then his wife—a tall, slender woman with hair as red as the roses she apparently loved. She walked toward him, a welcoming smile on her face. "Detective Foster, it's a pleasure to meet you."

David tried to imagine this beauty and Camellia as friends. They must have turned every male head in New Orleans. He bowed over her hand. "The pleasure is mine, Mrs. Baxter."

"Please, call me Jane." She smiled up at him. "I'm anxious to hear news of Camellia. How is her little girl doing? And Jonah? You must tell me everything."

They moved into the dining room, and David found himself comfortable with his gracious hosts. After regaling the couple with news from Les Fleurs, their conversation turned to the dismal economy and President Grant's latest scandal.

"Speaking of scandals, I suppose Camellia and Lily are quite upset that Jasmine is working as an actress."

David leaned forward, his gaze sharpening at Jane's comment. He couldn't believe news of the runaway had fallen into his lap like an overripe plum. "You've seen Jasmine here in Vicksburg?"

Jane sipped from her glass of lemonade before answering. "I didn't recognize her at first, but I know it was Jasmine. Those eyes of hers are so distinctive, almost purple in color. I always told Camellia her name should be Violet or maybe Iris."

"Where did you see her?"

Jane looked a little surprised at his intensity. "She was on one of those showboats."

He should have known. If not for his concern over the bank robberies, he might have even thought of looking for her on a showboat. It was an easy way for her to reach her destination, earn some money, and gain experience. Jasmine might be selfish and stubborn, but no one could accuse her of being dimwitted. "Camellia's been frantic since she disappeared from Les Fleurs a few days ago. I'd like to find her and send her back home. What was the name of the showboat?"

"It had one of those Greek-sounding names. Do you remember, Harry? Was it Portia?"

"That doesn't sound quite right." Her husband pushed back from the table. "I think I kept a playbill. Would you like to see it?"

"Yes." David could hardly believe he had found Jasmine. At least once he sent her home he could concentrate on his real job.

Harry returned with the gaudy advertisement in his hand.

As soon as David saw the name at the top, his heart clenched. He took the paper in his hand and stared down at it, his mind spinning. He couldn't believe it. Jasmine had taken a job on a ship called the *Ophelia*. Another name in bold typeface drew his attention, and the final piece of the puzzle fell in place. *Vance Hargrove.* He was the reason Jasmine had gotten a position on the showboat. And he was the common link for all of the bank robberies as well. "May I keep this?"

Both Baxters nodded.

David knew he had to find the boat right away. Explaining the gravity of the situation, he took his leave of them and half-ran, half-walked back to the waterfront. A city of boats rested there, some tied to the piers while others were roped together, forming floating islands. Dogged determination pushed him from deck to deck, posing as the concerned brother of a runaway as he made his inquiries. Finally he found a captain who knew the *Ophelia*.

"She left outa' here a few days back." The swarthy man scratched his beard. "I heard tell they was going to Memphis for a week or so, and then on to St. Louis, mebbe all the way to Chicago."

David's jaw clenched so hard he thought his teeth might break. "You're sure?"

The captain nodded. "I hope you find your sister."

"I will." He stomped away, his mind boiling. Should he send a message to Camellia and Jonah? What if Jasmine was no longer with the *Ophelia* by the time he caught up with the boat? He didn't want to raise their hopes at this point and have to disappoint them later. It would be better to wait. By this time tomorrow night he would have his hands on her. He would read her the riot act. . .as soon as he was certain she was okay. Then he would send her home and concentrate on his real job of collaring criminals.

≈❧

David wasted no time in locating the *Ophelia* as soon as he arrived in Memphis. A performance was about to begin, so he decided the easiest way to gain entry was as a theatergoer. He smiled at the lady who sold him a ticket and entered the room that held the theater. Impressed by the number of people in the audience, he chose a seat toward the back and looked at the new playbill in his hand.

Her name jumped out at him. The part of the nurse was being played by none other than Jasmine Anderson. She hadn't even had the sense to choose a pseudonym. Jane Baxter had said Jasmine was playing a minor part, but that must have changed. Was her rapid rise due to her talent? He hoped that was the reason. He ground his teeth at the idea that Vance Hargrove might use his influence on her behalf for his own dissolute purposes.

He ought to march himself to the crew quarters and confront Jasmine right now. But something held him back. What was it? He couldn't be reluctant to end her foolishness—her attempt to earn fame and fortune. Jasmine should be back at Les Fleurs dancing with men from her social circle, not consorting with philanderers and loose women. She should be surrounded by the protection of her sisters and extended family. Jasmine might not—would not—agree, but only because the little minx was as blind to the dangers around her as a field mouse being stalked by an owl.

Fish Out of Water, the first offering, was an uncomplicated farce about a series of misunderstandings between a couple that led to all sorts of trouble, including infidelity.

David found himself embarrassed by the sexual innuendos. This was exactly why working in the theater was not something an innocent girl should do. Jasmine probably didn't even understand the worst of the bawdy jokes, but it wouldn't be long before some helpful soul explained them to her.

He crossed his arms over his chest when the farce ended with much laughter and applause. David was growing increasingly anxious for the entertainment to end so he could get to Jasmine and get her out of here.

After the stage was reset, the curtain rose once more, and the two-woman chorus began telling the audience of the tragic events about to unfold in front of them. He recognized Jasmine the moment she stepped on the stage, even though she was playing the part of a much older woman. It was ludicrous. Tabitha Barlow might have been hired to play the part of Juliet, but she was much too mature. The drama would be more believable if she and Jasmine switched parts.

He had to admit, though, that Jasmine had talent. She played the part with understanding and energy. Shakespeare had written the role as comic relief, and Jasmine brought laughter to the audience with her facial expressions and gestures, even during heartrending scenes of the tragedy.

At the end of the play, David leaped to his feet, adding his applause to that of the rest of the crowd around him. A part of him wished it was possible for Jasmine to be an actress on the scale she dreamed of. God had obviously showered her with talent. But she needed a way to use her abilities in an uplifting, moral manner. If she remained a part of this world, she would lose the very spark that made her stand out from the other actors in the production.

He fought his way against the crowd and managed to reach the edge of the stage. Where would Jasmine be? Eating? Sleeping? Flirting with Hargrove? He thrust the curtains out of his way and found a door leading to a different part of the barge. As he reached for the handle, the door opened toward him, and two young women carrying mops stepped through. The first was a brunette, a girl he didn't recognize.

David forgot all about her when the second female gasped and let her mop fall. Jasmine looked like a startled fawn. He reached out and caught her arm before she could bolt. "What a surprise to find you here."

"Let go of my friend." The other girl rapped his knuckles with the handle of her mop. "I'll scream for help."

He winced but kept his grip on Jasmine. She would not escape so easily.

"Camellia must have sent you to track me down."

The other girl's mouth snapped shut at Jasmine's accusation.

David couldn't let her reveal his true identity. "Who better than your brother?"

"Well, you can just go back home to Natchez and tell Camellia—and Lily, too—that I'm fine. In fact, I'm more than fine. I've found a job and several friends. People who understand me and share the same interests. None of you needs to worry about me anymore."

"He's your brother?" The other girl picked up Jasmine's mop and handed it back to her.

His glare warned Jasmine to agree. She was the one who had first claimed he was a brother to her, after all. And it gave him the perfect cover story.

After a moment she nodded. "Would you give us a few minutes, Clem?"

"Ummm, o–kay." Clem emphasized the last syllable, infusing it with a great deal of curiosity. She must be an actress, too.

David dropped his hold on Jasmine's arm as soon as they were alone. "How soon can you be packed?"

"Packed?" She tossed her head like a restive horse. "Why should I pack? I'm not leaving. You are."

"Don't be ridiculous. You can't stay here."

"Yes, I can."

David gave her another warning glare. "I don't intend to argue with you. This boat is at best inappropriate for a lady with even the barest of morals; at worst it's dangerous."

"What on earth are you talking about?"

He glanced around to make sure no one lurked in the large room. "I have reason to believe that this showboat is involved in the bank robberies I'm investigating."

"That's ridiculous."

"No, it's not. In fact, it makes a great deal of sense. Before he was murdered, one of the robbers I was working with managed to tell me one word—*Ophelia*."

He saw the gooseflesh prickling her arms. Good. Jasmine needed to realize how much danger she was in.

"What makes you think he was referring to this *Ophelia*? There must be dozens of other reasons he would mention a woman's name.

Or you might have misunderstood him." Her eyes widened. "Or maybe he lied to you. He was a thief, wasn't he?"

"He wouldn't have any reason to lie when he knew he was dying, and I've looked for any other connection. The *Ophelia* was in New Orleans during the robbery there, and in Vicksburg. It wouldn't surprise me at all if a bank in Memphis was the next target."

"So were dozens of other boats."

He should have known Jasmine would argue. She had never seen him as someone deserving respect.

The stage door creaked open behind them. "Jasmine? Clem sent me to check on—" Vance Hargrove stopped short as he stepped onto the stage. "Mr. Anderson. What brings you to Memphis?"

"I'm retrieving my sister."

Hargrove frowned at Jasmine. "I thought you said your family agreed for you to come."

David would have laughed if he hadn't been so exasperated at this further evidence of Jasmine's duplicity. "She didn't bother to ask permission."

"I didn't need to." Jasmine moved toward the other man. "I'm an adult. In spite of my brother's threats, I have every right to stay with you."

David wanted to step between them. He wouldn't be surprised if steam started pouring from his ears. Jasmine was not going to stay on the *Ophelia*, no matter what she thought. "You can't prevent my putting you on the next boat heading to Natchez with instructions to deliver you to Les Fleurs."

"Maybe not, but it won't matter. I'll run away again as soon as Camellia's back is turned. I've tasted freedom now, and I refuse to accept a life of bondage any longer."

He wanted to remove Vance's smirk by fastening a set of handcuffs around his wrists. But he couldn't let himself be distracted by pleasant fantasies. "Jasmine, I don't care if you have to spend the rest of your days locked in your bedroom, you're not staying here."

"The thing I don't understand is how your brother figured out you're on the *Ophelia* if your family didn't know."

Feeling like he'd been doused with a bucket of cold water, David shut his mouth at the suspicious words.

"I think I know what must have happened." Jasmine stepped into the uneasy silence. "Do you remember my hesitation the first time I took the stage?"

Hargrove turned his suspicious gaze toward her.

"Jane Baxter was in the audience. She lives in Vicksburg, but she's my—our—sister Camellia's best friend."

"Yes, she's the one who put me on your trail." Perhaps Jasmine would make a better detective than he did. Her story was convincing and stayed close enough to the truth that neither of them would be tripped up by contradictory details. He allowed a tight smile to loosen his mouth. "I promised Camellia I'd stop you from ruining your life, and I'm going to keep my promise."

"Wait, wait, wait." Vance took a step away from Jasmine and snapped his fingers.

David raised an eyebrow, wondering what Vance was going to say next. Was the man going to accuse him of an ulterior motive?

"I have the perfect answer to satisfy both of you. Your brother is worried about your reputation, and you're determined to stay on board because this is your dream, right?" Hargrove turned to him. "Do you have to return to Mississippi right away?"

David shook his head. He thought he might be getting an inkling of the other man's train of thought. "The rest of the family will get along fine without me for a while."

"Our tugboat captain is always losing his hands to more lucrative jobs, and you're bound to have some experience since you come from a riverboat family. You can work there and keep an eye on your sister until you're convinced she's safe with us." Hargrove beamed at both of them, expecting compliments on his brilliance.

"I don't think that's a good idea." Jasmine glared at David. "Having my *brother* close by is bound to inhibit my performances."

"Perfect. I'll do it." David grinned at her stormy expression. He offered a hand to the actor. "You've solved everything."

Jasmine stomped away from them, her outrage plain in every step. But David was pleased. He could nose around and gather more evidence before making arrests, starting with the self-satisfied Hargrove. And he could make sure Jasmine was safe. . .even if he had to threaten her with an arrest for conspiracy.

Chapter Twenty-two

Clem pushed Jasmine's arm up until it was parallel to the floor. "Be still or I won't be able to get your measurements right."

Jasmine didn't mean to drop her arm, but she was having a hard time with her concentration. David had sent a telegram to Camellia this morning and returned after breakfast with the information that they would be having dinner with Eli and Renée Thornton this evening. Had a man ever been more high-handed? If he hadn't been a longtime family friend, she wouldn't put up with his arrogance.

"I'm glad your brother got a job on the *Miss Polly*." Clem shoved a pin through the navy-blue material of the dress.

"Why?" Jasmine couldn't believe her friend was taking his side over hers. Did Clem want her to be bundled back to Mississippi?

"He's...he's single, isn't he?"

Jasmine's arm dropped, and a dozen pins pricked her side. "Ow."

"I told you to stand still."

"I know." She raised her arm again. "Please don't tell me you're developing an interest in David."

"He is handsome." Clem's face suffused with color. "And you can tell he's honorable by the way he treats all the women on board, even Miss Barlow and Miss Fenwick."

"He's not honorable. He's overbearing and egotistical. And a stick in the mud."

"He is not. You don't know how lucky you are to have a brother who loves you enough to come looking for you." Clem's sigh lingered in the quiet room. "It's so romantic."

David's popularity on the *Ophelia* amazed her. What did these women see in him? He had been here only a little more than twelve hours, and he was already the darling of every woman from Miss Barlow to the cook. He was David—solid, practical, bossy David. "Believe me, Clem. He doesn't have a romantic bone in his body."

Clem snorted her disbelief. "You can get down now."

Jasmine stepped off the stool.

"You only think he's romantic because you don't know my. . .brother." She couldn't help the waspish tone. Everything had gotten so mixed up. Convincing the others to ignore him was not getting her anywhere. Even the men seemed drawn to him. Mr. Easley had better watch out, or he might find himself replaced by her "brother."

She could only think of one way to get rid of him—tell everyone that he was a Pinkerton detective. But she couldn't betray him. She couldn't expose his real reason for taking the position on their tugboat, even though she knew David was wrong about the *Ophelia*'s connection to the bank robberies. She was as certain of that as she was her own name. Absolutely, positively certain.

The actors on board the showboat had their weaknesses, but not a one of them was evil. Last night and again at breakfast this morning, she found herself looking for something sinister in the people around her. But it was ridiculous. From the gruff Mr. Easley to sweet Clem, each and every one of the people on this boat was focused on providing quality entertainment. Besides, the *Ophelia* was making good money. Why would someone want to risk a lucrative income on a hanging offense?

Clem helped her pull the dress over her head. "I know I'm being foolish. No one as kind and handsome as your brother would ever look at someone like me."

Jasmine emerged from the dress with a gasp. "Don't you ever say anything like that again. Don't even think it. You're talented and beautiful and very special. You're worth a dozen Davids."

"Me? I'm just a farm girl who didn't want to spend her life plucking chickens and milking cows." Clem smoothed her hand over the material of the dress. "I once got a switching because I cut up Ma's curtains to make a dress for wearing to church on Easter Sunday."

Jasmine had been in trouble plenty of times, but Lily had never spanked her. "She must have been very upset."

"Especially when it turned out the dress I made ended about halfway between my knees and my ankles."

The picture that formed in her mind made Jasmine giggle. "What did you wear to church?"

"The same old dress I'd been wearing all year long. Ma made me cut my curtain dress into squares for making a quilt. It was pretty, but not nearly as pretty as the dress I'd dreamed of wearing." Clem's giggle joined hers.

Their shared laughter restored the camaraderie between them. Jasmine began picking up the scraps from the floor when an idea came to her. David had once told her he conducted interviews to get information. An interview was nothing but a bunch of questions, wasn't it? Maybe she could conduct her own interviews and prove to him that his suspicions were unfounded.

"Where was your parents' farm?"

"A small town in Ohio. The name wouldn't mean anything to you."

Jasmine nodded. This interview stuff was easy. "How long have you been on the *Ophelia*?"

"Only a year."

"What made you look for a job here?"

Clem got out her thread and picked up the dress. "You sure are curious this afternoon. Are you checking to see if I would be an acceptable wife for your brother?"

Feeling like she'd fetched upon a hidden snag, Jasmine blinked. "Of course not. I just thought I'd find out more about you. . .since we're friends and all."

The needle flashed up and down in quick motions. "I guess that makes sense. But sometimes people don't want to be asked about their pasts. Some might think you were being nosy or that you were trying to figure out their weaknesses."

So much for her future as a detective. Jasmine wondered how David managed to avoid raising people's suspicions. Especially people who had a reason to hide something from a lawman.

"I'm sorry. I was just interested in you, Clem. Will you forgive me for being a bother?"

"You're not a bother." Clem pulled on a seam to check its strength. "I just don't want you to make enemies here. You're pretty and talented, which is sure to make all the women jealous. Miss Fenwick in particular. Didn't I tell you earlier that she's the type to scratch your eyes out? If you go asking her questions, she may push you overboard."

"I'll remember that." Jasmine checked her appearance in the full-length mirror attached to one of the walls in the dressing room. "Mr. Easley called a rehearsal this morning. If you're done with me for now, I'll go read over my lines."

"Don't leave right away." Clem looked up. "Tell me more about your brother."

"I. . .I can't." She escaped before Clem could continue asking her about things she didn't want to answer. Her interrogation skills would have to improve if she was going to help solve David's case and get him out of her way.

❧

"Your garden is so beautiful, Renée." Jasmine smiled at the petite woman. "I don't know how you have time to tend it while taking care of your houseful of men."

She glanced up at the crescent moon and starlit sky above them, glad Renée had offered to walk through her flower garden instead of sitting in the drawing room while the men finished their dinner. Iona, Brandon's fiancée, had remained inside, concerned that the night air and pollen would give her a headache.

Renée settled her shawl around her shoulders. "It does take some time in the spring, but I think it's worth the effort."

"I never enjoyed the work, but the result you've achieved is breathtaking." Yellow daisies, pink and lavender dahlias, and lacy purple carnations swayed gently in the evening breeze. Jasmine breathed deeply, enjoying the fragrances almost as much as the carpet of blooms surrounding them.

"Your namesake is growing over here." Renée led her to a trellis in one corner of the garden. Delicate white blossoms peeked out from between velvety green leaves. She plucked a couple of blooms and tucked them into Jasmine's hair.

The sweet scent of the flowers brought a smile to her lips. "Thank you."

"It's my pleasure." Renée put her arm around Jasmine's waist. "I've been praying for your safe return ever since Lily and Blake told us you went missing."

Why did she have to bring that up? Jasmine pulled away from Renée's arm. She didn't want another homily about setting out on her own. Why didn't anyone understand her? All during dinner, Renée and Eli's sons had peppered her with questions about the showboat. She had enjoyed the attention and the admiration.

"I know you think you're a grown woman, Jasmine, but in Lily's mind you'll always be a little girl who needs her guidance. I feel the same way about my boys. My eyes can see that they're young men, but my heart knows how vulnerable they are, how much they still have to learn."

"Brandon's about to get married and start a family of his own." Jasmine liked Iona—a pretty girl from Memphis with a tinkling laugh and big brown eyes that seemed locked on her fiancé. "Surely you don't still see him as a child."

Renée pinched a dead bloom from the top of a rose bush. "But I do, dear. I know how quickly he can forget the lessons his father and I have tried to instill in him. Whenever I look at my sons, I think of

Jesus' parable of the sower. The dangers of this world are so pervasive."

Jasmine wanted to scoff, but the serious expression on the other woman's face warned her to remain quiet.

Renée swept her hand out to indicate the plants around them. "I've seen firsthand how easily seeds can be destroyed. Birds, heat, weeds, all three of the examples Jesus talked about have threatened my flowers."

The problem with Renée's comparison was evident to Jasmine. She might be named after a flower, but she was a person. She had the sense to stay out of the sunlight in the heat of summer, and neither birds nor weeds were a threat to her.

"It's only through watchful tending and God's provision that these plants reach maturity. Even then they can be destroyed if some insect or blight gains entry. That's how Satan operates. He's always quick to attack unwary souls. Lily wants you to thrive in the garden of life, but even more than that, she wants to make sure you follow the path God set out for you."

That's what Jasmine was trying to do. If everyone would leave her be. Their problem was not being able to see that her path was not a traditional one. She had so much to offer the world, much more than the women who were tied down with husbands and households.

Remington opened the door and ran to them, his impulsiveness propelling him forward. "Can I come to the showboat to see you acting?"

Renée shook her head. "I don't know if that's a good idea. We don't want to make Jasmine nervous."

"Don't worry. I've had a lot of practice performing for people I know. It will probably make things even easier."

Remington begged his mother to attend as they walked back to the house. Cameron was talking to David and his father in one corner of the parlor while Brandon and Iona had their heads together, intent on the magazine she held.

"We'll ask your father what he thinks." Renée pulled off her shawl and laid it on the back of the sofa.

"Pa, can we go see Jasmine tomorrow?" Remington was as tenacious as a bull terrier.

Following in his wake, Jasmine wondered if the Thorntons' youngest son would choose a path his parents approved of. Both Brandon and Cameron seemed more serious, more interested in working in the family business. But Remington was different. Perhaps he would like to join her in the theater. He was only sixteen now. By the time he was old enough to leave home, she would be established enough to give him a helping hand.

"What did your mother say?" Eli queried.

"To ask you."

Jasmine couldn't help smiling at Remington's hopeful expression. "I wish you would. I can speak to the manager about holding five seats for you."

"Make it six." Eli pointed his chin toward his oldest son. "They're inseparable these days."

The engaged couple were too engrossed in each other to realize they were being discussed.

As she nodded agreement, David cleared his throat. "I imagine we need to get back. You need a good night's sleep, and I am supposed to tend the boiler in a little while."

Renée's mouth turned down. "Must you go so soon?"

"I'm afraid so."

Jasmine would have disagreed, but she had to admit she was tired. Rehearsals, fittings, and two performances had made the day long. She wasn't sleeping well, either, worried about David dragging her back to Les Fleurs. The idea of resting her head on a soft pillow was so appealing that the sudden need to yawn made her eyes water. "I suppose we should." She had the satisfaction of seeing surprise in David's green gaze. Maybe that would teach him that he didn't know her as well as he thought.

They thanked the family for inviting them, even managing to pull Brandon away from his love long enough to say good-bye.

Eli walked them to the front door. "Are you sure you don't want to take our carriage back to the boat?"

Of course David answered for both of them, claiming the evening too perfect for being cooped up in a carriage. It was a good thing she didn't mind the walk. Raising her chin, Jasmine marched down the stairs without waiting for his escort.

He caught up with her in a few steps, of course, reaching for her arm. Jasmine tried to pull free of him, but his grip was too strong. Fine. He might be able to compel her to walk beside him, but he couldn't make her talk to him.

"It's a nice evening."

She ignored his puny attempt at conversation.

"I thought Brandon's fiancée was a sweet girl."

Jasmine kept her lips pressed tight. A nearby street lamp showed her the frown on his face.

"Do you hate me that much?"

His question hit her with the power of a lightning bolt. "I don't hate you."

"That's a relief." David pushed back his hat and wiped his brow.

He could be so silly at times. And his highhandedness, his failure to consult her most of the time, proved that he lied. "You don't really care what I think."

David stopped walking, forcing her to halt or risk straining her arm. "I care far too much about your feelings."

"You have hidden talents, Mr. Foster. You may earn a role in our next production."

"Don't call me that. Remember that everyone on the *Ophelia* thinks we're siblings."

She wrinkled her nose at him. "That wasn't my idea. I still don't understand why you introduced yourself as my brother back in New Orleans."

His laugh was closer to a dog's bark than a sound of amusement. Shaking his head, he resumed walking. "Did you enjoy dinner?"

"Yes, more than I thought I would. And she is a sweet girl."

It seemed to take him a minute before realizing she was referring to his earlier statement. "What was her name again?"

"Iona Woods." She choked back a giggle. What had possessed her parents to choose such a name for their daughter?

David's laugh sounded more natural this time. "I suppose it's better than naming her Piney."

Piney Woods. She doubled over with laughter. The sound of their merriment blended together like a harmonious chord, and suddenly she was once again the barefoot girl who loved running across the deck of the *Water Lily*. Jasmine turned toward him like she would have done back then, putting her hands on his shoulders as she allowed free rein to her mirth.

It felt natural when his arms went around her, held her close to his chest. For a moment no warning bells sounded in her mind, and when they did she found them easy to ignore. This was David after all, not some stranger.

His heartbeat thumped against her cheek even as his laughter began to lessen. She knew she should straighten, but it felt so good to be this near to him. David wasn't as tall as Vance, and he didn't wear a cologne to compete with the earthy, masculine scent that was uniquely his.

"Jasmine?" David's tentative voice made her tilt her head back.

The walls between them fell with the suddenness of Jericho's fortifications. The yearning look in his face touched her heart in a place so deep that it almost hurt. She caught her breath and watched as his eyelids drooped low, hiding half of his serious green gaze. On some level she knew he was going to kiss her. She wanted it, wanted to feel his lips on hers, wanted to draw even closer.

Her blood thickened, slowing her heart and making her ears ring. When his hooded gaze dropped to her mouth, she thought she might die. Yet how could she die when every inch of her was alive in a way it never had been before.

One of her hands reached up and pulled his head lower, throwing caution and sense to the wind. His lips captured hers, and she felt the earth shake below her feet. Joy filled her as they clung together. It was heady, exciting. . .and absolutely impossible.

The warning bells clanged loud and deep. What was she doing? This would never work. It was all wrong. Her hands pushed against his shoulders. "Stop."

"Jasmine."

"Don't ever touch me again." She spat the words at him, picked up her skirts, and started running. She didn't stop until she reached the *Ophelia*. But even when she found her room and readied for bed, her mind still ran in directions she dared not follow.

Chapter Twenty-three

David wasn't at breakfast the next morning. After the third female asked her where he was, Jasmine threw up her hands and left the dining hall. *Am I my brother's keeper?*

Vance followed her into the hallway. "I missed seeing you after the performance last night."

Jasmine stopped walking and pinned a smile to her face. At least Vance wouldn't want to know where David was. "I had to go to dinner with some family friends."

"Should I be jealous?" Vance put his hand on the wall above her right shoulder.

She raised her left shoulder in a shrug. "They're coming to the boat this afternoon. You can see for yourself."

"Something's different about you today." He put a finger under her chin and tilted it upward, studying her face.

Jasmine pulled her head back, banging it on the wall behind her. "I don't know what you're talking about."

"Vance, leave the girl alone and take this money to the bank. You know what we need." Mr. Easley's voice brought scalding hot blood into Jasmine's cheeks.

"I have to go." She ducked under Vance's arm and ran to her room. Closing the door with a snap, she leaned against it and concentrated on breathing deeply. Rubbing the back of her head, she wondered what Vance had seen in her. Something had changed inside her, but was it obvious on the outside, too?

The question that had burned in her mind last night returned. Why had David's kiss been so devastating? The difference between his kiss and Vance's attempt was like the difference between the painting inside the Sistine Chapel and the scribbles of a child. Vance's touch had been repugnant, nasty, and wet. With David she had felt as though their souls touched, as though their hearts had been soldered together.

Was this one of the assaults Renée had tried to warn her about last night? Would her attraction to David destroy the seed of her talent? Her chin hardened. She wouldn't allow it. With a nod of her head, she straightened and opened the door. She would not be distracted.

After the third time she had to be cued for her next line, Jasmine realized it would take more than determination to overcome the effect of the previous night. Tears of hopelessness threatened to spill from her eyes.

"We need a break." Miss Barlow's voice rang out across the theater. The manager checked his pocket watch. "Be back in thirty minutes."

Miss Barlow grabbed her hand. "Come with me."

Long nails dug into her arm, but Jasmine was too downhearted to complain. She didn't even pay any attention when the older woman led her down a separate passage. But when Miss Barlow dropped her hand and opened the door to her dressing suite, Jasmine balked.

"Get in here."

Jasmine crossed the threshold, her eyes wide. The large room was filled with open trunks overhung by skirts, blouses, dressing gowns, and silk chemises. Feather boas in one corner of the room looked like a litter of kittens, and shoes in all colors of the rainbow were scattered across the floor like autumn leaves.

Miss Barlow ignored the chaos, picking her way to a slipper chair and sitting. "What's wrong with you?"

"I don't... I—"

A snort interrupted her. "I thought you were made of stronger stuff than this. You've only been acting for a few weeks, but everyone who sees you knows you're talented. You have something special, something few people—even fewer ladies—have."

The color rushed upward again. "Thank you."

"I invited you to my room so we can talk frankly, just the two of us." Miss Barlow settled back against her chair. "You and I have many things in common. I was about the same age as you when I first started."

Jasmine wished she could sit down, but she didn't want to appear too forward by either perching on the edge of Tabitha's bed or sitting at her dressing table.

"In some ways those days seem like yesterday. But then I look in the mirror and I realize how long it's been—almost two decades. I wanted to be rich and famous. I wanted to read about my performances in the newspaper. I dreamed of the whole world knowing my name, of my photograph being the most recognizable in this country, in the whole world."

"But you *are* famous." Jasmine glanced at all the clothes around them. "And rich."

"Pah, this is nothing. And yet it's all I have." The other woman stood up and kicked a shoe out of her way. Reaching inside one of the trunks, she grabbed up a skirt. "I wore this on a stage in Virginia the day before the war began. Those were hard days. Never knowing when one army or the other might lock us away as spies." A harsh laugh came from her throat, and she tossed the skirt down. "Of course I did my fair share of passing along information on troops and plans. All for naught."

Jasmine didn't know what to say. Miss Barlow had been a spy? The very thought of doing something so dangerous made her heart trip.

"That's all ancient history now." Miss Barlow uncovered a wooden chair and pointed her finger at it. "Sit."

As soon as Jasmine settled down, the actress returned to her slipper chair. "Even though you're talented, you'll need help to see your dreams come true. Someone who has contacts in the world of the theater. Someone who can get you noticed by the right people. Someone like me."

Shock held her still. Of all the things she thought Miss Barlow might offer her, sponsorship was not one of them. "I don't know what to say."

"Thank you is sufficient."

When Jasmine hesitated, Miss Barlow's eyes narrowed. "Oh, I see how it is. Vance Hargrove has turned your head. You think he's all you need to get ahead."

"I—"

"Do you think you're the first pretty girl he's gotten a job for?" A harsh laugh came from the older woman. "Has he already kissed you?"

Jasmine put her hands to her burning cheeks. How did Miss Barlow know? Was it true that Vance didn't care about her? What about his words this morning?

"No need to answer, I can see it on your face. You're lucky I've decided to take an interest in you. After he is through using you, he'll be on to his next conquest."

She wanted to cover her ears to shut out Miss Barlow's words. Could they be true? Was Vance using her for his own purposes? And what about Miss Barlow? "Why do you want to help me?"

"Good. I knew you were a quick study." Miss Barlow's laugh sounded harsh to Jasmine's ears. "Everyone has their reasons, even me. If you become as famous as I think you will, you'll soon leave this country and become a sensation abroad. That's when I'll want your help. But in all honesty, if I really wanted to help you, Jasmine, I'd tell you to go to your handsome brother and beg him to take you home. Leave before you're as washed up as I am."

"You're not washed up."

Another callous laugh answered her statement. "I'm a long way from the theaters in New York. It's too late for me, but you can still get out."

"I don't want out. I want to see the world."

The other woman leaned forward, her chin propped on her hand.

"The world is not the exciting place you're imagining. It's mostly unwashed farmers, empty promises, and mud."

Jasmine pushed herself up from her chair. She'd heard enough.

"You can run if you want, but I'm trying to give you the benefit of my experience. I've been snubbed by ladies who think they're better than me. I've been pelted with rotten vegetables when the audience decides they're not getting their money's worth. I've had to run for my life with nothing but the clothes on my back."

Picking her way through the mess, Jasmine finally reached the door and jerked it open.

Before she could get out, though, Miss Barlow added her parting shot. "If you don't take my advice to escape, come back to see me. I can help you more than you realize."

The words reverberated in her mind as Jasmine went back to her room. She was embarrassed and upset by the interview with Miss Barlow. It was all too much for her. Everyone wanted something from her, each one demanding something different. She didn't know which way to turn anymore. Feeling dazed and confused, Jasmine threw herself across the bed and let the tears flow. How had everything gone so wrong?

❧

David wondered what he was going to say to Jasmine the next time he saw her. Guilt scoured him every time he thought of the way she'd run from him. He was an idiot. All these years he'd remained silent. And for what? So he could frighten her away when she realized he didn't think of her as a sister?

He saw the Thornton family from a distance as they boarded the showboat. He wished he could visit with them again, but the only time he could search the *Ophelia* was during the two hours that the performance had everyone occupied.

Judicious questioning of the unsuspecting Titus Ross, the tugboat captain, supplied him with the location of the actors' rooms. He started with Vance Hargrove's. A large bed covered with crimson silk sheets made his stomach churn. He had no doubt the actor was a master seducer, although what women saw in him was a mystery to David.

A thorough search of the nooks and crannies turned up no notes or incriminating evidence. David found a strongbox concealed in one of the man's trunks and wished he could open it without alerting Hargrove to the fact that it had been discovered. But the box was too small to hold much. He would have to find a more blatant connection before he risked showing his hand.

Someone walking down the hallway had him diving for cover, but the footsteps passed Hargrove's room. David knew it was time to get out before he had to explain his presence in the actor's quarters.

After listening for other activity, he opened the door an inch. The hall looked empty so he crept out of the room, closed the door without making a noise, and tiptoed back to the room where the props were stored. He could always feign some excuse if he was found there.

"There you are." Clem's voice made him jump. "I wondered if we would see you at all today."

He turned to her and smiled. Of all the people on the *Ophelia*, he prayed Clem was not involved. "I had some business to do in town this morning. Do you ever get off the boat to see some of the countryside?"

Her round face turned pink, and David wished he'd kept his mouth shut. He hadn't meant to give her the idea that he wanted to pursue her. All he wanted to do was eliminate her as a suspect.

"I'd love to see Memphis." Her smile made Clem's face transform from average to pretty.

How was he supposed to ignore such a blatant invitation? He didn't want to hurt her feelings. Maybe she would be satisfied with a quick walk through downtown to see the shops. "We'll have to do something about that."

A sound at the door made David look over his shoulder. His heart dropped to his toes as he recognized coal black hair and dark eyes the color of violets. He'd imagined many scenarios during the long hours of the night, but none of the meetings he'd dreamed of included Jasmine overhearing him making plans with another girl.

"Excuse me, Clem, but I need to talk to my brother before the two of you leave on your outing." Jasmine's voice was cool and calm.

David ran a finger around the collar of his shirt.

"If you can tear yourself away, of course." Her tone suggested he'd be sorry if he didn't.

Clem looked at both of them, muttered some excuse, and left them alone.

Jasmine's eyes burned his skin. "What do you think you're doing?"

Was she jealous? The thought was ludicrous. Wasn't it? Now that he really looked at Jasmine, he realized something he had not before. The skin around her eyes looked bruised. "Have you been crying?"

She shook her head. "I— of course not. It's just been a trying few days. Everything'll be better once you leave."

Here was the condemnation he'd expected. "I'm sorry, Jasmine. I never meant to—"

"Hush." She put a hand to her lips and glanced around. "I don't want to talk about it. We were both carried away by the moment. The sooner we move past what happened, the sooner things can go back to normal."

"If you didn't come to talk about. . .last night, then what?"

"I think I might have a clue."

Fear stole into his veins, pushed his heart all the way up his throat. "You're supposed to leave that to me. I don't want you putting yourself at risk."

Her eyes widened.

He wanted to shake some sense into her. "Don't you realize that some of these people are killers? One of them, maybe someone who works on this boat, stabbed a man in cold blood. Charles Petrie died in front of my eyes. I couldn't bear it if something happened to you."

One of the minor actors stuck his head in the door but backed away when David sent him a warning glare. "Hurry up and tell me what you learned before someone else comes in."

"Mr. Easley sent someone to the bank today."

David waited a minute for her to continue. When she didn't, he sighed, the urge to shake her growing stronger with each passing second. Jasmine couldn't still think this was all play. She had to grasp the gravity of the situation. "What else?"

"Nothing." She closed her mouth, but he could tell she was holding something back.

"Does it have something to do with Vance Hargrove?"

"Yes—well—maybe. But I'm certain he's innocent."

"Tell me, Jasmine, and let me decide who's innocent and who's guilty. That's what I'm trained to do."

She huffed. "It wasn't much really. Only that Mr. Easley gave Vance a huge pile of money and told him to go to the bank. Then he said, 'You know what to do.'"

The way she dropped her voice an octave and thrust out her chest was so cute. Jasmine might be an actress, but no one would confuse her with the two-hundred-pound manager. He wanted to laugh but knew he couldn't. That's what had gotten them in trouble last night. He needed to keep his focus on the case.

"Thanks for keeping your ears open, but I don't want to tell you again to keep your nose out of my business. I don't need your help."

She rolled her eyes, obviously not heeding his warning at all. "Have you made any progress?"

"A little." David didn't want to go into detail. He could imagine her outrage if he told her he'd searched Hargrove's room. "Look, there's something else I want you to think about."

She crossed her hands over her chest, a sure sign she wasn't in a receptive mood.

He had to tell her anyway. "I'm not asking you to ignore Hargrove, but don't let him talk you into doing anything. . .well. . .anything you're uncomfortable with."

Her face hardened. "You mean like letting him kiss me? I hate to tell you, David, but you're too late with your warning. Vance has already kissed me, and it was. . . Well, it was more pleasant than some experiences I've had."

When the import of her words percolated through his brain,

jealousy shut out all other emotions. He wanted to tear Hargrove limb from limb. He wanted to stalk back to the man's room and rip that strongbox open with his bare hands. "If you let him touch you again, I don't care what you say, you're going back to Les Fleurs."

She stepped back a pace. "Are you threatening me? After last night?"

"I'm not the same kind of man as Vance Hargrove."

"No. No, you're not." Her whisper was as sharp as a knife. "You're the kind who'll kiss one girl at night and romance a different one the next day."

"I don't care about your opinion of me, Jasmine Anderson. I've seen enough to know he's the worst kind of hardened rake. If you don't stay away from him and quit asking questions of the actors, I will stop you."

"You don't get to make those kinds of decisions, David Fos—Anderson. And the sooner you figure that out, the better things will be between us." A slow, dangerous smile appeared on her face. "Whether you like it or not, I'm going to help you solve this mystery. You can either work with me or ignore me. But I'm going to do everything I can to get you off of this boat, hopefully before we leave Memphis."

He watched as she spun on her heel and marched toward the door, her nose leading the way. He stomped on the floor once and had the satisfaction of seeing her scamper several feet forward before she realized he was not actually chasing her.

David decided he could keep an eye out for her safety, even though he would rather work alone. Something about the idea of working with her eased the pain in his heart, reminded him of happier times when they'd been as close as his next breath. They had enjoyed each other so much back then. Why had adulthood gotten in their way?

Chapter Twenty-four

"Another bank was robbed yesterday afternoon."

Jasmine caught her breath. "It can't be a coincidence."

David shook his head. He had singled her out right after breakfast, telling her to meet him outside. They left the boat together and walked uphill toward the center of town.

"When did it happen?"

"During the matinee." He pounded a fist against his pants leg. "I can't quite make the connection to the showboat, but I know there has to be one. I know it."

"Don't worry, we'll find it."

"I've searched your boat from stem to stern. Hargrove is the only one with the means and opportunity. He's got to be the one."

Jasmine couldn't help but feel that David was prejudiced against poor Vance because of his relationship with her. "I don't see how he can be. He was right here all afternoon."

"Are you sure he was there the whole time?"

A fresh breeze grazed her neck, and Jasmine wished she could loosen the bun at the back of her head and let her hair fly around her face like she'd done when she was a child. "He's the star, remember? Vance has lines in most of the scenes. He couldn't have left in the middle of the play without it being noticed. It has to be someone else."

"I don't believe it's a coincidence that every town he's been in for the past year has been robbed while he was there. Unless he's some kind of albatross."

She knew better than to believe David was superstitious. He had a stronger relationship with God than she did. He must really be desperate to catch the robbers. "We're supposed to leave for Cairo tomorrow."

He looked off into the distance.

"David, are you listening to me?"

His green gaze lost its faraway look and focused on her. "Yes, of course. But I need to do a couple of things before we leave Memphis."

"What things?"

He shook his head and flicked her nose with a finger. "Nothing that needs to concern you."

She wanted to stomp her foot. When would David learn to treat her like an adult? As she watched him walk away, she gave in to the impulse to stick out her tongue at his retreating back. Maybe if she solved his mystery, David would finally admit she was a grown woman.

ஐ&

Lily moved across the parlor as Aunt Dahlia stood, and she kissed the air next to the older woman's cheek. "You sleep well. We'll see you in the morning."

Aunt Dahlia's nose wrinkled. "Unless the Good Lord sees fit to take me home tonight."

"We're not going to worry about that, dear." Uncle Phillip put an arm around his wife's shoulders. He winked toward Lily and the others. "According to what I remember of my classical studies, Herodotus said, 'Whom the gods love dies young; Best go first.'"

Aunt Dahlia's face turned suspicious. "Are you making fun of me?"

"Of course not." He led her out of the room, bending toward Aunt Dahlia, and placating her with tender words.

Lily put a hand over her mouth to keep from laughing out loud as she, Blake, Camellia, and Jonah waited for the pair to get out of earshot.

"When did your uncle Phillip develop such a sense of humor?" Blake kept a straight face, but the twinkle in his blue eyes told her he shared her amusement.

Camellia, sitting on one of the pair of sofas, smiled at him. "He's been much happier since he realized Jonah and I are not going to let the plantation go to rack and ruin."

"I think he enjoys teasing your aunt." Jonah walked to the window and opened the drapes to let a breeze into the room.

Lily shook her head and settled on the sofa opposite her sister. "Every time we come home, things seem a little more comfortable than the time before. I'm so glad the fire didn't slow you down."

"When will you ever get over your wanderlust and come back home to stay?" Camellia opened her fan and waved it in front of her face.

"Not for another century or so." Blake took a seat next to his wife.

Lily thanked God for a husband who understood her so well. She tilted her head to look at him. "Don't let Blake fool you by blaming our absence on me. He would like for us to go even farther afield than we do presently."

"Tell us what you found out in Memphis." Jonah lounged against the open window.

"Eli and Renée are certain we need to make an investment right away, while the opportunities are wide open." Lily turned toward him. "Your brother is even considering leaving Memphis and moving out West to take better advantage of the situation."

Blake stretched out his legs and crossed them at the ankles. "I'm trying to convince Lily that we need to take a trip out there to see for ourselves."

"Where would you go?" asked Camellia.

"I'd like to travel all the way to California on the Pacific Railroad." Blake glanced toward her.

Lily nodded. She understood her husband's reasoning, but she wasn't quite ready to commit to spending a month or more away from the river. Especially now that Jasmine was running about on her own, getting into who knew what kind of trouble.

"What towns are you planning to visit?" Jonah straightened and moved toward the sofas.

Blake uncrossed his legs and stood. "Let's go look at that map in the library. I'll show you the exact route we'll take."

Before the two men could leave, the parlor door opened. Lily looked up, smiling when she saw her father's familiar visage. His smile sent her back to the distant past, the days of her childhood. A pang of sadness settled in her heart. Papa hadn't looked this happy since before Mama died. While she didn't want him to live the rest of his life mourning his first wife, his interest signaled the end of an era. . .at least in her mind.

"Where are the two of you going?"

"Blake's going to show me where he's taking your eldest daughter." Jonah moved toward the door. "Why don't you come with us?"

"Hold on just a minute." Camellia closed her fan and pointed it at Papa. "You're not going to leave until we hear a report about your evening with Aunt Tessie."

Papa's face was ruddy from years sailing the river, but Lily could still see a blush darken his cheeks. Her eyebrows rose. "I have to agree with Camellia. We want to hear every salacious detail."

When he rolled his eyes at her sally, Lily couldn't help thinking of her youngest sister. Jasmine had followed Papa's every footstep for years, picking up so many of his mannerisms. How she wished Jasmine would walk in that door right now. But when Jonah opened it, the hallway was empty.

"Can I not count on my own daughters to respect my privacy?"

Camellia shook her head. "Not when Aunt Tessie's heart may be at risk."

Papa sat on a chair, his hands hanging between his knees. "I guess you girls have noticed that Tessie and I have been spending some time together."

Lily exchanged a glance with her sister.

"She's a nice woman." He cleared his throat and looked up at the ceiling. "I may be asking her to marry me soon."

"Papa, that's wonderful." Camellia jumped up and ran to him, catching him in an enthusiastic hug. "She's the smartest, most thoughtful, kindest woman I know."

"I don't know how to take that." Lily used irony to cover her surprise. Love? Although she had known Papa had spent some time with Tessie during their recent trip to New Orleans, she hadn't realized how serious their relationship had become in just a few short weeks.

Camellia shot a laughing glance at her over one shoulder. "Present company excepted, of course."

"I hope you girls understand." Papa trained his gaze on Lily's face. "It's just that when you get as old as I am, you begin to realize your time on earth may be very limited. Tessie and I have no time to waste."

"Now Papa, don't talk like that." Lily's heart swelled with love for her father. "We want you around for many more years, and we want you to be happy. Tessie is a very lucky lady. She's going to make a welcome addition to our family."

Papa had stood when Camellia came to him. Now he gestured for Lily to join them. She rose and walked to where they stood, putting her arms around both her father and her sister. Lily was reminded of the verse that promised God's presence whenever two or more of His followers came together. The Holy Spirit was here.

Finally they separated. Lily felt the healing in her heart, relieved that the poignancy she had felt was only a fleeting echo of the past. As Lily returned to her seat on the sofa, she pulled her father along with her. Camellia also sat down once more.

Papa sighed. "I only wish Jasmine were here with us."

"She would be as happy for you and Aunt Tessie as Lily and I are." Camellia's voice was a little shaky.

Lily wished Camellia could let go of her guilt over Jasmine's disappearance. She'd been adamant in telling her middle sister that she was not at fault. Jasmine's decision to leave had been made long before she actually walked out the door. Any blame for their youngest sister's actions would be more properly placed at Lily's feet. She was the one who had tried to curtail Jasmine in New Orleans. If she had been a little less inflexible, Jasmine might still be here at Les Fleurs.

"I know you're right." The smile on his face was not as bright as it had been moments earlier. "I just miss the little minx."

"I do, too, Papa." Lily's throat constricted. It was hard to push the words out without letting go of her emotions. "I do, too."

Camellia's wobbly smile also hinted at unstable emotions. "At least we know she's safe, thanks to David."

"That's true." Papa gave a gentle smile. "But let's not forget that God is the One watching over both of them."

Lily lifted her chin. Why were they all sitting here moaning about the situation? It was time for action. "I think I'll go get Jasmine."

Camellia's gaze locked on her face. "What do you mean?"

"I know she's on a boat called the *Ophelia*. It shouldn't be that hard to find it. As Blake is fond of pointing out to me, river traffic is much reduced. We can go up to Cape Girardeau and farther if necessary. Even if I have to go all the way to Chicago, I'll find her."

"Do you think that's a good idea?" Camellia's cornflower blue eyes mirrored the doubt in her voice.

Lily nodded, growing more certain as she considered her plan. "I think it's a wonderful idea. Much better than doing nothing."

Papa cleared his throat and waited until she looked in his direction. "I disagree."

What could he possibly mean? What was wrong with going to look for Jasmine?

Her father looked like he was trying to marshal his thoughts. "Lily, Jasmine is twenty years old."

"But she's still—"

"I know." He interrupted her protest with a raised hand. "You are my oldest child, and I've always been proud of the way you've shouldered the responsibility for raising both of your sisters. In a way, they are your children."

Lily could feel the frown on her face. What did he mean? Yes, she loved Camellia and Jasmine in the same way she loved her children.

Wasn't that the way it was supposed to be? Shouldn't she want the best for them the way she did for Noah, Magnolia, and Benjamin? Of course, Camellia was settled. She had a husband and a home—a family of her own to raise. But Jasmine was different. Jasmine still needed her.

"I'm speaking to you now as a parent, Lily. Don't you remember the first time Noah scraped his knee on your gangplank?"

A picture formed in her mind of that day almost five years ago. Noah had been barely able to walk, but he had pulled away from her hand, insisting he could cross to the *Water Lily* by himself. Papa's voice described the scene exactly the way she remembered it. A bright spring day, the river overflowing its banks as it often did. "Noah fell and scraped his knee." She felt Papa had vindicated her concern. "But he could have fallen into the river. He might have drowned."

"That's true, Lily. Isn't that why you and Blake taught him how to swim? In case he ever did fall overboard? You didn't try to stop him from exploring the world. You gave him the tools he needed to conquer it. You have to trust that you and your sister have outfitted Jasmine so she can face whatever obstacles life throws at her. You won't always be there for her, Lily."

"I can be there for her now, though." Lily wasn't ready to give up the argument. She glanced at Camellia for support. "What would you do if we were talking about Amaryllis?"

Instead of taking her side, Camellia laughed. "I don't think comparing the needs of my three-year-old is quite fair. Like Papa said, Jasmine is twenty years old. Remind me again how old you were when you purchased the *Hattie Belle*, your first boat?"

"That's different." Lily voiced the objection, but it didn't ring true, even to her own ears.

Camellia raised her hand and held up one finger. "When you were even younger than Jasmine is right now, you bought a boat"—a second finger went up—"moved Jasmine and me onto it"—three fingers—"took off for New Orleans without any idea of what we would find there"—a fourth finger—"and failed to tell us the true identity of our captain." She dropped her hand back into her lap.

Lily felt misused and misunderstood. Everything she'd done had been for them, after all. To make sure both Camellia and Jasmine had choices. "It didn't turn out too badly, though, did it?"

"Of course not." Papa's emphatic answer made her feel a little less betrayed. "That's exactly the point, Lily. All three of my daughters have a bit of the Anderson stubbornness, and you are determined to make your own way in life."

Comprehension dawned. Unshed tears made her eyes sting. The tip of her nose was probably crimson.

"I know we all wish Jasmine had chosen a more proper vocation." Camellia sighed. "But we cannot force her into the mold we would choose."

"Do you think she's safe?" Lily felt one of her tears escape. She swiped it away with an impatient finger. "I'm so scared she'll make a mistake she can't recover from."

Camellia's eyes widened. "She's got a Pinkerton detective with her. David will make sure she's not swept away. And I predict he'll bring her back to us as soon as he thinks she's had enough of freedom."

"Why don't we take our fears to Jesus?" Papa's face rediscovered its smile. "He has promised to listen to our hearts' desires."

Lily nodded. "I'm sorry, Papa."

He patted her shoulder. "You don't have anything to be sorry about, Lily. You love your sisters. I know that. Sometimes you just get a little eager to solve all their problems for them."

Camellia moved from the sofa she'd been using and plopped down between Lily and Papa. Reaching for both their hands, she squeezed her eyes shut. "Thank You, Lord, for watching over Jasmine. We know You love her even more than we do, and we are putting our trust in You to call her back into Your fold."

As her sister spoke, Lily felt peace soak into her heart. When Camellia stopped, she took a deep breath. "God, please help me to lean on You instead of my own strengths, which are puny beyond belief. Thank You for my family, for a father and a sister who have my best interests at heart, even if they are a little harsh at times."

Camellia's choked laughter made her grin.

"Lord, our Father, the One who loves us beyond all understanding, we give thanks to You for sending Your Son to die on the cross for our sins. Sometimes we forget who is in control. Please forgive us for that. Be with my wondrous daughters in all their endeavors. Strengthen them, be with them, and help us all remember Your promises. You've created us for Your pleasure and called us for Your purpose. We rest in You, Lord. . . Amen."

The parlor door opened as her father ended their prayer. Lily could tell by the looks on Blake's and Jonah's faces that they had heard at least some of the conversation.

"Have you solved all the problems of the world?" Blake's question made Camellia giggle once more.

"I may wring Lily's neck. Would you believe she complained to God because Papa and I were giving her a little advice?"

Except for Lily, everyone in the parlor laughed. Camellia patted her knee before returning to her former seat on the other side of the tea table.

Blake took her place between Lily and her father, his concern plain on his features.

Lily fished in the waist of her skirt for her handkerchief, wiping away the telltale tears that had slipped down her cheeks during their prayer. "Everything's fine, honey. They were just setting me straight."

Her husband's dark eyebrows climbed toward his hairline. "They're braver than I am."

This time Lily was able to join in the laughter, even though she swatted her husband's shoulder. "Don't you start on me, too."

As Papa told his sons-in-law about his intentions with regard to Tessie, Lily mused about the advice she had received from him and Camellia. If she wasn't going to look for Jasmine—and she was beginning to agree that it would be a poor idea—maybe it was time for her to take that trip Blake had his heart set on. At least she would have something new to focus on. Something that would have nothing to do with the paths her sisters chose.

Chapter Twenty-five

The *Ophelia* remained in Memphis for longer than planned because of the number of people attending each performance. Jasmine realized the Easleys wanted to rake in all the money possible, but she was ready to head north. She didn't want to look out into the audience and realize Lily had caught up with them. And she was anxious to begin rehearsing for their Fourth of July production, a series of one-act vignettes on the highlights of America's founding. Clem had told her it would end with everyone on stage singing patriotic numbers. Jasmine hoped she could fake her part in the singing since she couldn't carry a tune in a bushel basket.

Jasmine was still excited about the production because Mr. Easley had slated her for the part of Princess Pocahontas. She would finally be the star on stage instead of second fiddle for Tabitha. If only they would leave Memphis.

Over the past week, life had fallen into a humdrum rhythm. The manager gave the actors mornings off unless they flubbed their lines the night before. She had visited Renée and Eli Thornton once but usually spent her mornings with Clem, helping the other girl with the never-ending work of keeping the costumes mended and altered.

The only times she saw David were immediately after each evening performance and before the dinner meal, when he escorted her and Clem back and forth from their room. She suspected it was his way of covering his real goal of hanging about to look for evidence. The more time that passed, the more she became convinced he was on the wrong trail. But she'd given up trying to convince him.

A part of her was anxious for him to stay with them. She'd grown accustomed to his protective presence. Besides, he needed to remain on board for as long as it took for him to agree with her staying when he did leave.

"I don't believe it." Clem's voice held more than a trace of irritation.

Jasmine put down the chemise she was stitching. "What's wrong?"

"Angelica has pulled another seam apart." Clem dug into a large bag that held scraps. "I don't have the right color to make a patch."

"What color do you need?"

"Magenta."

Jasmine snapped her fingers. "When I was in Tabitha's room last week, a torn scarf was lying on her chair. I wonder if she would donate it to the cause."

"You and Tabitha sure have gotten close lately."

"She's writing to some of her theater friends about me." Jasmine didn't know why she felt defensive. It wasn't like she was betraying their friendship. Clem had no wish to become a famous actress.

"Humph." Clem took out her scissors and started removing the stitches on Angelica's dress. "I hope you don't wake up one day and find her knife planted in your back. Women like Miss Barlow never do something unless it will benefit them."

"Maybe she wants to relive her glory days through me."

"Perhaps."

Jasmine blew out an irritated breath. "Do you want me to ask her about the scarf or not?"

"Yes, go ahead." Clem kept her gaze on the cloth in her lap.

Making her way to the other corridor that housed the first-billed actors, Jasmine wondered what Clem would say if she knew Jasmine's plans for the future included her. Once she was making enough money to support herself in style, she would need a talented dressmaker. Clem had an eye for the right color and style. If she was given free rein to create what she wanted, the result would probably be stunning.

Jasmine was surprised to see Tabitha's door ajar when she reached it. The actress was usually very particular about her privacy. Her heart thumped as she knocked on the door.

A scuffling sound from the room made her think the actress might be in trouble.

"Tabitha?" She pushed at the door but found she could not open it. "Tabitha, are you okay?"

"Who's there?" The voice that answered did not belong to Tabitha. Not unless she had learned how to mimic a man.

"David?"

The door stopped resisting her pressure and swung open, revealing David's blazing green gaze. "What are you doing here?"

Quashing the uncomfortable idea that he might have an assignation with the actress, she put her hands on her hips. "I have an irreproachable errand. What excuse do you have for being in a woman's boudoir?"

He pulled her inside the room by one elbow. "I'm looking for evidence, of course."

"In Tabitha's room? You've lost your mind. Do you really think a female can be your culprit?" She noticed he was wearing a workman's apron. Was he supposed to be on duty on the *Miss Polly*?

David dropped her elbow and stepped back. "No one's above suspicion, even though I agree that a female is not the probable culprit."

"If Tabitha catches you in here, she'll make sure you get sacked. Then what will you do?"

"I suppose I could depend on you to get me the information I need."

For a moment she thought he was serious. Then she saw the gleam in his gaze. He was about as serious as a clown.

Before she could counter with a biting remark, he raised a hand to signify his capitulation. "She's gone on another of her shopping expeditions." He picked up a feather boa from the floor and draped it over the back of Tabitha's slipper chair. "I saw her leave half an hour ago, so I have at least that much more time before I have to worry about her return."

"Have you found anything?" She winced at the derision in her voice. The inflection was uncomfortably close to Tabitha's.

"She spends more on jewelry and geegaws than she can afford on her current salary."

Jasmine glanced over his shoulder at a large bouquet of fresh flowers. "She has a lot of male admirers. Did you stop to think some of them might be giving her gifts of jewelry and geegaws?"

His shoulders drooped, and David nodded. "I know. But it's getting frustrating. I have to find something soon or admit defeat." When David spoke the words out loud, dismay filled her. Not that she needed him, of course. But his presence was reassuring. She even found herself looking forward to meeting him each evening after she had removed her makeup and changed back into her regular clothes. She would miss telling him about her impressions of the other actors and giggling with him over the odd world of the theater. "What about Mr. Easley? Did you find out what he sends Vance to do?"

A half-grin appeared on David's face. "He's a passable director, but your Mr. Easley is not much of a businessman. At least not when it comes to mathematics. Vance counts the money for him and takes it to the bank where he gets change. I'm sure that's what he was talking about."

"Will you finally admit Vance is innocent?"

"Of bank robbery, maybe. But that man doesn't have an innocent bone in his body."

Jasmine found herself unable to argue the point. Vance was much more circumspect whenever her "brother" was around. If David was working on the *Miss Polly*, Vance was becoming more and more insistent toward her. He made personal remarks and touched her with increasing frequency, brushing back a strand of her hair or running a finger along the back of her arm. Jasmine didn't want to offend him. Vance was the reason she was here, after all. But if he didn't tone down his gestures and words, she was going to have to tell him in no uncertain terms that she was not a woman of ill repute.

She wasn't ready to share that side of Vance with David. He was already too suspicious of the man. She turned her attention to the part of the room where she'd last seen the scarf she wanted, her cheeks heating as she caught sight of a pair of Tabitha's lacy pantaloons. "You really shouldn't be in here."

"I've seen lady's undergarments before." David's grin widened.

Grabbing up the brightly colored material she'd come for, Jasmine tucked it into her pocket. "We need to leave."

David's smile disappeared. He raised both hands this time, a mock surrender.

With a huff, she opened the door. "Come on." Stepping into the hallway, she waited for him to close the door.

"What are you two doing down here?" Vance's accusing voice startled Jasmine.

She whirled to face him, wishing she'd looked to make sure they were alone before leaving Tabitha's room. "I. . .I. . ."

"Miss Barlow's hinges weren't working properly. She complained that they squeaked like a herd of pigs whenever she opened or closed her door. Jasmine brought me down to see what I could do about them."

"Where are your tools?" Vance's suspicious gaze looked like it might bore a hole into David's head.

Reaching into his pocket, David produced an oil can, a wrench, and a hammer. "Any other questions, Mr. Hargrove?"

Jasmine breathed a sigh of relief. David was prepared as always. She glanced up at him. "Thanks."

He leaned over and kissed her cheek. "Anything for you, Sis." Whistling a merry tune, he walked away.

After putting her hand to the cheek he'd kissed, Jasmine shot a glance at Hargrove. "Excuse me, I have to get back to Clem."

By the time she'd negotiated the separate hallways, her heart had slowed its furious pace. She slipped through the door to the costume room and pulled out the scarf. "Will this do?"

Clem studied the material and pursed her lips. "I think so. What did Tabitha say about donating something for Angelica?"

"She doesn't know."

Clem reached for the scarf. "What do you mean?"

"She wasn't there." Surrendering the cloth, Jasmine giggled. "I helped myself."

"Are you saying you stole something from our star?" Clem's smile teased her. "I knew you weren't as sweet as you pretend to be."

"She did offer it to me." Jasmine resumed her seat. "All I did was wait a day or two before accepting her gift."

"As soon as I finish this, we'll talk about your costume. I have some ideas I want to try." Clem stitched as she talked, her fingers seeming to fly. "How daring are you feeling?"

Excitement curled in Jasmine's stomach. The Fourth of July pageant might be her ticket to stardom. She would do almost anything to ensure her success.

Chapter Twenty-six

The blue waters of the Ohio River mingled with the chocolate waters of the Mississippi at the town of Cairo, ensuring its importance both during and after the war. Fort Defiance still guarded the port, and plans had begun to build a customs house because of the volume of goods passing through the area.

Jasmine wrinkled her nose as she picked her way across the mushy ground between the ship landing and the open area where the Fourth of July celebration would be held. On one side of the field, a group of men worked with saws and hammers, building a raised platform for the stage. As she drew near, they stopped their work, one by one, elbowing each other and grinning.

One would think they had never seen a lady before. Cairo might be little more than a swamp, but it was not the very end of the earth. She lifted her chin and turned her back on them. Where was everyone? Mr. Easley had said they would begin rehearsals precisely at 10:00 a.m.

The buildings of the town were huddled against the clearer waters of the Ohio. She put her hand above her eyes and looked in that direction to see if she could spy any of the others. Had they gone to the fort instead of meeting here? Had she misunderstood the directions?

After several moments, she saw Clem walking in her direction and waved a greeting. At least the two of them could talk while they waited for the rest of the actors to appear.

The clanging and banging of the workers began again as Clem reached her. "What is all of that clatter?"

"Progress." Jasmine had to shout over the noise. "Shall we try to find a quieter spot?"

They strolled in the opposite direction of the workers until the sound diminished a bit.

Clem scuffed at the dirt with the toe of her slipper. "Have you been here before?"

"Yes, although we didn't land here often. My brother-in-law has family and several friends in Cape Girardeau, so that's where we usually stop." Jasmine looked back toward the tree-lined bank that hid the Mississippi from their view. "What about you?"

"Yes, many times. Did you know three states come together here?" Jasmine pointed to the Ohio River's blue water, busy with small flatboats ferrying goods from the riverboats and railroad to destinations on its far side. "Kentucky. And the mud beneath our feet is in the state of Illinois."

Clem nodded. "The Mississippi River separates Illinois from Missouri. The first time we stopped here, I didn't believe the person who told me."

Trust Clem to find something romantic about Cairo. "Even if ten states met in this same space, Cairo is still so flood-prone that it's little more than a mud hole at times."

"True." Clem laughed. "I like to think that one day it will be a beautiful town with wide streets and stunning vistas."

"I don't know how you do it, Clem."

"What's that?"

"You always look for the best in life." Jasmine linked arms with her friend, and they walked along in silence for a moment.

"Has anyone seen your costume yet?"

Jasmine looked down toward her knees. Her dark brown skirt was narrower than what she was used to, but that was not its most noticeable feature. It was short, ending right below her knees. Below its hem her limbs were encased in brown leggings. The outfit was daring, making her feel bold, brave, and intrepid. "I don't know yet, but I think I was the topic of conversation over by the stage."

Both of them giggled.

"Not everyone could carry it off." Clem stepped back and looked at her.

Jasmine held out her hands and turned around to model her dashing clothing. "What do you think?"

"You'll turn every head in the town. The women may hate you, but the men will flock to see you from all over."

"Do you really think so?" Jasmine turned back in the other direction.

"I guarantee it."

They reached a lane of sorts and turned to follow it. Jasmine looked over her shoulder and realized the workmen had stopped their labor once more. "If they take this many breaks, we won't have a stage to perform on until August."

Clem didn't look back. Her gaze focused on a man walking toward them. "Here comes David."

Jasmine smoothed the skirt of her gown. What would he think?

She didn't have long to wonder as he pointed at her knees. "What on earth are you wearing, Jasmine?"

"It's my Princess Pocahontas outfit." She twirled once more. "Do you like it?" When she stopped moving, she looked to gauge his reaction.

If a thundercloud had landed on his brow, it could not be any darker. "I don't know why I expect you to behave with any decorum. If Lily could see you right now, she would be ashamed."

His words tore at her like the bite of a rabid animal, but she raised her chin and glared back at him. "You obviously need to build a house and raise a family in Cairo. We all know what it's like here when it floods. What better location for someone who is a stick in the mud."

David's jaw tightened. "Get back to the *Ophelia* and put on something less shocking, or I'm going to put you over my shoulder and throw you on the next boat to Natchez."

"I'm tired of your threats, David Foster. You're not going to intimidate me any longer."

Clem's eyes widened. "But I thought you were Jasmine's brother."

Jasmine bit her lip. She should not have let her anger loose. Now she'd ruined everything.

"I am." David took off his coat and wrapped it around Jasmine. "My full name is David Foster Anderson."

Jasmine was grateful he had managed to cover her gaffe, but it still didn't excuse her stupidity.

"Oh, I see. I misunderstood." Clem's wrinkled brow smoothed out. "I have an idea that may resolve your problem with your sister's outfit."

His hands squeezed Jasmine's shoulders, a warning to keep silent. "What is that?"

She leaned forward and turned up the edge of Jasmine's skirt. "I made a wide hem because I wasn't certain how short the dress should be. I can let it out and add a layer of lace to the bottom of her leggings so they look more like a flounce than. . .well, you understand."

"But I—" Another squeeze stopped her protest. Jasmine fumed but acquiesced. . .for the moment.

"Don't you realize you're asking for the wrong kind of attention from men? Is that the kind of reputation you want? Can't you understand yet there's a reason for rules? A reason to guard your reputation? I know you don't want to shame our whole family with your actions, so I have to wonder if the reason you do these kinds of things is a lack of confidence in your acting ability. Do you think you have to stoop to sensationalism to draw attention?"

Shame and anger mingled in her blood. Was David right? Had she gone from daring to scandalous? Or was he being too old-fashioned?

"Let out the hem." David's hands relaxed, kneading the taut muscles of her shoulders. "We'll see if the change will allow her sufficient modesty."

David pulled her up close to his body, shielding her from the glances of the workers as the three of them started back toward the showboat. Clem chattered nonstop about the weather, the town, and the patriotic celebration in an attempt to fill the silence.

Jasmine thought back to the day Tabitha had first offered to help her. She'd mentioned being snubbed. Was that what David was trying to protect her from? Should she care? Jasmine had her morals, her boundaries. For all he knew, the ill will of others might spring from jealousy rather than moral indignation. It might be part of the payment for the notoriety she craved.

They crossed the gangplank, and David removed his coat. "Don't forget to show me the outfit first."

Jasmine rolled her eyes. She would not let him see how ambivalent she felt. Reaching their bedroom, she unbuttoned the shirtwaist and jerked it off.

"I'm sorry." Clem sat on the edge of her bed.

"It's not your fault." Jasmine summoned a smile for her friend. "I wanted to wear it."

"It would be acceptable on the stage in a big city, but David may be right in thinking that the people here won't be as progressive in their attitudes."

Jasmine snorted. David didn't know everything. He wasn't an arbiter of decorum or fashion.

"He only has your best interests at heart." Clem's face shone with admiration. "I wish he were my brother. I would love feeling so cherished."

"You can have him with my blessing." What Clem didn't understand, what she couldn't explain to her, was that the man posing as her brother had only one goal—to ruin her life. And he was doing a fair job of it.

Jasmine pulled on her most conservative dress. His condemnation had stung. She would show David Foster—Anderson—that she would do as she pleased.

$$\approx$$

Jasmine still refused to speak to him by the end of the week. At least her anger ensured she wouldn't try to help him with his investigation.

Not that he'd intended to make her angry, but that girl knew how to push every boundary to its utmost extent. He refused to stand aside and watch her self-destruct, and if her enmity was the price, he considered it worth the cost.

This morning he had finally gained entrance to Angelica Fenwick's bedroom, the last on his list. He glanced around the crowded room. Were all actresses clotheshorses? Although David could understand that they might need a few extra items to supplement the costumes they wore, he was amazed at the number of outfits both Miss Fenwick and Miss Barlow carried around with them.

Even Camellia wasn't this bad. At least he didn't think she was. Of course, Jonah had once claimed that his wife had enough outfits to avoid repeating any particular one for a year. At the time David had thought the man was exaggerating. Now he was less certain.

He picked up an armful of crinolines to search the bottom of one of her trunks, his eyes widening to find a child's doll dressed in a pink gown and matching bonnet hidden under the actress's undergarments. He would never have thought Miss Fenwick the nostalgic type, but the proof was before him. The doll must be a treasured reminder of her childhood.

Replacing the contents, he moved to the dressing table in one corner of the room. The drawers were filled with brushes, perfumes, and bottles of rouge. Nothing to indicate that Miss Fenwick was guilty. Not that he'd really thought she would be. He couldn't imagine a female working with a gang of hardened thieves and murderers. But that didn't mean she couldn't be involved in some way—as a go-between or accomplice of some sort. As hard as it was to invade a woman's privacy, he had to be thorough.

Mentally reviewing the list of suspects one more time, David slipped out of the actress's room. He was beginning to agree with Jasmine's assertions that no one on board was connected to the robberies. What was he missing? The *Ophelia* had to be the clue Charlie Petrie had tried to tell him about with his dying breath. David shook his head. It didn't make sense.

Everyone on board both the *Ophelia* and its tugboat was talking about the big race that would begin the Fourth of July festivities tomorrow morning. Some of the tugboat crew even wanted Captain Ross to enter the race. David was glad the man had refused. His intuition told him that if the robbers were nearby, they would use the distraction of the celebration to their advantage. He planned to set up watch outside the bank and catch them red-handed. Once he had arrested the culprits, he would wire the home office that he was taking some time off and redouble his efforts to get Jasmine away from this band of gypsy actors.

The sound of a distant bell brought his head up. It was time for church. Clem had asked him last night if he planned to attend, but if he didn't hurry, he was going to be late. He squinted in the bright sunlight as he reached the outside deck, surprise and pleasure filling him at the sight of both Clem and Jasmine apparently awaiting his escort.

"See, I told you he was coming." Clem pointed her finger at Jasmine. "You owe me a forfeit."

Holding out an elbow for each of them, he grinned. "No one's ever placed a bet on me before."

"Don't act so conceited." Jasmine ignored his arm, stepping onto the gangplank. "Clem wouldn't leave until you appeared, even though I told her you'd make all of us late."

"I suppose we'd better hurry then."

Clinging to his arm for support, Clem managed to keep up with his long strides. Rebellious Jasmine was having more trouble. He could hear her huffing and puffing, but he refused to be manipulated by the sound. She had turned down his offer of support, so unless she asked for help, she could make her own way.

"Will you take part in the pageant?" Clem sounded breathless, so David slowed his pace a little.

"I doubt it. I'm not interested in racing. I'll probably just wander around town and visit the booths." He had no intention of letting Clem or anyone else know his real plans.

Disappointment made her smile droop. "I see."

Jasmine caught up with them as David and Clem reached the dirt lane on the edge of town. The deserted streets didn't surprise him. Shopkeepers were either attending church or sleeping late on their one day off. Even the ferries would not run until after midday in observance of the Lord's Day.

As they reached the street the church faced, a movement at the end of a nearby alley made David turn his head. He only caught a glimpse but thought he recognized the dark hair and tall frame of Rafe Griffin. Expecting to see the man as they turned the corner, he immediately grew suspicious when no one appeared. Why was Rafe skulking about?

The question continued bothering him as they entered the one-room church. The center aisle was flanked on both sides by rows of benches. David would have preferred finding an empty spot in the back of the sanctuary, but Clem tugged him forward until they reached the front.

The preacher, a gray-haired man with a weathered face, smiled at the three of them. "Welcome."

David shook the man's hand. "Thank you." He stood in the aisle, feeling the combined gazes of the good people of Cairo on his face, as first Clem and then Jasmine sat on the first pew. When he sat, Jasmine put her hand on her skirt and pulled it closer to her body as though she didn't want him to touch her at all. He crossed his hands over his chest and ignored her.

"I was going to talk to you about the importance of stewardship today, but God helped me come awake before the sun this morning. He filled my mind with another sermon, one that I feel compelled to share with you." The pastor opened his Bible. "For those of you who brought your Bibles, I'll be reading from the thirteenth chapter of the Gospel of Matthew. I'm always amazed when I read this chapter about the sower of seeds."

David heard the intake of Jasmine's breath. He was glad she was listening. She had not been showing him much sign that she still turned to God on a daily basis. Maybe this trip to church would help her renew her faith.

"I've often wondered about the man sowing the seeds in this parable.

Many of you are farmers, and I know you wouldn't bother to plant your precious seed out there on top of rocks, would you?"

A couple of the men answered in the negative.

"Would you plant them so shallowly that animals could eat them or fail to pull the weeds from your fields before you planted your seed?"

No one answered the question this time, but David could tell by the silence behind him that the pastor had everyone's attention.

"Of course you wouldn't. If you did, your families would starve. So why does Jesus tell us about someone being so foolish?" The pastor stopped to let the question settle in. "Because He knows that any one of us can have a stony heart. He knows that any of us can become shallow and self-absorbed. We can forget our faith when we become distracted by the pleasures of this world."

David sat a little straighter in the pew. He hoped Jasmine was paying close attention. He knew God must have meant for the pastor to choose these verses for her sake.

"But that's not the only point of this story. It's not the only lesson Jesus wants us to learn. So why didn't He tell us about only sowing seed in rich, prepared soil?" The pastor looked straight at David, the fire of his message lighting his eyes. "Friends, you and I need to remember that we as Christians are the sowers. We're not supposed to worry about the fruit of the Gospel. We can't make the seed we spread grow. All God wants us to do is sow His seed. He will take care of the rest."

David's mouth fell open. He forgot all about Jasmine and her lack of faith as the truth pierced his own heart. He had been so busy trying to correct Jasmine's behavior, trying to make her act like he thought a Christian sister should. That wasn't his job. All God wanted him to do was sow the seed. He was trying to change Jasmine, an impossible task for a human being. Only Jesus could change someone.

As God continued to speak to him through the preacher, David determined to be the witness God needed him to be. He sent a prayer heavenward for the strength he knew it would take.

Chapter Twenty-seven

Folding chairs lined the decks of the two larger steamboats for the addition of paying guests during the race. Vance purchased tickets for himself and Jasmine—and with a little prodding, Clem—on the *Marc Antony*. The sun had barely escaped the horizon as they took their seats on the spotless deck. Streamers hung limply from the rails in preparation for the extreme speeds the boat would attain during the contest.

"Do you think we'll win?" Clem wore a hat with a wide brim to shade her face. She had secured it to her head with a blue lawn scarf that matched the color of her dress.

Jasmine could imagine an artist capturing her friend's excited face and fashionable appearance for use in *Harper's Bazaar*. "It doesn't really matter. All we have to do is enjoy the scenery."

A white-coated server appeared with steaming cups of chocolate to warm them against the cool, damp air. Vance handed her a cup, and Jasmine held it close to her face, inhaling the sweet fragrance.

"It's a shame your brother couldn't join us." Clem sipped from her mug.

Vance's face showed his disagreement with the statement, although he made no comment. "I don't see how we can lose. In fact, I've wagered a large sum of money on it. The *Marc Antony* is a modern boat with the latest innovations. She's only been on the water for half a year."

Jasmine slid a glance in his direction. "I hope you're not disappointed. It's not always the date on the boiler that decides the victor. The *Davy Crockett* may be older, but she has a knowledgeable pilot and an experienced crew. She might have been a better choice."

His unsettled glance toward her made Jasmine wonder if Vance needed to win his bet. The idea took root in her mind like an evil weed. If he was having money problems, it would make him more likely to join himself with bank robbers. But that made no sense, either. The man who had been working with the robbers wouldn't have money troubles. He'd be flush with his ill-gotten gain.

The boat filled up with other passengers—twenty in all—and the gangplank was lifted away from the bank.

Jasmine turned to Vance. "How long will the race take?"

"We'll be traveling downriver ten miles to a small island. Each boat must circumnavigate the island before returning to Cairo. The captain estimates that it will take less than two hours total to get back to the finish line at that cottonwood." He pointed to a large tree overhanging the bank some yards away. Someone had plaited its thick limbs with wide lengths of red. "The first boat to capture a ribbon will be declared the winner."

"We won't miss anything while we're gone, will we?" Clem leaned forward, her gaze fixed on the people beginning to line up on the riverbank. "I noticed the fliers mentioned races and equestrian exhibitions."

"I doubt it." Jasmine put her free hand on the arm of Clem's chair. "Most everyone is going to be waiting to see who wins the race."

"Yoo-hoo." A feminine voice gained her attention. "Look, it's Angelica and Rafe. They're on the *Davy Crockett*."

"Too bad they chose the losing steamboat." Vance's smug words were as irritating as a swarm of gnats.

Jasmine gritted her teeth and waved at the other couple. "As long as everyone has a good time, it doesn't really matter."

They watched as a short, barrel-chested man climbed onto the stage that would be the central focus of the day's activities and addressed the crowd. "Good morning, ladies and gentlemen. I know everyone's eager to begin our patriotic celebration, but please bear with me for a few moments while I cover some of the rules we'll be observing."

A general groan or two from the crowd showed their disapproval, but the man continued anyway. He warned that no weapons were to be discharged except the starter gun and asked everyone to maintain polite and civil manners. He went on to point out the doctor's tent next to the stage and expressed his hope that no one would be in need of medical service. He reminded them of the various contests that would be going on during the day, the dramatic performance that would begin at dusk, and the fireworks spectacular that promised to end the day with a "bang." A louder groan answered his sally, and a grin split the man's face. Reaching into his pocket, he pulled out a small pistol and aimed it toward the sky.

Jasmine saw the puff of smoke before she heard the report of his weapon. The crowd cheered as the deck below her feet began to shudder. Thick, black plumes of smoke poured from the twin stacks above their heads, while behind them, the paddlewheel roared to life. The race had begun.

Clem jumped to her feet, leaning over the rail and waving at the people they swept past. Jasmine would have joined her, but Vance reached over and put a hand on her arm. "If this race goes like I expect, things are going to be different for me in the future, and I hope different for you, too."

The girl she'd been when she first ran away would have been ecstatic because of his words and the intense look he gave her. Jasmine found herself hoping she misunderstood his intent. The direction of her thoughts surprised her. She had never thought of herself as being fickle, but whatever feelings she'd had about Vance seemed to have disappeared.

Was it her or him? Had she ever really loved Vance? She wasn't sure anymore. Jasmine shook off his hand without an answer and stood next to Clem, looking to see whether they were still in the lead.

At the moment it was hard to tell who would win. Their boat rode the choppy waters of the confluence with steady purpose, as did the

Davy Crockett. The smaller boats were out in front for the moment, but she knew that would probably change on the way back to Cairo when they fought the strong currents of the swift water.

"Look, is that the island?" Clem pointed toward a small spot of green ahead.

Jasmine shook her head. "If it's that close, the race won't last fifteen minutes, much less two hours."

Vance made a space for himself between them, but his eyes focused on her face. "Would you like to take a tour of the boat?"

She looked past him to Clem, who nodded. "I don't think there will be much to see out here until we reach the halfway point."

The three of them picked their way between the seats of the other onlookers and headed for the main room on the lower deck. A large table in the center of the room was piled high with an array of breakfast foods. Biscuits, fresh fruit, bacon, scrambled eggs, jams, and jellies looked tempting. They were welcomed by the staff and offered delicate porcelain plates and gleaming silverware.

Jasmine's stomach growled. She looked at Vance. "How much did our tickets cost?"

He shrugged, a smile on his face. "You're worth the price, Jasmine."

Clem rolled her eyes, accepted a plate, and began heaping food onto it. "I, for one, am glad she is."

Jasmine chose a fluffy biscuit and a spoonful of eggs, glad she hadn't taken time to eat before leaving the *Ophelia.* The food was delicious, and Clem's enthusiasm was contagious. She hoped the rest of the day would be equally enjoyable.

They had barely finished when one of the passengers came running inside. "We're about to reach the island."

Jasmine looked around to see that all four boats were running very close. She had no idea who would reach the finish first.

~

"I don't have any hard evidence." David blew out an exasperated breath. It was often difficult working with local law enforcement. He should know by now that patience was the best defense against suspicion and resistance.

"But you still want me to assign a deputy to stay at the bank in case it is robbed?" Sheriff Ambrose Cunningham wore his uniform well. Although not as tall as David, his thick chest and muscled arms would inspire fear in any criminal. "This is one of the busiest days of the year. I only have two men working for me, and they need to be visible, not hidden away waiting for someone who's probably not coming anyway."

"What better time to rob the bank than when everyone is focused on the celebration?"

"I thought you said these bank robbers know all the details about the inside of a bank before they strike. What gives you the idea they'll try to get into our bank while it's closed?"

David relaxed his shoulders with an effort. The sheriff was a nice man, and by all accounts honest, but he obviously didn't like to depart from his routine. "Because it's the easiest way to commit a robbery. Why take the chance that someone might surprise them during normal working hours, when the Fourth of July activities give them the perfect opportunity to slip in, help themselves to the cash inside, and disappear before anyone realizes they're here?"

"I'm spread too thin today anyway. I don't see how I can help you."

"I understand." At least he had tried to work with the authorities. "You don't mind if I keep watch over the bank, do you?"

"Go ahead, young man. I've heard a lot of stories about you Pinkertons. I'm sure you can handle yourself if your fellows do show up."

David left the jail and put his hat on his head as he considered his next step. A glance toward the sky told him it was going to be another warm day. The population of Cairo was swollen with strangers from nearby villages. It was the perfect time for strangers to mingle unnoticed. He knew the one bank in town was too easy a target for Hargrove and his gang to resist. That's where he would wait.

Brick with wide windows, the two-story building offered no place for him to hide. David walked around to the alley alongside the building. Shadows filled the area. He stretched his hearing to its limit. If the robbers planned ahead, they might already be here. His hand rested on the gun he had strapped on before leaving the *Miss Polly*.

A sound in the shadows at the back of the alley made him slip off the leather guard holding his weapon in its holster. A rat dashed out of the darkness, closely followed by a scrawny cat. David grimaced at his jumpiness and reholstered his gun. Taking a deep breath, he entered the alley, looking for a place to hide while he waited for the robbers to strike.

This had to be the day, the day he would finally catch the robbers and end this assignment. He would take great pleasure in fastening a pair of handcuffs on Vance Hargrove and dragging him off to prison. He knew the man was guilty, felt it in his heart. He knew Jasmine didn't agree, but she didn't have his experience.

He stopped the thought as the pastor's message from the day before returned to him. Was he making the same mistake again? Was his smug self-righteousness keeping him from seeing the truth? David sank to his knees at the edge of the alley, locked his hands in front of him, and closed his eyes.

Lord, thank You for showing me the error of my ways. I know I'm apt to act before I think. Help me to wait on Your leading. You're in control. Please help me stop these men before they hurt anyone else. And God, forgive me for ignoring the beam in my own eye while I was so concerned with the mote in Jasmine's. I'm going to leave that problem up to You. . .or at least I'm going to try.

Feeling much more calm, David got back to his feet. When he looked in the alley this time, he saw a stairwell that led to the bank's roof. With an additional thanks to God, he ran to the wooden steps and climbed up. The view from the roof showed him every entrance to the bank. The thieves would not be able to get away. All he had to do now was wait.

Cheers from the riverbank told him that the boats must be within sight once more. Was Jasmine down there somewhere? Or was she still asleep on the *Ophelia*? He hoped it was the latter. Maybe she would have a good time at the fair and forget about the robberies.

A couple of young boys ran down the street, their laughter bringing a smile to his face. They dashed past the bank and disappeared, leaving him alone once more. David lay back on the flat roof and put his hands behind his head. Was this what his future would be like? Would he always be so alone?

He reached for his shirt pocket and pulled out the letter from his father. Turning it over in his hands, he heard Marguerite Trahan's question once again. Who would it hurt if he forgave his pa? If he let go of the past, of the terrible choices his mother had made, of the way he'd had to rely on the charity of others to survive?

A laugh floated upward on the breeze, interrupting his thoughts. Jasmine? David raised his head over the edge of the roof and looked down into the street. A couple was strolling past the bank. It was hard to tell who the woman was because her large hat hid her features from him. But the man was certainly not Vance. His hair was a lighter brown, and he walked with a slight limp.

As David watched, the limping man stopped, pulled the female into his arms, and began kissing her. She didn't struggle, instead reaching a hand up to caress his cheek. The man pulled her even closer, deepening the kiss. Suddenly realizing that he was spying on a private moment, David drew back.

They moved on, and his thoughts turned back to his father. Blake had told him Christ would help him figure out how to forgive Pa. But how? A scripture from Psalms floated to the surface of his mind. *"Be still, and know that I am God."* Was that the answer? He had rushed from one goal to the next for so long now that he'd not taken much time to still his mind and listen for God's voice. He felt his lips turn up in a smile. Only God would use a time like this—while he was watching for criminals to appear—to speak to him in that still, small voice.

David closed his eyes. *God, I'm listening.* Warmth enveloped him, a warmth that had nothing to do with the roof beneath him or the sun above. This feeling came from his heart, from the depths of his soul. And he knew. Forgiveness flowed to him and through him, targeting the emotions he had clung to for so long. With God filling his heart, the bitterness lost its hold. No matter what his parents had done or not done, his heavenly Father would never abandon him. The sadness that had weighted his soul for so long was lost in the realization that God had plans for his future, good plans. The words of the prophet Jeremiah sounded in his mind. *"For I know the thoughts that I think toward you, saith the Lord, thoughts of peace, and not of evil, to give you an expected end."* He basked in the love and understanding of his Father as he continued his vigil.

Multiple blasts from steamboat whistles indicated that the race was over, and he wondered who had won. The thought disappeared as David heard someone approaching the bank. His heart doubled its speed. Had his hunch been right?

Peeking over the roof edge, he saw nothing at first. David was beginning to think he'd imagined the sounds when a pair of men moved out of a shadowed doorway across the street, guns drawn. A thump below him was followed by the sound of shattering glass. The bank's plate glass window. David drew back and stood, easing his way to the street as he drew his own weapon. He breathed a prayer for protection as he rounded the corner of the bank building.

Two men stood at the busted window, their attention centered on the interior of the building.

David raised his weapon. "Hold it right there."

A rain of bullets answered him as both the robbers swung in his direction.

David ducked back around the corner of the building.

"Did we kill him?" He heard one of the men ask the question.

The only answer was the sound of footsteps running away from David's position.

"What's going on?" Another voice sounded, this one from farther away, probably the man inside.

"Get out o' there." The man who had spoken first yelled the warning as he, too, ran in the opposite direction.

David came out from his hiding place as the third man dove through the window back onto the street, rolled to a standing position, and took off toward the busy street where the fair was going on. A few steps behind, David centered his attention on catching the robber before anyone else's life was endangered.

ജ

"You should have consulted Jasmine before making your wager. She comes from a riverboat family, after all." Clem's voice sounded less helpful than her words indicated. "Or David would have been happy to advise you."

Jasmine knew her friend didn't trust Vance any more than David did, but she felt sorry for him. He looked so hurt because the *Marc Antony* had lost. "Let's go see the flea circus."

Vance shook his head. "That's nothing but a sham."

"I don't care." Jasmine tugged on his arm. "Sham or not, it'll still be fun to watch. I've never seen one before."

Rafe and Angelica walked toward them.

"Maybe next time you'll buy a ticket on the winning boat like we did." Angelica sounded giddy. "I really thought your boat would win until your captain got you caught in that snag."

Vance grimaced. "Come on."

Jasmine sent the pair an apologetic glance as they headed down the street. Her gaze met Clem's. Vance needn't be such a sorehead. It was his own fault for making a bet in the first place.

They walked past booths and stalls that had been set up all along the street, stopping to watch a man hide a seed under one of three walnut shells. He slid the shells around on the surface of his board, his hands moving so fast Jasmine's eyes couldn't follow his movements. Then he offered to double the money of anyone who could guess which shell hid the seed. When he tried to get her to guess, she laughingly declined, and the three of them walked on.

The flea circus was a fun novelty, with tiny swings that moved back and forth and balls that rotated under their own power. Vance said they were run by mechanical means, like a pocket watch. Jasmine and Clem refused to believe him, pointing out the tiny insects who were currently "resting" in a jar beside the exhibition.

Tabitha stood in front of a stall that displayed handmade jewelry, haggling with the owner. She smiled when she saw them. "Clem, I have found the most beautiful length of cloth. I just know you'll be able to make me a new outfit with it."

Clem's face brightened. "Let me see it."

Vance expressed an interest in competing in a three-legged race. Jasmine encouraged him with a smile but stayed behind with Clem.

Losing interest as the two other women discussed lengths and styles, she watched a juggler who was tossing some very sharp knives above his head. A group of boys followed close behind him, nudging each other and exclaiming over the juggler's skills. One of them was liable to be hurt if he got any closer.

Jasmine darted out into the street to warn them just as someone ran out from a nearby building, a gun in his hand. Distracted by whoever was chasing him, the man zigzagged at the last moment to avoid colliding with the juggler. Panting, he ran straight toward her, his head turned to judge the distance of his pursuer.

"Look out!" Clem called out the warning, but Jasmine ignored her.

The man was definitely not part of the Fourth of July celebration, so he must be up to no good. She stood her ground and put out her hands to stop him.

David rounded the corner, his eyes widening when he saw her. In an instant, she knew the fleeing man was one of the robbers David had been chasing since the trip to New Orleans. The robber still didn't realize she was there, so he crashed into her full tilt. Down they both went, raising a cloud of dust when they struck the ground.

The world went dark. When the light returned, the heavy weight pinning her was lifted. She heard David yelling her name as though he were a long way away. Jasmine tried to take a breath, but something was wrong with her chest. She couldn't draw air in. Was she going to die? Fear as deep and cold as the river clawed at her. Jasmine put a hand on her chest and tried again. Finally her mouth began working. Air rushed into her lungs.

Someone grabbed her shoulders and pulled her into a sitting position. "Are you okay?" She recognized David's voice.

Jasmine managed a nod. Where was the man who had run her down? Before she could ask the question, David pulled her into a tight hug, burying his face into her shoulder. "Jasmine, Jasmine, what am I going to do with you?"

She wanted to push him away, but he was holding her tight, as though he would never let her go. Someone else was patting her on the back. Clem. While Jasmine appreciated the concern for her welfare, she was beginning to get irritated. Had they let the robber get away?

"Where is he?"

David lifted his head, the green of his eyes almost completely hidden by his irises. "I thought I'd lost you." He stood, grabbed her arm, and jerked her to her feet, his face hardening into exasperation. "I may shoot you myself."

"If you let that man get away, I may shoot you." Out of the corner of her eye, Jasmine could see Clem shaking her head.

David turned her around. Sprawled on the ground was a man with a long, skinny face and dirty blond hair. His hands were under him, his ankles tied together with a length of rope. She hoped his hands were similarly bound.

"Are you hurt?" David stepped around her, positioning himself between her and his prisoner.

"Don't be silly." She blocked out the memory of not being able to breathe. At least her sacrifice had been worthwhile. And she could breathe fine now.

"You should have seen your brother." Clem clasped her hands in front of her, adoration spilling from her eyes. "I've never seen anything like it. He jumped so high, it was like he flew across that street. I thought he would be shot for sure, but your brother kicked the weapon out of the man's hand and roped and tied him as fast as a flash of lightning. He ought to be in one of those cowboy rodeos. He would win for sure."

David looked sheepish, almost embarrassed by Clem's extravagant praise.

Jasmine's stomach quivered. She'd never thought about David getting hurt. He was supposed to be invincible. Her knees buckled, and she met his gaze. Something happened in that moment. Her world shifted. Everything changed, like the landscape after a flood. It was all so clear to her now. Clear and yet muddled beyond comprehension. She bit her lip and turned away. What else could she do?

Chapter Twenty-eight

*L*et's try this one more time." David sighed and leaned his elbows on the table between himself and the man he'd managed to capture. "I need the name of your boss."

"Jack Sprat."

"His real name."

"How 'bout Abraham Lincoln?"

Irritation rolled down his back along with a drop of perspiration. He hadn't planned to spend the whole afternoon in the stuffy jail, but Hiram Daniels was proving to be a hard nut to crack. "If you'll cooperate with me now, I'll put a word in with the judge. Who knows? He might not even hang you."

Hiram, if that was even his real name, didn't seem too impressed with the offer. He was leaning back in his chair, his legs sprawled out in front of him. "I don't plan to stay in here long enough to get hanged."

David shook his head. "Who said you'd be here?"

The other man straightened and scratched his ear. He had a face only a mother could love—small eyes, a long nose, and a weak chin. "So where you gonna take me?"

"I ought to drag you back to New Orleans. See if they can't charge you with Charlie Petrie's murder."

Hiram shook his head. "I wasn't part of that. Felix is the one who did in poor ol' Charlie."

"Where is he?"

"Dead."

David raised an eyebrow at that news. It sounded to him like the members of this gang weren't under much control. They seemed to prey on each other as much as they preyed on the innocent. "How did he die?"

Hiram relaxed, a smile on his thin lips. "Fell off his horse and hit his head. Weren't nothing we could do. Leastwise that's what my buddies said."

It sounded like his buddies might have murdered Felix and made it look like an accident. Had they been worried Felix was working with the police? "When was that?"

"Near about two weeks ago, I guess." Hiram looked off into the distance, counting the days.

"Yep." He nodded. "I remember it clear. It was right before we got our orders to come up here and wait."

"How long have you been in Cairo?"

"Not in Cairo." The thief corrected David. "We been living in the woods."

David gritted his teeth. He was ready to get this interrogation behind him and catch the real culprit. "All right, how long have you been living in the woods nearby?"

" 'Bout a week. We been sitting around doing nothing until we got our instructions last night."

"What did they say?"

"To rob the bank." Hiram looked at David, his eyes flat.

"So you and the rest of your gang sat around for a week. You didn't do anything at all until you got a note telling you to rob the bank."

"That's right."

David slammed a fist on the table. Although the action caused his hand to ache, Hiram sat up, and the distant look in his eyes disappeared.

"That's not right. I know you got more information than to 'rob a bank.' Someone is giving you specific information on the strengths and weaknesses of every bank you've hit. I want to know who that person is and how he gets his information."

Hiram shook his head. "Listen to me, lawman. I ain't scared of you. I ain't scared of your threats. In fact, there's only one thing I am scared of."

"What's that?"

"Getting stabbed in the back by the man you want to know the name of."

"I'll protect you."

"Like you protected poor ol' Charlie?"

David felt his cheeks flush. "That was an accident."

"Well, I don't want no accident happening to me." Hiram grinned at him. "I know how to keep my skin whole."

The jailhouse door opened, and Sheriff Cunningham strolled back in. "Did you find out what you need, Pinkerton?"

"Yes." David nodded. "Hiram has been very helpful."

"What?" Hiram sat up, a shocked look on his his face. "I didn't tell you nothing."

The sheriff chuckled. "Apparently you're wrong. I wonder if the fellow he arrests will think you're innocent."

"That's not fair." Hiram's whine made David grin. "You're gonna get me killed for sure."

"I don't think you need to worry about it." David held out a hand to indicate the sheriff. "I'm sure there's more than one cell here. You should be safe."

Sheriff Cunningham nodded his agreement as he walked toward Hiram. "Come on, let's get you settled in and comfortable before your friend arrives."

David wished he could've gotten Hiram to give up Vance's name, but it didn't really matter. It was obvious Vance had orchestrated the whole affair. Nothing would convince him the actor was innocent. All he had to do now was arrest Vance and put him in the jail next to Hiram. He was certain he could get a confession from one of them before the week was out.

Leaving the jail, David was surprised to see how dark the sky had become. Was a storm brewing? A glance upward told him otherwise. He'd wasted the whole afternoon inside the jail with his prisoner. All the booths that had earlier lined the street were either gone or deserted. The celebration had moved to the raised stage where the actors from the *Ophelia* would perform.

At least he knew where to find Vance. David strode down the street, considering his next move. Although he knew Vance was guilty, others might be working with him from the *Ophelia*. Rafe, for example, had been skulking about town in a guilty manner. Was he another conspirator? Until David knew for certain, he needed to continue protecting his real identity. He would have to claim he'd been looking for Jasmine when he came upon the bank robbery, and his instinct had kicked in when he realized his "sister" was in danger. Any man in town might have done the same to protect the women in his family.

Blending in with the audience, David watched as Jasmine, modestly attired in her altered costume, beseeched Rafe, resplendent in a feathered Indian headdress, to save Captain John Smith from a beheading.

The gallant captain—alias Vance Hargrove—knelt at center stage, his head bowed and his hands tied behind him as an Indian brave menaced him with a raised tomahawk. As she cried out and ran to stand between Hargrove and the brave, David found himself caught up in the drama along with the rest of the audience. The fear on Jasmine's face was so real, her every gesture so natural that she seemed to have become Pocahontas.

She put her arms around Captain Smith's shoulders and hugged him tight. "You will free him, great Powhatan, or I will die with him."

David blinked and fell out of the trance Jasmine had woven. Of course she could play the part of Pocahontas with convincing authenticity. She and the Indian girl shared the same strength of will and imperious bravery. If she had to play a different part, Katherine from *The Taming of the Shrew* for example, he doubted she would be nearly as credible.

Powhatan relented, the brave retreated, and Pocahontas helped Captain Smith rise to his feet. He thanked her for saving him and pledged to reward her with endless wonders from his homeland in exchange for her bravery.

Jasmine smiled up at him. "You owe me nothing, good captain. You have been a kind and honorable man. How could I let others harm you? Return to your people and tell them they are welcome here. You will live in peace among us. We are thirsty for the knowledge you will share with us. Together we will become a great nation."

They bowed and walked off the stage to thunderous applause.

It was time for him to act. David slipped through the crowd as Rafe, now dressed in a gray Colonial suit and white wig, escorted Angelica onto the stage for their skit about George and Martha Washington. Four tents had been set up behind the stage so the actors could change costumes. All he had to do was find out which one belonged to Hargrove and wait. He hoped to get him away from the area with a minimum of fuss.

Clem rushed past him, a blue scarf trailing from a mountain of material in her arms.

He reached out a hand to stop her. "Have you seen Vance?"

"He's changing in that far tent. He ought to be out in a minute or two."

Tabitha Barlow appeared at the flap of a different tent. "Clem, are you coming? I have to be on stage next."

"I'm right here." Clem grimaced and hurried away.

Several minutes ticked by, and David's shoulders tensed. Did Vance suspect he'd been identified?

"Did you find out anything from that man?" Jasmine's voice behind him distracted David from his worried thoughts.

He turned and smiled at her. "You made a very convincing Pocahontas."

"Do you think so?"

"I would have freed John Smith myself."

For a moment the chaos surrounding them seemed to disappear. Jasmine's lips parted, and her eyes widened. Like a moth drawn to a candle's flame, David felt himself yearning to caress her beautiful face, feel its softness beneath his fingers.

"If I didn't know better, I would think the two of you weren't even related." The sound of Miss Barlow's voice stung him, making David jerk back.

"Of course they are." Vance finally made an appearance, a stovepipe hat tucked under one arm. "Can't you see the resemblance? They have the same strong chins and high cheekbones."

David didn't want this conversation to continue. "I need you to come with me, Vance."

The actor looked surprised for a moment, but then he nodded, his face showing comprehension. "You've figured it out, haven't you?"

⁊❦

"Tell Mr. Easley I won't be able to deliver the Gettysburg Address after all." Vance reached for Jasmine's hand and pressed a swift kiss on it. "If only you had been wrong about that race, this evening would be turning out very differently."

Jasmine pulled her hand from his. "What are you talking about? What's going on?"

"Nothing." David sounded so cold, so different than he had only a moment earlier.

Tabitha looked as surprised as she felt. "I think I'll go find Mr. Easley. . .make sure he knows about the change in the program." She walked away from them, leaving Jasmine to stare after her.

"You should go with her." David's voice brought her attention back to him.

"Not until you tell me where you're taking Vance and why he won't be back in time for his performance."

"Someone else can recite the address." Vance's gaze was sad, defeated. Guilt poured from him like a spring flood.

Jasmine shook her head. "I don't believe it. I can't. He hasn't done anything wrong."

"Of course he has." David blew out an exasperated breath. "You're just blind to the truth, as always. When will you stop ignoring the evidence right in front of you?"

Was he still talking about Vance? Jasmine had the odd feeling that David's words had a completely different meaning. She snapped her mouth shut.

David held a hand out to Vance. "Why don't you show us what's in your pockets?"

"Do we have to do that out here?" Vance glanced around. "I don't want everybody to know what's going on."

"They'll have to know sooner or later." David's face was implacable.

"Not if you tell them I decided to leave the *Ophelia* on my own."

Jasmine watched the debate, unable to accept the implications of their words. Could Vance have fooled all of them for so long? It didn't seem possible. Vance had kissed her. A chill went down her spine. If he really was all that David said, he could just as easily have stabbed her.

The three of them moved a few feet away from the stage, standing behind one of the tents where no one could see them. Jasmine prayed David was wrong. But her heart dropped to her toes when Vance reached into his pocket and pulled out a handful of bills. He avoided meeting her gaze as he slapped the money into David's palm.

"Do you believe it now, Jasmine? Vance is the one who's been going to the banks at every stop your showboat makes. He trades on his notoriety as a successful actor and his dubious charms to ferret out information from the tellers and officers at the banks. They never realize what he's doing."

Jasmine couldn't think of anything to say in the face of Vance's silence.

"Didn't I hear you tell Clem earlier that he missed the rehearsal last night?" David continued reciting the evidence of the actor's guilt. "By a strange coincidence, that's when the rest of the gang got the instructions they were waiting for. He's their leader—the reason the bank robberies are so successful. If I hadn't been there when they struck this time, he would've gotten away with it again."

Vance's head jerked up. "What are you talking about?"

"It's too late for you to claim innocence now, Hargrove." David folded the money and put it into his own pocket. "I've got all the proof I need."

"Wait a minute. Do you think I'm a bank robber?"

The incredulity in Vance's voice could not be faked. Hope sprang anew in Jasmine's chest. Something was wrong. She put an arm through his. "You won't take him to jail unless I go, too."

David's glance speared her. "You're not Pocahontas, and he's not the noble Captain Smith. He's a bank robber at best and a murderer at worst. Stand back and let me get him out of here."

She lifted her chin, ready to mount a strong defense.

But Vance shook his head and pulled her arm away from his. "Don't worry, Jasmine. We'll get this all sorted out. I may not be as honest as I should be, but there's no way I can be convicted of robbery."

"That's where you're wrong, Hargrove." David gave a shallow bow and spread his hand out in the direction of the town. "We'll see what the prisoner has to say about it when he sees your face."

Jasmine wanted to go with them, but she knew neither of the men would agree. She turned away and went in search of Clem, finding her standing near the stage, a worried look on her face.

"Where have you been?" Clem's question came out in a squeak. "Do you know what's going on? Where's Mr. Hargrove? Is he hurt? Miss Barlow is telling everyone he won't be back for his skit or the final pageant. I know he missed rehearsal last night, but this is inexcusable. Mr. Easley will have his head."

"Clem, I need your help." Jasmine kept her voice low and even. "I need some advice from someone I can trust."

"What's wrong? Does it have to do with Mr. Hargrove?" Her eyes widened. "Are he and David going to have a duel?"

Now it was Jasmine's turn to gape. "Of course not. What gave you that idea?"

"David was asking for him earlier, and I know how protective he can be. I thought maybe he'd heard that. . ." Clem stuttered to a stop. "I mean, I heard that. . ." She stopped again.

"What have you heard, Clem?"

"The doctor in Cairo told someone that we'll soon have a baby traveling with us." Clem's face turned as red as a beet. "And I knew it wasn't me, so I just thought. . ."

Jasmine's head buzzed as she jumped to the conclusion Clem was so hesitant to voice. "You think I'm pregnant?"

Clem nodded. "Aren't you?"

"No!" Jasmine's shout carried out over the audience. She pulled Clem away from the stage. "As soon as the performance is over, we've got to get back to the boat."

It took another hour, but they finally entered their bedroom and closed the door. Clem helped her out of her Pocahontas costume, and they both clambered onto the bed. "Clem, before I can tell you what's really going on, I need you to promise you won't say a word to anyone."

Clem's gaze turned solemn. She raised her right hand. "I promise."

Jasmine took a deep breath. Where should she start? "The first thing you need to know is that David isn't my brother."

"He's not?"

"No, we grew up together on my sister's riverboat, but we're not related at all."

"Then why is he—"

"He's a Pinkerton detective, and he's been trying to catch a gang of bank robbers who seem to have some connection to the *Ophelia*."

"Mr. Hargrove?" The other girl drawled the name, making his last name three distinct syllables. She might be from Ohio, but her voice sounded like she'd been born and raised much further south.

Jasmine nodded. "At least that's what he thinks. But something isn't right. At first Vance acted guilty, but when David mentioned the bank robberies, he seemed surprised. I don't know what Vance may have done, but I'm sure he's not part of any gang."

"What do we need to do?" Clem whispered the question as if concerned that the walls might overhear them.

"We've got to find out who the real culprit is." Jasmine lifted her chin when she saw the dubious look from Clem. But what else could they do? They couldn't stand by and let an innocent man hang.

⁊❧

"I am not a robber."

"That's right." Hiram leaned against the wall of his neighboring cell. "Didn't you hear him? He's just a thief."

Vance put his head in his hands and groaned. "I know how it must sound, but you have to believe me."

David wondered why Vance continued to insist on his innocence. It made no sense to him. When confronted several hours earlier, he'd immediately produced money that proved his guilt. Why claim now that he was skimming money from the *Ophelia*'s manager? Why not just go ahead and admit the whole truth? "If you'll steal from the people you work with, how do you expect me to believe that you wouldn't take part in robbing a bank? Especially once you figured out how to keep your own hands clean in the process."

Vance's bleary eyes focused on his face. "Because it's the truth."

A part of David wanted to believe the man in spite of all the evidence to the contrary. But he was an actor. He could be playing the part of the innocent victim.

"It's like I told you. This morning I put a rather large wager on the *Marc Antony* to win the race. I was sure I'd double my money. It was a safe bet. That boat should have won."

"But it didn't." David stated the obvious.

"That's right. I know you won't believe me, but I'd decided to stop taking money from the Easleys. As soon as I won the wager, I knew I'd have enough to keep myself comfortable. I wouldn't have to pad my salary anymore. If only that stupid boat captain hadn't run us into a snag."

"And you don't have anything to do with the bank robberies?"

"No." Vance stood up and walked to the door of his cell. "But if someone aboard the *Ophelia* is working with the robbers, I may know who it is."

Hiram's face lost its grin. He sat up. "You'd best stubble it."

263

Vance hunched the shoulder closest to Hiram and looked toward David. "If nothing else does, his reaction just now should tell you that I'm not the man you're looking for."

"I was pulling your leg." Hiram settled back once more, assuming an uncaring expression. "Go on and tell him your idea. I need a good laugh anyway."

David wondered which of them made the better actor.

"Haven't you noticed how Rafe Griffin has been absent from rehearsals lately?"

The question was like the tiniest leak in a levee. David thought about seeing Rafe sneaking through town Sunday morning. The man had been acting strange lately, less jovial than when David had first joined the *Ophelia*. Was he the real culprit? Was he worried the authorities would catch him after the death of one—no two—of his men? The questions swirled in his mind, making it hard to think.

"I need to get some sleep." David pushed himself up from the seat that had grown hard over the past hour. "They ought to be wrapping up the pageant by now. Sheriff Cunningham said he'd be back as soon as it's over."

"You have to listen to me." Vance put his arms through the bars of his cell and rested his weight on them. "Go back to the *Ophelia* and at least talk to Rafe. You owe me that much."

"I don't owe you anything." He had to give it to Vance Hargrove. The man had an overrated sense of his own importance. Not only did he try to convince David that he was innocent, but now he was trying to throw suspicion on another man.

And what about his plans for Jasmine? The very idea of the two of them together made him physically ill. David still remembered how Jasmine had sounded when she told him that Vance's kiss was better than his. He'd wanted to drag her back into his arms right then and prove to her that he could make her swoon. Maybe he should have. And maybe he should have gotten her off the *Ophelia* back then. At least she wouldn't be in danger of falling in love with a felon. David hoped she hadn't lost her heart to Vance. He hated to think of her mourning the man while he served a life term in prison, or worse, ended up dangling from a noose.

The sky outside the jailhouse lit up, and David walked to the window. Spider webs of blue, yellow, and red sparkled against the black sky before fading away. He had missed a large part of the celebration, but at least he'd been able to watch Jasmine perform, and now he had a front row seat to the grand finale. It was a fitting end to his mission.

The Illinois Central Railroad ran between Cairo and Chicago. The territorial marshal shouldn't have any trouble getting the criminals back for a trial. All David had left to decide was what to do about Jasmine. He couldn't leave her on the *Ophelia*. And he knew her well enough to know she wouldn't go back to Les Fleurs if he didn't take her there. She was more likely to board the train to Chicago herself, eager to prove Vance's innocence to the authorities in that town.

For a moment he considered the attractive idea of Jasmine in Chicago...but then discarded it. Now that he no longer had to focus on the gang of bank robbers, David knew he needed to get her back to the people who loved her, the people who would protect her from her worst enemy—her own driving ambition.

He left Sheriff Cunningham at the jailhouse and trudged back to the *Ophelia*. His stomach was empty, his heart weary. He didn't even know what he was going to say to the other actors on the showboat. Should he tell them the truth about Vance? If the man was as guilty as he believed, he wouldn't be returning. But what if David had arrested the wrong man? What if it was Rafe? Or Mr. Easley? Or some other man he hadn't even considered? The questions in his head were absurd, the product of an exhausted mind. Vance Hargrove wasn't innocent. He couldn't be. The man was playing some kind of game for his own purposes, maybe trying to muddy the water enough so he could swim away, free to continue his wicked enterprise somewhere new. David could never let that happen.

Chapter Twenty-nine

Clem's quiet snores weren't the reason Jasmine couldn't sleep. Like a beaver worrying the bark from a sapling, her mind kept working at the question of Vance's guilt or innocence. David was smart and knew how to do his job. He wouldn't have arrested Vance if he wasn't sure the actor was guilty.

But how could Vance be guilty? After spending weeks in his company, she had realized he was not the dashing hero she'd thought in New Orleans. But a bank robber? She refused to believe Vance Hargrove was that evil. And what about the man who had been murdered? Could Vance have ordered his death? How could she reconcile this image of a cold-blooded criminal with the man who had, for the most part, been kind to her?

No matter how she looked at it, Jasmine could only find two possible answers, each of which excluded the other—believe Vance was innocent or believe David was right. She hadn't known Vance for even a year, and she had known David all her life. The choice was simple. Jasmine wished it was easy, as well.

She threw off her sheet and blanket, unable to lie still any longer.

Claustrophobia clamped anxious fingers around her throat. If she stayed in this room, Jasmine was afraid she would lose her mind. Rising from her bed, she exchanged her gown for the clothes she'd draped across the end of her bed and slipped out of the room.

Candles flickered in the hallway as she picked her way upstairs. Relief eased the tension in her neck and shoulders when she opened the door and sucked the cool night air into her lungs. The only sound out here was the soft sigh of a midnight breeze and the gentle slap of the water against the edge of the barge. Above her head God had flung a giant saltshaker of stars into the blackness of the sky. The trees on the opposite shore stood shoulder to shoulder, an army of enemy soldiers intent on subduing the countryside. The river was a dark and mysterious highway, capturing a sliver of light from the moon above as it rushed ever southward. She breathed deeply of the pine-scented air, trying to calm the melee in her head.

Turning her back on the river, Jasmine leaned into the rail, her gaze combing the bleak landscape of this side of the river for answers. The town of Cairo was dark, its citizens resting from the exciting day. A movement startled her as a shadow separated from one of the spindly pine trees between the riverbank and the town. Someone was walking toward her. Thoughts of murder and robbery came roaring back into her head. Was the real culprit sneaking back to the *Ophelia*?

Her heart clenched in fear, but before she could decide whether to run or scream—or both—an errant beam from the moon illuminated his face. David. Her terror abated with the recognition, replaced by curiosity.

His head was down; his shoulders drooped. Something was wrong. David should be elated by his success. Putting aside her own confusion, Jasmine called his name.

His head jerked up. "Who's there?"

"It's me, Jasmine."

"What are you doing out here at this hour?" He changed direction, walking toward the gangplank that connected the barge to the riverbank.

"I could ask you the same thing."

"I had to wait for Sheriff Cunningham to return. I didn't want to leave the prisoners alone." David reached her side, and she could see the frown on his face. "Your turn."

"I couldn't sleep." Jasmine left out the part about the walls of the bedroom closing in on her. "I decided to come out for some fresh air."

"You know the rest of Vance's gang is camped out somewhere near. I don't like the idea of your standing out here all alone."

She should be upset at his complaint, but Jasmine could hear the concern in David's voice. It echoed the way she'd felt earlier in the day when she had come face-to-face with the idea that David could have been hurt trying to protect her. It was time to apologize for adding to his burdens. "I'm sorry for causing so much trouble."

David said nothing. His face, half in shadow, didn't betray his thoughts. As the silence lengthened, she began to wonder if he would accept her apology. Had she finally pushed him so hard that he no longer cared about their friendship?

Another minute passed, and she couldn't stand it any longer. "Aren't you going to say something?"

"I'm just trying to overcome my shock. What's changed? Is it because of Vance, or have you finally seen what kind of people you're living with?"

Jasmine blinked. Maybe she was sleepier than she'd realized. "What are you talking about, David?"

"I'm talking about the loose morals and decadent lifestyles of the theater."

"And you think that's why I want to be a famous actress? So I can lead a shameful life? Sometimes I think you don't understand me at all."

"I know you're doing this for all the wrong reasons, Jasmine. You've said yourself that you want to be famous. Can't you see how destructive such a goal can be?"

She straightened. "Fame and fortune are not bad things. I can hold onto my morals and still be a part of this world."

David's eyes closed, and he shook his head. "I wish that were true."

"What about you? Don't try to convince me that you don't enjoy the slaps on the back for a job well done."

Jasmine waited for his answer.

"You're right to an extent. When I foiled an attempt to rob the coach I was on last year, I was pretty proud of myself. The passengers were so complimentary. It felt good. I accepted a job offer with the Pinkerton Agency with the idea that I wanted to spend my life repeating that experience." He paused and swallowed. "One day God tapped me on the shoulder. I was riding along with a payroll train that was attacked. I killed one of the robbers and wounded one, a kid too young to shave. A pastor on the train stepped forward and shared the Gospel with that kid right there in the middle of nowhere. He was saved that day—I watched as he changed. God used that pastor, but He also used me and the talents He's given me to make a difference. I like to think that if I save a man's life, maybe he'll have time to repent and turn to God."

What made him think God wasn't using her talents, too?

As if he had read her mind, David shook his head. "Providing an hour or two of entertainment isn't a bad thing in itself. I was proud of you back in Natchez when you were helping the orphanage, but what you're doing now is for your own purposes."

Jasmine was beginning to wish she'd never come up on deck. But she couldn't let his condemnation go unchallenged. "How can you say I won't touch lives? When I get to be famous, I can use my resources to rebuild dozens of orphanages."

"Like you're doing right now?" He cocked his head.

"That's not fair. I'm just starting out. Once I become a star, everything will be different."

"No it won't, Jasmine. That's just the point. Jesus said if we are unjust in the least things, we'll be unjust in greater ones. You can't wait to become rich or famous. You can't expend all of your talent getting the things this world labels valuable and expect to hold onto what's really important."

The words rang with power and truth. For a moment Jasmine felt like a curtain had been lifted. Was she already growing calloused and hard? Immoral? *No.* She was still the same person she'd always been.

"What about my obligation to Mr. and Mrs. Easley? To the other actors on the *Ophelia*? I know it's not your fault that Vance is guilty." There. Maybe by admitting that he was right, David would see that she was not the selfish, heartless person he accused her of being. "But that doesn't change the fact that we can't hope to replace him before getting to St. Louis. And my part may not be as vital as his, but I'm filling in for Angelica. If I leave now, the whole company might fold."

"All right, Jasmine, have it your way." He sounded so defeated. So tired. "I'll stay on board the *Ophelia* until it reaches St. Louis, since that's the end of its current run. But that's it. I think you're trying to run from God. Be careful that you don't get too far away to call on Him."

She watched him cross the gangplank with a heavy heart. Had she thrown away something precious by refusing to listen to David? Had she forfeited his protection? Jasmine hugged her arms as a damp gust of air blew against her face. Why couldn't David see that she was the same person she'd always been?

She would show him the truth. She would reach her goals in spite of his doubts. And she would use her influence to make changes in the world that impressed even David Foster.

❧

Jasmine awoke to the low tone of a steam whistle very close by. What time was it? She rolled over in her bed and groaned when she realized Clem was already dressed and gone. She had overslept again, thanks to her sleeplessness during the night. Ever since her talk with David, slumber had eluded her each night until the wee hours of the morning.

The past few days had been difficult for everyone. Hot, long days that led to short tempers, outbursts, and arguments. Jasmine had gone to visit Vance once before the U.S. marshal arrived. It had been an uncomfortable experience, and she was relieved she wouldn't have to repeat it.

Angelica had talked the Easleys into letting her reassume her role as the second leading lady, reducing Jasmine to the status of an understudy. No matter which play they performed, the most she got to do was the bit parts, the same as the rest of the stock troupe who received no recognition.

So much for her determination to show David how she could use her talents. At least they were supposed to leave Cairo today. The residents had seen all the plays in the *Ophelia*'s repertoire, even a reprise of their patriotic vignettes. Last night, the audience even booed poor Rafe.

The barge shook under her feet as she considered whether or not to bury her head in her pillow again. Were they already underway? Deciding it was too late to fall back asleep, Jasmine got up, hurried through her toilette, and headed for the dining room. Maybe a cup of coffee would clear the cobwebs from her head.

"Here's Miss Johnny-Come-Lately to join us. Clem said you needed your beauty sleep, and I have to say I agree with her." Tabitha's words contained the sting of a wasp.

Jasmine felt like sticking her tongue out at the snippy female. "I didn't realize we were on a schedule."

The others in the room paused for a moment before returning to their meals, except for Mr. Easley, who looked at her from his seat at the head of the dining table, his eyes narrowed. "Are you ill?"

"No, sir." She picked up a plate and chose some crisp bacon and a piece of toast from the buffet before sliding into a vacant chair next to Clem and across from Rafe and Angelica.

Jasmine noticed that Angelica's face looked blotchy and swollen, like she had been crying. What was she so upset about? From her woebegone expression, anyone would think she'd lost her best friend... but Rafe was sitting next to her.

"I hope not." Mrs. Easley took a sip from her coffee cup. "We've had enough of bad luck lately."

It was the same thing Jasmine had heard again and again since Vance was arrested. At first everyone had been shocked and unbelieving, but as the days wore on, they adjusted. Rafe was not as convincing as the male lead, and Mr. Easley was beginning to lose patience. She glanced at the man across from her, wondering what was bothering him. Maybe she should try to get him alone and question him. Offer him a sympathetic ear and even give him helpful advice.

"Everything will be better once we reach St. Louis." Rafe glanced at Angelica, a question in his eyes.

Perhaps she should start with Angelica. Whatever was bothering him most likely involved her as well and might be the root of the blond actress's obvious distress.

"I doubt you'll be much better." Mr. Easley sent a dark frown his direction. "But that may not be my problem by then anyway."

Angelica pushed back from the table and ran from the room. Tabitha made a face but said nothing.

Jasmine exchanged a confused glance with Clem. Something she didn't understand was going on. Her stomach churned. Even though she'd grown up with two older sisters, she had never liked emotional scenes. Especially at breakfast.

Clem cleared her throat and glanced toward the door—a signal for Jasmine to follow as soon as possible—before excusing herself. She must know something that she couldn't discuss in front of the others.

Jasmine toyed with the food on her plate, sipped her coffee, and covertly watched the others. What had happened before she arrived? The Easleys exited next, leaving Tabitha, Rafe, and Jasmine in the dining room. Time to make her escape. She tossed her napkin over her plate and stood. "See you later."

Neither of the other two said anything as she exited. She looked for Clem on deck, in the theater, and in the prop room but found no sign of her friend until she returned to her room. "What's going on?"

"It's Angelica." Clem opened her eyes wide and twisted her mouth.

Jasmine understood she was supposed to infer something from Clem's expression, but she had no idea what. "What about Angelica? I saw she was upset. I don't understand why unless she's afraid I'm going to get her parts again."

"Angelica is the one." Again that odd twist to Clem's mouth.

Jasmine shook her head.

Finally Clem made a disgusted noise. "She's the one who is going to— She's going to be a mother."

"What?" Jasmine couldn't believe what her friend was saying. With all the extra drama lately, she had forgotten the rumor that someone was in the family way. Everything fell into place. The way Angelica had been gaining weight. Her moodiness.

"The truth was bound to come out sooner or later."

"Is Rafe the. . .the one who. . ." Her face colored. She couldn't get the words out.

Clem raised her shoulders in a shrug. "Who knows? But you still don't get it. Have you thought what this is going to mean for you?"

First Vance turned out to be a criminal. Now Angelica was— *Disgraced* was the only word she could assign to Angelica's scandalous condition. What was wrong with these people? At this point she wouldn't have been surprised to find out that Tabitha was an alcoholic or that the Easleys ran a gambling den. Now Clem wanted her to be happy about assuming Angelica's roles on a permanent basis? "I can't believe you said that."

Clem looked as though Jasmine had slapped her. "Why? Haven't you heard that 'It's an ill wind blows no good'?"

"Angelica is far from the most pleasant woman on board, but I can't take pleasure in such a thing. Her life is going to change dramatically. She needs our prayers."

"When did you turn into such a goody-goody?"

Jasmine caught her breath. Had she strayed so far from her beliefs that her best friend on the *Ophelia* didn't know where she stood on spiritual matters? Did she even know anymore? Although Clem's cutting words hurt, Jasmine found herself more disturbed by the realization that David had been right that night. She had strayed a long way from what she once held dear.

It was time to find her way back to the person she used to be, back to the important things in life, back to God and her faith. She would start by trying to help Angelica. "I'm sorry you're disappointed in me, but we'll sort things out when I get back."

"Where are you going?" Clem's voice followed her into the hallway.

Jasmine continued on her mission without answering. She would tell Clem later. Right now she needed to talk to Mr. and Mrs. Easley before they did anything rash.

She passed Angelica's room on her way to find the manager and his wife, coming to a halt as she realized she could hear sobs coming from within. Her heart ached for the actress. She couldn't ignore Angelica's distress. Jasmine knocked on the door, turning the knob when the weeping continued. "Angelica, may I come in?"

"Go away." The actress was lying face down across her bed, her hair loose.

Ignoring Angelica's order, Jasmine sat on the edge of the bed and rubbed the actress's back. "It's going to be okay, honey."

Angelica turned her head toward the wall. "No, it's not. My life is over."

"You do have some difficult days ahead of you." Jasmine knew that sugarcoating the situation would not help Angelica. She needed someone who would help her face her future and perhaps even appreciate the blessings in her life. "You also have a lot of things going for you."

"You don't know anything about it." Angelica sniffed and sat up. "If I don't do something, I'm going to have a baby. My life will be over if that happens."

"What do you mean. . .if?"

"Tabitha says she knows of a doctor in St. Louis who can take care of my problem."

Jasmine was horrified at the suggestion. "You cannot be serious, Angelica."

"What do you know about anything?" Angelica could be a pretty girl, but the sneer on her face distorted her features, making her look like she was wearing an evil mask. "You waltz in here all fresh and innocent like you aren't planning to step into my shoes the minute the Easleys dismiss me. I know you want to steal my career."

"I have to admit I've enjoyed playing larger roles, Angelica. I want to be a serious actress, too. But I've always been eager to give them back to you."

"Well, you can have them now, unless I decide to go see Tabitha's doctor."

"You can't do that, Angelica." Jasmine reached out and pushed Angelica's hair away from her face. "You're carrying a life inside you. A life God has given you."

Angelica didn't pull away from her touch. An encouraging sign. Jasmine decided to risk going a step further. "I can't say I approve of the way you went about this—and we both know God is not pleased when we go against His Word and choose our own pleasure over His will. But you can't change the situation now. What you have to consider at this moment is the precious baby you'll get to love and care for."

"But what about my career?"

"That has to come secondary to the precious life you will bring into this world. That's what any loving parent does: put what's best for the child before his or her own dreams and wishes." Jasmine felt an inward prick as Lily came to mind. She knew deep down her oldest sister always wanted what was best for her. She pushed aside her guilt for now, as she needed to concentrate on Angelica. "Who's the father?"

"Rafe, of course." Angelica frowned at her.

"What does he say about the baby?"

Angelica twisted her hair and pushed it behind her shoulders. "He says he'll marry me."

"See? There's your answer." Jasmine paused as another thought occurred to her. "Do you love him?"

"I suppose so. But even if we do get married, I still won't be able to continue acting."

"That's true. But you'll be busy with an even more important role. You'll be raising a beautiful son or daughter."

Angelica rubbed her nose with the heel of her hand. "Do you think I can do that?"

"I'm sure you can. God gave you this baby because He knows it, too. You and Rafe can make a good life for your child. God has a plan for all three of you. All you have to do is follow Him."

A tiny smile appeared on the other woman's mouth. "You remind me of a lady from my hometown. She was always telling me about God and Jesus, too. You know, you're not as bad as I thought you were."

Jasmine couldn't help laughing at the backhanded compliment. "I'm glad to hear that."

Angelica pushed herself up from the bed, a look of hope on her face. She moved to her dressing table and pinned her hair in a bun. "Thanks, Jasmine. I'm going to think about what you said. I may even go talk to Rafe."

Feeling better than she had since David arrested Vance, Jasmine left Angelica's room. She didn't know if the couple would turn to God, but she prayed they would.

☙

David heard the *Miss Polly's* paddlewheel stall. He looked back to see if he could identify the problem. No sign of a snag or sandbar. What was wrong?

A hint of black smoke rising past the blades of the paddlewheel made him wonder if something had happened to the pistons under the deck. The engineer stuck his head out of the boiler room. "I've got pressure building up in here."

Several of the crew ran away from the engineer, but David moved toward him. Boiler explosions were the most common reasons for the loss of a riverboat. And for the deaths of passengers and crew. If the boiler exploded, the ship often sank. Those who survived the initial explosion were in danger of drowning. In his years with Jasmine and her family, he had seen the ghastly remains of more than one such incident.

David threw open the door and ran to help Sal Benson, the engineer. Outside the cramped room, men yelled, and he thought he heard a splash. Had someone decided to jump before knowing whether or not it was necessary?

Throwing his weight against the largest valve, David prayed for the safety of the tugboat, the showboat it was pushing, and the lives of everyone aboard both vessels.

Sal kept one eye on his gauges as he tackled the other valves. "I think we're getting ahead of the problem. The needles are beginning to drop."

"Thank You, Lord." David grabbed one of the coal shovels and used it to jam his valve open.

Sal pulled a filthy handkerchief from his pocket and staunched the beads of sweat from his broad forehead. A gray streak caused by the swipe of the dirty cloth stood out in stark relief to his parchment-hued face. "That was a close one."

"What do you think happened?"

"I have no idea. I had just added fresh coal to the boiler when I realized it was too quiet. Even tossing a bucket of water on them wasn't enough to stop the pressure from building up. If you hadn't come to help me. . ." His voice trailed off.

Captain Ross's face appeared at the boiler room door. "Is everything all right in here?"

Sal nodded. "Thanks to David. He was the only one who wasn't too scared to help me get the boiler shut down."

"Is the *Ophelia* okay?" David didn't want to dwell on his actions. He hadn't been any braver than the engineer standing beside him.

"Yes, but we're going to have to land and figure out what's happened to our paddlewheel. Luckily we're only a few miles north of Wittenberg, Missouri. I hope to negotiate a safe landing there." He tugged on his cap and left them alone.

When David left the engineer, he helped the others knot lengths of rope around several grappling hooks. The plan was to hurl the hooks toward trees or any other targets that could hold their boat against the current of the river. He was glad they were far enough north of Cairo that the rough water of the confluence wouldn't be a danger.

A glance toward the barge showed that most of the passengers were on deck watching the activity on the tug. He caught a glimpse of Jasmine's windblown dark hair. Even though David told himself that he was no longer responsible for her safety, he knew better. Just seeing her tentative wave brought a smile to his face and made the muscles of his stomach loosen. Who was he kidding? As long as he drew breath, he would love Jasmine. But if she didn't soon change her ways, he would have to sever their contact. Watching her destroy her life was something he couldn't do.

After some tense moments, they managed to get the *Miss Polly* secure against the riverbank at Wittenberg. The showboat suffered no visible damage, but he knew the ride had been rougher than the actors were used to as the river current tried to separate the two boats. Finally it was done.

He crossed to the showboat and began searching for Jasmine and Clem, finding them in the prop room picking up the costumes and props that had become jumbled up during the maneuvers. "Are the two of you okay?"

Clem picked up a bouquet of silk flowers. "What's wrong with the *Miss Polly?*"

"A piston rod splintered."

Jasmine looked at him. "That's serious. I wonder how long it will take to replace it."

David shrugged and shoved his hands into his pockets. He had been avoiding Jasmine for days in an attempt to give her time to think about what she wanted to do with her life. Had his tactic worked? Had she considered her future from a different point of view, or was she still clinging to the belief that she could serve two masters?

"I've got to go check on something in our room." Clem put the flowers on a table before leaving.

A backdrop painted to resemble *Macbeth*'s Great Birnam Wood leaned against a papier-mâché arch. David pushed the plywood stage set against the wall. "I heard you've been busy over the past week."

"I don't have that much to do." Jasmine folded the costume in her hands and put it in one of the open trunks. "I mostly spend my time helping Clem."

"That's not what I mean, and you know it."

He heard her soft laugh. "I didn't do anything worth mentioning."

David stopped trying to straighten the arch. It would need professional attention. "Rafe has been singing your praises to anyone who will listen. He says you intervened on his behalf with the Easleys. That you begged them to keep him on since he's about to be a father. That took a lot of pluck."

"I was worried about him and Angelica. They're going to be a family. I know they should have gotten married first, but Angelica told me they're going to see a pastor as soon as we get to St. Louis."

"Which is going to take several days longer than expected." David picked up a skull, shuddered, and set it on a table as Hamlet's soliloquy about death rang in his ears. "I just wanted you to know how proud I am of you."

"Will it take that long to replace the piston rod?"

"I can't believe Wittenberg will have the proper replacement parts. We'll probably have to order it from St. Louis."

"If that's not the definition of irony, I don't know what is. To get to St. Louis we need to purchase a part from St. Louis."

This time his laughter joined hers.

"Did I see someone jump off the *Miss Polly*?"

David sobered. "Yes. The idiot apparently decided he'd rather take his chances in the water. He was lucky to be fished out a mile or so downriver. It's a wonder he didn't drown."

Jasmine nodded.

Silence filled the room for several moments until Jasmine stopped working and tossed a glance at him.

"Is something wrong?"

A tentative smile appeared on her lips, making her look so sweet... so vulnerable. "I've been thinking about what you said."

His heart thumped. "And?"

"You made a lot of sense, David, but I'm not sure I want to leave the *Ophelia* when we reach St. Louis."

David put a hand to his forehead. Nothing had changed. All his prayers, all his heartfelt words had meant nothing to Jasmine. Disappointment weighted his shoulders. What could he say to her?

She forestalled his words. "Before you start in on me again, please let me explain."

He put his hand down, offering a silent plea to God for fortitude. "Go ahead."

"Angelica cannot continue acting for obvious reasons. Someone will have to replace her." She stopped and looked at him.

Was she waiting for his agreement? If so, she would have a long wait. He could already see where this was going.

When he said nothing, she sighed. "You remember how I took over for her on a temporary basis when the Easleys thought her problem was overeating. My name was even on the playbill. I saved a copy as a reminder. Even if I can't go on to Chicago or New York, at least I'll be able to say I was a serious actress. That playbill is a memento of the time I—we—have spent on the *Ophelia*."

He shook his head. "You're falling into a trap. Even though I've never received applause for what I do, the praise I get makes me feel good—it brings me pleasure. If I'm not careful, though, those good feelings begin to replace something important. I start thinking I deserve the praise. That it's because I'm special—smarter or faster or stronger. It's like an addictive drug. The more praise you receive, the more you want."

"You still don't get it, David. It's not so much the applause that I want to hold onto, although that is part of it. I want to remember making others happy, helping the Easleys and Tabitha, Angelica and Rafe, Clem and all the others who depend on the *Ophelia* for their livelihood. I want to remember spending this time with you, too."

David considered her words. He still thought she should go home, but he had to admire her spirit. Jasmine was maturing. She was beginning to sound like a woman he had always hoped she would become. Should he agree? If he insisted on her immediate return, would he risk destroying the bridge forming between them? A bridge that could bring them together?

She smiled, her eyes lighting with mischief, reminding him of the girl he'd grown up adoring. "There's something else I wanted to talk to you about. I've already mentioned it to Clem, and she thinks it's a great idea."

"What's that?" He let go of his concerns for the moment. He would have to pray about St. Louis.

"Since Rafe is having to take over for Vance, we've struggled to find someone who can do his parts."

"I find that hard to believe." David frowned. Why was she talking to him about acting problems? "Don't you have several men in the stock company?"

"Yes, but none of them seems quite right. Ever since the trouble in Cairo, we've been losing people. The ones who are left are either too inexperienced or too old. They're not convincing, and the Easleys are worried our performances will fall short if we don't find a strong second lead."

"You're beginning to sound more like a manager than an actress."

She tilted her head, her violet eyes serious. "Clem said the same thing."

"So what will you do?" David's heart seemed to grow wings. Perhaps he should not worry so about Jasmine's plans. He sensed the change in her was deeper than he'd first thought.

"I thought maybe you could join us on the barge."

"What?" His mouth fell open in shock. "Please tell me you're not serious."

"Come on. It'll be fun. Remember how we used to act for our friends and family back home? You already know the stories, and the lines will come back to you after a few rehearsals." She stood and walked to him, her eyes begging for his agreement.

When would he stop being an idiot for this woman? "What about my work on the tugboat?"

"Don't worry about that. The Easleys will explain to Captain Ross. He'll have to find someone else to take over your duties." Jasmine hugged him. "I can't wait to tell Clem."

Relishing the feel of her arms around his waist, David gave in. It couldn't be that bad, could it?

Chapter Thirty

Tabitha stood on a crate, only her upturned face and steepled hands showing above Juliet's balcony. "O Romeo, Romeo! Wherefore art thou Romeo? Deny thy father and refuse thy name! Or, if thou wilt not, be but sworn my love, and I'll no longer be a Capulet."

Standing in the wings in the nurse's costume, Jasmine mouthed the familiar lines, her heart wrung once again by Shakespeare's words. No matter how often they were repeated or who actually performed them, her imagination carried her to the Capulets' garden.

"You should be Juliet." The words in David's slow drawl sent a shiver down her spine.

She turned in the crowded space, her elbow grazing his arm. "I doubt Tabitha would agree with you."

His mouth was only a breath away. Her awareness shrank until all she could see was his mouth. The memory of the night in Memphis returned to her in full force. The thrill of their lips pressed together, the strength of his hands cupping her face, the love and devotion in his gaze. The aftermath of his touch returned to her, too. She'd pushed him away, left him standing all alone. And when he'd tried to do the honorable thing and apologize to her, she had scoffed at his words, even taunting him. . .lying to him about Vance's kiss.

When he took a step back, Jasmine remembered to breathe. Fiery coals burned her cheeks. Jasmine put her hands to them, her mind skittering.

"Are you ready for your scene?"

"All I have to do is shout, 'Madam!' from the edge of the stage." His question refocused her attention, giving her something to think about besides the past. She looked him up and down. "I never realized how long your legs were until tonight."

He laughed, the sound warming her heart. "Thanks. Now I feel less self-conscious about these ridiculous tights."

"They look fine on you, better than they did on Rafe." She bent her head toward the stage. "You would make a better Romeo than he does."

"I doubt he would agree with you." He winked at her as he paraphrased her previous answer. "Besides, Rafe seems to have grown into his new role. I think it's because he knows his position is secure on the *Ophelia*."

"I'll be happier once he and Angelica are safely married."

David glanced toward the curtain between them and the audience. "I'm sure she's sitting out there watching to make sure he doesn't stray."

"She doesn't have to worry about that. Rafe has made it abundantly clear he loves her. He is constantly hovering over her. It would drive me crazy."

"You've always been too independent for your own good."

Jasmine pretended indignation. "And here I was thinking we were beginning to understand each other. I see now that you're still clinging to your mistaken opinion of my obvious strengths."

"You're wrong about that. I've always admired your strengths, Jasmine, even when I disagreed with your use of them."

"You used to like playacting with me." She squeezed her lips into a pout. "Or at least you always went along."

His face sobered. "That's because I care about you. Why else would I let you talk me into donning this ridiculous costume and making a fool of myself?"

She didn't know what to think about his statement. Did he really still care? Even after all she'd done?

"Jasmine, that's your cue." Mr. Easley hissed the warning at her.

Already? She moved to the edge of the curtain and put a hand to her mouth. "Madam!"

Tabitha answered her, impatience in her voice.

"Madam!" She repeated the summons before moving back to where David stood. "That's it for me until after your next scene."

When he didn't answer, she searched his face. "You're not still nervous are you?"

A twist of his lips told her the truth. And she'd been teasing him. Contrite, she assumed a serious expression. "You're doing a wonderful job. Mercutio is one of the hardest characters to portray—"

"You're not helping me feel much better."

"If you'd let me finish without interrupting." She put her hands on her hips. "I was going to say that you've conveyed his scornful wit perfectly. The people out there are laughing at the right times and staying silent when they should. You have them in the palm of your hand."

"Don't worry, Jasmine. You don't have to exaggerate. I'm not about to run off and leave you in the lurch." He touched her nose with the tip of his finger. "I've really enjoyed parts of the past week. Especially getting to watch all of you so serious about your art. It's given me a new respect for the theater."

"It's about time." She was glad to hear that David was not still angry about lingering aboard the *Ophelia*. "Now get out there and make me proud."

He saluted before moving past her. "Where the devil should this Romeo be? Came he not home tonight?"

Jasmine's heart soared as she watched him. Was it any wonder Vance had been such a disappointment to her? Even before she found out he was a thief and a bank robber, Jasmine had known the man couldn't hold a candle to David. What Vance lacked had nothing to do with looks or occupation. Although she'd been blinded by both of those attributes when she first met him, she had eventually come to recognize the emptiness in Vance's soul where his faith should be.

She hadn't suspected him like David had, but at least she'd known enough to keep Vance at arm's length. Even when she was denying her connection to God, He had kept her heart safe.

David returned to her side of the wings, but Jasmine had no time to compliment him on his scene. It was her turn to take center stage. In front of the audience, she delivered her lines with all the right gestures and inflections. Odd that she could perform even though being on stage no longer triggered the same heady surge of pleasure.

The performance ended to thunderous applause, and Jasmine took her place on the stage. She went through the motions of curtsying and smiling, moving forward with the other principals for an additional curtsy before stepping back to let Tabitha and Rafe bask in their stardom. When the curtain calls ended, David was surrounded by the rest of the cast. He was the new actor in their midst and deserved their congratulations.

Why did she feel so odd to see him being hailed? She wasn't jealous of his success. She was happy for David. Happy to see him enjoying the moment. Jasmine pinned a smile on her lips and added her thanks to the rest of the cast and the Easleys before slipping back downstairs to help Clem with the cleanup.

"I can't believe it's over." Clem stood in the middle of an avalanche. "How did David do?"

"He was extraordinary. If he didn't already have another job, he could succeed in the theater."

"If anyone can change his mind, it's you."

"I doubt David would agree with you." Jasmine smiled as she recalled their offstage banter. She would treasure those silly moments no matter what their futures held. As for his words about his feelings, she had no doubt she would lie awake considering them once she sought her bed. "And I doubt I would want to even if he did."

Clem rolled her eyes. "We'll see if you change your mind once we get to St. Louis."

"Don't count on it." Jasmine began to sort the mountain of costumes into two piles—one for washing, the other for mending.

For a brief moment she had a vision of being married to David, traveling around the world with him at her side. But then it faded. She knew better. David had his priorities, priorities that had nothing to do with the theater. Besides, she was starting to lose the passion for that dream herself. Jasmine didn't know if her feelings were a temporary aberration or a more permanent change, but she was leaning toward the latter.

As each day passed, she found herself more content with the idea of returning to Les Fleurs. Wouldn't Lily and Camellia be surprised to hear her admit that they'd been right all along? Although Jasmine couldn't regret her time with the people on the *Ophelia*, her brief stint in the public eye had taught her that life was more than accolades and applause.

What Renée Thornton had tried to tell her all those months ago— that she was supposed to being sowing the seeds of faith in this world— made sense to her now. Jasmine hoped to one day tell the sweet woman how much she appreciated her advice.

Once all of the costumes were sorted, Clem put a hand on her back and stretched. "That's all we can do for tonight, but we'll have to get up early if we're going to get all of these things ready for our arrival in St. Louis."

Jasmine was grateful that Clem had turned her attention from speculation about the future. Tomorrow would take care of itself. All they had to do was deal with today.

"Where is my script?" Jasmine upturned the pile of clothes on her bed. "I wanted to read through that scene once more before dinner."

Clem's hand halted midstroke through her loose hair as she twisted on the stool in front of their dressing table. "Stop making a mess. It's obviously not here. Do you think it's upstairs?"

Jasmine considered the question. She had not had it when she went to visit Angelica in her room after rehearsal. "It must be. I wouldn't worry about it, but I need to read through those Latin words once more.

I kept stumbling over them this afternoon."

"Are you sure you don't have another reason for going back upstairs? Perhaps you and David need more practice. . ."

With a shake of her head, Jasmine exited the room. Ever since they started rehearsing *The Taming of the Shrew* back in Wittenberg, Clem had teased her about playing the part of sweet-natured Bianca opposite David's portrayal of the love-stricken Lucentio. At least they weren't Katherine and Petruchio. She was sure she'd never manage to be convincing in submitting to Petruchio's unreasonable demands. Jasmine much preferred sweet-natured, discerning Bianca, the pretty younger sister who chose David—Lucentio—from her bevy of admirers.

It was only a performance, after all. That's what Clem didn't understand. Rafe, or even Vance if he was not in prison, could be playing the part of Lucentio. The fact that she was looking into David's velvety green gaze had nothing to do with the way she stumbled over the Latin words in her lines. It was a difficult scene. That was all. David was only playing a part when he told her of his love during the scene. The same was true for her.

Jasmine knew she could overcome the problem by studying—by embracing the character of Bianca and forgetting everything but the performance. She had to. The Easleys would expect her to perform flawlessly at the St. Louis premiere tomorrow evening, and she was determined not to let them down.

Stepping into the theater, Jasmine was surprised to find it shrouded in darkness. Had Mr. or Mrs. Easley decided they could save money by extinguishing all the candles now that rehearsals had ended? The vast room was like a cave. She would have a hard time finding her script now. She stood still wondering if she should return to her bedroom for a candle on her own or fumble around on the stage and risk running into something.

"I thought I heard someone." A male voice coming from the back of the theater made her heart attempt to escape from her chest.

She recognized Tabitha's answering voice. "You're just nervous. Why do you think I snuffed all the candles? If anyone wandered in here, we'd hear them stumbling about. It's an effective way to ensure privacy."

"Are you sure?"

"I am. Now tell me why you think we should get rid of Hiram Daniels."

The name sounded familiar to Jasmine, but she couldn't quite place him. She left the question for now and concentrated on identifying the man's voice.

"Because he could still testify I had something to do with Charlie Petrie's death."

Jasmine put a hand over her mouth to keep from making any noise as understanding dawned on her. Charlie Petrie was the man who had died in David's arms. He was one of the bank robbers. And Hiram was the man who had mowed her down in Cairo.

Tabitha's laugh made the hair on her arms stand up. "Vance Hargrove will take the blame for that, not you and certainly not me. Hiram is too smart to say anything that could come back on us. He knows what happens to snitches."

"I hope you're right." The unseen man sounded less certain than Tabitha. "If a lawman knocks on my door, it won't be long before he also knocks on yours."

Jasmine placed the man's voice. Adam. . .no, Arnold Garth, one of the stock cast she had never paid much attention to. He and Tabitha were the bank robbers! They were the connection with the *Ophelia*.

Her first inclination was to go find David and tell him what she'd heard. But she needed to get proof first. Undeniable, incontrovertible proof. But what proof was there? Tabitha and Arnold would deny their conversation, and it would be their word against hers. She needed to continue listening. Maybe they would say something she could use against them.

"Don't worry about Hiram. We need to focus on getting this job done here. Then you and I can put our plans into action. It's about time to cut our losses here anyway."

"What are you talking about?"

"Things haven't been the same since New Orleans. Since Petrie's arrest." Tabitha's voice carried clearly through the empty theater. "There's something odd about that David Foster, too. I'm not sure what he had to do with catching Hiram and Vance, but he was involved in it somehow. Make sure you stay clear of him."

"I will. I may look for work out West." Arnold's laugh raised the hair on Jasmine's arm. "Maybe we can hook up in the future for another lucrative venture."

"Maybe. But listen, I visited two banks this morning. The best target is going to be Boatmen's Savings Institution." Tabitha lowered her voice, and Jasmine strained her hearing to its limits. "I wrote out most of the instructions this afternoon, but I didn't quite finish. It won't take me long to get it done. I'll give it to you after dinner. And this time I want you to stay with the men until it's done. I don't want any more mistakes or arrests."

"That wasn't my fault. Someone was waiting for us in Cairo. I never saw him, but I heard the gunshots. I almost didn't escape in time."

"It was a mistake to rob a town as small as Cairo." Tabitha's voice sounded hesitant, reluctant. "I thought it would do because of the Fourth of July celebration, but I was wrong. The bank must have hired a guard. Here in St. Louis, it'll be like it was before. The men will walk in, help themselves, and walk out. And we'll all be rich."

Jasmine had heard enough. She knew what to do. She had to get to Tabitha's room, find the note, and take it to David.

Thankful the unexpected darkness had kept her from stepping past the edge of the curtain, Jasmine felt behind her for the doorknob. She had to hurry. Slipping through the door, she held her breath and closed it without a sound. Glad she'd not changed out of the slippers she wore to rehearsals, she tiptoed down the stairs and broke into a run as she reached the corridor.

She didn't see anyone as she turned to the left and headed for Tabitha's suite. Opening the door, she was surprised to find it much tidier than her last visit. Was Tabitha packing in preparation for her departure?

With a sense of urgency, she looked for a note on Tabitha's dresser, opening each drawer to nothing but jewelry and face paint. A quick look through two trunks yielded nothing, but when Jasmine opened the top drawer in the table beside Tabitha's bed, she found it. A note on thick vellum. Her hand shook so hard, she could barely read the words. But she knew she had the proof David needed.

"What do we have here?" Tabitha's voice brought her head up.

The piece of paper drifted from her hand as Jasmine realized she was in serious trouble. Both Tabitha and her henchman stood in the door.

Arnold pulled a gun from the waist of his pants and trained it on Jasmine. "I told you someone was upstairs."

"It looks like you were right for once."

Jasmine closed her eyes and prayed for a miracle.

Chapter Thirty-one

David knew he was a little early for escorting the girls to dinner, but he wanted them to see the boat about to dock next to the *Ophelia*. Elephants, lions, and a hippopotamus were sights one didn't see every day. He knocked on their door and waited.

"Who's there?"

He recognized Clem's voice. "It's me, David."

She opened the door a crack. "I'm almost ready. But I don't know about Jasmine. She left several minutes ago to retrieve her script."

"I just came through there and didn't see her." He frowned. "I don't know how I missed her."

"She wasn't sure where it was. Maybe she went to see if she left it in Angelica's room. I'm sure she'll be right back."

"I hope so. I've got a special treat for the two of you."

Clem opened the door an inch wider. "What is it?"

"You'll have to wait and see."

She made a face and snapped the door shut.

David tapped his foot on the floor and waited. Other actors passed and spoke, but Jasmine still had not appeared by the time

Clem came out of the room.

"Still no sign of her?" Clem looked down the hall as if she expected Jasmine to be hiding behind him in the corridor.

David took her arm. "Let's go to the dining hall and see if she went ahead of us."

"I doubt that." Clem's face wrinkled in a frown. "She hadn't changed out of her costume. I can't imagine where she's gotten to. You're sure she wasn't in the theater?"

"Unless she was hiding from me." David was beginning to grow worried. It wasn't like Jasmine to disappear. "Let's go up and make sure, though. If we don't find her there, at least I'll be able to show you the surprise."

The theater was dimly lit by a small number of sconces. Clem called out her name while David went to look behind the Padua backdrop. "Jasmine, are you back here?"

"Look, David, I found her script." Clem held up the booklet. "She must have gone somewhere else."

He tried to quiet the alarm bells in his head. Jasmine had to be somewhere near. She was no longer a child with a tendency to wander off. "Let's go on outside. Maybe she's already discovered the surprise."

Clem folded the booklet and tucked it under her arm before meeting David at center stage. "I'm sure she's fine."

They walked through the auditorium side by side. He could tell Clem's unease matched his own. They would find her outside. Anything else was unthinkable.

He couldn't see anyone on the deck when they emerged from the stage entrance, but he could hear voices from the far side of the *Ophelia*, the side where the circus boat would dock.

"What's going on?" Clem glanced up at him, her eyes clouded with worry.

David led her around the front of the barge to the other side without explaining anything. Several people were crowded together, pointing at the barge floating toward them, its paddlewheel tugboat slowly guiding it toward the dock.

"I see a tiger." Clem's concern was temporarily shelved as she stared at the boat.

"That's my surprise. A floating circus." He moved her to the rail so she could get a better view, still looking for Jasmine's dark hair and the flowing blue costume she'd worn during the rehearsal.

Clem pointed to the large signs ruffling in the breeze as the barge inched forward: AMAZING ANIMALS, ASTONISHING ACTS, AND ASTOUNDING ACROBATICS.

David nodded, but his attention was still on the group of people leaning against the rail. Where was Jasmine?

The caged tiger Clem had first noticed paced back and forth, its growls bringing shrieks and exclamations from the women on the *Ophelia* as well as from the onlookers who lined the dock. Had Jasmine gotten off the *Ophelia* for some reason? Was she watching the excitement from there? His gaze raked the crowd but could not pick her out.

As he was about to leave the deck and return to the lower level of the barge, a man in a three-piece suit appeared on the upper deck of the floating circus. A monkey sat on his shoulder, its tail wrapped around his neck. "Come closer and be amazed. Watch in horror as one of our most experienced entertainers places his own head in the mouth of a man-eater. Hold your breath as a beautiful Egyptian princess lays her tender tresses beneath the huge paw of a ten thousand pound African pachyderm. Watch vicious hippopotamuses battle against prehistoric armored crocodiles, brought directly to you from the bloody waters of the Zambezi River in the dangerous wilds of darkest Africa."

Clem backed up closer to David. At first he thought it was because of the horrific description of the barker. But then he realized she was pointing in a different direction. Had she spotted Jasmine? "What is it?"

She gave a little hop. "Isn't that boat coming too close to us?"

David centered his attention on the tugboat guiding the floating circus. Something was wrong. He could see the men running back and forth, pointing toward the dock.

When he realized the problem, David's breath caught. Nothing was holding the two vessels together. Without the guidance of the tug, the barge would be completely at the mercy of the river current.

When he looked back at the floating circus, his heart climbed into his throat. "Get back! It's going to ram us."

Screams and shouts erupted all around them. David grabbed Clem's arm, but before he could get her to safety, a horrific crash sounded and the deck beneath his feet lifted into the air. He felt himself falling, his body rolling toward the opposite rail. His fingers scrabbled for anything to stop his momentum. The door to the theater slammed open, and he grabbed for it, nearly tearing his arm out of its socket in the process.

The squeal of grinding metal hulls drowned out the screams of the others. David dragged himself to his feet and staggered toward Clem, who had fetched up against the rail. He squatted next to her and helped her sit up. "Are you okay?"

She put her hands over her ears to shut out the noise and nodded.

David stood. "Good girl. You're going to have to get up and help the rest of the people out here get off the *Ophelia*."

The squealing stopped, and the deck leveled out once more. But David could hear an ominous sound of rushing water. The other barge must have torn a hole in the side of the *Ophelia*. A sizeable hole by the sound of it.

Clem put her hands down, terror visible in her wide eyes. "What are you going to do?"

"I'm going to find Jasmine." He helped her stand and gave Clem a little push. "We'll be out in a few minutes."

≈

"Why?" Jasmine asked the question uppermost in her mind. "Why would you do this when you have so much, Tabitha?"

Tabitha's right eyebrow rose. "You can ask me that? You, the sweet young ingenue who is already being groomed to take my place?"

"You're wrong about that." Jasmine shook her head. "I'm leaving the *Ophelia* after this stop."

"Don't argue with her." Arnold looked much more formidable with a gun in his hand. She'd not paid much attention to him since getting a position on the *Ophelia*. Arnold Garth was just one of the background actors—easily forgotten. Effortlessly overlooked. Making him the perfect criminal. He was a little taller than Tabitha, with a wiry build and a hard face. "We've got work to do."

"Whether it's you or someone else doesn't really matter." Tabitha's sneer distorted her features as she continued talking to Jasmine. "You weren't there the first time an oafish theater manager relegated me to a smaller part because a younger actress needed a chance to shine. I can read the handwriting on the wall. I knew what was happening. There's no work for washed-up actresses. At least no decent work."

Jasmine's heart thumped so loudly it sounded like a bass drum in her ears. She wondered if she might be having a fit of apoplexy. Wouldn't it be ironic if she fell dead at Arnold and Tabitha's feet?

Tabitha moved to her dressing table, sitting and gazing at her reflection in the mirror. "You know, it only seems like yesterday that I was the starry-eyed girl who dreamed of seeing her name featured on a marquee."

Arnold shifted his weight from one foot to the other, a longsuffering expression on his face. Had he heard her story before? How long had the two been working together? How had they managed to carry out their plans under everyone's noses? What would they do with her now that she knew their secret?

"Hand me that note." Arnold gestured with the gun in his hand.

Jasmine bent to pick it up and moved toward him. Could she hold the slip of paper out far enough that he would have to reach for it? Grab his weapon when his attention was diverted? Her heart stuttered before resuming its hard thumps, twice as fast this time. She wasn't a Pinkerton detective. It would take him only a second to shoot her. Jasmine sought a safer solution.

"You said it yourself when you first came aboard the *Ophelia*." Tabitha's gaze locked onto hers through the mirror. "I've been in the theater since you were a child. Do you have any idea what kind of things I had to do to get the parts you're so eager to perform?"

Wishing she had never been so thoughtless, Jasmine looked toward the older woman. She wanted to put her arms around Tabitha and reassure her. Tell her that God loved her no matter how old she was or what she had done. But she was already so lightheaded, she didn't know if she could say what was needed before losing consciousness.

Tabitha balled up her fist and shook it at Jasmine's reflection. "My fame and glory tarnish a little more with each sunset, while you or girls like you swarm the theater, eager to grab my triumphs for yourselves."

Jasmine couldn't believe she had ever wanted to be like the pitiful woman sitting amid her tawdry finery. She understood that all the store-bought goods crowded into the suite were Tabitha's attempts to bolster her self-confidence. David's warning about replacing God with the sound of applause returned to her as Jasmine realized Tabitha was using jewelry, clothing, and money to bolster her fear of failure. She thought material wealth could fill the void in her heart, stave off the emptiness threatening to consume her. "I never meant to hurt you."

"Hurt me?" Tabitha pushed herself up and turned to face Jasmine. "You can't hurt me. Your name may one day replace mine on a playbill, although that remains to be seen. But I've made provisions already. I'm smarter than all the people on this boat. While you memorized your lines and offered pat answers for every situation, I've put together a profitable business."

Arnold chuckled. "You mean *we* have."

"I hope you're not trying to imply that you could have set up all of this without me." Tabitha turned on the man, exposing him to a full measure of fury.

The mask that Tabitha wore every day melted away, leaving her exposed in that moment. Jasmine wondered if the woman had ever been an innocent, decent girl. If so, the choices she had made in pursuing her goals had changed her into a cold, vicious liar. Someone who had to be more important than anyone else around her. Someone who would sacrifice everything, every decent impulse, to her god of fame and success.

Driving, relentless ambition had engulfed her soul. It was a high price, one that Jasmine knew she could not pay. If she lived through this, she would quit. She closed her eyes. *Lord, I choose You. I'm sorry, and I hope it's not too late. If You're listening, please believe me. I never should have tried to serve both my ambition and You.*

"What should we do with her?" Arnold shifted the focus off himself, apparently realizing how unstable Tabitha was at this moment.

Tabitha tilted her head, her eyes dangerously empty. "I like you, Jasmine. You're a bright girl. I could use someone like you. What do you say to throwing in your lot with me? I can promise you furs and jewels, excitement and recognition. You could be the distraction we need to keep our little group together."

Jasmine shook her head. She had already made her choice. God was the only One she would follow. Her heart slowed down and peace filled her. No matter what happened now, she knew He was in control.

"No?" Tabitha's voice held a note of disappointment. "I suppose it was a bad idea."

The older woman returned her attention to Arnold. "It's almost time for dinner. You get her off the boat while I go make an excuse for Jasmine's absence. We don't want anyone to suspect what's going on. Once we finish this job, we'll decide what to do with her."

A look passed between them. Jasmine translated it without any trouble. She knew they were going to kill her. They couldn't afford to leave her alive. She needed help if she was going to escape. She needed David to come to her rescue. A laugh tried to erupt, making Jasmine wonder if she would give in to hysteria after all. David had told her she would need him someday and he wouldn't be there. How right he'd been.

Lord, I know I don't deserve it, but I'm asking You to save my life if that is Your will. Please send David to rescue me, or show me a way to get free. And if I'm to die here—

The feel of the cold muzzle in her back cut off her thoughts. "Have a seat, Jasmine." Arnold's voice whispered the command in her ear. "We've got a little time before we leave."

Tabitha's lips twisted into a tight smile as she grabbed a black lace shawl. "Make sure you don't forget to deliver the message to—" She stopped speaking as the boat rocked under their feet. "What's going on?"

Their barge was safely tied to the dock so it couldn't be a problem with the *Miss Polly* again. Maybe a paddlewheeler had come too close to their berth before slowing.

Tabitha opened her mouth to say something, but the words were drowned out by a tremendous crash—like a volley of cannon fire— followed by the unearthly squeal of metal against metal.

Jasmine covered her ears, looking around for the source of the terrible sound. The word formed in her mind. *Collision!* Something large had crashed into the *Ophelia*.

Chapter Thirty-two

David ran through the dark theater and pushed through the door leading to the living area of the barge. "Jasmine. Jasmine, are you down here?"

A cry answered him. Weak, terrified. His mind refused to consider what might have happened to her. He just knew he had to reach Jasmine. He had to get her off of the barge before it sank.

He stood still a moment and listened intently. Where had the cry come from? The only thing he could hear now was the hiss of water. Brown and muddy, an inch of water pooled at the base of the stairs. It didn't look too bad. Maybe the *Ophelia* wouldn't sink.

Down the hallway to his right, a door banged in time with the rocking motion of the barge. Without hesitation, David ran in that direction, entering the room without pause. At first glance he thought the room was empty, but then he heard a weeping sound and looked again at the bed. "Angelica."

The blond actress was huddled in the center of the bed. Pillows, cushions, and a blanket bunched around her. She put an arm around her stomach in a protective gesture.

David held out a hand to her. "Come on. You need to go upstairs."

"What's happened?" She shrank back against the headboard.

"A floating circus got loose and has run into the *Ophelia*. Water's coming in somewhere. Come on, I'll help you."

Angelica nodded and slid from the bed. She drew back when her feet touched the water puddled on the floor. "It's cold."

"I know. But we have to go anyway." He forced a calm smile onto his face and clung to his patience even though he knew time was slipping away. He couldn't leave poor Angelica cowering in her room.

Footsteps ran down the hall toward them. "Angelica?"

David recognized Rafe's voice. "She's in here."

The tall leading man ducked into the room and scooped Angelica from the bed, picking her up as though she weighed no more than a ragdoll. "Let's get out of here."

"You get her out. I've got to find Jasmine."

Rafe looked back over his shoulder. "Could she be outside?"

David shook his head and waved the actor toward the staircase.

"Be careful." The other man tossed the warning back as his long legs negotiated the stairs. "Some of the animals escaped the other barge."

Wondering if the cry he'd heard earlier was from a wounded animal, David set his jaw. It shouldn't take him too long to search the rooms. Heading back to the left corridor, he threw open the door to the stateroom Jasmine shared with Clem, praying he would find her huddled on her bed like Angelica had been. But this room really was empty.

"David, come on." Mr. Easley waded through the water in the hallway, a determined look on his face. David realized the water covered the man's ankles. "We've got to get out of here."

He shook his head. "I can't find Jasmine."

Easley thrust a thumb over his shoulder. "No one's back there. I'm the last one out. Could she be with Clem?"

"No. I think Tabitha's missing, too." David could hear the fear in his own voice. He took a deep breath. "They weren't in Angelica's room, but I haven't checked Tabitha's yet. Maybe they're both there."

"I'll go with you." Mr. Easley slipped and fell backward into the rising water.

"You get out of here." David helped him up and gave him a push toward the stairs. "I'll be better off by myself."

Easley hesitated a moment, weighing the truth of David's words. Then he nodded and turned toward the exit. "Hurry."

David could see the hole when he turned down the right corridor once more. Something swam past, sloshing even more water past the barge's hull. A hippopotamus in the Mississippi River?

He forgot what he'd seen in the next instant as the loud bark of a gun dumped an extra measure of terror into his blood. As he ran forward, David prayed he wasn't already too late to save Jasmine.

Tabitha looked around, her eyes wild. As water began to trickle under the doorway, she grabbed an empty trunk and threw it onto her bed.

"What are you doing?" Arnold tried to catch hold of her arm, but Tabitha pulled free.

"I have to get my things." She picked up two pairs of shoes and threw them into the trunk. Then she ran to her dressing table, picked up her jewelry box, and added it to the luggage. "Help me!"

Arnold shook his head and tucked away his pistol. "You're crazy, Tabitha. We've got to get out of here now."

She didn't slow down. Gathering up armloads of clothes from all over the room, she shoved them into the trunk, quickly filling it up.

Jasmine edged toward the door. If the two of them wanted to stay here and argue, it was okay with her. She knew how quickly the barge would sink once the water weighed it down. If she could slip past Arnold, she would make a run for it. He might chase her, but she'd stand a better chance of getting away once she was out of Tabitha's suite.

"Don't move another step." Arnold stopped trying to reason with Tabitha and aimed his weapon at Jasmine's head.

Jasmine froze. It looked like she wouldn't make it out alive after all. Water slipped around her ankles, raising the hair on her arms as she waited for the blast of Arnold's pistol.

"Put down that gun and help me." Tabitha shouted. She slammed the lid on the overfilled trunk and jerked it off the bed. Something happened then. Either the bed moved or Tabitha's feet slipped, Jasmine wasn't exactly sure. But the effect was disastrous. The heavy trunk became a missile, slamming Tabitha into the wall beside her. With a loud thud, the woman's head struck the wall, and she slid to the floor, her eyes shut.

Instinct sent Jasmine plunging toward Tabitha as the pistol went off, the bullet whizzing harmlessly past her. She didn't have time for thought. All she knew was that Tabitha would drown if they couldn't rouse her. "Put that stupid gun down and come help me. We've got to get her out of here."

"Aren't you something?" The contempt in Arnold's voice coupled with the icy water that rose with every passing second sent a cold shiver down her back. "I promise she wouldn't waste any time saving you."

The door slammed open, David's blazing green gaze locking onto her face.

"Watch out!" Jasmine called out the warning as Arnold threw himself at David, a murderous glint in his eyes.

She watched helplessly as the two men struggled, wincing as Arnold managed to land several blows. But then David began to gain the upper hand, his fists punishing the other man until Arnold finally stopped fighting and threw up his hands in a defensive posture. David stepped back, breathing hard, and swiped away a trickle of blood from the edge of his mouth. "Get your hands behind your back."

Arnold's expression turned fearful. "What are you going to do?"

"I'm going to arrest you as soon as we get out of here." David glanced around, his gaze lighting on a scarf draped across Tabitha's dressing table. As he moved forward to get it, Arnold shoved him hard. David went down to one knee. Before he could recover his balance, the other man fled through the open door.

Jasmine looked down at Tabitha's pale face. A large lump had formed on the woman's forehead, probably the reason she was still out cold. "Help me with Tabitha."

David glanced toward the doorway, shook his head, and moved toward her. "You go on. I'll get her."

Screams from somewhere nearby made her catch her breath. It sounded like Arnold had met his match. Even if he had been ready to kill her, she could not find any pleasure in whatever caused his shrieks. "I'm not leaving you alone."

David's sigh was louder than the water rushing into the room. "You never do what I tell you to do."

Heedless of the danger surrounding them, she smiled at him. "I'm just trying to save her life so she'll have a chance to know the Lord. Someone once reminded me how important a job that is."

His eyes softened. "Come on." He put his hands under Tabitha's knees and back, lifting her with a grimace. "When Rafe picked up Angelica, he made it look effortless."

Jasmine was glad to hear the couple was safe. Time was running out. She stood and realized the water had risen to the height of her knees. Would they be able to get out before the barge was completely engulfed?

When she stepped into the hall, Jasmine could see the hole in the side of the barge. A movement close to the opening made her squint toward it. She raised a hand and pointed. "Is that a lion?" A growl answered her question.

"A floating circus hit us." David whispered the information. "Rafe said some of the animals got loose."

As Jasmine's eyesight adjusted to the dim corridor, she saw the snarl that revealed the animal's deadly teeth. She clutched David's arm. "Is that what happened to Arnold?"

He nodded and inclined his head toward the other end of the hallway. "We need to get back to the staircase now. I don't think the lion will attack us unless he feels cornered, but I don't really want to test that theory."

They pushed through the rising water, reaching the stairs after what seemed an eternity. As they climbed out of the water, Jasmine realized how tense her shoulders were. She had expected every moment to feel the lion's claws tear into her back. She held open the door to the theater, expecting to see further evidence of the devastation caused by the collision. The room was canted at an odd angle, but that was the only indication something was wrong. Jasmine picked up her wet skirts and hurried after David.

When they reached the door to the outside, she felt like she was walking into a maelstrom. Voices shouted, and people were running back and forth from the *Ophelia* to the floating circus. A pair of elephants stood on the bank, their giant ears moving back and forth like great gray wings. Monkeys chattered and ran between the legs of the circus performers like rambunctious children. A large tiger, thankfully still confined, paced the length of its cage and growled at anyone who dared approach.

"There they are!" Jasmine heard Clem's voice and saw her friend jumping up and down as though her feet were made of coils.

Rafe ran across the gangplank and took Tabitha from David. "Did the lion attack you?"

David shook his head. "Arnold Garth wasn't so lucky."

"I see." Rafe settled the unconscious woman against his shoulder before heading back to the riverbank.

"I didn't think you would come for me, David." A shudder shook Jasmine's aching shoulders as they followed a few steps behind Rafe. She let her skirts drop to keep from displaying her legs to the curious onlookers. "You said you were done pulling me out of scrapes."

He looked straight ahead, his stride long. "Old habits die hard."

"Thank you anyway." Jasmine's wet skirts made it impossible to keep up with him. When he realized she had fallen behind, David turned around, his green gaze seeing more than she wanted. With a roll of his eyes, he came back and lifted her into his arms. "Don't you know yet that I'll always come rescue you?"

She put an arm around his shoulders and let her head drop down to his chest. She might be wet and exhausted, but Jasmine had never felt quite so treasured in her whole life.

Chapter Thirty-three

 still find it hard to believe Tabitha Barlow is a bank robber." Clem sat on the bright, dimity-covered window seat, her scissors and a large square of cloth in her hands.

"I know." Jasmine wandered over and sat next to her, looking down at a carriage traveling along First Street. She was glad their boardinghouse faced the river. It afforded them an ever-changing view of the traffic and people. "I was so shocked when I heard her and Arnold discussing their plans."

"You were very brave to go to her room for the evidence."

"That's not how David phrased it."

Clem giggled. "He was upset because he doesn't like the idea of you getting hurt. That man loves you."

"Do you really think so?" Jasmine could feel the heat burning her cheeks. "He hasn't been by but once since the accident."

"He's got a lot to do. Trust me, he'll be here as soon as he can."

"I still can't believe the *Ophelia* is gone."

Clem snipped at a corner of the cloth and sighed. "I know. All those lovely costumes."

"Now you sound like Tabitha."

"Heaven forbid. Did she really try to get all her clothes packed into trunks?"

"And her shoes and jewelry." Jasmine could hardly believe it either. She still cringed to think of Tabitha's compulsion to save her material belongings over her life. The poor woman really didn't understand what was important.

Anyone looking at the dock today would never realize the drama that had played out there three days earlier. She sighed and turned away from the window. "I suppose it's a blessing how few people actually died that afternoon."

"Poor Arnold." Clem pursed her lips as she studied the material. "Imagine running directly into the path of that dangerous beast."

"The newspaper said the animals are being kept in several warehouses while new cages are made to replace those that couldn't be salvaged from the wreck." Jasmine wandered to the writing desk in one corner of their room, looking at the note she had written to her sisters. She had spent all morning on that task, trying to apologize for her actions. It was difficult to explain the choices she had made over the past months. Looking back, she barely understood the reasons herself. At least the letter would let them know she was unhurt and that she was coming home.

Clem picked up a doll and measured the length of cloth against it. "Do you think Rafe and Angelica will be happy?"

Jasmine watched her friend work on her project. "Is that who the doll is for?"

"Oh, no. It's for Mrs. O'Hara's daughter."

"The lady who owns the boardinghouse?" Jasmine was surprised Clem would put so much effort into a dress for a stranger's child. "I hope she appreciates getting an original design by a seamstress as talented as you."

"Since Mr. and Mrs. Easley have decided not to buy another showboat, I need something to do." Clem took out her needle and a spool of white thread.

"You could get a job on a different showboat. I'm sure the Easleys would give you a good reference."

Clem stitched away with her usual speed. "I'm tired of living on the river."

Jasmine was surprised by her friend's statement. She thought Clem loved the theater, or at least the costume work she did. Did she share Jasmine's disillusionment because of the immorality and greed rampant among the *Ophelia*'s actors? "What will you do?"

"Mrs. O'Hara's sister owns a millinery shop. She thinks I can probably get a job there if I prove I have sufficient talent." Clem grinned at her. "So now you see that my charitable work will benefit me as well as our landlady's daughter."

"I'm glad you've decided not to return to the theater." Jasmine tapped the table with one finger. "It's so different from what I expected. So debauched. I expected a world of excitement and adulation, not lechers and bank robbers."

"So you're not going to be an actress anymore?" Clem's needle halted midstitch. "What will you do?"

"Go home, I guess." Jasmine sighed. "I'm not really sure."

Choked laughter answered her sigh. "Save your melodrama for somebody else. I know a certain handsome detective who's not going to let you get very far away."

"Perhaps." Jasmine remembered the way David had carried her across the gangplank. "All I know is I need to pray about what God wants me to do for the future."

"You really are serious about this God stuff, aren't you?" Clem put down the doll dress, her gaze sober.

"I know I haven't been a very good example to you and the others on the *Ophelia*." Jasmine found the words difficult to say out loud. "Being a Christian is a very serious matter, something I forgot for a while. Christ lives in my heart. He's the One I want to keep my eyes on, the One I want to follow, no matter what. In a way, Tabitha helped me see how silly I had been. When she started packing that trunk as the ship was sinking, it dawned on me that I was guilty of the same thing—putting emphasis on the things of this world, things that have no eternal value. Jesus said that our hearts would be in the same place as our treasures. I forgot that for a while."

"I can't tell you I'm ready to make a commitment today, but I have seen a difference in you. And I like it." Clem resumed her handwork. "I hope you'll pray for me."

"I always do." Jasmine found encouragement in Clem's words. "But don't delay too long. We never know when death may be lurking around a corner. Arnold's death was terrible, the circumstances of course. But the worst thing of all is that he may not have been saved when he left this world. The idea of anyone having to be separated from God forever is too horrifying to consider."

"I see what you mean." Clem's thoughtful gaze raked her face.

Deciding to leave the subject for now, Jasmine made a promise to herself to redouble her prayers for Clem's salvation. She knew God loved Clem as much as she did. And His business was calling people to Him.

ॐ

"What will happen to Vance?"

David winced at Jasmine's question. Did she still care for the man, after all? He had hoped, dreamed even, that she returned his feelings. They had seemed to grow so close after leaving Cairo. Had it been nothing more than an act on her part? "The charges of murder and armed robbery were dropped, but he's pled guilty to theft. He'll have to serve time."

Standing on the deck of the *Coriander*, he watched as they once again reached the intersection of the Ohio and Mississippi Rivers. How appropriate. His feelings were as turbulent as the merging currents below their boat.

He angled a look at Jasmine. Her beauty had deepened to a new level, a realization that made his heart ache.

"I still can't believe he stole money from the Easleys. From all of us on the *Ophelia*." A strand of her coal-black hair escaped from Jasmine's coiffure and brushed her cheek.

David's fingers itched to smooth it back, let his fingers caress her soft skin. He gripped the rail tighter instead. "He proved unworthy of the trust you placed in him."

"Maybe he'll change while he's in prison."

He should be warmed by her obvious faith in the man, but he was too human to completely avoid a wave of resentment. He cleared his throat and searched for a different subject. "Tabitha's facing more serious charges. She was involved in two murders and more than a dozen robberies. I don't see how she'll avoid being hanged."

Jasmine brushed the hair away from her face. "I can't help but remember how she tried to warn me away from the theater when I first began to gain recognition aboard the *Ophelia*. I didn't realize at the time that she had my best interests at heart."

"I imagine her motives were more about self-protection than altruism." He didn't want to hurt Jasmine, but she needed to understand how evil Tabitha really was. He remembered the interview he'd conducted after she was placed under arrest. She had tried to place blame on everyone but herself, painting herself as victim rather than villain. First it was Arnold Garth who had led her astray, then Vance Hargrove. She had even accused Clem and Jasmine of trying to usurp her position on the *Ophelia*. "She was jealous of you."

The errant strand of hair returned to Jasmine's cheek, tempting his fingers once more. "She may never change, but at least we gave her time to consider eternity. I hope she'll listen to God's voice before it's too late."

David's pain receded a little. Even if they were not meant to be together, at least he could rejoice in Jasmine's resurgent faith. "You're really serious about all this now, aren't you?"

"I'm sorry for my rebellion." She sighed and pushed her hair back once more. "I see now what you and my sisters were trying to tell me. I thought life in the theater was a magical existence, but now I understand that it's nothing more than a dangerous illusion."

"I don't know if you should rush to the other extreme, Jasmine. Over the past weeks, I've seen you and the others work together to create something special. Who knows what lives you may have touched, what lessons your plays might teach about the hazards of making immoral choices?"

David hoped she understood his point. While he didn't like the loose lifestyles of the actors on the *Ophelia*, he could see that a troupe of actors who were Christians might be able to use the stage to advance sound principles and even plant the seeds of salvation.

Her violet eyes widened in surprise. "I can't believe you said that."

"Why not? The theater is not evil in itself."

"That may be true, but it's still not the life for me." Her chin jutted out.

David suppressed his smile. No matter what happened to Jasmine, she would always be headstrong. He loved that about her. "What do you plan to do once you return to Natchez?"

"Rest for a while, I guess. Maybe I'll help Camellia teach the local children. I'm not really sure what God wants me to do at this point."

"I have an idea." David wanted to bite his tongue off. When would he learn to keep his mouth shut? He hadn't planned to say anything to Jasmine about what she should do next. It wasn't any of his business. If he'd ever thought they might have a future together, she had made her choice abundantly clear when she'd sighed over Vance's fate.

Shivering, Jasmine pulled her shawl up over her shoulders. "Are you going to tell me what it is or leave me guessing?"

"Are you cold?"

Jasmine raised her eyebrows. "A little, but I'm not going in until you tell me your idea."

"I was thinking about your work with the cast." David decided he might as well take the plunge. The worst she could do was laugh at him. "You witnessed to Angelica, helped Rafe keep his job, and even talked me into joining the performance. You have a real talent for management. If you combine that with your love for all things theatrical, maybe you could have your own theatrical company."

He held his breath and refused to look at Jasmine while she considered the idea.

"I don't know. . . ."

He let out his breath, interrupting her attempt to let him down easy. "Forget it. It's a stupid idea."

"No, it's not. It's brilliant." She put a hand on his arm. "You're brilliant. I was going to say that I don't know why I didn't think of it myself. It doesn't have to be on a grand scale like the theater on the *Ophelia*. I could teach young men and women how to act while keeping their Christian values intact."

David nodded, glad to see her so excited.

Jasmine stared up at him, her violet gaze suddenly serious. "Would you come to see the productions?"

"I'm sure I could visit Natchez from time to time." Although he wasn't sure if he could stand seeing her married to anyone else.

"So you're going back to Chicago?" Her hand fell away from his arm. "I had hoped you might find—"

He waited for her to finish her sentence, sighing when she turned away and hid her face from him. "What did you hope I would find?"

"Oh, never mind. It was a silly idea, anyway." Her words were whipped away by the wind, their meaning unclear.

He would never understand her. David wanted to walk away, leave her standing on the deck by herself. But something. . .some One whispered that he should stay. "Please tell me what you were going to say."

Were her shoulders shaking? He hadn't meant to make her cry.

David locked his own emotions away and reached for Jasmine, pulling her into a brotherly embrace. "I'm sorry. I didn't mean to upset you. Of course I'll be there for you. At least until you have a husband to watch out over you. It's the least a brother can do."

Jasmine gasped and pulled away from his embrace. When she turned to face him, her beautiful eyes were filled with annoyance instead of tears. "I am not and never have been your sister, David Foster. Don't you know yet that you're the only man I could ever love?"

Her words broke down the barriers between them. But he didn't take her in his arms yet. He still had a matter that needed to be straightened out. "I thought you liked Vance's kisses more than mine."

She shook her head, a blush spreading across her cheeks. "I was upset when I told you that. Vance kissed me once, but it was nothing to compare to the way I feel in your arms."

His last reservation disappeared. David opened his arms to her, his mind full of thankfulness. Even the river seemed to sing with joy as their lips met in a kiss that warmed his blood and sealed the bond between them.

Epilogue

Natchez, Mississippi
December 10, 1870

Lily stood on tiptoe and draped a pine garland over the door to the dining room. "It seems like only a few weeks ago that you were the one getting married on the *Water Lily*."

Camellia's gaze looked past her shoulder, and a smile curved her lips upward. "Yes, but then again sometimes it seems like Jonah and I have been together for decades."

"In a way you have. Or at least you've known him for that long." Lily stepped back to assess their decorations.

The smell of pine permeated the room. Holly boughs festooned with red berries decorated the row of windows. Camellia had brought crystal vases from Les Fleurs and gossamer tulle swags for the tables that would hold Papa and Tessie's wedding dinner in a few short hours. They still needed to place the chairs for the families, but then everything would be ready.

Jasmine walked into the room, her cheeks as red as the holly berries. "I'm so glad it stopped raining."

"Is the change in temperature the reason for those roses in your cheeks?" Camellia bent a playful frown in her direction.

Lily couldn't hide her smile as Jasmine's cheeks darkened further. It was sweet to see their little sister so much in love. Especially since she had finally come to her senses and realized what everyone else had known for a while—she was deeply in love with David Foster. "I imagine it has more to do with her escort than the weather."

Jasmine blew out an impatient breath. "Stop it."

As her laughter blended with Camellia's, Lily opened her arms wide and caught Jasmine in a brief hug. "I'm sorry, honey. It's just that we're so happy for the two of you."

"That's right." Camellia nodded, her blond curls bobbing around her face. "But I don't understand why you're waiting until spring to marry. You and David should join Papa and Tessie at the altar today."

Jasmine emerged from the hug and shook her head. "Today's their day. We can wait. Besides, I've always wanted to be a June bride. The flowers are so abundant then. I can just imagine how beautiful the garden at Les Fleurs will be."

"I think Jasmine is saying she doesn't care for our decorations." Lily put her hands on her hips and pursed her lips.

Camellia gasped and pointed a finger in her direction. "You look so much like Aunt Dahlia when you do that."

"Please." Lily relaxed her mouth.

"No, it's true." Jasmine looked from her face to Camellia's. "And she also looks a little like Grandmother, don't you think?"

Now Lily's cheeks were redder than Jasmine's. Her sisters circled around her, their frowns nearly identical. "No matter what you say, I refuse to believe I'll ever be as sour as our aunt."

"Of course you won't." Camellia stopped in front of her. "I love Aunt Dahlia, but she's mired in the past. You've got your sights on the future with this new shipping venture."

Lily let a relieved breath escape. She'd always wanted to be as adventurous as their mother. "I'm glad you and Jonah decided to invest, too. Eli and Renée are going to handle getting river shipments onto the rails from their office in Memphis. The only ones we have left to get involved are Jasmine and David."

"Perhaps later." Jasmine started to pull off her cloak. "Once we get more settled."

Lily had news she could hardly wait to share with her younger sister. "Blake and Jean Luc were talking about hiring the Pinkerton Agency to protect our shipments from bandits and Indians. I'm hoping they can insist on having David oversee the operations."

Jasmine's motions halted. "Really? That would be exciting. Maybe he and I could even travel together."

Camellia stomped her foot to get their attention. "Why is everyone so interested in leaving Natchez?"

Lily put a comforting hand around Camellia's waist. "This will always be our home. You and Jonah are doing a wonderful job with the sharecroppers and the family's assets. You're the linchpin that holds us together."

Jasmine nodded, her beautiful violet eyes wide. "Besides, you know you're the only one who can reason with Aunt Dahlia."

Camellia's eyes were suspiciously moist, but she laughed at Jasmine's mischievous expression. "You're a minx."

"I know."

Lily was nearly overcome with her own tears, her heart threatening to explode with pride and joy over her sisters. "I love you."

Jasmine's face lost its playfulness. "One thing I realized while I was on the *Ophelia* is how much I owe to you, Lily. I'm ashamed of my blindness to all the sacrifices you've made over the years."

"They're not sacrifices to me." Emotion clogged Lily's throat, making it difficult to talk.

"Jasmine's right." Camellia put both arms around her. "You fought everyone to make sure we could live our lives in the ways we chose."

Lily tightened the muscles in her throat to keep from melting into a puddle of tears. She felt Jasmine's hug in addition to Camellia's. Had anyone ever been so blessed?

After a few minutes, peace settled over her. Lily returned the hugs from her sisters. "It's an honor to help you when I can. I just hate the times we've been at cross-purposes."

"We're together now." Jasmine's voice sounded as choked as her own. "And we'll always be sisters."

Lily closed her eyes. "Dear Lord, thank You for all the blessings. Thank You for wiping away our tears and giving us 'beauty for ashes, the oil of joy for mourning, the garment of praise for the spirit of heaviness; that they might be called trees of righteousness, the planting of the Lord, that He might be glorified.'"

A brief silence filled the room before Camellia picked up the prayer. "Lord, I want to say thanks for my sister. You're the One who describes a virtuous woman as having a price above rubies. Thank You for filling Lily with all the characteristics that have made her a virtuous woman and a wonderful sister."

Jasmine's voice took over when Camellia stopped. "Thanks, God, for my wonderful Christian sisters. And thank You for watching over all of us so well. Bless our Papa and Tessie as they begin this new chapter of their lives. Help us to be ever mindful of Your love and sovereignty. May we sow Your seeds at every opportunity as we live out our lives in Your service."

"Amen." As she ended the prayer, Lily knew this would be a moment she would always cherish. A moment in which every fear was quieted and only peace remained.

❧

Benjamin stood between Lily and Blake, each of his hands in one of theirs. Noah and Magnolia were immediately ahead of them, their high-pitched whispers betraying their excitement at attending the wedding.

"Shhh." Lily put her free hand across her lips. "You're supposed to be as quiet as little mice, remember?"

Noah looked over his shoulder, his blue eyes full of mischief. "Magnolia doesn't believe Grandpapa is going to be a broom."

Blake chuckled. "Son, I'm afraid I have to agree with your sister."

Magnolia stuck her tongue out at her brother.

Lily prayed for patience. "Magnolia, that is not a ladylike gesture. Noah, Grandpapa is going to be a *groom*. It means a husband."

Noah looked to his father for confirmation, grimacing at Blake's nod. "I was almost right."

"Jensen says, 'A miss is as good as a mile.'" Magnolia raised her chin, a familiar gesture that Lily knew her daughter had learned from her. At least she didn't stick out her tongue again.

Suddenly Lily wanted to gather her family close and try to stop anything from changing them. She could remember Jasmine being as young as Magnolia was now.

She looked into the room they were about to enter, her gaze skipping over the decorations, past the expectant gazes of the guests, and fastening on Anna standing in front of the altar as Tessie's bridesmaid. Her eyes, the same bright blue color as her brother Blake's, matched her silk dress. It was made up in the modern style, with narrowed skirts and a bustle at the back. Lily wasn't sure she liked the bustle, but Camellia had insisted that all of their gowns should reflect the newest fashion.

Jensen and Papa stood on the other side of the altar. Papa looked as nervous as she'd ever seen him. He wiped his hands on the black material of his slacks. It was hard to tell Jensen's mood. His scarred face rarely showed emotion. As she watched, he leaned over and said something to Papa. A smile broke out on Papa's face, and he nodded.

Lily knew it was time. She focused on Noah. "Escort your sister to her place like we practiced."

Her gaze met Blake's as their oldest son held out his arm and Magnolia put her small hand on it. Could anything be more adorable? As she and Blake followed, helping Benjamin between them, she passed Uncle Phillip and Aunt Dahlia, who wore identical smiles this afternoon.

As they reached the front row, she looked to her left and nodded to Mrs. Champney and Jean Luc. His son, Achille, fussed and fidgeted in Jean Luc's lap. Tamar, sitting next to the Champneys, fished in her reticule and produced a stick of candy that the little boy accepted and immediately popped into his mouth.

Jasmine, her hand in David's, grinned at Noah and Magnolia as they sat next to her. On David's far side, Camellia dabbed at her eyes with a lace-edged white handkerchief, the smile on her face indicating that her tears had nothing to do with grief. Seated next to Camellia, her daughter, Amaryllis, swung her legs back and forth. The motion lifted her velvet skirt up with each kick until her father, Jonah, shook his head at her. She subsided with a pout as Lily sat in one of the two remaining seats on this row. Blake sat beside her and put Benjamin in his lap.

A rustle from the back of the room indicated that Tessie had arrived at the doorway. Lily stood with the rest and watched as Anna and Blake's aunt stepped into the room. Dressed in a white dress with deep flounces, the older woman radiated joy. Her veil floated around her like a rising mist as she moved forward, her gaze fastened on Papa's face. For an instant Lily was transported back in time as she glanced toward her father. The smile on his face was one she'd forgotten. She hadn't seen it since her mother died. In that moment, she knew Papa and Tessie would be happy together.

Time collapsed and expanded. Past, present, and future seemed to come together in one confusing instant as intense longing swept Lily. Where had the years gone? It seemed she'd only blinked her eyes and her baby sister Jasmine was all grown up and ready to leave home. Would it be the same with Magnolia? The future seemed so uncertain at times. How would she ever cope? What would their lives be like in another fourteen or fifteen years? Tears burned at the corners of her eyes.

"Is everything okay?" Blake's gaze met hers, at once concerned and empathetic.

"Yes." Lily could feel the pain ebbing as God covered her confusion with His grace. "I'm just being silly."

A smile chased away her husband's frown. "I love you, Lily."

She lifted her chin and returned his smile. "I love you, too."

As they sat side by side and listened to Papa and Tessie repeat their vows, a verse from the last book of the Bible came to her. *"And God shall wipe away all tears from their eyes; and there shall be no more death, neither sorrow, nor crying, neither shall there be any more pain: for the former things are passed away."* She and Blake—all the members of her family—had endured trials and tears, from the ever-changing fortunes of life on the river to the deaths of loved ones. But no matter what happened, faith guided them like a beacon in the night. Whatever the future held, she could rejoice knowing that God's promises transcended all else.

 **Diane T. Ashley,** a "town girl" born and raised in Mississippi, has worked more than twenty years for the House of Representatives. She rediscovered a thirst for writing, was led to a class taught by Aaron McCarver, and became a founding member of the Bards of Faith.

Aaron McCarver is a transplanted Mississippian who was raised in the mountains near Dunlap, Tennessee. He loves his jobs of teaching at Belhaven University and editing for Barbour Publishing. A member of ACFW, he is coauthor with Gilbert Morris of the bestselling series "The Spirit of Appalachia." He now coauthors with Diane T. Ashley on several historical series.